P9-CNE-149

RED RISING

BY PIERCE BROWN

Red Rising

Golden Son

Morning Star

Iron Gold

Dark Age

RED RISING

Pierce Brown

DEL REY
NEW YORK

Red Rising is a work of fiction. Names, places, characters, and incidents either are the product of the author's imagination or are used fictitiously. Any resemblance to actual persons, living or dead, events, or locales is entirely coincidental.

Published in the United States by Del Rey, an imprint of Random House, a division of Random House LLC, a Penguin Random House Company, New York.

DEL REY and the HOUSE colophon are registered trademarks of Random House LLC.

Library of Congress Cataloging-in-Publication Data
Brown, Pierce
Red Rising / Pierce Brown.
pages cm
ISBN 978-0-345-53978-6 (acid-free paper)—ISBN 978-0-345-53979-3 (e-book)
1. Government, Resistance to—Fiction. 2. Dystopias.
3. Science fiction. I. Title.
PS3602.R7226R43 2013
813'.6—dc23 2013020634

Printed in the United States of America on acid-free paper.

www.delreybooks.com

16 18 19 17

Book design by Caroline Cunningham

To Father, who taught me to walk

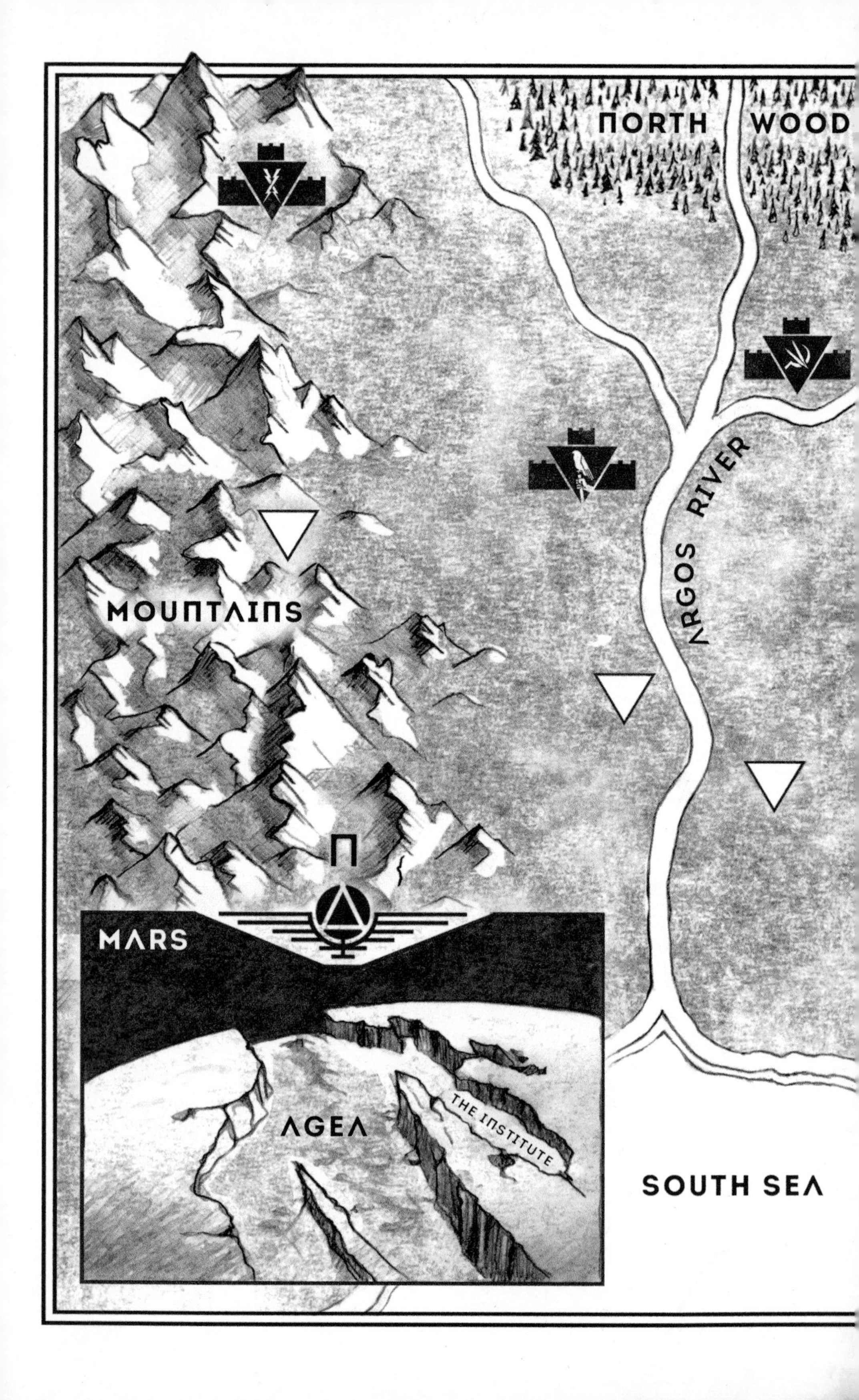
NORTH WOOD
ARGOS RIVER
MOUNTAINS
MARS
AGEA
THE INSTITUTE
SOUTH SEA

HIGHLANDS
POSTERN HILLS
GREATWOODS
HOUSE APOLLO
HOUSE CERES
HOUSE DIANA
HOUSE JUNO
HOUSE JUPITER
HOUSE MARS
HOUSE MINERVA
UNKNOWN HOUSE

ACKNOWLEDGMENTS

If writing is a work of the head and heart, then thank you to Aaron Phillips, Hannah Bowman, and Mike Braff, who burnish my head with their wisdom and advice.

Thank you to my parents, my sister, friends, and the Phillips Clan who guard my heart with their love and loyalty.

And to the reader, thank you. I hope you bloodydamn love these books.

I would have lived in peace. But my enemies brought me war.

I watch twelve hundred of their strongest sons and daughters. Listening to a pitiless Golden man speak between great marble pillars. Listening to the beast who brought the flame that gnaws at my heart.

"All men are *not* created equal," he declares. Tall, imperious, an eagle of a man. "The weak have deceived you. They would say the meek should inherit the Earth. That the strong should nurture the gentle. This is the Noble Lie of Demokracy. The cancer that poisoned mankind."

His eyes pierce the gathered students. "You and I are Gold. We are the end of the evolutionary line. We tower above the flesh heap of man, shepherding the lesser Colors. You have inherited this legacy," he pauses, studying faces in the assembly. "But it is not free.

"Power must be claimed. Wealth won. Rule, dominion, empire purchased with blood. You scarless children deserve nothing. You do not know pain. You do not know what your forefathers sacrificed to place you on these heights. But soon, you will. Soon, we will teach you why Gold rules mankind. And I promise, of those among you, only those fit for power will survive."

But I am no Gold. I am a Red.

He thinks men like me weak. He thinks me dumb, feeble, subhuman. I was not raised in palaces. I did not ride horses through meadows and eat meals of hummingbird tongues. I was forged in the bowels of this hard world. Sharpened by hate. Strengthened by love.

He is wrong.

None of them will survive.

PART I

SLAVE

There is a flower that grows on Mars. It is red and harsh and fit for our soil. It is called haemanthus. It means "blood blossom."

1

HELLDIVER

The first thing you should know about me is I am my father's son. And when they came for him, I did as he asked. I did not cry. Not when the Society televised the arrest. Not when the Golds tried him. Not when the Grays hanged him. Mother hit me for that. My brother Kieran was supposed to be the stoic one. He was the elder, I the younger. I was supposed to cry. Instead, Kieran bawled like a girl when Little Eo tucked a haemanthus into Father's left workboot and ran back to her own father's side. My sister Leanna murmured a lament beside me. I just watched and thought it a shame that he died dancing but without his dancing shoes.

On Mars there is not much gravity. So you have to pull the feet to break the neck. They let the loved ones do it.

I smell my own stink inside my frysuit. The suit is some kind of nanoplastic and is hot as its name suggests. It insulates me toe to head. Nothing gets in. Nothing gets out. Especially not the heat. Worst part is you can't wipe the sweat from your eyes. Bloodydamn stings as it goes through the headband to puddle at the heels. Not to mention the stink when you piss. Which you always do. Gotta take in a load of water through the drinktube. I guess you could be fit with a catheter. We choose the stink.

The drillers of my clan chatter some gossip over the comm in my ear as I ride atop the clawDrill. I'm alone in this deep tunnel on a machine built like a titanic metal hand, one that grasps and gnaws at the ground. I control its rockmelting digits from the holster seat atop the drill, just where the elbow joint would be. There, my fingers fit into control gloves that manipulate the many tentacle-like drills some ninety meters below my perch. To be a Helldiver, they say your fingers must flicker fast as tongues of fire. Mine flicker faster.

Despite the voices in my ear, I am alone in the deep tunnel. My existence is vibration, the echo of my own breath, and heat so thick and noxious it feels like I'm swaddled in a heavy quilt of hot piss.

A new river of sweat breaks through the scarlet sweatband tied around my forehead and slips into my eyes, burning them till they're as red as my rusty hair. I used to reach and try to wipe the sweat away, only to scratch futilely at the faceplate of my frysuit. I still want to. Even after three years, the tickle and sting of the sweat is a raw misery.

The tunnel walls around my holster seat are bathed a sulfurous yellow by a corona of lights. The reach of the light fades as I look up the thin vertical shaft I've carved today. Above, precious helium-3 glimmers like liquid silver, but I'm looking at the shadows, looking for the pitvipers that curl through the darkness seeking the warmth of my drill. They'll eat into your suit too, bite through the shell and then try to burrow into the warmest place they find, usually your belly, so they can lay their eggs. I've been bitten before. Still dream of the beast—black, like a thick tendril of oil. They can get as wide as a thigh and long as three men, but it's the babies we fear. They don't know how to ration their poison. Like me, their ancestors came from Earth, then Mars and the deep tunnels changed them.

It is eerie in the deep tunnels. Lonely. Beyond the roar of the drill, I hear the voices of my friends, all older. But I cannot see them a half klick above me in the darkness. They drill high above, near the mouth of the tunnel that I've carved, descending with hooks and lines to dangle along the sides of the tunnel to get at the small veins of helium-3. They mine with meter-long drills, gobbling up the chaff. The work still requires mad dexterity of foot and hand, but I'm the earner in this crew. I am the Helldiver. It takes a certain kind—and I'm the youngest anyone can remember.

I've been in the mines for three years. You start at thirteen. Old enough to screw, old enough to crew. At least that's what Uncle Narol said. Except I didn't get married till six months back, so I don't know why he said it.

Eo dances through my thoughts as I peer into my control display and slip the clawDrill's fingers around a fresh vein. *Eo*. Sometimes it's difficult to think of her as anything but what we used to call her as children.

Little Eo—a tiny girl hidden beneath a mane of red. Red like the rock around me, not true red, rust-red. Red like our home, like Mars. Eo is sixteen too. And she may be like me—from a clan of Red earth diggers, a clan of song and dance and soil—but she could be made from air, from the ether that binds the stars in a patchwork. Not that I've ever seen stars. No Red from the mining colonies sees the stars.

Little Eo. They wanted to marry her off when she turned fourteen, like all girls of the clans. But she took the short rations and waited for me to reach sixteen, wedAge for men, before slipping that cord around her finger. She said she knew we'd marry since we were children. I didn't.

"*Hold. Hold. Hold!*" Uncle Narol snaps over the comm channel. "*Darrow, hold, boy!*" My fingers freeze. He's high above with the rest of them, watching my progress on his head unit.

"What's the burn?" I ask, annoyed. I don't like being interrupted.

"*What's the burn, the little Helldiver asks.*" Old Barlow chuckles.

"*Gas pocket, that's what,*" Narol snaps. He's the headTalk for our two-hundred-plus crew. "*Hold. Calling a scanCrew to check the particulars before you blow us all to hell.*"

"That gas pocket? It's a tiny one," I say. "More like a gas pimple. I can manage it."

"A year on the drill and he thinks he knows his head from his hole! Poor little pissant," old Barlow adds dryly. *"Remember the words of our golden leader. Patience and obedience, young one. Patience is the better part of valor. And obedience the better part of humanity. Listen to your elders."*

I roll my eyes at the epigram. If the elders could do what I can, maybe listening would have its merits. But they are slow in hand and mind. Sometimes I feel like they want me to be just the same, especially my uncle.

"I'm on a tear," I say. "If you think there's a gas pocket, I can just hop down and handscan it. Easy. No dilldally."

They'll preach caution. As if caution has ever helped them. We haven't won a Laurel in ages.

"Want to make Eo a widow?" Barlow laughs, voice crackling with static. *"Okay by me. She is a pretty little thing. Drill into that pocket and leave her to me. Old and fat I be, but my drill still digs a dent."*

A chorus of laughter comes from the two hundred drillers above. My knuckles turn white as I grip the controls.

"Listen to Uncle Narol, Darrow. Better to back off till we can get a reading," my brother Kieran adds. He's three years older. Makes him think he's a sage, that he knows more. He just knows caution. *"There'll be time."*

"Time? Hell, it'll take hours," I snap. They're all against me in this. They're all wrong and slow and don't understand that the Laurel is only a bold move away. More, they doubt me. "You are being a coward, Narol."

Silence on the other end of the line.

Calling a man a coward—not a good way to get his cooperation. Shouldn't have said it.

"I say make the scan yourself," Loran, my cousin and Narol's son, squawks. *"Don't and Gamma is good as Gold—they'll get the Laurel for, oh, the hundredth time."*

The Laurel. Twenty-four clans in the underground mining colony of Lykos, one Laurel per quarter. It means more food than you can eat. It means more burners to smoke. Imported quilts from Earth. Amber swill with the Society's quality markings. It means winning. Gamma clan has had it since anyone can remember. So it's always been about the Quota for us lesser clans, just enough to scrape by. Eo says the Laurel is the carrot the Society dangles, always just far enough beyond our grasp. Just enough so we know how short we really are and how little we can do about it. We're supposed to be pioneers. Eo calls us slaves. I just think we never try hard enough. Never take the big risks because of the old men.

"Loran, shut up about the Laurel. Hit the gas and we'll miss all the bloodydamn Laurels to kingdom come, boy," Uncle Narol growls.

He's slurring. I can practically smell the drink through the comm. He wants to call a sensor team to cover his own ass. Or he's scared. The drunk was born pissing himself out of fear. Fear of what? Our overlords, the Golds? Their minions, the Grays? Who knows? Few people. Who cares? Even fewer. Actually, just one man cared for my uncle, and he died when my uncle pulled his feet.

My uncle is weak. He is cautious and immoderate in his drink, a pale shadow of my father. His blinks are long and hard, as though it pains him to open his eyes each time and see the world again. I don't trust him down here in the mines, or anywhere for that matter. But my mother would tell me to listen to him; she would remind me to respect my elders. Even though I am wed, even though I am the Helldiver of my clan, she would say that my "blisters have not yet become calluses." I will obey, even though it is as maddening as the tickle of the sweat on my face.

"Fine," I murmur.

I clench the drill fist and wait as my uncle calls it in from the safety of the chamber above the deep tunnel. This will take hours. I do the math. Eight hours till whistle call. To beat Gamma, I've got to keep a rate of 156.5 kilos an hour. It'll take two and a half hours for the scanCrew to get here and do their deal, at best. So I've got to pump out 227.6 kilos per hour after that. Impossible. But if I keep going and squab the tedious scan, it's ours.

I wonder if Uncle Narol and Barlow know how close we are. Probably. Probably just don't think anything is ever worth the risk. Probably think divine intervention will squab our chances. Gamma has the Laurel. That's the way things are and will ever be. We of Lambda just try to scrape by on our foodstuffs and meager comforts. No rising. No falling. Nothing is worth the risk of changing the hierarchy. My father found that out at the end of a rope.

Nothing is worth risking death. Against my chest, I feel the wedding band of hair and silk dangling from the cord around my neck and think of Eo's ribs.

I'll see a few more of the slender things through her skin this month. She'll go asking the Gamma families for scraps behind my back. I'll act like I don't know. But we'll still be hungry. I eat too much because I'm sixteen and still growing tall; Eo lies and says she's never got much of an appetite. Some women sell themselves for food or luxuries to the Tinpots (Grays, to be technic about it), the Society's garrison troops of our little mining colony. She wouldn't sell her body to feed me. Would she? But then I think about it. I'd do anything to feed her . . .

I look down over the edge of my drill. It's a long fall to the bottom of the hole I've dug. Nothing but molten rock and hissing drills. But before I know what's what, I'm out of my straps, scanner in hand and jumping down the hundred-meter drop toward the drill fingers. I kick back and forth between the vertical mineshaft's walls and the drill's long, vibrating body to slow my fall. I make sure I'm not near a pitviper nest when I throw out an arm to catch myself on a gear just above the drill fingers. The ten drills glow with heat. The air shimmers and distorts. I feel the heat on my face, feel it stabbing my eyes, feel it ache in my belly and balls. Those drills will melt your bones if you're not careful. And I'm not careful. Just nimble.

I lower myself hand over hand, going feetfirst between the drill fingers so that I can lower the scanner close enough to the gas pocket to get a reading. The heat is unbearable. This was a mistake. Voices shout at me through the comm. I almost brush one of the drills as I finally lower myself close enough to the gas pocket. The scanner flickers in my hand as it takes its reading. My suit is bubbling and I smell something sweet and sharp, like burned syrup. To a Helldiver, it is the smell of death.

2

THE TOWNSHIP

My suit can't handle the heat down here. The outer layer is nearly melted through. Soon the second layer will go. Then the scanner blinks silver and I've got what I came for. I almost didn't notice. Dizzy and frightened, I pull myself away from the drills. Hand over hand, I tug my body up, going fast away from the dreadful heat. Then something catches. My foot is jammed just underneath one of the gears near a drill finger. I gasp down air in sudden panic. The dread rises in me. I see my bootheel melting. The first layer goes. The second bubbles. Then it will be my flesh.

I force a long breath and choke down the screams that are rising in my throat. I remember the blade. I flip out my hinged slingBlade from its back holster. It's a cruelly curved cutter as long as my leg, meant for taking off and cauterizing limbs stuck in machinery, just like this. Most men panic when they get caught, and so the slingBlade is a nasty halfmoon weapon meant to be used by clumsy hands. Even filled with terror, my hands are not clumsy. I slice three times with the slingBlade, cutting nanoplastic instead of flesh. On the third swing, I reach down and jerk free my leg. As I do, my knuckles brush the edge of a drill. Searing pain shoots through my hand. I smell crackling flesh, but I'm up and off, climbing away from the hellish heat, climbing back to my holster seat and laughing all the while. I feel like crying.

My uncle was right. I was wrong. But I'll be damned if I ever let him know it.

"*Idiot,*" is his kindest comment.

"*Manic! Bloodydamn manic!*" Loran whoops.

"Minimal gas," I say. "Drilling now, Uncle."

The haulBacks take my pull when the whistle call comes. I push myself out of my drill, leaving it in the deep tunnel for the nightshift, and snag a weary hand on the line the others drop down the kilometer-long shaft to help me up. Despite the seeping burn on the back of my hand, I slide my body upward on the line till I'm out of the shaft. Kieran and Loran walk with me to join the others at the nearest gravLift. Yellow lights dangle like spiders from the ceiling.

My clan and Gamma's three hundred men already have their toes under the metal railing when we reach the rectangular gravLift. I avoid my uncle—he's mad enough to spit—and catch a few dozen pats on the back for my stunt. The young ones like me think we've won the Laurel. They know my raw helium-3 pull for the month; it's better than Gamma's. The old turds just grumble and say we're fools. I hide my hand and duck my toes in.

Gravity alters and we shoot upward. A Gamma scab with less than a week's worth of rust under his nails forgets to put his toes under the railing. So he hangs suspended as the lift shoots up six vertical kilometers. Ears pop.

"*Got a floating Gamma turd here*," Barlow laughs to the Lambdas.

Petty as it may seem, it's always nice seeing a Gamma squab something. They get more food, more burners, more everything because of the Laurel. We get to despise them. But then, we're supposed to, I think. Wonder if they'll despise us now.

Enough's enough. I grip the rust-red nanoplastic of the kid's frysuit and jerk him down. Kid. That's a laugh. He's hardly three years younger than I.

He's deathly tired, but when he sees the blood-red of my frysuit, he stiffens, avoids my eyes, and becomes the only one to see the burn on my hand. I wink at him and I think he shits his suit. We all do it now and then. I remember when I met my first Helldiver. I thought he was a god.

He's dead now.

Up top in the staging depot, a big gray cavern of concrete and metal, we pop our tops and drink down the fresh, cold air of a world far removed from molten drills. Our collective stink and sweat soon make a bog of the area. Lights flicker in the distance, telling us to stay clear of the magnetic horizonTram tracks on the other side of the depot.

We don't mingle with the Gammas as we head for the horizonTram in a staggered line of rust-red suits. Half with Lambda *L*s, half with Gamma canes painted in dark red on their backs. Two scarlet headTalks. Two blood-red Helldivers.

A cadre of Tinpots eye us as we trudge by over the worn concrete floor. Their Gray duroArmor is simple and tired, as unkempt as their hair. It would stop a simple blade, maybe an ion blade, and a pulseBlade or razor would go through it like paper. But we've only seen those on the holoCan. The Grays don't even bother to make a show of force. Their thumpers dangle at their sides. They know they won't have to use them.

Obedience is the highest virtue.

The Gray captain, Ugly Dan, a greasy bastard, throws a pebble at me. Though his skin is darkened from exposure to the sun, his hair is gray like the rest of his Color. It hangs thin and weedy over his eyes—two icecubes rolled in ash. The Sigils of his Color, a blocky gray symbol like the number four with several bars beside it, mark along each hand and wrist. Cruel and stark, like all the Grays.

I heard they pulled Ugly Dan off the frontline back in Eurasia, wherever that is, after he got crippled and they didn't want to buy him a new arm. He has an old replacement model now. He's insecure about it, so I make sure he sees me give the arm a glance.

"Saw you had an exciting day, darling." His voice is as stale and heavy as the air inside my frysuit. "Brave hero now, are you, Darrow? I always thought you'd be a brave hero."

"You're the hero," I say, nodding to his arm.

"And you think you're smart, doncha?"

"Just a Red."

He winks at me. "Say hello to your little birdie for me. A ripe thing for piggin'." Licks his teeth. "Even for a Ruster."

"Never seen a bird." Except on the HC.

"Ain't that a thing," he chuckles. "Wait, where you going?" he asks as I turn. "A bow to your betters won't go awry, doncha think?" He snickers to his fellows. Careless of his mockery, I turn and bow deeply. My uncle sees this and turns from it, disgusted.

We leave the Grays behind. I don't mind bowing, but I'll probably cut Ugly Dan's throat if I ever get the chance. Kind of like saying I'd take a zip out to Venus in a torchShip if it ever suited my fancy.

"Hey, Dago. Dago!" Loran calls to Gamma's Helldiver. The man's a legend; all the other divers just a flash in the pan. I might be better than him. "What'd you pull?"

Dago, a pale strip of old leather with a smirk for a face, lights a long burner and puffs out a cloud.

"Don't know," he drawls.

"Come on!"

"Don't care. Raw count never matters, Lambda."

"Like bloodyhell it doesn't! What'd he pull on the week?" Loran calls as we load into the tram. Everyone's lighting burners and popping out the swill. But they're all listening intently.

"Nine thousand eight hundred and twenty-one kilos," a Gamma boasts. At this, I lean back and smile; I hear cheers from the younger Lambdas. The old hands don't react. I'm busy wondering what Eo will do with sugar this month. We've never earned sugar before, only ever won it at cards. And fruit. I hear the Laurel gets you fruit. She'll probably give it all away to hungry children just to prove to the Society she doesn't need their prizes. Me? I'd eat the fruit and play politics on a full stomach. But she's got the passion for ideas, while I've got no extra passion for anything but her.

"Still won't win," Dago drawls as the tram starts away. "Darrow's a young pup, but he is smart enough to know that. Ain't you, Darrow?"

"Young or not, I beat your craggy ass."

"You sure 'bout that?"

"Deadly sure." I wink and blow him a kiss. "Laurel's ours. Send your sisters to my township for sugar this time." My friends laugh and slap their frysuit lids on their thighs.

Dago watches me. After a moment, he drags his burner deep. It glows bright and burns fast. "This is you," he says to me. In half a minute the burner is a husk.

After disembarking the horizonTram, I funnel into the Flush with the rest of the crews. The place is cold, musty, and smells exactly like what it is: a cramped metal shed where thousands of men strip off frysuits after hours of pissing and sweating to take air showers.

I peel off my suit, put on one of our haircaps, and walk naked to stand in the nearest transparent tube. There are dozens of them lined up in the Flush. Here there is no dancing, no boastful flips; the only camaraderie is exhaustion and the soft slapping of hands on thighs, creating a rhythm with the whoosh and shoot of the showers.

The door to my tube hisses closed behind me, muffling the sounds of music. A familiar hum comes from the motor, followed by a great rush of atmosphere and a sucking resonance as air filled with antibacterial molecules screams from the top of the machine and shoots over my skin to whisk away dead skin and filth down the drain at the bottom of the tube. It hurts.

After, I part with Loran and Kieran as they go to the Common to drink and dance in the taverns before the Laureltide dance officially starts. The Tinpots will be handing out the allowances of foodstuffs and announcing the Laurel at midnight. There will be dancing before and after for us of the dayshift.

The legends say that the god Mars was the parent of tears, foe to dance and lute. As to the former, I agree. But we of the colony of Lykos, one of the first colonies under Mars's surface, are a people of dance and song and family. We spit on that legend and make our own birthright. It is the one resistance we can manage against the Society that rules us. Gives us a bit of spine. They don't care that we dance or that we sing, so long as we obediently dig. So long as we prepare the planet for the rest of them. Yet to remind us of our place, they make one song and one dance punishable by death.

My father made that dance his last. I've seen it only once, and I've heard the song only once as well. I didn't understand when I was little, one about distant vales, mist, lovers lost, and a reaper meant to guide us to our unseen home. I was small and curious when the woman sang it as her son was hanged for stealing foodstuffs. He would have been a tall boy, but he could never get enough food to put meat on his bones. His mother died next. The people of Lykos did the Fading Dirge for them—a tragic thumping of fists against chests, fading slowly, slowly, till the fists, like her heart, beat no more and all dispersed.

The sound haunted me that night. I cried alone in our small kitchen, wondering why I cried then when I had not for my father. As I lay on the cold floor, I heard a soft scratching at my family's door. When I opened the door, I found a small haemanthus bud nestled in the red dirt, not a soul to be seen, only Eo's tiny footprints in the dirt. That is the second time she brought flowers after death.

Since song and dance are in our blood, I suppose it is not surprising that it was in both that I first realized I loved Eo. Not Little Eo. Not as she was. But Eo as she is. She says she loved me before they hanged my father. But it was in a smoky tavern when her rusty hair swirled and her feet moved with the zither and her hips to the drums that my heart forgot a couple of beats. It was not her flips or cartwheels. None of the boastful foolery that so marks the dance of the young. Hers was a graceful, proud movement. Without me, she would not eat. Without her, I would not live.

She may tease me for saying so, but she is the spirit of our people. Life's dealt us a hard hand. We're to sacrifice for the good of men and women we don't know. We're to dig to ready Mars for others. That makes some of us nastyminded folks. But Eo's kindness, her laughter, her fierce will, is the best that can come from a home such as ours.

I look for her in my family's offshoot township, just a half mile's worth of tunnelroad away from the Common. The township is one of two dozen townships surrounding the Common. It is a hivelike cluster of homes carved into the rock walls of the old mines. Stone and earth are our ceilings, our floors, our home. The Clan is a giant family. Eo grew up not a stone's throw from my house. Her brothers are like my own. Her father like the one I lost.

A mess of electrical wires tangle together along the cavern's ceiling like a jungle of black and red vines. Lights hang down from the jungle, swaying gently as air from the Common's central oxygen system circulates. At the center of the township dangles a massive holoCan. It's a square box with images on each side. Pixels are blacked out and the image is faded and fuzzy, but never has the thing faltered, never has it turned off. It bathes our cluster of homes in its own pale light. Videos from the Society.

My family's home is carved into the rock a hundred meters from the bottom floor of the township. A steep path leads from it to the ground, though pulleys and ropes can also bear one to the township's greatest heights. Only the old or infirm use those. And we have few of either.

Our house has few rooms. Eo and I only recently were able to take a room for ourselves. Kieran and his family have two rooms, and my mother and sister share the other.

All Lambdas in Lykos live in our township. Omega and Upsilon neighbor us just a minute's worth of wide tunnel over to either side. We're all connected. Except for Gamma. They live in the Common, above the taverns, repair booths, silk shops, and trade bazaars. The Tinpots live in a fortress above that, nearer the barren surface of our harsh world. That's where the ports lie that bring the foodstuffs from Earth to us marooned pioneers.

The holoCan above me shows images of mankind's struggles, which are then followed by soaring music as the Society's triumphs flash past. The Society's sigil, a golden pyramid with three parallel bars attached to the pyramid's three faces, a circle surrounding all, burns into the screen. The voice of Octavia au Lune, the Society's aged Sovereign, narrates the struggle man faces in colonizing the planets and moons of the System.

"Since the dawn of man, our saga as a species has been one of

tribal warfare. It has been one of trial, one of sacrifice, one of daring to defy nature's natural limits. Now, through duty and obedience, we are united, but our struggle is no different. Sons and daughters of all Colors, we are asked to sacrifice yet again. Here in our finest hour, we cast our best seeds to the stars. Where first shall we flourish? Venus? Mercury? Mars? The Moons of Neptune, Jupiter?"

Her voice grows solemn as her ageless face with its regal cast peers down from the HC. Her hands shimmer with the symbol of Gold emblazoned upon their backs—a dot in the center of a winged circle—gold wings mark the sides of her forearms. Only one imperfection mars her golden face—a long crescent scar running along her right cheekbone. Her beauty is like that of a cruel bird of prey.

"*You brave Red pioneers of Mars—strongest of the human breed—sacrifice for progress, sacrifice to pave the way for the future. Your lives, your blood, are a down payment for the immortality of the human race as we move beyond Earth and Moon. You go where we could not. You suffer so that others do not.*

"I salute you. I love you. The helium-3 that you mine is the lifeblood of the terraforming process. Soon the red planet will have breathable air, livable soil. And soon, when Mars is habitable, when you brave pioneers have made ready the red planet for us softer Colors, we will join you and you will be held in highest esteem beneath the sky your toil created. Your sweat and blood fuels the terraforming!

"Brave pioneers, always remember that obedience is the highest virtue. Above all, obedience, respect, sacrifice, hierarchy . . ."

I find the kitchen room of the home empty, but I hear Eo in the bedroom.

"Stop right where you are!" she commands through the door. "Do not, under any condition, look in this room."

"Okay." I stop.

She comes out a minute later, flustered and blushing. Her hair is covered in dust and webs. I rake my hands through the tangle. She's straight from the Webbery, where they harvest the bioSilk.

"You didn't go in the Flush," I say, smiling.

"Didn't have time. Had to skirt out of the Webbery to pick something up."

"What did you pick up?"

She smiles sweetly. "You didn't marry me because I tell you everything, remember. And do not go into that room."

I make a lunge for the door. She blocks me and pulls my sweatband down over my eyes. Her forehead pushes against my chest. I laugh, move the band, and grip her shoulders to push her back enough to look into her eyes.

"Or what?" I ask with a raised eyebrow.

She just smiles at me and cocks her head. I back away from the metal door. I dive into molten mineshafts without a blink. But there are some warnings you can buck off and others you can't.

She stands on her tiptoes and pecks me good on the nose. "Good boy; I knew you'd be easy to train," she says. Then her nose wrinkles because she smells my burn. She doesn't coddle me, doesn't berate me, doesn't even speak except to say, "I love you," with just the hint of worry in her voice.

She picks the melted pieces of my frysuit out of the wound, which stretches from my knuckles to my wrist, and pulls tight a webwrap with antibiotic and nervenucleic.

"Where'd you get that?" I ask.

"If I don't lecture you, you don't quiz me on what's what."

I kiss her on the nose and play with the thin band of woven hair around her ring finger. My hair wound with bits of silk makes her wedding band.

"I have a surprise for you tonight," she tells me.

"And I have one for you," I say, thinking of the Laurel. I put my sweatband on her head like a crown. She wrinkles her nose at its wetness.

"Oh, well, I actually have two for you, Darrow. Pity you didn't think ahead. You might have gotten me a cube of sugar or a satin sheet or . . . maybe even coffee to go with the first gift."

"Coffee!" I laugh. "What sort of Color did you think you married?"

She sighs. "No benefits to a diver, none at all. Crazy, stubborn, rash . . ."

"Dexterous?" I say with a mischievous smile as I slide my hand up the side of her skirt.

"Reckon that has its advantages." She smiles and swats my hand away like it's a spider. "Now put these gloves on unless you want jabber from the women. Your mother's already gone on ahead."

3

THE LAUREL

We walk hand in hand with the others from our township through the tunnelroads to the Common. Lune drones on above us on the HC, high above, as the Goldbrows (Aureate to be technic) ought to be. They show the horrors of a terrorist bomb killing a Red mining crew and an Orange technician group. The Sons of Ares are blamed. Their strange glyph of Ares, a cruel helmet with spiked sunbursts exploding from the crown, burns across the screen; blood drips from the spikes. Children are shown mangled. The Sons of Ares are called tribal murderers, called bringers of chaos. They are condemned. The Society's Gray police and soldiers move rubble. Two soldiers of the Obsidian Color, colossal men and women nearly twice my size, are shown along with nimble Yellow doctors carrying several victims from the blast.

There are no Sons of Ares in Lykos. Their futile war does not touch us; yet again a reward is offered for information on Ares, the terrorist king. We have heard the broadcast a thousand times, and still it feels like fiction. The Sons think we are mistreated, so they blow things up. It is a pointless tantrum. Any damage they do delays the progress of making Mars ready for the other Colors. It hurts humanity.

In the tunnelroad, where boys compete to touch the ceiling, the people of the townships flow in merriment toward the Laureltide dance. We sing the Laureltide song as we go—a swooping melody of a man finding his bride in a field of gold. There's laughter as the young boys try running along the walls or doing rows of flips, only to fall on their faces or be bested by a girl.

Lights are strung along the lengthy corridor. In the distance, drunk Uncle Narol, old now at thirty-five, plays his zither for the children who dance about our legs; even he cannot scowl forever. He wears the instrument suspended on shoulder straps so that it rests at his hips, with its plastic soundboard and its many taut metal strings facing up toward the ceiling. The right thumb strums the strings, except when the index finger drops down or when the thumb picks single strings, all while the left hand picks out the bass line string by string. It is maddeningly difficult to make the zither sound anything but mournful. Uncle Narol's fingers are equal to the task, though mine only make tragic music.

He used to play to me, teaching me to move to the dances my father never had the chance to teach me. He even taught me the forbidden dance, the one they'll kill you for. We'd do it in the old mines. He would hit my ankles with a switch till I pirouetted seamlessly through the swooping movements, a length of metal in my hand, like a sword. And when I got it right, he would kiss my brow and tell me I was my father's son. It was his lessons that taught me to move, that let me best the other kids as we played games of tag and ghosts in the old tunnels.

"The Golds dance in pairs, Obsidians in threes, Grays in dozens," he told me. "We dance alone, because only alone do Helldivers drill. Only alone can a boy become a man."

I miss those days, days when I was young enough that I didn't judge him for the stink of swill on his breath. I was eleven then. Only five years ago. Yet it feels a lifetime.

I get pats on the back from those of Lambda and even Varlo the baker tilts me his brow and tosses Eo a fist of bread. They've heard about the Laurel, no doubt. Eo tucks the bread into her skirts for later and gives me a curious look.

"You're grinning like a fool," she says to me, pinching my side. "What did you do?"

I shrug and try to wipe the grin from my face. It is impossible.

"Well, you're very proud of something," she says suspiciously.

Kieran's son and daughter, my niece and nephew, patter by. Three and three, the twins are just fast enough to outrace both Kieran's wife and my mother.

My mother's smile is one of a woman who has seen what life has to offer and is, at best, bemused. "It seems you've burned yourself, my heart," she says when she sees my gloved hands. Her voice is slow, ironic.

"A blister," Eo says for me. "Nasty one."

Mother shrugs. "His father came home with worse."

I put my arm around her shoulders. They are thinner than they used to be when she taught me, as all women teach their sons, the songs of our people.

"Was that a hint of worry I heard, Mother?" I ask.

"Worry? Me? Silly child." Mother sighs with a slow smile. I kiss her on the cheek.

Half the clans are already drunk when we arrive in the Common. In addition to a dancing people, we're a drunken people. The Tinpots let us alone in that. Hang a man for no real reason and you might get some grumblings from the townships. But force sobriety upon us, and you'll be picking up the pieces for a bloodydamn month. Eo is of the mind that the fungus, grendel, which we distill, isn't native to Mars and was instead planted here to enslave us to the swill. She brings this up whenever my mother makes a new batch, and my mother usually replies by taking a swig and saying, "Rather a drink be my master than a man. These chains taste sweet."

They'll taste even sweeter with the syrups we'll get from the Laurel boxes. They have flavors for alcohol, like berry and something called cinnamon. Perhaps I'll even get a new zither made of wood instead of metal. Sometimes they give those out. Mine is an old, frayed thing. I've played it too long. But it was my father's.

The music swells ahead of us in the Common—bawdy tunes of improvised percussion and wailing zithers. We're joined by Omegas and Upsilons, jostling about merrily toward the taverns. All the tavern doors have been thrown open so their smoke and sound billow into the Common's plaza. Tables ring the plaza and a space is left clear surrounding the central gallows so that there is room to dance.

Gamma homes fill the next several levels, followed by supply depots, a sheer wall, and then, high above in the ceiling, a sunken metal dome with nanoGlass viewports. We call that place the Pot. It is the fortress where our keepers live and sleep. Beyond that is the uninhabitable surface of our planet—a barren wasteland that I've only seen on the HC. The helium-3 we mine is supposed to change that.

The dancers and jugglers and singers of the Laureltide have already begun. Eo catches sight of Loran and Kieran and gives them a holler. They're at a long, packed table near the Soggy Drop, a tavern where the oldest of our clan, Ol' Ripper, holds court and tells tales to drunken folks. He's passed out on the table tonight. It's a shame. I would have liked for him to see me finally get us the Laurel.

At our feasts, where there's hardly food enough for each soul to hold a bit in their gob, the drink and dance take center. Loran pours me a mug of swill before I even sit down. He's always trying to get others to drink so he can put ridiculous ribbons in their hair. He clears the way for Eo to sit beside his own wife, Dio, her sister, twin in looks if not birth.

Loran has a love for Eo like her brother Liam would, but I know he was once as taken with her as he ever was with Dio. In fact, he bent a knee to my wife when she turned fourteen. But then again, half the lads joined him in that. No sweating it. She made her choice right and clear.

Kieran's children swarm him. His wife kisses his lips; mine kisses his brow and tousles his red hair. After a day in the Webbery harvesting spiderworm silk, I don't know how the wives manage to look so lovely. I was born handsome, face angular and slim, but the mines have done their part to change me. I'm tall, still growing. Hair still like old blood, irises still as rust-red as Octavia au Lune's are golden. My skin is tight and pale, but I'm pocked with scars—

burns, cuts. Won't be long till I look hard as Dago or tired as Uncle Narol.

But the women, they're beyond us, beyond me. Lovely and spry despite the Webbery, despite the children they bear. They wear layered skirts down past their knees and blouses of half a dozen reds. Never anything else. Always red. They're the heart of the clans. And how much more beautiful they will look wrapped in the imported bows and ribbons and laces contained in the Laurel boxes.

I touch the Sigils on my hands, a bonelike texture. It's a crude Red circle with an arrow and cross-hatching. It feels right. Eo's doesn't. Her hair and eyes may be ours, but she could be one of the Goldbrows we see on the holoCan. She deserves it. Then I see her smack Loran hard on the head as he throws back a mug of Ma's swill. God, if he's placing about the pieces, placed her well. I smile. But as I look behind her, my smile fades. Above the leaping dancers, amid the hundred swirling skirts and thumping boots and clapping hands, sways a single skeleton upon the cold, tall gallows. Others do not notice it. To me, it is a shadow, a reminder of my father's fate.

Though we are diggers, we are not permitted to bury our dead. It is another of the Society's laws. My father swayed for two months till they cut his skeleton down and ground his bones to dust. I was six but I tried to pull him down the first day. My uncle stopped me. I hated him because he kept me from my father's body. Later, I came to hate him again because I discovered he was weak: my father died for something, while Uncle Narol lived and drank and squandered his life.

"He's a mad one, you'll see someday. Mad and brilliant and noble, Narol's the best of my brothers," my father once said.

Now he's just the last.

I never thought my father would do the Devil's Dance, what the oldfolk call death by hanging. He was a man of words and peace. But his notion was freedom, laws of our own. His dreams were his weapons. His legacy is the Dancer's Rebellion. It died with him on the scaffold. Nine men at once doing the Devil's Dance, kicking and flailing, till only he was left.

It wasn't much of a rebellion; they thought peaceful protest would convince the Society to increase the food rations. So they performed the Reaping Dance in front of the gravLifts and removed bits of machinery from the drills so that they wouldn't work. The gambit failed. Only winning the Laurel can get you more food.

It's on eleven when my uncle sits down with his zither. He eyes me something nasty, drunk as a fool on Yuletide. We don't share words, though he has a kind one for Eo and she for him. Everyone loves Eo.

It's when Eo's mother comes over and kisses me on the back of my head and says very loudly, "We heard the news, you golden boy. The Laurel! You are your father's son," that my uncle stirs.

"What's the matter, Uncle?" I ask. "Have gas?"

His nostils flare wide. "You little shiteater!"

He launches himself across the table and soon we're a muddle of fists and elbows on the ground. He's big, but I flip him down and pound his nose with my bad hand till Eo's father and Kieran pull me off. Uncle Narol spits at me. It's more blood and swill than anything else. Then we're drinking again at opposite ends of the table. My mother rolls her eyes.

"He's just bitter he didn't do a bloodydamn thing to get the Laurel. Shown up is all," Loran says of his father.

"Bloodydamn coward wouldn't know how to win the Laurel if it landed in his lap," I say, scowling.

Eo's father pats me on the head and sees his daughter fixing my burned hand under the table. I slip my gloves back on. He winks at me.

Eo's figured out the fuss about the Laurel by the time the Tinpots arrive, but she's not excited as I'd hoped she'd be. She twists her skirts in her hands and smiles at me. But her smiles are more like grimaces. I don't understand why she's so apprehensive. None of the other clans are. Many come to pay their respects; all of the Helldivers do, except Dago. He's sitting at a group of shiny Gamma tables—the only ones with more food than swill—smoking down a burner.

"Can't wait for the sod to be eating regular rations," Loran chuckles. "Dago's never tasted peasant fare before."

"Yet somehow he's thinner than a woman," Kieran adds.

I laugh along with Loran and push a meager piece of bread to Eo.

"Cheer up," I tell her. "This is a night for celebrating."

"I'm not hungry," she replies.

"Not even if the bread has cinnamon on it?" Soon it will.

She gives me that half smile, as if she knows something I do not.

At twelve, a coterie of Tinpots descend in gravBoots from the Pot. Their armor is shoddy and stained. Most are boys or old men retired from Earth's wars. But that's not what matters. They carry their thumpers and scorchers in buckled holsters. I've never seen either weapon used. There's no need. They've got the air, the food, the port. We haven't a scorcher to shoot. Not that Eo wouldn't like to steal one.

The muscle in her jaw flexes as she watches the Tinpots float in their gravBoots, now joined by MineMagistrate, Timony cu Podginus, a minute copper-haired man of the Pennies (Copper to be technic).

"Notice, notice. Grubby Rusters!" Ugly Dan calls. Silence falls over the festivities as they float above us. Magistrate Podginus's gravBoots are substandard things, so he wobbles in the air like a geriatric. More Tinpots descend on a gravLift as Podginus splays open his small, manicured hands.

"Fellow pioneers, how wonderful it is to see your celebrations. I must confess," he titters, "I have a fondness for the rustic nature of your happiness. Simple drink. Simple fare. Simple dance. Oh, what fine souls you have to be so entertained. Why, I wish I were so entertained. I cannot even find pleasure off-planet in a Pink brothel after a meal of fine ham and pineapple tart these days! How sad for me! How your souls are spoiled. If only I could be like you. But my Color is my Color, and I am cursed as a Copper to live a tedious life of data, bureaucracy, and management." He clucks his tongue and his copper curls bounce as his gravBoots shift.

"But to the matter: All Quotas have been met, save by Mu and Chi. As such, they will receive no beefs, milks, spices, hygienics, comforts, or dental aid this month. Oats and substantials only. You understand that the ships from Earth orbit can only bring so many supplies to the colonies. Valuable resources! And we must give them to those who *perform*. Perhaps next quarter, Mu and Chi, you will dally less!"

Mu and Chi lost a dozen men in a gas explosion like the one Uncle Narol feared. They did not dally. They died.

He prattles on awhile before coming to the real matter. He produces the Laurel and holds it in the air, pinched between his fingers. It's painted in fake gold, but the small branch sparkles nonetheless. Loran nudges me. Uncle Narol scowls. I lean back, conscious of the eyes. The young take their cues from me. The children adore all Helldivers. But the older eyes watch me too, just as Eo always says. I'm their pride, their golden son. Now I'll show them how a real man acts. I won't jump up and down in victory. I'll just smile and nod.

"And it becomes my distinct honor to, on behalf of the Arch-Governor of Mars, Nero au Augustus, to award the Laurel of productivity and monthly excellence and triumphant fortitude and obedience, sacrifice, and . . ."

Gamma gets the Laurel.

And we don't.

4

THE GIFT

As the Laurel-wreathed boxes come down to Gamma, I think about how clever it really is. They won't let us win the Laurel. They don't care that the math doesn't work. They don't care that the young scream in protest and the old moan their same tired wisdoms. This is just a demonstration of their power. It is their power. They decide the winner. A game of merit won by birth. It keeps the hierarchy in place. It keeps us striving, but never conspiring.

Yet despite the disappointment, some part of us doesn't blame the Society. We blame Gamma, who receives the gifts. A man's only got so much hate, I suppose. And when he sees his children's ribs through their shirts while his neighbors line their bellies with meat stews and sugared tarts, it's hard for him to hate anyone but them. You think they'd share. They don't.

My uncle shrugs at me and others are red and mad. Loran looks like he might attack the Tinpots or the Gammas. But Eo doesn't let me boil in it. She doesn't let my knuckles turn white as I clench my fists in fury. She knows the temper I have inside me better even than my own mother, and she knows how to drain the rage before it rises.

My mother smiles softly as she watches Eo take me by the arm. How she loves my wife.

"Dance with me," Eo whispers. She shouts for the zithers to get going and the drums to get rolling. No doubt she's pissin' fire. She hates the Society more than I do. But this is why I love my wife.

Soon the fast zither music swells and the old men slap their hands on tables. The layered skirts fly. Feet tap and shuffle. And I grasp my wife as the clans flow in dance throughout the square to join us. We sweat and we laugh and try to forget the anger. We grew together, and now are grown. In her eyes, I see my heart. In her breath, I hear my soul. She is my land. She is my kin. My love.

She pulls me away with laughter. We wend our way through the crowd to be alone. Yet she does not stop when we are free. She guides me along metal walkways and low, dark ceilings to the old tunnels, to the Webbery, where the women toil. It is between shifts.

"Where are we going exactly?" I ask.

"If you remember, I have gifts for you. And if you apologize for your own gift going flat, I'll smack you in the gob."

Seeing a bloody-red haemanthus bulb peeking out from the wall, I snatch it up and hand it to her. "My gift," I said. "I did intend to surprise you."

She giggles. "Well then. This inner half is mine. This outer half is yours. No! Don't pull at it. I'm keeping your half." I smell the haemanthus in her hand. It stinks like rust and Mother's meager stews.

Inside the Webbery, thigh-thick spiderworms of brown and black fur, with long skeletal legs, knit silk around us. They crawl along the girders, thin legs disproportionate to their corpulent abdomens. Eo leads me into the Webbery's highest level. The old metal girders are laced with silk. I shiver in looking at the creatures above and below; pitvipers I understand, spiderworms I do not. The Society's Carvers made the creatures. Laughing, Eo guides me to a wall and pulls back a thick curtain of webbing, revealing a rusted metal duct.

"Ventilation," she says. "Mortar on the walls gave way to reveal it about a week ago. An old tube too."

"Eo, they'll lash us if they find us. We're not allowed . . ."

"I'm not going to let them ruin this gift too." She kisses me on the nose. "Come on, Helldiver. There's not even a molten drill in this tunnel."

I follow her through a long series of turns in the small shaft till we exit out a grate into a world of inhuman sounds. A buzz murmurs in the darkness. She takes my hand. It's the only familiar thing.

"What is that?" I ask of the sound.

"Animals," she says, and leads me into the strange night. Something soft is beneath my feet. I nervously let her pull me forward. "Grass. Trees. Darrow, trees. We're in a forest."

The scent of flowers. Then lights in the darkness. Flickering animals with green abdomens flutter through the black. Great bugs with iridescent wings rise from the shadows. They pulse with color and life. My breath catches and Eo laughs as a butterfly passes so close I can touch it.

They're in our songs, all these things, but we've only ever seen them on the HC. Their colors are unlike any I could believe. My eyes have seen nothing but soil, the flare of the drill, Reds, and the gray of concrete and metal. The HC has been the window through which I've seen color. But this is a different spectacle.

The colors of the floating animals scald my eyes. I shiver and laugh and reach out and touch the creatures floating before me in the darkness. A child again, I cup them and look up at the room's clear ceiling. It is a transparent bubble that peers at the sky.

Sky. Once it was just a word.

I cannot see Mars's face, but I can see its view. Stars glow soft and graceful in the slick black sky, like the lights that dangle above our township. Eo looks as though she could join them. Her face is aglow as she watches me, laughing as I fall to my knees and suck in the scent of the grass. It is a strange smell, sweet and nostalgic, though I have no memories of grass. As the animals buzz near in the brush, in the trees, I pull her down, I kiss her with my eyes open for the first time. The trees and their leaves sway gently from the air that comes through the vents. And I drink the sounds, the smells, the sight as my wife and I make love in a bed of grass beneath a roof of stars.

"That is Andromeda Galaxy," she tells me later as we lie on our backs. The animals make chirping noises in the darkness. The sky above me is a frightening thing. If I stare too intently, I forget gravity's pull and feel as though I am going to fall into it. Shivers trickle down my spine. I am a creature of nooks and tunnels and shafts. The mine is my home, and part of me wants to run to safety, run from this alien room of living things and vast spaces.

Eo rolls to look at me and traces the steam scars that run like rivers down my chest. Farther down she'd find scars from the pitviper along my belly. "Mum used to tell me stories of Andromeda. She'd draw with inks given to her by that Tinpot, Bridge. He always liked her, you know."

As we lie together, she takes a deep breath and I know she has planned something, saved something to talk about in this moment. This place is leverage.

"You won the Laurel, we all know," she says to me.

"You needn't coddle me. I'm not angry any longer. It doesn't matter," I say. "After seeing this, none of that matters."

"What are you talking about?" she asks sharply. "It matters more than ever. You won the Laurel, but they didn't let you keep it."

"It doesn't matter. This place . . ."

"This place exists, but they don't let us come here, Darrow. The Grays must use it for themselves. They don't share."

"Why should they?" I ask, confused.

"Because we made it. Because it's ours!"

"Is it?" The thought is foreign. All I possess is my family and myself. Everything else is the Society's. We didn't spend the money to send the pioneers here. Without them, we'd be on the dying Earth like the rest of humanity.

"Darrow! Are you so Red that you don't see what they've done to us?"

"Watch your tone," I say tightly.

Her jaw flexes. "I'm sorry. It's just . . . we *are* in chains, Darrow. We are not colonists. Well, sure we are. But it's more on the spot to call us slaves. We beg for food. Beg for Laurels like dogs begging for scraps from the master's table."

"You may be a slave," I snap. "But I am not. I don't beg. I earn. I am a Helldiver. I was born to sacrifice, to make Mars ready for man. There's a nobility to obedience . . . ."

She throws up her hands. "A talking puppet, are you? Spitting out their bloodydamn lines. Your father had the right of it. He might not have been perfect, but he had the right of it." She grabs a clump of grass and tears it out of the ground. It seems like some sort of sacrilege.

"We have claim over this land, Darrow. Our sweat and blood watered this soil. Yet it belongs to the Golds, to the Society. How long has it been this way? A hundred, a hundred and fifty years of pioneers mining and dying? Our blood and their orders. We prepare this land for Colors that have never shed sweat for us, Colors that sit in comfort on their thrones on distant Earth, Colors that have never been to Mars. Is that something to live for? I'll say it again, your father had the right of it."

I shake my head at her. "Eo, my father died before he was even twenty-five because he had the *right of it.*"

"Your father was weak," she mutters.

"What the bloodydamn is that supposed to mean?" Blood rises into my face.

"It means he had too much restraint. It means your father had the right dream but died because he would not fight to make it real," she says sharply.

"He had a family to protect!"

"He was still weaker than you."

"Careful," I hiss.

"Careful? This from *Darrow,* the mad Helldiver of Lykos?" She laughs patronizingly. "Your father was born careful, obedient. But were you? I didn't think so when I married you. The others say you are like a machine, because they think you know no fear. They're blind. They don't see how fear binds you."

She traces the haemanthus blossom along my collarbone in a sudden show of tenderness. She is a creature of moods. The flower is the same color as the wedding band on her finger.

I roll on an elbow to face her. "Spit it out. What do you want?"

"Do you know why I love you, Helldiver?" she asks.

"Because of my sense of humor."

She laughs dryly. "Because you *thought* you could win the Laurel. Kieran told me how you burned yourself today."

I sigh. "The rat. Always jabbering. Thought that's what younger brothers were supposed to do, not elder."

"Kieran was frightened, Darrow. Not *for* you, like you might be thinking. He was frightened *of* you, because he can't do what you did. Boy wouldn't even think it."

She always talks circles around me. I hate the abstracts she lives for.

"So you love me because you believe that I think there are things worth the risk?" I puzzle out. "Or because I'm ambitious?"

"Because you've a brain," she teases.

She makes me ask it again. "What do you want me to do, Eo?"

"Act. I want you to use your gifts for your father's dream. You see how people watch you, take their cues from you. I want you to think owning this land, our land, is worth the risk."

"How much a risk?"

"Your life. My life."

I scoff. "You're that eager to be rid of me?"

"Speak and they will listen," she urges. "It is that bloody simple. All ears yearn for a voice to lead them through darkness."

"Grand, so I'll hang with a troop. I am my father's son."

"You won't hang."

I laugh too harshly. "So certain a wife I have. I'll hang."

"You're not meant to be a martyr." Sighing, she lies back in disappointment. "You wouldn't see the point to it."

"Oh? Well then, tell me, Eo. What is the point to dying? I'm only a martyr's son. So tell me what that man accomplished by robbing me of a father. Tell me what good comes of all that *bloodydamn* sadness. Tell me why it's better I learned to dance from my uncle than my father." I go on. "Did his death put food on your table? Did it make any of our lives any better? Dying for a cause doesn't do a bloodydamn thing. It just robbed us of his laughter." I feel the tears burning my eyes. "It just stole away a father and a husband. So what if life isn't fair? If we have family, that is all that should matter."

She licks her lips and takes her time in replying.

"Death isn't empty like you say it is. Emptiness is life without freedom, Darrow. Emptiness is living chained by fear, fear of loss, of death. I say we break those chains. Break the chains of fear and you break the chains that bind us to the Golds, to the Society. Could you imagine it? Mars could be ours. It could belong to the colonists who slaved here, died here." Her face is easier to see as night fades through the clear roof. It is alive, on fire. "If you led the others to freedom. The things you could do, Darrow. The things you could make happen." She pauses and I see her eyes are glistening. "It chills me. You have been given so, so much, but you set your sights so low."

"You repeat the same damn points," I say bitterly. "You think a dream is worth dying for. I say it isn't. You say it's better to die on your feet. I say it's better to live on our knees."

"You're not even living!" she snaps. "We are machine men with machine minds, machine lives . . . ."

"And machine hearts?" I ask. "That's what I am?"

"Darrow . . ."

"What do you live for?" I ask her suddenly. "Is it for me? Is it for family and love? Or is it for some dream?"

"It's not just *some* dream, Darrow. I live for *the* dream that my children will be born free. That they will be what they like. That they will own the land their *father* gave them."

"I live for you," I say sadly.

She kisses my cheek. "Then you must live for more."

There's a long, terrible silence that stretches between us. She does not understand how her words wrench my heart, how she can twist me so easily. Because she does not love me like I love her. Her mind is too high. Mine too low. Am I not enough for her?

"You said you had another gift for me?" I say, changing the subject.

She shakes her head. "Some other time. The sun rises. Watch it with me once, at least."

We lie in silence and watch light slip into the sky as though it were a tide made from fire. It is unlike anything I could have dreamed of. I can't stop the tears that well in the corners of my eyes as the world beyond turns to light and the greens and browns and yellows of the trees in the room are revealed. It is beauty. It is a dream.

I am silent as we return to the grimness of the gray ducts. The tears linger in my eyes and as the majesty of what I saw fades; I wonder what Eo wants of me. Does she want me to take my slingBlade and start a rebellion? I would die. My family would die. She would die, and nothing would make me risk her. She knows that.

I am puzzling out what her other gift may be when we exit the ducts for the Webbery. I roll first from the duct and extend a hand back to her when I hear a voice. It is accented, oily, from Earth.

"Reds in our gardens," it oozes. "Ain't that a thing."

5

THE FIRST SONG

Ugly Dan stands with three Tinpots. Their thumpers perch crackling in their hands. Two of the men lean on the metal rails of the Webbery's girders. Behind them, the women of Mu and Upsilon wrap silk from the worms around long silver poles. They shake their heads insistently at me, as if telling me not to be foolish. We've gone beyond the permitted zones. This will mean a flogging, but if I resist, it will mean death. They will kill Eo and they will kill me.

"Darrow . . . ," Eo murmurs.

I set myself between Eo and the Tinpots, but I don't fight. I won't let us die for a simple glimpse of the stars. I put my hands out to let them know I will surrender.

"Helldivers," Ugly Dan chuckles to the others. "The toughest ant is yet but an ant." He swings his thumper into my stomach. It's like being bitten by a viper and kicked by a boot. I fall gasping, hands on the metal grate. Electricity slithers through my veins. I taste the bile rising in my throat. "Take a swing, Helldiver," Dan coos. He drops one of the thumpers in front of me. "Please. Take a swing. Won't be any consequences. Just some fun between the boys. Take a piggin' swing."

"Do it, Darrow!" Eo shouts.

I'm not a fool. I thrust my hands up in surrender and Dan sighs in disappointment as he clacks the magnetic manacles around my wrists. What would Eo have had me do? She curses at them as they lock her arms together and drag us away through the Webbery to the cells. This will mean the lash. But it will be just the lash because I did not pick up the thumper, because I did not listen to Eo.

It's three days in a cell in the Pot before I see Eo again. Bridge, one of the old, kinder Tinpots, takes us out together; he lets us touch. I wonder if she'll spit at me, curse me for my impotence. But she only grips my fingers and brings her lips to mine.

"Darrow." Her lips brush my ear. The breath is warm, the lips cracked and trembling. She's frail as she hugs me—a little girl, all wire wrapped in pale skin. Her knees wobble and she shudders against me. The warmth I saw in her face as we watched the sun rise has fled and left her like a faded memory. But I hardly see anything but her eyes and her hair. I wrap my arms around her and hear the muttering of the crowded Common. The faces of our kin and clan stare at us as we stand at the edge of the gallows, where they will flog us. I feel like a child under their stares, under the yellowish lights.

It's like a dream when Eo tells me she loves me. Her hand lingers on mine. But there's something strange to her eyes. They should only whip her, yet her words are final, her eyes sad but not afraid. I see her making a goodbye. A nightmare is coming to my heart. I can feel it like a nail dragged along the bones of my spine as she murmurs an epigram in my ear. "Break the chains, my love."

And then I am jerked away from her by my hair. Tears stream down her face. They are for me, though I do not yet understand why. I cannot think. The world is swimming. I am drowning. Rough hands shove me to my knees, then jerk me up. I've never heard the Common so quiet. The shuffling of my captors' feet echoes as they move me around.

The Tinpots fit me into my Helldiver frysuit. Its acrid smell makes me think I am safe, I am in control. I am not. I'm dragged away from her into the very center of the Common and tossed at the edge of the gallows. The metal stairs are rusted and stained. I grip them with my hands and look to the top of the gallows. Twenty-four of the headTalks each have a cord of leather. They wait for me atop the platform.

"Oh, the horror of such occasions as this, my friends," Magistrate Podginus cries. His copper gravBoots hum above me as he floats through the air. "Oh, how the ties that bind us are stretched when one decides to break the laws which protect us all.

"Even the youngest, even the best, are subject to Law. To Order! Without these we would be animals! Without obedience, without discipline, there would be no colonies! And those few colonies there are would be torn asunder by disorder! Man would be confined to Earth. Man would wallow forevermore on that planet until the end of days. But Order! Discipline! Law! These are the things which empower our race. Cursed is the creature who breaks with these compacts."

The speech is more eloquent than usual. Podginus is trying to impress his intelligence upon someone. I look up from the stairs and see a sight I did not ever think to see with my own two eyes. It stings to look at him, to drink in the radiance of his hair, of his Sigils. I see a Gold. In this drab place, he is what I imagine angels would be like. Cloaked in gold and black. Wrapped in the sun. A lion roaring upon his breast.

His face is older, severe, and pure with power. His hair shines, combed back against his head. Neither a smile nor a frown mark his thin lips, and the only line I see is that of a scar, which runs along his right cheekbone.

I've learned from the HC that such a scar is borne only by the finest of the Golds. The Peerless Scarred, they call them—men and women of the ruling Color who have graduated from the Institute, where they learn the secrets that will permit mankind to one day colonize all the planets of the Solar System.

He does not speak to us. He speaks to another Gold, one tall and thin, so thin I thought it a woman at first. Without a scar, the man's face is coated with strange paste to bring out the color of his cheeks and cover the lines on his face. His lips shine. And his hair glistens in a way his master's does not. He is a grotesque thing to look upon. He thinks so of us. He sniffs the air, contemptuous. The older Gold speaks to him softly and not to us.

And why should he speak to us? We are not worthy of a Gold's words. I scarcely want to look at him. I feel like I dirty his gold and black finery with my red eyes. Shame creeps upon me and then I realize why.

His is a face I know. It is a face every man and woman of the colonies would know. Besides Octavia au Lune, this is the most famous face on Mars—that of Nero au Augustus. The ArchGovernor of Mars has come to see me flogged, and he has brought a retinue. Two Crows (Obsidians to be technic) float quietly behind him. Their skull helmets suit their Color. I was born to mine the earth. They were born to kill men. More than two feet taller than I. Eight fingers on each massive hand. They breed them for war, and watching them is like watching the coldblooded pitvipers who infest our mines. Reptiles both.

There are a dozen others in his retinue, including another, slighter Gold who seems his apprentice. He's even more beautiful than the ArchGovernor and he appears to dislike the thin, womanish Gold. And there is an HC camera crew of Greens, tiny creatures compared with the Crows. Their hair is dark. Not green like their eyes and the Sigils on their hands. Frenetic excitement shimmers in those eyes. It's not often they have Helldivers to make into an example, so they make a spectacle of me. I wonder how many other mining colonies are watching. All of them, if the ArchGovernor is here.

They make a show of stripping away the frysuit they only just dressed me in. I see myself on the HC display above, see my wedding band dangling from the cord around my neck. I look younger than I feel, thinner. They jerk me up the stairs and bend me over a metal box beside the noose where my father hung. I shiver as they lay me across the cold steel and tighten my hands in restraints. I smell the synthleather of the lashes, hear one of the headTalks cough.

"Forevermore, let justice be done," Podginus says.

Then the lashes come. Forty-eight in all. They aren't soft, not even my uncle's. They can't be. The lashes bite and wail into my flesh, making a strange keening noise as they arch through the air. Music of terror. I can barely see by the end of it. I pass out twice, and each time I wake I wonder if you can see my spine on the HC.

It's a show, all a show of their power. They let the Tinpot, Ugly Dan, act sympathetic, as though he pities me. He whispers encouragement in my ear loud enough for the cameras. And when the last lash slashes my back, he steps in as if to stop another from coming down. Subconsciously, I think he saves me. I'm thankful. I want to kiss him. He is salvation. But I know I've had my forty-eight.

Then they are dragging me to the side. They leave my blood. I'm sure I screamed, sure I shamed myself. I hear them bring out my wife.

"Even the young, even the beautiful cannot escape justice. It is for all the Colors that we preserve Order, Justice. Without, we would find anarchy. Without Obedience, chaos! Man would perish upon the irradiated sands of Earth. He would drink from the blasted seas. There must be unity. Forevermore, let justice be done."

MineMagistrate Podginus's words ring hollow.

No one is offended that I'm bloody and beaten. But when Eo is dragged atop the gallows, there are cries. There are curses. Even now she is beautiful, even drained of the light I saw in her three days ago. Even as she sees me and lets the tears come down her face, she is an angel.

All this for a little adventure. All this for a night under the stars with the man she loves. Yet she is calm. If there is fear, it is in me, because I feel a strangeness in the air. Her skin prickles as they lay her across the cold box. She flinches. I wish my blood had warmed it better for her.

When they whip Eo, I try not to watch. But it hurts more to abandon her. Her eyes find mine. They shine like rubies, twitch every time the lash falls. *Soon this will be over, my love. Soon we will go back to life. Just last the lash and we get everything back.* But can she even take so many lashes?

"End it," I say to the Tinpot beside me. "End it!" I beg of him. "I'll do anything. I'll obey. I'll take her lashes. Just end it, you bloodydamn bastards! End it!"

The ArchGovernor looks down at me, but his face is golden, poreless, and without care. I am nothing but the bloodiest of ants. My sacrifice will impress him. He'll feel compassion if I abase myself, if I throw myself into the fire for love. He'll feel pity. This is how the stories go.

"Your Excellency, give me her punishment!" I plead. "Please!" I beg because in my wife's eyes I see something that terrifies me. I see fight in her as they streak her back bloody. I see anger building inside her. There is a reason she is not afraid.

"No. No. No," I plead to her. *"No, Eo. Please, no!"*

"Gag that wretched thing! He prickles the ArchGovernor's ears," Podginus orders. Bridge forces a knot of stone into my mouth. I gag and cry.

As the thirteenth lash falls, as I mumble for her not to do it, Eo stares into my eyes one last moment and then she begins her song. It is a quiet sound, a mournful sound, like the song the deep mines whisper as wind moves in the abandoned shafts. It is the song of death and lament, the song that is forbidden. The song I have only heard once before.

For this, they will kill her.

Her voice is soft and true, never as beautiful as she. It echoes across the Common, rising up like a Siren's unearthly call. The lashes pause. The headTalks shiver. Even the Tinpots sadly shake their heads when they place the words. Few men truly like seeing beauty burn.

Podginus glances embarrassedly over at ArchGovernor Augustus, who descends on golden gravBoots to watch more closely. His shining hair glistens against his noble brow. High cheekbones catch the light. Those golden eyes examine my wife as though a worm had suddenly sprouted a butterfly's wings. His scar curves as he speaks with a voice dripping power.

"Let her sing," he says to Podginus, not bothering to hide his fascination.

"But, my lord . . ."

"No animal but man throws themselves willingly into the flames, Copper. Relish the sight. You'll not see it again." To his camera crew: "Continue recording. We will edit out the parts we find intolerable."

How futile his words make her sacrifice seem.

But never has Eo been more beautiful to me than in that moment. In the face of cold power, she is fire. This is the girl who danced through the smoky tav with a mane of red. This is the girl who wove me a wedding band of her own hair. This is the girl who chooses to die for a song of death.

My love, my love
Remember the cries
When winter died for spring skies
They roared and roared
But we grabbed our seed
And sowed a song
Against their greed

And
Down in the vale
Hear the reaper swing, the reaper swing
the reaper swing
Down in the vale
Hear the reaper sing
A tale of winter done

My son, my son
Remember the chains
When gold ruled with iron reins
We roared and roared
And twisted and screamed
For ours, a vale
of better dreams

As her voice finally swells and the song runs out of words, I know I have lost her. She becomes something more important; and she was right, I do not understand.

“A quaint tune. But is that all you have?” the ArchGovernor asks her when she is through. He looks at her but he speaks loudly, to the crowd, to those who will watch in the other colonies. His entourage chuckles at Eo’s weapon, a song. What is a song but notes unto the air? Useless as a match in a storm against his power. He shames us. “Do any of you wish to join her in song? I implore you, bold Reds of . . .” He looks to his assistant, who mouths the name. “. . . Lykos, join her now if you wish.”

I can barely breathe past the stone. It chips my molars. Tears stream down my face. No voices rise from the crowd. I see my mother trembling with anger. Kieran clutches his wife close. Narol stares at the ground. Loran weeps. They are all here, all quiet. All afraid.

“Alas, Your Excellency, we find the girl alone in her zealotry,” Podginus declares. Eo has eyes only for me. “ ’Tis clear her opinion is an outlier’s, an outcast’s. Mayhaps we should proceed?”

“Yes,” the ArchGovernor says idly. “I have an appointment with Arcos. Hang the rusty bitch lest she continue to howl.”

6

THE MARTYR

For Eo, I do not react. I am anger. I am hatred. Everything. But I hold her gaze even as they take her away and fit the noose around her neck. I look up at Bridge and he quietly takes the gag from my mouth. My teeth will never be the same. Tears build in the Tinpot's eyes. I leave him and stumble numbly to the bottom of the scaffold so Eo can see me as she dies. This is her choice. I will be with her to the end. My hands shake. Sobs come from the crowd behind me.

"The last words, to whom will you speak them before justice is done?" Podginus asks her. He drips sympathy for the camera.

I ready for her to say my name, but she does not. Her eyes never leave mine, but she calls her sister out. "Dio." The word trembles in the air. She is frightened now. I do not react as Dio climbs the scaffold stairs; I do not understand, but I will not be jealous. This is not about me. I love her. And her choice is made. I do not understand, but I will not let her die knowing anything but my love.

Ugly Dan has to help Dio climb the gallows; she's stumbling and senseless as she leans close to her sister. Whatever is said, I do not hear; but Dio lets loose a moan that will haunt me forever. She looks at me as she weeps. What did my wife tell her? Women are crying.

Men wipe their eyes. They have to stun Dio to pull her away, but she clings to Eo's feet, weeping. There is a nod from the ArchGovernor, though he doesn't even care enough to watch as, like my father, Eo is hanged.

"Live for more," she mouths to me. She reaches into her pocket and pulls out the haemanthus I gave her. It is smashed and flat. Then loudly she screams to all those gathered, "Break the chains!"

The trapdoor beneath her feet opens. She falls, and for one moment, her hair hangs suspended about her head, a flourish of red. Then her feet scramble at air and she falls. Her slim throat gags. Eyes open so wide. If only I could save her from this. If only I could protect her; but the world is cold and hard to me. It does not bend as I wish it to bend. I am weak. I watch my wife die and my haemanthus fall from her hand. The camera records it all. I rush forward to kiss her ankle. I cradle her legs. I will not let her suffer.

On Mars there is not much gravity, so you have to pull the feet to break the neck. They let the loved ones do it.

Soon, there is no sound, not even the creaking of the rope.

My wife is too light.

She was only just a girl.

Then the thumping of the Fading Dirge begins. Fists on chests. Thousands. Fast, like a racing heartbeat. Slower. A beat a second. A beat every five. Every ten. Then never again, and the mournful mass fades away like dust held in the palm as the old tunnels wail with deep winds.

And the Golds, they fly away.

Eo's father, Loran, and Kieran sit by my door through the night. They say they are there to keep me company. But they are there to guard me, to ensure I do not die. I want to die. Mother dresses my wound with silk my sister, Leanna, stole from the Webbery.

"Keep the nervenucleic dry, or you will scar."

What are scars? How little they matter. Eo will not see them, so why should I care? She will not run her hand along my back. She will never kiss my wounds.

She is gone.

I lie in our bed on my back so I can feel the pain and forget my wife. But I cannot forget. She hangs even now. In the morning, I will pass her on the way to the mines. Soon she will stink and soon she will rot. My beautiful wife shone too bright to live long. I still feel her neck cracking against my hands; they tremble now in the night.

There is a hidden tunnel I carved in my bedroom long ago in the rock so I could sneak out as a child. I use it now. I leave out the secret path, climbing stealthily down from my home, so my kin never see me slip away in the low light.

It is quiet in the township. Quiet except for the HC, which makes my wife die to a soundtrack. They intended to show the futility of disobedience. And they succeed in that, but there is something else in the video. They show my flogging, and Eo's, and they play her song throughout. And as she dies, they play it again, which seems to give the video the wrong effect. Even if she were not my wife, I see a martyr, a young girl's pretty song silenced by the rope of cruel men.

Then the HC flashes black for several moments. It has never gone to black before. And Octavia au Lune comes back on with the same old message. It almost seems as though someone has hacked into the broadcast, because my wife flickers onto the giant screen again.

"Break the chains!" she cries. Then she's gone and the screen is black. It crackles. The image comes back. She cries it again. Black once more. Standard programming goes up, then it cuts to her screaming one last time and then there's me pulling her legs. Then static.

The streets are quiet as I make my way to the Common. The nightshift will be returning soon. Then I hear a noise and a man steps into the street in front of me. My uncle's face leers at me from the shadows. A single bulb hangs over his head, illuminating the flask in his hand and his tattered red shirt.

"You are your father's son, little bastard. Stupid and vain."

My hands clench. "Come to stop me, Uncle?"

He grunts. "Couldn't stop your father from killing his bloody self. And he was a better bloodyman than you. More restraint in him."

I step forward. "I don't need your permission."

"Nay, you little squabber, you don't." He runs a hand through his hair. "Don't do what you're gonna do, though. It'll break your mother; you might think she didn't know you'd slip out. She did. Told me so. Said you were gonna go die like my brother, like your girl."

"If Mother knew, she would have stopped me."

"Nah. She lets us men make our own mistakes. But this ain't what your girl would've wanted."

I point a finger at my uncle. "You don't know a thing. Not a thing about what she wanted." Eo said I wouldn't understand being a martyr. I will show her I do.

"Righto," he says with a shrug. "I'll walk with you, then, since your head is full of rocks." He chuckles. "We Lambdas do love the noose."

He tosses me his flask and I fall into tentative step beside him.

"I tried to talk your father out of his little protest, you know. Told him words and dance mean as much as dust. Tried squaring up with him. I squabbed that one up. He laid me down cold." He throws a slow right. "Comes a time in life when you know a man has his mind set and it's an insult to gainsay."

I drink from his flask and hand it back. The swill tastes strange and thicker than usual. Strange. He makes me finish the flask.

"Your's set?" he asks, tapping his head. "Course it is. I forget, I taught you how to dance."

"Stubborn as a pitviper, wasn't that how you put it?" I say quietly, allowing a little smile.

I walk in silence for a moment with my uncle. He puts a hand on my shoulder. A sob wants to come out of my chest. I swallow it.

"She left me," I whisper. "Just left me."

"Musta had a reason. Not a dumb girl, that one."

The tears come as I enter the Common. My uncle takes me in a one-armed hug and kisses the crown of my head. It's all he can offer. He's not a man made for affection. His face is pale and ghostly. Thirty-five and so old, so tired. A scar twists his upper lip. Gray streaks his thick hair.

"Tell them hello for me in the vale," he says into my ear, his beard coarse against my neck. "Give my brothers a toast and my wife a kiss, specially Dancer."

"Dancer?"

"You'll know him. And if you see your gramp and gran, tell them we still dance for them. They won't be long alone." He walks away, then pauses and without turning says, "Break the chains. Hear?"

"Hear."

He leaves me there in the Common with my swaying wife. I know the cameras watch me from the can as I walk up the gallows. It is metal, so the stairs don't creak. She hangs like a doll. Her face is pale as chalk and her hair shifts slightly as the ventilators rasp above.

When the rope has been cut with the slingBlade I stole from the mines, I grab its frayed end and lower her down gently. I take my wife in my arms and together wend our way from the square to the Webbery. A nightshift is working their final hours. The women watch in silence as I carry Eo to the ventilation duct. There I see Leanna, my sister. Tall and quiet like my mother, she watches me with hard eyes, but she does nothing. None of the women do. They will not gossip about where my wife is buried. They will not speak, not even for the chocolate given to spies. Only five souls have been buried in three generations—someone always hangs for it.

This is the ultimate act of love. Eo's silent requiem.

Women begin to cry, and as I pass they reach to touch Eo's face, to touch mine and help me open the ventilation duct. I drag my wife through the tight metal space, taking her to where we made love beneath the stars, where she told me her plans and I did not listen. I hold her lifeless body and hope her soul sees me in a place where we were happy.

I dig a hole near the base of a tree. My hands, covered with the dirt of our land, are red like her hair as I take her hand and kiss her wedding band. I place the outer bulb of the haemanthus atop her heart and take the inner and put it near my own. Then I kiss her lips and bury her. But I sob before I can finish. I uncover her face and kiss her again and hold my body to hers till I see a red sun rising through the artificial bubbleroof. The colors of the place scald my eyes and I cannot stop my tears. When I pull away, I see my headband poking from her pocket. She made it for me to take my sweat. I give it my tears now and take it with me.

Kieran strikes me in the face when he sees me back in the township. Loran cannot speak, while Eo's father slumps against a wall. They think they failed me. I hear Eo's mother's cries. My mother says nothing as she makes me a meal. I don't feel well. It's hard to breathe. Leanna comes in late and helps her, kissing me on the head as I eat, lingering long enough to smell my hair. I must use one hand as I move the food from plate to mouth. My mother holds my other hand between her callused palms. She watches it instead of me, as though remembering when it was small and soft and wondering how it became so hard.

I finish the meal just as Ugly Dan comes. My mother does not leave the table as I'm pulled away. Her eyes stay fixed on where my hand lay. I think she believes if she does not look up, this will not happen. Even she can only bear so much.

They will hang me before a full assembly at nine in the morning. I'm dizzy for some reason. My heart feels funny, slow. I hear the ArchGovernor's words to my wife echo.

"Is that all your strength?"

My people sing, we dance, we love. That is our strength. But we also dig. And then we die. Seldom do we get to choose why. That choice is power. That choice has been our only weapon. But it is not enough.

They give me my last words. I call Dio up. Her eyes are bloodshot and swollen. She's a fragile thing, so unlike her sister.

"What were Eo's last words?" I ask her, though my mouth moves slowly, oddly.

She glances back to Mother, who finally followed but now shakes her head. There is something they are not telling me. Something they don't want me to know. A secret held back even though I am about to die.

"She said she loved you."

I don't believe her, but I smile and kiss her forehead. She can't handle more questions. And I'm dizzy. Hard to speak.

"I'll tell her you say hello."

I do not sing. I am made for other things.

My death is senseless. It is love.

But Eo was right, I don't understand this. This is not my victory. This is selfish. She told me to live for more. She wanted me to fight. But here I am, dying despite what she wanted. Giving up because of the pain.

I panic as suicides do when they realize their folly.

Too late.

I feel the door beneath me open. My body falls. Rope flays my neck. My spine creaks. Needles lance my lumbar. Kieran stumbles forward. Uncle Narol shoves him away. With a wink, he touches my feet and pulls.

I hope they do not bury me.

PART II

REBORN

There is a festival where we wear the faces of demons to ward evil spirits from our dead in the vale. The faces sparkle with fool's gold.

7

LAZARUS

I do not see Eo in death. My kin believe we see our loved ones when we pass on. They wait for us in a green vale where woodfire smoke and the scent of stews thicken the air. There is an Old Man with dew on his cap who makes safe the vale, and he stands with our kin waiting for us along a stone road beside which sheep graze. They say the mist there is fresh and the flowers sweet, and those who are buried pass along the stone road faster.

But I do not see my love. I do not see the vale. I see nothing but phantom lights in darkness. I feel pressure, and I know, as would any miner, that I am buried beneath the earth. I loose a soundless scream. Dirt enters my mouth. Panic fills me. I cannot breathe, cannot move. The earth hugs me till finally I claw my way free, feel air, gasp oxygen, pant and spit dirt.

It is minutes before I look up from my knees. I crouch in an abandoned mine, an old tunnel long deserted but still connected to the ventilation system. It smells of dirt. A single flare burns beside my grave, splaying weird shadows over the walls. It singes my sight like the sun did as it rose over Eo's grave.

I'm not dead.

The realization takes longer in coming than one might have thought. But there's a bloody wound around my neck where the rope cut the skin. There's dirt in the lashes on my back.

Still, I'm not dead.

Uncle Narol didn't pull my feet hard enough. But surely the Tinpots would have checked, unless they were lazy. Not a stretch to think that, but something else is at play. I was too woozy when I walked to the gallows. I feel something in my veins even now, a lethargy as though I've been drugged. Narol did this. He drugged me. He buried me. But why? And how would he escape being caught when he pulled my body down?

When a low rumbling comes from the darkness beyond the flare, I know I will have answers. A tumbler, like a metal beetle on six wheels, crawls over the crest of a long tunnel. Its front grille hisses steam as it comes to a stop in front of me. Eighteen lights singe my vision; shapes exit the sides of the vehicle, cutting across the glare of the headlights to grab me. I'm too stunned to resist. Their hands are callused like miners' and their faces are covered with Octobernacht demon masks. Yet they move me gently, guiding instead of forcing me into the tumbler's hatch.

Inside the tumbler, the globe light is red and bloody. I sit in a worn metal bucket seat across from the two figures that fetched me from my grave. The female's mask is pale white and gold, horned like a cacodemon. Her eyes glitter darkly out from the eyeholes. The other figure is a timid man. He's willowy and quiet, seemingly frightened of me. His snarling batface mask can't conceal his shy glances or the way in which he hides his hands—a trait of the frightened, as Uncle Narol always claimed when he taught me to dance.

"You're Sons of Ares, aren't you?" I guess.

The weakling flinches, while the woman's eyes are mocking.

"And you're Lazarus," she says. I find her voice cold, lazy; it plays with the ears as a cat plays with a caught mouse.

"I am Darrow."

"Oh, we know who you are."

"Don't tell him anything, Harmony!" the weakling gibbers. "Dancer didn't tell us to discuss anything with him till we get home."

"Thank you, *Ralph.*" Harmony sighs at the weakling and shakes her head.

After realizing his error, the weakling shifts uncomfortably in his bucket seat, but I've stopped paying him any mind. Here, the woman is king. Unlike the weakling's, her mask is like that of an old crone, one of the witches of Earth's fallen cities who made soup from the marrow of children's bones.

"You're a mess." Harmony reaches to touch my neck. I grab her hand and squeeze. Her bones are brittle as hollow plastic in a Helldiver's hand. The weakling reaches for his thumper, but Harmony motions him to calm down.

"Why am I not dead?" I ask. After the hanging, my voice is like gravel dragged over metal.

"Because Ares has a mission for you, little Helldiver."

She winces as I squeeze her hand.

"Ares . . ." My mind flashes to images of bomb blasts, disembodied limbs, chaos. Ares. I know what sort of mission he'll want. I'm too numb to even know what I'll say when he asks. My mind is on Eo, not this life. I am a shell. Why could I not have stayed in the ground?

"May I have my hand back now?" Harmony asks.

"If you take off your mask. Otherwise, I'm keeping it."

She laughs and strips away her mask. Her face is day and night—the right side a ragged and distended mess of skin running and folding together in smooth scar rivers. A steam burn. A familiar sight, but not on women. Rare for a woman to be on a drillteam.

Yet it is the unburned side of her face that startles. She is beautiful, more beautiful even than Eo. Skin soft, pale as milk, bones prominent and delicate. Yet she looks so cold, so angry and cruel. Her bottom teeth are uneven and her nails poorly maintained. She has knives in her boots. I can tell by the way she flinched down when I grabbed her hand.

The weakling, Ralph, is unremarkably ugly—dark face like a hatchet, teeth all ajar and grimy. He stares out the tumbler's window hatch as we drive through abandoned tunnels till we reach lit paved tunnelroads meant for fast moving. I do not know these Reds, and though they have the Red Sigil emblazoned on their hands, I do not trust them. They are not of Lambda or Lykos. Might as well be Silvers.

Eventually I glimpse other utility vehicles and tumblers out the hatch. I don't know where we are, yet that bothers me less than the swelling sadness in my chest. The farther we ride and the more time I'm given to my thoughts, the worse the pain becomes. I finger my wedding band. Eo is still dead. She's not waiting for me at the end of this ride. Why did I survive when she did not? Why did I pull her feet so hard? Could she have lived too? My guts feel like a black hole. A terrible weight compresses my chest, and I ache to just jump from the tumbler into the path of a utility vehicle. Death is easy when you've already tried to find it.

But I don't jump; I sit with Harmony and Ralph. Eo wanted more for me. I clench the scarlet headband in my fist.

The tunnelroad widens slightly when we come to a checkpoint manned by dirty Tinpots in worndown gear. The electric gate isn't even charged. They let the tumbler ahead of us through after scanning a panel on its side. Then it's our turn and I'm shifting uncomfortably in my seat right along with Ralph. Harmony chuckles disdainfully as the grey-haired Tinpot scans the side of the tumbler and waves us through the gate.

"We have a passcode. No brains in slaves. Mine Tinpots are idiots. It's the Grey elites, or the Obsidian monsters you watch out for. But they don't waste their time down here."

I am trying to convince myself that this all is not some Gold trick, that Harmony and Ralph are not enemies, when we pull off the main tunnelroad into a cul-de-sac of utility warehouses not much larger than the Common. Harsh sulfur lights hang down from utility fixtures. Half the bulbs are burned out. One flickers on and off above a garage near a warehouse marked with a queer symbol done in strange paint. We steer into the garage. The door closes and Harmony motions for me to get out of the tumbler.

"Home sweet home," she says. "Now time to meet Dancer."

8

DANCER

Dancer looks through me. He's near enough my height, which is rare. But he's thick and terribly old, maybe in his forties. White swirls from his temples. A dozen twin scars mark his neck. I've seen their sort before. Pitviper bites. The arm on the left side of his body hangs limp. Nerve damage. But his eyes arrest me; they are brighter than most, swirling with patterns of true red, not rust red. He has a fatherly smile.

"You must be wondering who we are," Dancer says gently. He's big but his voice is easy. Eight Reds are with him, all men except for Harmony, and they watch him with adoring eyes. All miners, I think, each with the scarred, strong hands of our kind. They move with the grace of our people. No doubt some were jumpers and boasters, as we call those who run along the walls and perform the flips at dances. Any Helldivers?

"He's not wondering." Harmony takes time with the words, rolling them along her tongue. She squeezes Dancer's hand as she passes around him to look at me. "Bloodydamn runt pegged it an hour ago."

"Ah." Dancer smiles softly at her. "Of course he did, otherwise Ares wouldn't have asked us to risk extracting him here. Do you know where 'here' is, Darrow?"

"It doesn't matter," I murmur. I look around at the walls, the men, the swaying lights. Everything is so cold, so dirty. "What matters is . . ." I fail to finish my own sentence. A thought of Eo severs my voice. "What matters is that you want something from me."

"Yes, that matters," says Dancer. His hand touches my shoulder. "But that can wait. I'm surprised you're standing. The wounds on your back are sullied. You'll need antibac and skinres to stop the scarring."

"Scars don't matter," I say. I stare at the two blood drops that trickle from my shirttail to the floor. My wounds reopened when I climbed from the grave. "Eo *is* . . . dead, yes?"

"Yes. She is. We couldn't save her, Darrow."

"Why not?" I ask.

"We just couldn't."

"Why not?" I repeat. I glare up at him, glare at his followers and hiss the words one by one. "You saved me. You could have saved her. She is the one you would have wanted. The bloodydamn martyr. She cared about all this. Or does Ares only need Sons, not Daughters?"

"Martyrs are a dime a dozen." Harmony yawns.

I slip forward like a serpent and grab her around the throat; waves of anger ripple through my face till it goes numb and I feel tears welling behind my eyes. Scorchers whine as they're primed around me. One jams into the back of my neck. I feel its cold muzzle.

"Let her go!" someone shouts. "Do it, boy!"

I spit at them, shake Harmony once and toss her aside. She crouches on the floor, hacking, and then a knife glimmers in her hand as she rises.

Dancer stumbles between us. "Stop it! Both of you! Darrow, please!"

"Your girl was a dreamer, boy," Harmony spits at me from Dancer's other side. "As worthless as a flame over water . . ."

"Harmony, shut your bloodydamn gob," Dancer barks. "Put those damn things away." The scorchers go quiet. A tense silence follows and he leans in close to speak with me. His voice lowers. My breath is fast. "Darrow, we're friends. We're friends. Now, I can't answer for Ares—why he couldn't help us save your girl; I am just one of his hands. I can't wash away the pain. I can't bring your wife back to you. But, Darrow, look at me. Look at me, Helldiver." I do. Right into those blood-red eyes. "I can't do many things. But I can bring you justice."

Dancer goes to Harmony and whispers something, likely telling her that we're to be friends. We won't be. But I promise not to choke her and she promises not to stab me.

She is quiet as she guides me from the others through cramped metal hallways to a small door opened by twisting a knob. Our feet echo over rusting walkways. The room is small and littered with tables and medical supplies. She has me strip and sit on one of the cold tables so she can clean my wounds. Her hands are not gentle as they scrub dirt from my lacerated back. I try not to scream.

"You're a fool," she says as she scrapes rock out of a deep wound. I wheeze in pain and try to say something, but she jams her finger into my back, cutting me short.

"Dreamers like your wife are limited, little Helldiver." She makes sure I don't speak. "Understand that. The only power they have is in death. The harder they die, the louder their voice, the deeper the echoes. But your wife served her purpose."

Her purpose. It sounds so cold, so distant and sad, as though my girl of smiles and laughter was meant for nothing but death. Harmony's words carve into me and I stare at the metal grating before turning to look into her angry eyes.

"Then what is your purpose?" I ask.

She holds up her hands, caked with dirt and blood.

"The same as yours, little Helldiver. To make the dream come true."

After Harmony scours my back of dirt and gives me a dose of antibac, she takes me to a room next to humming generators. The squat quarters are lined with cots and a liquid flush. She leaves me to it. The shower is a terrifying thing. Though it's gentler than the air of the Flush, half the time I feel like I'm drowning, the other half I find a mixture of ecstasy and agony. I turn the heat nozzle till steam rises thick and pain lances my back.

Clean, I dress in the strange garments they've set out for me. It's not a jumpsuit or homespun weave like I'm used to wearing. The material is sleek, elegant, like something someone of a different Color would wear.

Dancer comes into the room when I'm half dressed. His left foot drags behind him, almost as useless as his left arm. Yet still he's an impressive man, thicker than Barlow, handsomer than me despite his age and the bite scars on his neck. He carries a tin bowl and sits on one of the cots, which creaks against his weight.

"We saved your life, Darrow. So your life is ours, do you not agree?"

"My uncle saved my life," I say.

"The drunk?" Dancer snorts. "The best thing he ever did was tell us about you. And he should have done that when you were a boy, but he kept you a secret. He's worked for us since before your father's death as an informer, you know."

"Is he hanged now?"

"Now that he pulled you down? I should hope not. We gave him a jammer to shut off their ancient cameras. He did the work of a ghost."

Uncle Narol. HeadTalk, but drunk as a fool. I always thought him weak. He still is. No strong man would drink like him or be so bitter. But he never earned the disdain I gave him. Yet why did he not save Eo?

"You act like my uncle bloodydamn owed you," I say.

"He owes his people."

"*People.*" I laugh at the term. "There is family. There is clan. There may even be township and mine, but people? *People.* And you act as though you're my representative, as though you have a right to *my* life. But you are just a fool, all you Sons of Ares." My voice is withering in its condescension. "Fools who can do nothing but blow things up. Like children kicking pitviper nests in rage."

That's what I want to do. I want to kick, to lash out. That's why

I insult him, that's why I spit on the Sons even though I have no real cause to hate them.

Dancer's handsome face curls into a tired smile, and it's only then that I realize how feeble his dead arm really is—thinner than his muscular right arm, bent like a flower's root. But despite the withered limb, there's a twisted menace to Dancer, a less obvious sort than that in Harmony. It comes out when I laugh at him, when I scorn him and his dreams.

"Our informants exist to feed us information and to help us find the outliers so we can extract the best of Red from the mines."

"So you can use us."

Dancer smiles tightly and picks up the bowl from the cot. "We will play a game to see if you are one of these outliers, Darrow. If you win, I will take you to see something few lowReds have seen."

LowReds. I've never heard the term before.

"And if I lose?"

"Then you are not an outlier and the Golds win yet again."

I flinch at the notion.

He holds out a bowl and explains the rules. "There are two cards in the bowl. One bears the reaper's scythe. The other bears a lamb. Pick the scythe and you lose. Pick the lamb and you win."

Except I notice his voice fluctuate when he says this last bit. This is a test. Which means there is no element of luck to it. It must then be measuring my intelligence, which means there is a kink. The only way the game could test my intelligence is if the cards are both scythes; that's the singular variable that could be altered. Simple. I stare into Dancer's handsome eyes. It is a rigged game; I'm used to these, and usually I follow the rules. Just not this time.

"I'll play."

I reach into the bowl and pull free a card, taking care that only I can see its face. It is a scythe. Dancer's eyes never leave mine.

"I win," I say.

He reaches for the card to see its face, but I shove it in my mouth before he can take hold of it. He never sees what I drew. Dancer watches me chew on the paper. I swallow and pull the remaining card from the bowl and toss it at him. A scythe.

"The lamb card simply looked too good not to eat," I say.

"Perfectly understandable."

The red in his eyes twinkles and he sets the bowl aside. Warmth of character returns to him, as if he'd never been a menace. "Do you know why we call ourselves Sons of Ares, Darrow? To the Romans, Mars was the god of war—a god of military glory, defense of the hearth and home. Honorable and all. But Mars is a fraud. He is a romanticized version of the Greek god Ares."

Dancer lights a burner and hands a second one to me. The generators buzz freshly and the burner fills me with a similar haze as its smoke curls through my lungs.

"Ares was a bastard, an evil patron of rage, violence, bloodlust, and massacre," he says.

"So by naming yourselves after him, you're pointing to the truth of things within the Society. Cute."

"Something like that. The Golds would prefer for us to forget history. And most of us have, or were never taught it. But I know how Gold rose to power hundreds of years ago. They call it the Conquering. They butchered any who contested them. Massacred cities, continents. Not many years ago, they reduced an entire world to ash—Rhea. The Ash Lord nuked it to oblivion. It was with Ares's wrath that they acted. And now we are the sons of that wrath."

"Are you Ares?" I ask, voice hushed. Worlds. They've destroyed worlds. But Rhea is so much farther out from Earth than Mars. It's one of Saturn's moons, I think. Why would they nuke a world all the way out there?

"No. I'm not Ares," he answers.

"But you belong to him."

"I belong to no one but Harmony and my people. I am like you, Darrow, born to a clan of earth diggers, miners from the colony Tyros. Only I know more of the world." He frowns at my impatient expression. "You think me a terrorist. I am not."

"No?" I ask.

He leans back and takes a drag on his burner.

"Imagine there was a table covered with fleas," he explains. "The fleas would jump and jump to heights unknown. Then a man came along and upturned a glass jar over the fleas. The fleas jumped and hit the top of the jar and could go no farther. Then the man removed the jar and yet the fleas did not jump higher than they had grown accustomed, because they believed there to still be a glass ceiling." He breathes out smoke. I see his eyes glow through it like the ember tip of his burner. "We are the fleas who jump high. Now let me show you just how high."

Dancer takes me down a rickety corridor to a cylindrical metal lift. It's a rusty thing, heavy, and it squeals as we rise steadily upward.

"You should know that your wife didn't die in vain, Darrow. The Greens who help us hijacked the broadcast. We hacked in and played the true version over every HC on our planet. The planet, the clans of the hundred thousand mining colonies and those in the cities, have heard your wife's song."

"You tell tall tales," I grumble. "There aren't half that many colonies."

He ignores me. "They heard her song and they call her Persephone already."

I flinch and look over at him. No. That is not her name. She is not their symbol. She doesn't belong to these brigands with trumped-up names.

"Her name is Eo," I sneer. "And she belongs to Lykos."

"She belongs to her people now, Darrow. And they remember the old tales of a goddess stolen from her family by the god of death. Yet even when she was stolen, death could not forever keep her. She was the Maiden, the goddess of spring destined to return after each winter. Beauty incarnate can touch life even from the grave; that's how they think of your wife."

"She's not coming back," I say to end the conversation. It is futile debating with this man. He just rolls on.

Our lift comes to a halt and we exit into a small tunnel. Following it, we come to another lift of sleeker metal, better maintained. Two Sons guard it with scorchers. Soon we're going upward again.

"She will not come back, but her beauty, her voice, will echo until the end of time. She believed in something beyond herself, and her death gave her voice power it didn't have in life. She was pure, like your father. We, you and I"—he touches my chest with the back of his index finger—"are dirty. We are made for blood. Rough hands. Dirty hearts. We are lesser creatures in the grand scheme of things, but without us men of war, no one except those of Lykos would hear Eo's song. Without our rough hands, the dreams of the pure hearts would never be built."

"Cut to the point," I interrupt. "You want me for something."

"You tried to die before," Dancer says. "Do you want to do so again?"

"I want . . ." What do I want? "I want to kill Augustus," I say, remembering the cold Golden face as it commanded my wife's death. It was so distant, so uncaring. "He will not live while Eo lies dead." I think of Magistrate Podginus and Ugly Dan. I will kill them too.

"Vengeance then," he sighs.

"You said you could give it to me."

"I said I would give you *justice*. Vengeance is an empty thing, Darrow."

"It will fill me. Help me kill the ArchGovernor."

"Darrow, you set your sights too low." The lift picks up speed. My ears pop. Up and up and up. How far does this lift rise? "The ArchGovernor is merely one of the most important Golds on Mars." Dancer hands me a pair of tinted glasses. I put them on tentatively as my heart thuds in my chest. We're going to the surface. "You must widen your gaze."

The lift stops. The doors open. And I am blind.

Behind the glasses, my pupils constrict to adjust to the light. When at last I'm able to open my eyes, I expect to see a massive glowing bulb or a flare, some source to the light. But I see nothing. The light is ambient, from some distant, impossible source. Some human instinct in me knows this power, knows this primal origin of life. The sun. Daylight. My hands tremble and I step with Dancer from the elevator. He does not speak. I doubt I would hear him even if he did.

We stand in a room of strange makings, unlike any I've imagined.

There is a substance underfoot, hard but neither metal nor rock. Wood. I know it from the HC pictures of Earth. A carpet of a thousand hues spreads over it, soft under my feet. The walls around are of red wood, carved with trees and deer. Soft music plays in the distance. I follow the tune deeper into the room, toward the light.

I find a bank of glass, a large wall that lets the sun in to shine across the length of a squat black instrument with white keys, which plays itself in a tall room with three walls and a long bank of glass windows. Everything is so smooth. Beyond the instrument, beyond the glass, lies something I don't understand. I stumble toward the window, toward the light, and fall to my knees, pressing my hands against the barrier. I moan one long note.

"Now you understand," Dancer says. "We are deceived."

Beyond the glass sprawls a city.

9

THE LIE

The city is one of spires, parks, rivers, gardens, and fountains. It is a city of dreams, a city of blue water and green life on a red planet that is supposed to be as barren as the cruelest desert. This is not the Mars they show us on the HC. This is not a place unfit for man. It is a place of lies, wealth, and immense abundance.

I gasp at the grotesquerie.

Men and women fly. They shimmer Gold and Silver. Those are the only Colors I see in the sky. Their gravBoots carry them about like gods, the technology so much more graceful than the clumsy gravBoots our keepers wear in the mines. A young man soars past my window, his skin burnished, his hair fluttering loosely behind him as he carries two bottles of wine toward a nearby garden spire; he's drunk and his wobbling through the air reminds me of a time I saw a drillBoy's air system break down in his frysuit; he gasped for oxygen as he died, twitching and dancing. This Gold laughs like a fool and does a mirthful spin. Four girls, not at all older than me, fly after him in a merry hunt, giddy and giggling. Their tight dresses seem to be made of liquid and drip around their young curves. They look my age, in a way, but seem so bloody foolish.

I do not understand.

Beyond them, ships flit through the air along beacon-lit avenues. Small ships, ripWings, as Dancer calls them, escort the most intricate of air yachts. On the ground, I see men and women moving through wide avenues. There are automobiles, Color-coded lamps along the lower levels—Yellow, Blue, Orange, Green, Pink, a hundred shades of a dozen Colors to form a hierarchy so complex, so alien, I scarcely think it a human concept. The buildings through which the paths wind are huge, some of glass, some of stone. But many remind me of those I've seen on the HC, those buildings of the Romans, made this time for gods instead of man.

Beyond the city, which stretches nearly as far as I can see, Mars's red and barren surface is scarred with the green of grass and struggling woods. The sky above is blue, stained with stars. The terraforming is complete.

This is the future. It should not be this way for generations.

My life is a lie.

So many times has Octavia au Lune told us of Lykos that we are the pioneers of Mars, that we are the brave souls who sacrifice for the race, that soon our toils for humanity will be over. Soon the softer Colors will join us, once Mars is habitable. But they have already joined us. Earth has come to Mars and we pioneers were left below, slaving, toiling, suffering to create and maintain the foundation of this . . . this empire. We are as Eo always said—the Society's slaves.

Dancer sits in a chair behind me and waits till I can speak. He says a word and the windows darken. I can still see the city, but the sun no longer blinds my eyes. Beside us, the squat instrument, called a piano, whispers a dreary melody.

"They told us we were man's only hope," I say quietly. "That Earth was overcrowded, that all the pain, all the sacrifice, was for mankind. Sacrifice is good. Obedience the highest virtue . . ."

The laughing Gold has reached the nearby spire; he surrenders to the girls and their kisses. Soon they will drink their wine and have their amusement.

Dancer tells me how it is.

"Earth ain't overcrowded, Darrow. Seven hundred years back,

they expanded to their moon, Luna. Because it is so difficult to launch spacecraft through Earth's gravity and atmosphere, Luna became Earth's port through which it colonized the moons and planets of the Solar System."

"Seven hundred years?" I gasp, feeling suddenly very stupid.

"On Luna, efficiency and order became the chief concern. In space, every set of lungs must have a purpose. So the first Colors were gradually instituted and the Reds were sent to Mars to gather the fuel for mankind. The mining colonies were established there since Mars has the highest concentration of helium-3, which is used to terraform the other worlds and moons."

At least that wasn't a lie.

"Are they terraformed, the other moons and worlds?"

"The small moons, yes. Most of the planets. Obviously not the gas giants." He sits in a chair. "It was in the early stages of the Colonization when the wealthy of Luna began to realize Earth was nothing more than a drain on their profits. Even as Luna colonized the Solar System, they were taxed and owned by corporations and countries on Earth, but those same entities could not enforce their ownership. So Luna rebelled—the Golds and their Society against the countries of Earth. Earth fought back and Earth lost. That was the Conquering. Economics turned Luna into the power and port of the Solar System. And the Society began to change into what it is today—an empire built on Red backs."

I watch the Colors move about below. They are small, hard to distinguish from our height—and my eyes are not used to seeing so far or seeing so much light.

"Reds were sent to Mars five hundred years ago. The other Colors came to Mars about three hundred years back, while our ancestors still toiled beneath the surface. They lived in the paraterraformed cities—cities with bubbles of atmosphere over them—while the rest of the world terraformed slowly. Now the bubbles are coming down and the world is fit for any man.

"HighReds live as maintenance workers, sanitation, grain harvesters, assembly workers. LowReds are those of us born beneath the surface—the truest slaves. In the cities, the Reds who dance disappear. Those who voice their thoughts vanish. Those who bow their heads and accept the rule of the Society and their place in Society, as all Colors do, live on with relative freedom."

He exhales a cloud of smoke.

I feel outside my body, as though I'm watching the colonization of worlds, the transformation of the human species, through eyes that are not my own. The gravity of history drew my people into slavery. We are the bottom of the Society, the dirt. Eo always preached something of the like, though she never knew the truth. If she had known this, how much more passionately would she have spoken? This existence is worse than she ever could have imagined. It is not hard to understand the conviction with which the Sons of Ares fight.

"Five hundred years." I shake my head. "This is our bloodydamn planet."

"Through sweat and toil it was made so," he agrees.

"Then what will it take to take it back?"

"Blood." Dancer smiles at me like a township alleycat. There's a beast behind this man's fatherly smiles.

Eo was right. It comes to violence.

She was the voice, like my father. So what am I to be? The avenging hand? I cannot grasp that someone so pure, so full of love, would want me to play this part. But she did. I think of my father's last dance. I think of my mum, Leanna, Kieran, Loran, Eo's parents, Uncle Narol, Barlow, everyone I love. I know how hard they will live and how quickly they will die. And I now know why.

I look down at my hands. They are what Dancer called them—cut, scarred, burned things. When Eo kissed them, they grew gentle for love. Now that she is gone, they grow hard for hate. I clench them into fists till my knuckles are white as icecaps.

"What is my mission?"

10

THE CARVER

I grew up with a quicksmiling girl of fifteen so in love with her young husband that when he was burned in the mines and his wound festered, she sold her body to a Gamma in return for antibiotics. She was stronger than her husband. When he grew well and discovered what had been done on his behalf, he killed the Gamma with a slingBlade snuck from the mines. Easy to guess what happened after that. Her name was Lana and she was Uncle Narol's daughter. She lives no longer.

I think of her as I watch the HC in what Harmony called the penthouse as Dancer makes preparations. I flip through the many channels with the twitch of my finger. Even that Gamma had a family. He dug like me. He was born like me, went through the flush like me, and he never saw the sun either. He was just given a little packet of medicine by the Society, and look at the effect. How clever of them. How much hate they create between people who should be kin. But if the clans knew what luxury exists on the surface, if they knew how much had been stolen from them, they would feel the hatred I feel, they would unite. My clan is a hot-tempered breed. What would a rebellion of theirs look like? Probably like Dago's burner—burning hot but fast, till it was all ash.

I asked Dancer why the Sons streamed my wife's death to the mines. Why not instead show the lowReds the wealth of the surface? That would sow anger.

"Because a rebellion now would be crushed in days," Dancer explained. "We must take a different path. An empire cannot be destroyed from without till it is destroyed from within. Remember that. We're empire-breakers, not terrorists."

When Dancer told me what I am to do, I laughed. I do not know if I can do it. I am a speck. A thousand cities span the face of Mars. Metal behemoths sail between the planets in fleets carrying weapons that can crack the mantle of a moon. On distant Luna, buildings rise seven miles high; there the Sovereign Consul, Octavia au Lune, rules with her Imperators and Praetors. The Ash Lord, who made the world of Rhea cinders, is her minion. She controls the twelve Olympic Knights, legions of Peerless Scarred, and Obsidians as innumerable as the stars. And those Obsidians are only the elite. The Gray soldiers prowl the cities ensuring order, ensuring obedience to the hierarchy. The Whites arbitrate their justice and push their philosophy. Pinks pleasure and serve in highColor homes. Silvers count and manipulate currency and logistics. Yellows study the medicines and sciences. Greens develop technology. Blues navigate the stars. Coppers run the beauracracy. Every Color has a purpose. Every Color props up the Golds.

The HC shows me Colors I did not know existed. It shows me fashion. Ludicrous and seductive. There are biomodifications and flesh implants—women with skin so smooth and polished, breasts so round, hair so glossed that they appear a different species from Eo and all the women I've ever known. The men are freakishly muscular and tall. Their arms and chests bulge with artificial strength, and they flaunt their muscle like girls showing off new toys.

I am a Lambda Helldiver of Lykos, but what is that compared with all this?

"Harmony is here. Time to go," Dancer says from the door.

"I want to fight," I tell him as we ride the gravLift down with Harmony. They've doctored my Sigils so that they are brighter to match the highReds. I wear the loose garb of a highRed and carry a pack of street-scrubbing equipment. There's dye in my hair and contacts in my eyes, all so that I look a brighter shade of red. Less dirty. "I don't want *this* mission. Worse, I *can't* do it. Who could?"

"You said you would do anything that needed to be done," Dancer says.

"But this . . ." The mission he has given me is madness, yet that's not why I'm frightened. My fear is that I will become something Eo would not recognize. I'll become a demon from our Octobernacht stories.

"Give me a scorcher or a bomb. Let someone else do this."

"We brought you out for this," Harmony sighs. "And only this. It has been Ares's greatest goal since the Sons were born."

"How many others have you brought out? How many others have tried what you're asking me to try?"

Harmony looks over at Dancer. He says nothing, so she answers impatiently on his behalf. "Ninety-seven have failed the Carving . . . that we know of."

"*Bloodydamn,*" I curse. "And what happened to them?"

"They died," she says blandly. "Or they asked for death."

"Maybe Narol should have let me hang." I try to laugh.

"Darrow. Come here. Come." He grabs my shoulder and pulls me in. "Others may have failed. But you'll be different, Darrow. I feel it in my bones."

My legs go shaky when I first look up at the night sky and the buildings stretching around me. I slip into vertigo. I feel like I am falling, like the world is off its axis. Everything is too open, so much so that it seems as though the city should tumble into the sky. I look at my feet, look at the street, and try to imagine that I am in the tunnelroads from the townships to the Common.

The streets of Yorkton, the city, are a strange place at night. Luminescent balls of light line the sidewalks and streets. HC videos run like liquid streams along parts of the avenue in this hi-tech sector of the city, so most walk upon the moving pathways or ride in public transportation with their heads crooked down like cane handles. Garish lights make the night almost as bright as day. I see even more Colors. This sector of the city is clean. Teams of Red sanitation workers scour the streets. Its roads and walking paths stretch in perfect order.

There's a faint ribbon of red where we are to walk, a narrow ribbon in a broad street. Our path does not move like the others. A Copper woman walks along her wider path; her favorite programs play wherever she walks, unless she strides beside a Gold, in which case all the HCs go quiet. But most Golds do not walk; they are permitted gravBoots and coaches, as are any of the Coppers, Obsidians, Grays, and Silvers with the proper license, though the licensed boots are horribly shoddy things.

An advertisement for a blister cream appears on the ground in front of me. A woman of strangely slender proportions slinks out of a red lace robe. Suitably naked, she then applies the cream to a place on her body where no woman has ever before gotten a blister. I blush and look away in disgust because I've only ever seen one woman naked.

"You'll want to forget your modesty," Harmony advises. "It'll mark you worse than your Color."

"It is disgusting," I say.

"It's advertising, darling," Harmony purrs condescendingly. She shares a chuckle with Dancer.

An elderly Gold soars overhead, older than any human I've ever seen. We lower our heads as she passes.

"Reds up here have to get paid," Dancer explains when we are alone. "Not much. But they're given money and enough treats to make them dependent. What money they have, they spend on goods they're made to think they need."

"Same with all the drones," Harmony hisses.

"So they're not slaves," I say.

"Oh, they're slaves," Harmony says. "Enslaved by their suckling on the teats of those bastards."

Dancer struggles to keep up, so I slow down as he speaks. Harmony makes an irritated noise.

"Golds structure everything to make their own lives easier. They have shows produced to entertain and placate the masses. They give monies and handouts to make generations dependent on the seventh day of each new Earth month. They create goods to grant us a semblance of liberty. If violence is the Gold sport, manipulation is their art form."

We pass into a lowColor district where there are no designated walking paths. The storefronts are lined with electronic Green ribbons. Some stores peddle a month of alternate reality in an hour's time for a week's wages. Two small men with quick green eyes and bald heads studded with metal spikes and tattooed with shifting digital codes suggest for me a trip to someplace called Osgiliath. Other stores offer banking services or biomodifications or simple personal hygiene products. They shout things I don't understand, speaking in numbers and acronyms. I have never seen such commotion.

Brothels lined with Pink ribbon make me blush, as do the women and men in the windows. Each has a flashing price tag playfully hanging from a thread; it's a moving number that suits demand. A lusty girl calls to me as Dancer explains the idea of money. In Lykos, we traded only in goods and swill and burners and services.

Some blocks of the city are reserved for the use of high colors. Access to these districts depends on badges of warrant. I cannot simply walk or ride into a Gold or Copper district. But a Copper can always slum in a Red district, frequenting a bar or brothel. Never the other way around, even in the wild, free-for-all that is the Bazaar—a riotous place of commerce and noise and air heavy with the scents of bodies and food and automobile exhaust.

We walk deep into the Bazaar. I feel safer in the back alleys here than I did in the open avenues of the high-tech sectors. I do not yet like vast spaces, and seeing the stars above frightened me. The Bazaar is darker, though lights still shine and people still bustle. The buildings seem to pinch together. A hundred balconies form ribs in the alleyway's heights. Walkways crisscross above, and all around us, lights blink from devices. It is more humid here, dirty. And I see fewer Tinpots patrolling. Dancer says there are places in the Bazaar where even an Obsidian should not go. "In the densest places of man, humanity most easily breaks down," he says.

It is strange being in a crowd where no one knows your face or cares for your purpose. In Lykos, I would have been jostled by men I'd grown up with, run across girls I'd chased and wrestled with as a child. Here, other Colors slam into me and offer not even a faint apology. This is a city, and I do not like it. I feel alone.

"This is us," Dancer says, gesturing me into a dark doorway where an electronic flying dragon shimmers on the surface of the stone. A massive Brown with a modjob for a nose stops us. We wait for the metal nose to snort and sniff. He's bigger than Dancer.

"Dye in his hair," he growls at me, taking a whiff of my hair. "A Ruster, this one be."

A scorcher peeks out from his belt. He's got a shiv behind his wrist—I can tell by the way his hand moves. Another thug joins him on the stoop. He's got jewelry processors on his eyeballs, little red rubies that flicker when light catches them just right. I stare at the jewelry and the brown eyes.

"What's what with this one? He want a go?" the thug spits. "Keep eyein' me, and I'll take your liver to sell at market."

Thinks I'm challenging him. I'm actually just curious about the rubies, but when he threatens me I smile at him and give a little wink like I would in the mines. A knife flips into his hand. Rules are different up here.

"Boy, keep playin'. Dare ya. Keep playin'."

"Mickey is expectin' us," Dancer tells the man.

I watch Modjob's friend as he tries to stare me down like I'm some sort of child. Modjob smirks and leers at Dancer's leg and arm. "Don't know a Mickey, cripple." He looks to his friend. "You know a Mickey?"

"Nah. Ain't got no Mickey here."

"What a relief." Dancer sets a hand on the scorcher under his jacket. "Since you don't know Mickey, you won't have to explain to Mickey why my . . . generous friend couldn't reach him." He moves his jacket so they can see a glyph etched on the butt of his gun. The helmet of Ares.

When he sees the glyph, Modjob gulps and says, "Squab," then they fall over each other to open the door. "G-g-gotta take your shooters." Three others move toward us, scorchers half up. Harmony opens her vest and shows them a bomb strapped to her stomach. She rolls a blinking detonator over her nimble Red fingers.

"Nah. We're good."

Modjob swallows, nods. "You're good."

The interior of the building is dark. It is a darkness thick with smoke and throbbing lights—much like my mine. Music pulses. Glass cylinders stand as pillars amongst chairs and tables where men drink and smoke. Inside the glass, women dance. Some writhe in water, their strange webbed toes and sleek thighs moving to the music. Others gyrate to the thudding melody in environs of golden smoke or silver paint.

More thugs guide us to a back table that seems made of iridescent water. A slim man reclines there with several creatures of the strangest sort. I thought them monsters at first, but the closer I look, the more confused I become. They are humans. But they've been made differently. Carved differently. A pretty young girl, no older than Eo, sits looking at me with emerald eyes. The wings of a white eagle sprout from the flesh of her back. She's like something torn from a fever dream, except she should have been left there. Others like her lounge in the smoke and strange lights.

Mickey the Carver is a scalpel of a man with a crooked smile and black hair that hangs like a puddle of oil down one side of his head. A tattoo of an amethyst mask wreathed in smoke winds around his left hand. It is the Sigil of a Violet—the creatives—so it is always shifting. Other violet symbols stain his wrists. He's playing with a little electronic puzzle cube that has changing faces. His fingers are fast, thinner and longer than they should be, and there are twelve of them. Fascinating. I've never seen an artist before, not even on the HC. They're as rare as Whites.

"Ah, Dancer," he sighs without looking up from his cube. "I

could hear you from the drag in your step." He squints at the cube in his hands. "And Harmony. I could smell you from the door, my darling. Terrible bomb, by the bye. Next time you need real sneaky craftsmanship, look Mickey up, yes?"

"Mick," Dancer says, and seats himself at the table of dream-things. I can tell Harmony is growing a bit dizzy from the smoke. I'm used to breathing worse stuff.

"Now, Harmony, my love," Mickey purrs. "Have you given up on this cripple yet? Come to join my family, perhaps? Yes? Get yourself a pair of wings? Claws on your hands? A tail? Horns—you would look fierce in horns. Especially wrapped in my silken bedsheets."

"Carve yourself a soul and you might get a shot," Harmony sneers.

"Ah, if it takes being a Red to have a soul, on this I shall pass."

"Then to business."

"So abrupt, my darling. Conversation should be considered an art form, or like a grand dinner. Each course in its own time." His fingers fly over the cube. He's matching them based on their electronic frequency, but he's a bit too slow to match them before they change. He still hasn't looked up.

"We have a proposition for you, Mickey," Dancer says impatiently. He glances down at the cube.

Mickey's smile is long and crooked. He does not look up. Dancer repeats himself.

"Straight to the main course then, eh, cripple? Well, propose away."

Dancer swats the cube out of Mickey's hands. The table goes silent. The thugs bristle behind us and the music continues to pound. My heart is steady and I eye the scorcher on the thigh of the nearest thug. Slowly, Mickey looks up and cuts the tension with a crooked smile. "What's what, my friend?"

Dancer nods to Harmony and she slips a small box over to Mickey.

"A present? You shouldn't have." Mickey examines the box. "Cheap stuff. Such a tasteless Color, Red." Then he slides the box open and gasps in horror. He recoils from the table, slamming the box shut. "You stupid sodding bastards. What is this?"

"You know what they are."

Mickey leans forward and his voice becomes one lone hiss. "You brought them here? How did you get them? Are you insane?" Mickey glances at his followers, who peer down at the box wondering what has so unbalanced their master.

"Insane? We're bloodydamn manic." Dancer smiles. "And we need them attached. Soon."

"Attached?" Mickey starts laughing.

"To him." Dancer points at me.

"Leave!" Mickey screams at his entourage. "*Leave,* you simpering sycophantic miscreants! I'm talking to you . . . you *freaks*! Get out!" When his entourage has scurried away, he opens the box and dumps the contents onto the table. Two golden wings, the Sigils of a Gold, clatter onto the table.

Dancer sits. "We want you to make our boy here into a Gold."

11

MAD

"You're mad."

"Thank you." Harmony smiles.

"I assume you misspoke; pray repeat yourself," Mickey says to Dancer.

"Ares will pay you more money than you've ever seen if you can successfully attach those to my young friend here."

"Impossible," Mickey declares. He looks over to me, measuring me for the first time. He is unimpressed despite my height. I don't blame him. Once, I thought myself a handsome man of the clans. Strong. Muscular. Up here, I am pale and wiry, young and scarred. He spits onto the table. "Impossible."

Harmony shrugs. "It's been done before."

"By whom? I ask." He turns his head. "No. You cannot bait me."

"Someone talented," Harmony taunts.

"*Impossible.*" Mickey leans even farther forward; his thin face has not a single pore. "There's DNA matching him with the wings, cerebral extraction. Did you know they have subdermal markings in their skulls? Of course you didn't—datachips attached to their frontal cortexes to substantiate their caste? Then there's synapse linkage, molecular bonding, tracking devices, the Quality Control

Board. And there's the trauma and the associative reasoning. Say we make his body perfect, there's still one problem: we cannot make him smarter. One cannot make a mouse a lion."

"He can think like a lion," Dancer says plainly.

"Oho! He can think like a *lion*," Mickey snickers.

"And Ares wants it done." Dancer's voice is cold.

"Ares. Ares. Ares. It doesn't matter what Ares wants, you baboon. Never mind the science. His physical and mental dexterity is probably daft as a damn bowl cleaner's. And his tangibles won't match. He's not their species! He's a Ruster!"

"I'm a Helldiver of Lykos," I say.

Mickey raises his eyebrows. "Oho! A Helldiver! Clear the halls! A Helldiver, you say!" He mocks me, but he squints suddenly as if he's seen me before. My whipping was televised. Many know my face. "Bugger me blind," he mutters.

"You recognize my face," I confirm.

He pulls up the viral video and watches it, looking back and forth between it and me. "Aren't you dead with that girlfriend of yours?"

"Wife," I snap.

Mickey's jaw muscles flicker under his skin as he ignores me. "You're making a savior," he accuses, looking over at Dancer. "Dancer, you bastard. You're making a messiah for your gorydamn cause."

I never looked at it that way. My skin prickles uneasily.

"Yes" is Dancer's answer.

"If I make him a Gold, what will you do with him?"

"He will apply to the Institute. He will be accepted. There, he will excel well enough to reach the ranks of the Peerless Scarred; as a Scarred, he can train to be a Praetor, a Legate, a Politico, a Quaestor. Anything. He will advance to a prime position, the primer the better. From there, he will be in a position to do as Ares requires for the Cause."

"Mother of God," Mickey murmurs. He stares at Harmony, then at Dancer. "You want him to be a bona fide Peerless Scarred. Not a Bronzie?"

A Bronze is a faded Gold. Of the same class, but looked down on for inferior appearance, lineage, and capabilities. "Not a Bronze," Dancer confirms.

"Or a Pixie?"

"We don't want him to go to nightclubs and eat caviar like the rest of those worthless Golds. We want him to command fleets."

"*Fleets.* You lot are mad. Mad." Mickey's violet eyes settle on mine after a long moment. "My boy, they are murdering you. You are *not* a Gold. You cannot do what a Gold can do. They are killers, born to dominate *us;* have you ever met one of the Aureate? Sure, they may look all pretty and peaceful now. But do you know what happened in the Conquering? They are monsters."

He shakes his head and laughs wickedly. "The Institute is not a school, it is a culling ground where the Golds go to hack at one another till the strongest in mind and body is found. You. Will. Die."

Mickey's cube lies at the opposite end of the table. I walk over to it without saying a word. I don't know how it works, but I know the puzzles of the earth.

"My boy, what are you doing?" Mickey sighs in pity. "That is not a toy."

"Have you ever been in a mine?" I ask him. "Ever used your fingers to dig through a faultline at a twelve-degree angle while doing the math to accommodate eighty percent rotation power and fifty-five percent thrust so you don't set off a gas-pocket reaction while sitting in your own piss and sweat and worrying about pitvipers that want to burrow into your gut to lay their eggs?"

"This is . . ."

His voice fades as he sees how the clawDrill taught my fingers to move, how the grace with which my uncle taught me to dance is converted into my hands. I hum as I work. It takes a moment, maybe a minute or three. But I learn the puzzle and then solve it easily according to frequency. There seems another level to it, mathematical riddles. I don't know the math, but I know the pattern. I solve it and four more puzzles, then it changes once more in my hands, becoming a circle. Mickey's eyes widen. I toss the device back to him. He stares at my hands while working his own twelve fingers.

"Impossible," he murmurs.

"Evolution," Harmony replies.

Dancer smiles. "We will need to discuss price."

12

THE CARVING

My life becomes agony.

My Sigils are attached to the metacarpus in each hand. Mickey removes the old Red Sigils and cultivates new skin and bone over the wounds. Then he sets to installing a stolen subdermal datachip into my frontal lobe. I am told the trauma killed me and they had to restart my heart. I've died twice then. They say I was in a coma for two weeks, but to me it was nothing but a dream. I was in the vale with Eo. She kissed me on the forehead and then I woke and felt the stitches and the pain.

I lie in bed as Mickey tests me. He has me move marbles from one container into other containers coded by colors. I do this for what seems a lifetime.

"We are forming synapses, my darling."

He tests me with word puzzles and tries to make me read, but I don't know how to read. "You will have to learn that for the Institute," he giggles.

My dreams are cruel things to wake from. In them, Eo comforts me, but when I wake, she is nothing but a fleeting memory. I am hollow as I lie in Mickey's makeshift medical cell. An ion germ killer buzzes next to my bed. Everything is white, yet I can hear the thumping of music from his club. His girls change my diapers and empty my piss bags. A girl who never speaks bathes me three times a day. Her arms are willowy, her face soft and sad as when I first saw her sitting with Mickey at his liquid table. The wings that curl outward from her back are bound with a crimson ribbon. She never meets my eyes.

Mickey continues to make me develop synapse connections as he repairs the scar tissue from my neural surgery. He's all laughs and smiles and lingering touches on my forehead as he calls me his darling. I feel like one of his girls, one of the angels he sculpted for his own pleasure.

"But we must not be satisfied only with the brain," he says. "There is much work to be done on this Ruster body of yours if we want to make you into an iron Gold."

"And that is?"

"The golden ancestors, they call them the iron Golds. They were hard men. They stood lean and fierce upon their battlecruisers as they laid waste to the armies and republic fleets of Earth. What creatures they were." His eyes go distant. "It took generations of eugenics and biological tampering to make them. Forced Darwinism."

He's quiet for a moment, and it seems an anger builds in him.

"They say Carvers will never duplicate the beauty of the Golden Man. The Board of Quality Control taunts us. Personally, I do not want to make you a man. Men are so very frail. Men break. Men die. No, I've always wished to make a god." He smiles mischievously as he does some sketches on a digital pad. He spins it around and shows me the killer I will become. "So why not carve you to be the god of war?"

Mickey replaces the skin of my back and the skin of my hands where Eo applied bandages to my burns. This, he says, is not to be my real skin. It is only a homogeneous baselayer.

"Your skeleton is weak because Mars gravity is zero point three of Earth's, my delicate little bird. Also, you have a diet deficient in calcium. Gold Standard bone density is five times stronger than naturally occurring bone density on Earth. So we will have to make your skeleton six times stronger; you must be of iron if you want to last the Institute. This will be fun! For me. Not you."

Mickey carves me again. The agony is beyond language or comprehension.

"Someone has to dot God's i's."

The next day, he reinforces the bones of my arms. Then he does my ribs, my spine, my shoulders, my feet, my pelvis, and my face. He also alters the tensile qualities of my tendons and muscle tissue. Mercifully, he does not let me wake from this last surgery for several weeks. When I do wake, I see his girls around me applying new cultures of flesh and kneading my muscles with their thumbs.

Slowly, my skin begins to heal. I am a patchwork fleshquilt. They begin feeding me synthesized protein, creatine, and growth hormone to promote muscle growth and tendon regeneration. My body trembles in the nights and itches as I sweat through new, smaller pores. I cannot use pain medication strong enough to numb the agony, because the altered nerves must learn to function with the new tissue and my altered brain.

Mickey sits beside me on my worst nights telling me stories. It's only then that I like him, only then that I think he is not some monster cooked up by this perverted Society.

"My profession is to create, little bird," he says one night as we sit together in the darkness. Light from the machines bathes his face in queer shadows. "When I was young, I lived in a place they call the Grove. It was what you might think of as a circus culture. We had spectacles every night. Celebrations of color and sound and dance."

"Sounds terrible," I mutter sarcastically. "Just like the mines."

He smiles softly and his eyes find that distant place. "I suppose it may seem a plush life to you. Yet there was a madness to the Grove. They made us take pills. Pills that could make us fly between the planets on wings of dust to visit the faerie kings of Jupiter and the deep mermaids of Europa. My mind always separate from body. No peace to it. No end to the madness." He clapped his hands then. "And now I Carve the things I saw in my fever dreams, just as they always wished. I dreamed of you, I think. In the end, I suppose they'll wish I hadn't dreamed at all."

"Was it a good dream?" I ask.

"What?"

"The one with me."

"No. No, it was a nightmare. One of a man from hell, lover of fire." He's silent for a spell.

"Why is it so horrible?" I ask him. "Life. All this. Why do they need to make us do this? Why do they treat us like we're their slaves?"

"Power."

"Power isn't real. It's just a word."

Mickey ponders silently. Then he shrugs his thin shoulders. "Mankind was always enslaved, they'll say. Freedom enslaves us to lust, to greed. Take freedom away, and they give me a life of dreaming. They gave you a life of sacrifice, family, community. And society is stable. There is no famine. No genocide. No great wars. And when the Golds fight, they obey rules. They are . . . *noble* about it when the great houses bicker."

"Noble? They lied to me. Said I was a pioneer."

"And would you have been happier if you knew you were a slave?" Mickey asks. "No. None of the billion lowReds beneath Mars would be happy if they knew what the highReds knew—that they are slaves. So is it not better to lie?"

"It is better to not make slaves."

When I am ready, he inserts a forceGenerator into my sleeping tube to simulate increased gravity on my frame. I've never known pain like this. My body aches. My bones and skin and muscles scream against the pressure and the change till I'm on medication that turns the scream into a dull forever-moan.

I sleep for days. I dream of home and family. Every night I wake after seeing Eo hang yet again. She sways across my mind. I miss her warmth in bed beside me, even though they give me an HC immersion mask for distraction.

Gradually, I am weaned from the pain medication. My muscles still aren't used to the density of my bones, so my existence becomes a melodic ache. They begin to feed me real food. Mickey sits on the edge of my cot stroking my hair well into the nights. I don't care that his fingers feel like spider legs. I don't care that he thinks I am some piece of art, his art. He gives me something called a hamburger. I love it. Red meats and thick creams and breads and fruits and vegetables make my diet. I have never eaten so well.

"You need the calories," Mickey coos. "You have been so strong for me; eat well. You deserve this food."

"How am I doing?" I ask.

"Oh, the hard parts are over, my darling. You are a brilliant boy, you know. They have shown me the tapes from the other procedures where other Carvers tried this. Oh, how clumsy the other Carvers were, how weak the other subjects. But you are strong and I am brilliant." He taps my chest. "Your heart is like that of a stallion's. I've never glimpsed one like it before. You were bitten by a pitviper when you were young, I assume?"

"I was. Yes."

"I thought so. Your heart had to adjust to counteract the effects of the poison."

"My uncle sucked most of the poison out when I was bitten," I say.

"No," Mickey laughs. "That's a myth. The poison cannot be sucked out. It still runs through your veins, forcing your heart to be strong if you want to continue to live. You are something special, just like me."

"Then I will not die in here?" I manage.

Mickey laughs. "No! No! We are beyond that now. There will be pain. But we are past the threat of mortality. Soon we will have made man into god. Red into Gold. Even your wife would not recognize you."

That is all I've ever feared.

When they take my eyes and give me ones of gold, I feel dead inside. It's a simple matter of reconnecting the optic nerve to the "donor's" eyes, Mickey says. A simple thing he's done a dozen times for cosmetic purposes; the hard part was the frontal lobe surgery, he says. I disagree. There is the pain, yes. But with the new eyes, I see things I once could not. Elements are clearer, sharper, and more painful to bear. I hate this process. All it is is a confirmation of the superiority of the Golds. It takes all this to make me their physical equal. No wonder we serve them.

It's not mine. None of this is mine. My skin is too soft, too lustrous, too faultless. I don't know my body without scars. I don't know the back of my own hands. Eo would not know me.

Mickey takes my hair next. Everything is changed.

It is weeks of physical therapy. Walking slowly around the room with Evey, the winged girl, I'm left to my own thoughts. Neither one of us cares much to speak. She has her demons and I have mine, so we are quiet and calm except when Mickey comes to coo about what pretty children we would make together.

One day, Mickey even brings an antique zither for me, with a soundboard of wood instead of plastic. It is the kindest thing he's ever done. I do not sing, but I play the solemn songs of Lykos. The traditional ones of my clan that no one beyond the mine will ever have heard. He and Evey sit with me sometimes, and though I think Mickey a wretched sort of creature, I feel as though he understands the music. Its beauty. Its importance. And afterward, he says nothing. I like him then, too. At peace.

"Well, you're a bit sterner than I first measured," Harmony says to me one morning as I wake.

"Where have you been?" I ask, opening my eyes.

"Finding donors." She flinches as she sees my irises. "The world does not stop because you are here," she says. "We had work to do. Mickey says you can walk?"

"I am growing stronger."

"Not strong enough," she surmises, looking me over. "You look like a baby giraffe. I'll fix that."

Harmony takes me beneath Mickey's club to a grungy gymnasium lit by sulfurous bulbs. I like the feel of the cold stone on my bare feet. My balance has returned, and it is a good thing, because Harmony does not offer me her arm; instead, she waves to the center of the dark gymnasium.

"We bought these for you," Harmony says.

She points to two devices in the center of the dark space. The contraptions are silver and remind me of the suits knights wore in past centuries. The armor hangs suspended between two metal wires. "They are concentraction machines."

I slide my body into the machine. Dry gel hugs my feet, my legs, my torso and arms and neck, till only my head is free. The machine is built to resist my movements, yet it responds even to the tiniest stimuli. The idea of building muscle is to exercise it, which is nothing more than using the muscle intensely enough to create microscopic tears in the tissue fiber. This is the pain one feels in the days after an intense workout—torn tissue—not lactic acid. When the muscle repairs the tears, it builds on itself. This is the process the concentraction machine is built to facilitate. It is the devil's own invention.

Harmony slides the device's faceplate over my eyes.

My body is still in the gym, but I see myself moving across the rugged landscape of Mars. I'm running, pumping my legs against the concentraction machine's resistance, which increases according to Harmony's mood or the location of the simulation. Sometimes I venture to the jungles of Earth, where I race panthers through the underbrush, or I take to the pocked surface of Luna before it was populated. But always I return home to Mars to run across its red soil and jump over its violent ravines. Harmony sometimes accompanies me in the other machine so I have someone to race.

She pushes me hard, and sometimes I wonder if she's trying to break me. I don't let her.

"If you're not vomiting during a workout, you're not trying," she says.

The days are excruciating. My body is a misery of aches from the arches of my feet to the back of my neck. Mickey's Pinks massage me every day. There is no better pleasure in the world, but three days after beginning my training with Harmony, I wake up vomiting in my bed. I shiver and shake and hear cursing.

"There's a science to this, you wicked little witch," Mickey is shouting. "He will be a work of art, but not if you pour water on the paint before it's set. Do not ruin him!"

"He must be perfect," Harmony says. "Dancer, if he is weak in any way, the other children will butcher him like a freshmade drill-Boy."

"You are butchering him!" Mickey whines. "You are ruining him! His body cannot handle the muscle breakdown."

"He has not objected to the treatment," Harmony reminds him.

"Because he does not know he *can* object!" Mickey says. "Dancer, she has no understanding of the biomechanics involved in this. Do not let her ruin my boy."

"He is not *your boy*!" Harmony sneers.

Mickey's voice becomes softer. "Dancer, Darrow is like a stallion, one of the old stallions of Earth. Beautiful beasts that will run as hard as you push them. They will run. And run. And run. Until they don't. Until their hearts explode."

There is silence for a moment, then Dancer's voice.

"Ares once told me that it is the hottest fire that forms the sternest steel. Keep pushing the boy."

I resent two of my teachers after overhearing their words: Mickey for thinking me weak; Dancer for thinking me his tool. Only Harmony doesn't anger me. Her voice, her eyes, seethe with an anger I feel in my own soul. She may have Dancer now, but she lost someone. The unscarred part of her face tells me that. She is no schemer like Dancer or his master, Ares. She is like me—brimming with a rage that makes all else so inconsequential.

That night I cry.

Over the next days, they feed me drugs to expedite the protein synthesis and muscle regeneration. After my muscle tissue has recovered from the initial trauma, they train me harder than before, even Mickey—though his eyes are underlined with dark rings and his thin face is sallow, he does not object. He has grown distant these last weeks, no longer telling me stories—as though he fears what he has created, now that I'm taking fuller shape.

Harmony and I speak very little to one another, but there is a subtle shift in our relationship, some sort of primal understanding that we are the same sort of creature. But as my body grows stronger, Harmony can no longer keep up even though she is a hardened woman of the mines. That is after only two weeks. The distance between our capabilities continues to grow. After another month, she is like a child to me. Even then I do not plateau.

My body begins to change. I thicken. My muscles become strong and corded in the concentraction machine, which I now supplement with weight workouts in highGrav. Gradually, strength builds. My shoulders grow broader, rounded; I see tendons emerge in my forearms; a tense mass of hard muscles bind my torso, like armor. Even my hands, which were always stronger than the rest of me, grow more powerful in the concentraction machine. With a simple squeeze, I can pulverize rock. Mickey jumped up and down when he saw that. No one shakes my hand any longer.

I sleep in highGrav, so that when I move about on Mars, I feel fast, quick, more agile than ever before. My fasttwitch fibers form. My hands move like lightning, and when they hit the gymnasium's human-shaped punching bag, it leaps like it's been struck by a scorcher. I can punch through it now.

My body is becoming that of a Gold, one of the prime stock, not a Pixie, not a Bronze. This is the body of the race that conquered the Solar System. My hands are freaks. They are smooth, tanned, and dexterous, as any Gold's should be. But there is a power in them out of proportion with the rest of me. If I am a blade, they are my edge.

My body is not all that changes. Before I sleep, I drink a tonic laden with processing enhancers and speed-listen to *The Colors, The Iliad, Ulysses, Metamorphosis,* the Theban plays, *The Draconic Labels, Anabasis,* and restricted works like *The Count of Monte Cristo, Lord of the Flies, Lady Casterly's Penance, 1984,* and *The Great Gatsby*. I wake knowing three thousand years of literature and legal code and history.

My last day at Mickey's comes two months after my last surgery. Harmony smiles with me after our workout as she drops me off in my room. Music thuds in the background. Mickey's dancers are going full tilt tonight.

"I'll get you your clothing, Darrow. Dancer and I want to have dinner with you to celebrate. Evey will clean you up."

She leaves me alone with Evey. Today, as always, her face is as quiet as the snow I've seen on the HC. I watch her in the mirror as she cuts my hair. The room is dark but for the light over the mirror. It shines from above, so she looks like an angel. Innocent and pure. But she's not innocent, not pure. She's a Pink. They breed them for pleasure, for the curves of their breasts and hips, for the tautness of their stomachs and the plump folds of their lips. Yet she is a girl and her spark has not yet gone out. I remember the last time I failed to protect one like her.

And me? It's hard to look at myself in the mirror. I'm what I know the devil to be. I am arrogance and cruelty, the sort of man who killed my wife. I am Gold. And I am as cold as it.

My eyes shine like ingots. My skin is soft and rich. My bones are stronger. I feel the density in my lean torso. When Evey is done cutting the golden hair, she stands back and stares at me. I can feel her fear, and I suffer it in myself. I am no longer a human. Physically, I've become something more.

"You're beautiful," Evey says quietly, touching my golden Sigils. They're much smaller than her feather wings. The circle is set in the center of each hand's backside. Wings swoop back along the flesh, curving like scythes up the sides of my wristbones.

I look at Evey's white wings and know how ugly she must think them to be on her back, how she must hate them. I want to say something kind to her. I want to make her smile, if she can. I would tell her that she is beautiful, but she's lived a life of men saying that for some gain or another. She wouldn't believe a boy like me. And I don't believe her words to me. Eo was beautiful. I still remember the flush of blood in her cheeks as she danced. She had all the raw colors of life, the crude beauty of nature. I am the human concept of beauty. Gold made soft and supple into man's form.

Evey kisses the top of my head before darting away and leaving me alone to watch the HC in the mirror's reflection. I did not notice her slip a feather from her wings into my breast pocket.

I'm tired of watching the HC. I know their history now and I'm learning more every day. But I'm tired of being inside, tired of listening to Mickey's club thump its music and smelling the minty leaves he smokes. Tired of seeing the girls he brings into his family only to sell away when someone bids high enough. Tired of seeing all the full eyes go hollow. This is not Lykos. There is no love, no family or trust. This place is sick.

"My boy, you look fit to captain a fleet of torchShips," Mickey says from the door. He slides in, smelling like his burners. His spindly fingers take Evey's feather from my breast pocket and roll it back and forth over his knuckles. He taps the feather to each of my golden Sigils. "Wings are my favorite. Aren't they yours? They go to mankind's better aspirations."

He comes up behind me as I sit staring into the mirror. His hands go to my shoulders and he speaks down at my head, resting his chin upon it as though I am his property. It's easy to see he thinks I am. My left hand goes to the sigil on my right, lingering there.

"I told you you were brilliant. Now it's your time to fly."

"You give the girls wings, but you don't let them fly. Do you?" I ask.

"It's impossible for *them* to fly. They are simpler things than you. And I can't afford to buy a license to have gravBoots. So they dance for me." Mickey explains. "But you, you'll fly, won't you, my brilliant boy?"

I stare at him but say nothing. His lips slice into a smile because I unnerve him. I always have. "You're frightened of me," I tell him.

He laughs. "Am I? Oho! Am I now, my boy?"

"Yes. You're used to knowing what's what. You think like the rest of them." I nod to the HC's reflection. "Things are set in stone. Things are well ordered. Reds at the bottom, everyone else standing on our backs. Now you're looking at me and you're realizing that we don't bloodydamn like it down there. Red is rising, Mickey."

"Oh, you've got far to go . . ."

I reach up and grab his wrists so that he cannot move. He stares at me in the mirror's reflection, struggling against my hold. Nothing is stronger than a Helldiver's grip. I smile into the mirror, locking my golden eyes with his violet ones. He smells like fear. Primal terror. Like a mouse cornered by a lion.

"Be kind to Evey, Mickey. Don't make her dance. Give her a plush life or I'll come back to pull your hands off your body."

13

BAD THINGS

Matteo is a tall wisp of a Pink with long limbs and a lean, beautiful face. He is a slave. Or was a slave for carnal pleasures. Yet he walks like a water lord. Beauty in his step. Manners and grace in the wave of his hand. He has a penchant for wearing gloves and sniffing at even the smallest bit of dirt. Body maintenance has been his life's purpose. So he doesn't find it strange when he helps me apply a hair follicle killer to my arms, legs, torso, and privates. But I do. When we're done, we're both cursing—me from the sting, him from the punch I threw at his shoulder. I accidentally dislocated it just by punching it. I still don't know my own strength. And they do make their Pinks fragile. If he is the rose, I am the thorns.

"Bald as a toddler, you frenetic little baby," Matteo sighs as properly as one can say such a thing. "Just as the *newest* Luna fashion requires. *Now,* with a bit of eyebrow sculpting—oh, how your brows are like fungus-nibbling caterpillars—and nose-hair eradication, cuticle readjustment, teeth whitening on those slick new chompers—which, if I may say, are yellow as mustard dappled with dandelions . . . tell me, have you ever brushed your new teeth?—and blackhead removal (which shall be like probing for helium-3), toner adjustment, and melatonin injections, and you'll be prim and rose proper–ish."

I snort at the foolishness of it all. "I already look like a Gold."

"You look like a Bronze! A fool's Gold! One of the lowbred bastards who looks more khaki than Gold. You must be perfect."

"You're a bloodydamn odd lark, Matteo."

He smacks me. "Mind yourself! A Gold would rather die than use that slithering mineslang. 'Gorydamn' or 'gory'; and 'slag' instead of 'squab.' Every time you say 'bloody' or 'bloodydamn,' I will smack not your gob, but your mouth. And if you say 'squab' or 'gob,' I will kick you in the scrotum—which I do know my way around—as I will do if you do not get rid of that *horrible* accent. You sound like you were born in a gorydamn dumpster."

He frowns and sets his hands on his narrow hips.

"And then we'll have to teach you manners. And culture, culture, *goodman.*"

"I have manners."

"By the maker, we are so, *so* going to have to make you forswear that brogue as well as the cursing."

He pokes me as he lists out my flaws.

"Might try adopting some manners of your own, *buttboy,*" I growl.

He pulls off one of my gloves and slaps me across the face and takes a bottle in hand and holds it to my throat. I laugh.

"You'll have to get your Helldiver reflexes back soon to go with that gawky new body."

I eye the bottle.

"Going to poke me to death?"

"It is a polyenne sword, *goodman.* A razor, in other words. One moment it is soft as hair, but with an organic impulse, it turns harder than diamond. It is the only thing that will cut through a pulseShield. One moment a whip, the next moment a perfect sword. It is the weapon of a gentleman. A Gold. For any other Color to carry it is death."

"It is a bottle, you daft—"

He jams me in the throat so that I gag.

"And it was your manners that forced me to draw my razor and challenge you, thereby precipitously ending your impudent life. You may have fought with fists for honor in that hovel you called home. You were a bug then. An ant. An Aureate fights with a blade at the slightest provocation. They have honor the likes of which you know nothing about. Your honor was personal; theirs is personal, familial, and planetary. That is all. They fight for higher stakes, and they do not forgive when the bloodletting is done. Least of all the Peerless Scarred. Manners, *goodman*. Manners will protect you until you can protect yourself from my *shampoo* bottle."

"Matteo . . . ," I say, rubbing my throat.

"Yes?" he sighs.

"What is shampoo?"

Another stint in Mickey's carving room might have been preferable to Matteo's tutelage. At least Mickey was afraid of me.

The next morning Dancer tries to rename me.

"You will be the son of a relatively unknown family from the far asteroid clusters. Soon, the family will be dead in a shipping accident. You will be the lone survivor and the only heir to their debts and poor status. His name, your name, will be Caius au Andromedus."

"Slag that," I reply. "I will be Darrow or I will be nothing."

He scratches his head. "Darrow is an . . . odd name."

"You have made me give up the hair Father gave me, the eyes Mother left me, the Color I was born to, so I will keep the name they granted me, and you can make it work."

"I liked it better when you didn't act like a Gold," Dancer grumbles.

"Now, the key to dining like an Aureate is to eat slowly," Matteo says as we sit together at a table in the penthouse where Dancer first showed me the world. "You will find yourself subjected to many

Trimalchian feasts. On such occasions, there will be seven courses—appetizer, soup, fish, meat, salad, dessert, and libations."

He gestures to a small tray laden with silverware and explains the various methods for eating with each.

Then he tells me, "If you must urinate or defecate during the meal, you hold it in. Controlling one's bodily functions is expected of an Aureate."

"So these namby-pamby Goldbrows aren't allowed to shit? And when they do, I wonder, does it come out gold?"

Matteo slaps my cheek with his glove. "If you're so eager to see red again, let your tongue slip in their presence, *goodman,* and they'll be happy to remind you what color all men bleed. Manners and control! You have neither." He shakes his head. "Now, tell me what this fork is used for."

I want to tell him it's used for picking his arse, but I sigh and give him the correct answer. "Fish, but only if the bones are still in the dish."

"And how much of this fish are you to eat?"

"All of it," I guess.

"No!" he cries. "Were you even listening?" His small hands clutch his hair and he takes a deep breath. "Must I remind you? There are Bronzies. There are Golds. And there are Pixies."

He leaves the rest for me to finish.

"Pixies have no self-control," I remember aloud. "They take in all the treats of power, but do pissall to merit them. They are born and they chase pleasure. Righto?"

"Prime, not *righto*. Now what is expected of a Gold? Of a Peerless Scarred?"

"Perfection."

"Which means?"

My voice is cold as I mimic a Gold's accent. "It means control, *goodman.* Self-control. I am permitted to indulge in vices so long as I never permit them to usurp control. If there is a key to understanding Aureates, it is found in understanding control in all its forms. Eat the fish, leave twenty percent to indicate its deliciousness did not overpower my resolve or make slaves of my taste-buds."

"So you were listening after all."

Dancer finds me the next day as I practice my Aureate accent in the penthouse's holomirror. I can see a three-dimensional depiction of my head in front of me. The teeth move strangely, catching my tongue as I try to roll my words. I am still becoming used to my body, even months after the last of the surgeries. My teeth are larger than I initially thought them. It also doesn't help that the Goldbrows speak as though they've had golden shovels stuck up their bloodydamn stinkholes. So I find it easier to speak like one if I see that I am one. The arrogance comes easier.

"Soften your *r*'s," Dancer tells me. He sits attentively as I read from a datapad. "Pretend as though there is an *h* in front of each one." His burner reminds me of home and I remember how ArchGovernor Augustus seemed in Lykos. I remember the man's serenity. His patient condescension. His smirk. "Elongate the *l*'s."

"*Is that all the strength you have?*" I say into the mirror.

"Perfect," Dancer praises with a humorous shiver. He claps his good hand on his knee.

"Soon I'll be dreaming like I'm a bloodydamn Goldbrow too," I say in disgust.

"You shouldn't say 'bloodydamn.' Say 'gory' or 'gorydamn' instead."

I glare at him. "If I saw myself on the street, I would hate me. I would want to take a slingBlade and carve me from pucker to stinker and then burn the remains. Eo would puke to look at me."

"You're young still," Dancer laughs. "God, I sometimes forget how young." He takes a flask out of his boot and downs some before tossing it to me.

I laugh. "Last time I drank, Uncle Narol drugged me." I take a drink. "Maybe you've forgotten what the mines are like. I'm not young."

Dancer frowns. "I didn't mean to insult, Darrow. It's just you understand what you're to do. You understand why you're to do it. But you still lose perspective and judge yourself. Right now you probably get sick looking at your golden self. Righto?"

"Righto there." I drink deep from the flask.

"But you're only playing a part, Darrow." He twitches his finger and a blade slips from the ring on his finger. My reflexes are back and quick enough that I might have shoved it up into his throat if I thought he meant me harm, but I let him swipe the blade across my index finger. Blood wells out. Red blood. "Just in case you need reminding what you really are."

"Smells like home," I say, sucking on the finger. "Mum used to make blood soup out of the pitvipers. Not half bad to the truth of it."

"You dip flaxbread in it and sprinkle in okrablossom?"

"How'd you know?" I ask.

"My mum did the same," Dancer laughs. "We'd have it at Dancetide, or before the Laureltide when they'd announce the winner. Always squabbing Gamma."

"Here's to Gamma." I laugh and finish another swig.

Dancer watches me. The smile eventually slips from his face and his eyes grow cold. "Matteo's to teach you to dance tomorrow."

"Thought you'd be the one doing that," I say.

He thumps his bad leg. "Been a while since I've done that. Best dancer in Oikos. I could move like a deeptunnel draft. All our best dancers were Helldivers. I was one for several years, you know."

"I figured."

"Did you, now?"

I gesture to his scars. "Only a Helldiver would be bit so many times without drillBoys around to help pull the vipers off. Been bitten too. Got a bigger heart for it, at least."

He nods and his eyes go distant. "Fell into a nest when fixing to repair a nodule on the clawDrill. They were up in one of the ducts and I didn't see them. They were the dangerous kind."

I see where he's going with this. "They were babies," I say.

He nods.

"They have less venom. Much less than their parents, so they weren't burrowers bent on laying eggs inside of me. But when they bit, they used all the evil in them. Fortunately, we had antivenom with us. Traded some Gammas for it." In Lykos we had no antivenom.

He leans toward me.

"We're tossing you into a nest of baby vipers, Darrow. Mark that. Admissions testing is three months from now. I will be tutoring you in conjunction with your lessons from Matteo. But if you do not quit judging yourself, if you continue to hate your guise, then you will fail the test or worse—you will pass it and then slip up and be found out while at the Institute. And everything will be squabbed."

I shift in my seat. For once, there's another fear in me—not of becoming something Eo would not recognize, but a more primal fear, a mortal fear of my enemies. What will they be like? I already see their sneers, their contempt.

"Doesn't matter if they find me out." I clap Dancer's knee. "They've taken what they can from me already. That is why I am a weapon you can use."

"Wrong," Dancer snaps. "You're of use because you're more than a weapon. When your wife died, she didn't just give you a vendetta. She gave you her dream. You're its keeper. Its maker. So don't be spitting anger and hate. You're not fighting against them, no matter what Harmony says. You're fighting *for* Eo's dream, *for* your family that is still alive, your people."

"Is that Ares's opinion? I mean, is it yours?"

"I am not Ares," Dancer repeats. I don't believe him. I've seen the way his men look at him, how even Harmony pays him deference. "Look into yourself, Darrow, and you'll realize that you are a good man who will have to do bad things."

My hands are unscarred and feel strange when I clench them till the knuckles turn that familiar shade of white.

"See. That's what I don't get. If I am a good man, then why do I want to do bad things?"

14

ANDROMEDUS

Matteo cannot teach me to dance. He shows me what each of the five form dances of the Aureate looks like and we are through. More emphasis is put on your partner in Gold dances than the dances my uncle taught me, but the movements are similar. I perform all five with greater skill than he can manage. To show off, I blindfold myself and perform each dance again in succession without music, by memory. Uncle Narol taught me to dance, and with a thousand nights of filling time with nothing but dance and song, I am masterful in recording the motions of my body, even this new body. It can do things my old one could not. The muscle fibers contract differently, the tendons stretch farther, the nerves fire faster. There's a sweet burn in the muscles as I flow through the movements.

One dance, the Polemides, has a nostalgic feel. Matteo has me hold a baton as I move about in swirling steps, baton arm outstretched as though fighting with a razor. Even as my body moves, I hear the echoes of the past. I feel the vibrations of the mine, the scent of my clan. I have seen this dance before, and I perform it better than all the others. It is a dance my body is made for, one so very similar to the illegal Reaping Dance.

When I finish, Matteo is angry.

"Is this some sort of game?" he snarls.

"What do you mean?"

He glares at me and taps his foot. "You have never been beyond the mines?"

"You know that answer," I reply.

"You have never fought with a sword or shield?"

"Yes. I have. I've also captained starcruisers and dined with Praetors." I laugh and ask what this is about.

"This is *no* game, Darrow."

"Did I say it was?" I'm confused. What did I do to provoke him? I make a mistake in laughing to relieve the tension.

"You laugh? Boy, this is the Society with which you tangle. And you laugh? They are not some distant idea. They are cold reality. If they find out who you are, they will not hang you." His face looks lost as he says it. As though he knows only too well.

"I know this."

He ignores me. "The Obsidians will catch you and give you to the Whites and they will take you to their dark cells and they will torture you. They will pull out your eyes and cut away anything that makes you a man. They have more sophisticated methods, but I wager information won't be their only aim; they have chemicals for that if they want. Soon after you tell them everything, they will kill me, Harmony, Dancer. And they will kill your family with fleshPeelers and stomp on the heads of your nieces and nephews. These are the things they don't put on the HC. These are the consequences when the rulers of planets are your enemies. *Planets,* boy."

I feel a chill creep into my bones. I know these things. Why does he keep hammering me with them? I'm already frightened. I don't want to be, but I am. My task is swallowing me whole.

"So I ask you again, are you who Dancer says you are?"

I pause. *Ah.* I assumed that trust ran deep with the Sons of Ares, that they were of one mind. Here is a crack, a division. Matteo is Dancer's ally, but not a friend. Something in my dancing made him think twice. Then I realize it. He did not see Mickey carve me. He is taking this all on faith that I was once a Red, and how difficult that must be. Something in my dancing made him think I was born to this. Something to do with that last dance, the one called the Polemides.

"I am Darrow, son of Dale, Lambda's Helldiver of Lykos. I have never been anyone else, Matteo."

He crosses his arms. "If you are lying to me . . ."

"I do not lie to lowColors."

Later that evening, I research the dances I performed. *Polemides* is Greek for "child of war." It is the dance that reminded me so much of Uncle Narol's dances. It is the Gold's dance of war, the one they teach young children to prepare them for the motions of martial warfare and the use of the razor. I watch a holo of Golds in battle, and my heart falls into my stomach. They fight like a summer song. Not like the thunderous, monstrous Obsidians. But like birds banking into a fresh wind. They fight in pairs, swerving, dancing, killing, ripping through a field of Obsidian and Gray as though they were at play with scythes and all the bodies that fell to them were like stalks of grain that sprayed blood instead of sallow chaff. Their golden armor shines. Their razors flash. They are gods, not men.

And I mean to destroy them?

I sleep poorly in my bed of silk that night. Long after kissing Eo's haemanthus blossom, I fall asleep and dream of my father and what it would have been like to have known him into manhood, to have learned to dance from him instead of from his drunken brother. I clutch the scarlet headband in my hand as I wake. Holding it as dearly as I clutch my wedding band. All those things that remind me of home.

Yet they are not enough.

I am afraid.

Dancer finds me at my morning breakfast.

"You'll be happy to know, our hackers have spent two weeks hacking into the Board of Quality Control's cloud to change Caius au Andromedus's name to Darrow au Andromedus."

"Good."

"That's all you have to say? Do you know how much— Never mind." He shakes his head and gives a chuckle. "Darrow. It is so *offColor.* There will be raised eyebrows."

I shrug to conceal my fear. "So I'll butcher their gorydamn test and they'll care less than a lick."

"Spoken like a Gold."

The next day, Matteo takes me by ship to the stables of Ishtar, not far from Yorkton. It's a place by the sea, where green fields stretch over rolling hills. I've never been in so wide a place. I've never seen the land curve away from me. Never seen a true horizon or animals so terrifying as the beasts Matteo arranged for our lesson. They stomp and stamp and snort, flicking their tails and baring their monstrous yellow teeth. Horses. I've always been scared of horses, despite Eo's story of Andromeda.

"They're monsters," I whisper to Matteo.

"Nevertheless," he whispers back, "it is the gentleman's way. You must ride well, lest you find yourself embarrassed in some formal situation."

I look at the other Golds riding past. There are only three at the stables today, each accompanied by a servant like Matteo, Pinks and Browns.

"A situation like this one?" I hiss at him. "Fine. Fine." I point to a massive black stallion with hooves that paw the ground. "I'll take that beast."

Matteo smiles. "This one is more your speed."

Matteo gives me a pony. A big pony, but a pony. There is no social interaction here; the other riders trot past and tip their heads to say good day, but that is all. So their smiles are enough for me to know how ridiculous I look. I do not take to riding well. And I take to it even more poorly when my pony bolts as Matteo and I navigate a path into a copse of trees. Out the other side of the copse, I jump off the creature and land deftly in the grass. Someone laughs in the distance, a girl with long hair. She rides the stallion I pointed to earlier.

"Maybe you ought to stick to the city, Pixie," she shouts at me, then kicks her horse away. I rise from my knee and watch her ride into the distance. Her hair spills out behind her, more golden than the setting sun.

15

THE TESTING

My test comes after two months of training my mind with Dancer. I do not memorize. I do not even really learn when with him. Instead, his training is designed to help my mind adapt to paradigm shifts. For instance, if a fish has 3,453 scales on its left side and 3,453 on its right side, which side of the fish has the most scales? The outside. They call it extrapolational thinking. It was how I knew that I should eat the scythe card when I first met Dancer. I am very good at it.

I find it ironic that Dancer and his friends can create a fake history for me, a fake family, a fake life, but they cannot fake my admittance test. So, three months after my training begins, I take the test in a bright room next to a noisy mouse of a Goldbrow girl who incessantly taps her stylus on a jade bracelet. She may be part of the test for all I know. When she's not looking, I snatch the stylus from her fingers and hide it down my sleeve. I am a Helldiver of Lykos. So yes, I can steal a stupid girl's stylus without her knowing anything about it. She gawks around as if magic has been done. Then she begins to whine. They don't give her another stylus, so she runs out in tears. Afterward, the Penny Proctor looks at his datapad and rewinds a video from a nanoCamera. He looks at me and smiles. Such traits are apparently admirable.

A Golden razor blade of a girl disagrees and sneers "Cutter" in my ear as she slices past me in the hall outside. Matteo told me not to speak to anyone because I am not yet ready to socialize, so I barely bite back a very Red reply. Her words linger. Cutter. Cutthroat. Machiavellian. Ruthless. They all describe what she thinks of me. Funny thing is, most Golds would see the term as an accolade.

A musical voice addresses me.

"I think she actually just paid you a compliment. So don't mind her. She's pretty as a peach, but she's all rotten inside. I took a bite once, if you catch my flow. Tasty, then putrid. Fantastic grab in there, by the by. I was about to rip that ninny's eyes from her skull myself. Damnable tapping!"

The shining voice comes from a young man torn from Greek verse. Arrogance and beauty drip off of him. Impeccable breeding. I've never seen a smile so wide and white, skin so smooth and lustrous. He's all I despise.

He claps me on the shoulder and grasps my hand in one of the several ways of semiformal introduction. I squeeze slightly. He has a firm grip too, but when he tries to establish dominance, I squeeze his hand till he jerks it back. A flash of worry in his eyes.

"By God, your hand is like a vise!" He chuckles. He calls himself Cassius very quickly, and I'm lucky he gives me little time to speak, because his brow wrinkles when I do. My accent is still not perfect.

"Darrow," he repeats. "Well, that's quite the offColor name. Ah . . ." He looks at his datapad, pulling up my personal history. "Well, you come from no one at all. A farplanet hayseed. No wonder Antonia sneered your way. But listen, I'll forgive you for it if you tell me how you fared on the test."

"Oh, you'll forgive me?"

His brows knit together. "I'm trying to be kind here. We Bellonas aren't reformers, but we know that good men can come from low origins. Work with me, mate."

Because of the way he looks, I feel a need to provoke him.

"Well, I daresay I expected the test to be more difficult. I might have missed the one about the candle, but besides that . . ."

Cassius watches me with a forgiving grin. His lively eyes dance over my face as I wonder if his mother coils his hair with golden irons in the morning.

"With hands like yours, you must be a terror with the razor," he says leadingly.

"I'm fair," I lie. Matteo won't let me touch the thing.

"Modesty! Were you raised by the Whitecowls, man? Never mind, I'm off to Agea after the physical tests. Join me? I hear the Carvers have done some splendid work with the new ladies at Temptation. And they just had gravfloors installed at Tryst; we can float about without gravBoots. What say you, man? Does that interest you?" He taps one of his wings and winks. "Plenty of peaches there. None of them rotten."

"Unfortunately, I cannot."

"Oh." He jumps as if just remembering I'm a farplanet hayseed. "Don't worry about it, my goodman, I'll pay and all that."

I politely decline, but he's already moving on. He taps my datapad before he leaves. The holoscreen cast over the inside of my left arm flickers. The dimensions of his face and information about our conversation are left behind—the address for the clubs he spoke of, the encyclopedic reference for Agea, and his family's information. Cassius au Bellona, it reads. Son of Praetor Tiberius au Bellona, Imperator of the Society's Sixth Fleet and perhaps the only man on Mars to rival ArchGovernor Augustus in power. Apparently the families hate one another. Seems like they have a nasty habit of killing each other off. Baby pitvipers indeed.

I thought I would be frightened of these people. I thought they would be little godlings. But aside from Cassius and Antonia, many are unimpressive. There are only seventy in my testing room. Some look like Cassius. But not all are beautiful. Not all are tall and imperious. And very few strike me as men and women. For all their physical stature, they are children with exaggerated senses of self-worth; they don't know hardship. Babies. Pixies and Bronzies, mostly.

They test my physical properties next. I sit naked in an airchair in a white room as the Copper testers of the Quality Control Board watch me through nanoCams. "Hope you're getting a good look," I say.

A Brown worker comes in and applies a pinch to my nose. His eyes are blank. No fight in this one, no contempt for me. His skin is pallid and his movements awkward and clumsy.

I am instructed to hold my breath as long as my lungs will allow. Ten minutes. Afterward, the Brown removes the clamp and leaves. Next, I'm to take a breath and exhale. I do and realize there is suddenly no oxygen in the chamber. When I start to tilt in my seat, the oxygen returns. They freeze the room and measure how long it takes for me to shiver uncontrollably. Then they heat it to see when my heart begins to struggle. They amplify the grav in the room till my heart can't push sufficient blood and oxygen to my brain. Then they see how much motion I can take till I vomit. I'm used to riding a ninety-meter drill, so they have to give up.

They measure the flow of oxygen to my muscles, the beats of my heart, the density and length of my muscle fibers, the tensile ratings of my bones. It's like a walk in the park after my hell with Harmony.

They have me throw balls, then line me up against a wall and ask me to stop small balls that they shoot at me with a circular machine. My Helldiver hands are faster than their machine, so they bring in a Green techie to adjust the thing till it's shooting veritable rockets. Eventually, I'm hit with a ball in the forehead. I black out briefly. They measure that too.

An eye, ear, nose, and mouth test later and I am done. I feel vaguely distant from myself after the test. Like they measured my body and my brain but not me. I've had no personal interactions except that one with Cassius.

I stumble into the locker rooms, sore and confused. There's a couple others changing, so I take my clothes and move along to a more discreet section of the long rows of plastic lockers. Then I hear a strange whistling. A tune I know. One that echoes through my dreams. The one Eo died to. I follow the sound and come upon a girl changing in the corner of the locker room. Her back is to me, muscles lean as she dons her shirt. I make a noise. She turns suddenly, and for an awkward moment, I stand there blushing. Golds are not supposed to care about nudity. But I can't help my reaction. She's beautiful—heart-shaped face, full lips, eyes that laugh at you. They laugh like they did as she rode away on the horse. It's the same girl who called me a Pixie when I rode the pony.

One of her eyebrows arches upward. I don't know what to say, so, in a panic, I turn and walk fast as I can out of the locker rooms.

A Gold wouldn't have done that. But as I sit with Matteo on the shuttle as it ferries us back home, I remember the girl's face. She blushed too.

It is a short flight, not long enough. I watch Mars through the duroglass floor. Though the planet is terraformed, vegetation is sparse along our flightpath. The planet's surface is streaked with ribbons of green in its valleys and around her equator. The vegetation looks like green scars that cut across her pocked surface.

Water fills her impact craters, creating grand lakes. And the Borealis basin, which stretches across the northern hemisphere, brims with fresh water and teems with bizarre marine life. Great plains where dust devils gather cloaks of topsoil and tear through croplands. Storms and ice rule the poles where the Obsidians train and live. The weather there is said to be brutal and cold, though temperate climes are prevalent throughout much of Mars's surface now.

There are one thousand cities on Mars, each ruled by a Governor, the ArchGovernor presiding over all. Each city is set in the center of a hundred mining colonies. The Governors manage these colonies, with the individual MineMagistrates like Podginus overseeing the day-to-day.

With so many mines and so many cities, it was chance, I suppose, that brought the ArchGovernor to my home with his camera crew. Chance and my position as a Helldiver. They wanted to make an example out of me; Eo was an afterthought. And she would not have sung if the ArchGovernor had not been there. Life's ironies are not charming.

"What will the Institute be like if I get in?" I ask Matteo as I peer out the window.

"Full of classes, I imagine. How should I know?"

"Is there no intel?"

"No."

"No?" I ask.

"Well, some, I suppose," Matteo admits. "Three sorts of people graduate: the Peerless Scarred, the Graduates, and the Shamed. The Peerless can ascend in society; the Graduates can as well, but their prospects are relatively limited and they still must earn their scars; and the Shamed are sent to the distant, hard colonies like Pluto to oversee the first years of terraforming."

"How does one become a Peerless?"

"I imagine there is some sort of ranking system; *perhaps* a competition. I do not know. But the Golds are a species built upon conquest. It would make sense if that were to be part of your competition."

"How vague." I sigh. "You're as helpful as a legless dog sometimes."

"The game, *goodman,* in Gold society is patronage. Your actions in the Institute will serve as an extended audition for that patronage. You need an apprenticeship. You need a powerful benefactor." He grins. "So if you want to help our cause, you'll do as *bloodydamn* well as you can. Imagine if you became an apprentice to a Praetor. In ten years' time, you could be a Praetor yourself. You could have a fleet! Imagine what you could do with a fleet, my *goodman.* Just imagine."

Matteo never speaks about such flights of fancy, so the excitement in his eyes is contagious. It makes me imagine.

16

THE INSTITUTE

My test results come when I am practicing my cultural recognition and accent modulation with Matteo in our high-rise penthouse. We have a view of the city, the setting sun behind. I'm midway through a clever retort about the Yorkton Supernova faux-War sports club when my datapad beeps with a priority message sent to my datapad stream. I almost spill my coffee.

"My datapad has been slaved by another," I said. "It's the Board of Quality Control."

Matteo shoots up from his chair. "We have perhaps four minutes." He runs into the suite's library, where Harmony is reading on an ergocouch. She jumps up and is down and out of the suite in less than three breaths. I make sure that the holopictures of me with my fake family are arranged in my bedroom and throughout the penthouse. Four hired servants—Browns and a Pink—go about domestic tasks in the penthouse. They wear the Pegasus livery of my fake family.

One of the Browns goes to the kitchen. The other, a Pink woman, massages my shoulders. Matteo shines my shoes in my room. Of course there are machines to do these things, but an Aureate would never use a machine for something a person could do. There is no power in that.

The towncraft appears like a distant dragonfly. It grows as it buzzes closer and hovers outside my penthouse window. Its boarding door slides open and a man in a Copper suit gives a bow of formality. I let my datapad open the duroglass window and the man floats in. Three Whites are with him. Each has a white Sigil upon their hands. Members of the Academians and a Copper bureaucrat.

"Do I have the pleasure of addressing one Darrow au Andromedus, son of the recently deceased Linus au Andromedus and Lexus au Andromedus?"

"You have the honor."

The bureaucrat looks me up and down in a very deferential, but impatient manner. "I am Bondilus cu Tancrus of the Institute's Board of Quality Control. There are some questions we must beg to ask of you."

We sit across from one another at my oak kitchen table. There, they hook my finger to a machine and one of the Whites dons a pair of glasses that will analyze my pupils and other physiological reactions. They will be able to tell if I am lying.

"We will start with a control question to assess your normal reaction when telling truths. Are you of the Family Andromedus?"

"Yes."

"Are you of the Aureate genus?"

"Yes." I lie through my teeth, ruining their control questions.

"Did you cheat in your admissions test two months prior?"

"No."

"Did you use nervenucleic to stimulate high comprehension and analytical functions during the test itself?"

"No."

"Did you use a networkwidget to aggregate or synthesize outside resources in real time?"

"No." I sigh impatiently. "There was a jammer in the room, ergo it would have been impossible. I'm glad you've done your research and are not wasting my time, Copper."

His smile is bureaucratic.

"Did you have prior knowledge of the questions?"

"No." I deem an angry response proper at this point. "And what is this about? I'm not accustomed to being called a liar by someone of your ilk."

"It is procedure with all elite scorers, Lord Aureate. I beg your understanding," the bureaucrat drones. "Any upward outlier far removed from the standard deviation is subject to inquiry. Did you slave your widget to that of another individual during the test?"

"No. As I said, there was a jammer. Thank you for keeping up, pennyhead."

They take a sample of my blood and scan my brain. The results are instantaneous, but the bureaucrat will not share them. "Protocol," he reminds me. "You will have your results in two weeks."

We receive them in four. I pass the Quality Control examination. I did not cheat. Then comes my exam score, two months after I took the damn thing, and I realize why they thought I did cheat. I missed one question. Just one. Out of hundreds. When I share the results with Dancer, Harmony, and Matteo, they simply stare at me. Dancer falls into a chair and begins to laugh; it's an hysterical sort.

"Bloodyhell," he swears. "We've done it."

"He did it," Matteo corrects.

It takes Dancer a minute before he has wits enough to fetch a bottle of champagne, but I still feel his eyes watching me as though I am something different, something strange. It's like they suddenly don't understand what it is they have created. I touch the haemanthus blossom in my pocket and feel the wedding band around my neck. They didn't create me. She did.

It is when a valet arrives to escort me to the Institute that I say my goodbyes to Dancer inside the penthouse. He holds tight to my hand as we shake and gives me the look my father gave me before he was hanged. It's one of reassurance. But behind that is worry and doubt. Did he prepare me for the world? Did he do his duty? My father was twenty-five when he looked at me like that. Dancer is forty-one. It makes no difference. I chuckle. Uncle Narol never gave me such a look, not even when he let me cut Eo down. Probably because he'd taken enough of my right hooks to know the answer. But if I think about my teachers, my fathers, Uncle Narol shaped me the most. He taught me to dance; he taught me how to be a man, perhaps because he knew this would be my future. And though he tried to stop me from being a Helldiver, it was his lessons that kept me alive. I've learned new lessons now. Let's hope they do the trick.

Dancer gives me the knifeRing he used to slice my finger months before. But he's reshaped it to look like an *L*.

"They will think it the chevron the Spartans bore on their shields," he said. "*L* for Lacadaemonia." But it is for Lykos. For Lambda.

Harmony surprises me by taking my right hand, kissing where once my Red sigil was emblazoned. She's got tears in one eye, the cold, unscarred eye. The other cannot cry.

"Evey will be coming to live with us," she tells me. She smiles before I can ask why. It looks strange on her face. "You think you're the only one who notices things? We'll give her a better life than Mickey would."

Matteo and I share a smile and a bow. We exchange proper honorifics and he extends his hand. It doesn't grasp mine. Instead, it snatches the flower from my pocket. I reach after it, but he's still the only man I've ever met who is faster than me.

"You cannot take this with you, *goodman*. The wedding band on your hand is queer enough. The flower is too much."

"Give me a petal then," I say.

"I thought you would ask for that." He pulls out a necklace. It is the sigil of Andromedus. My sigil, I remember. It is iron. He drops it in my hand. "Whisper her name." I do and the Pegasus unfurls like a haemanthus bud. He sets a petal in the center. It closes again. "This is your heart. Guard it with iron."

"Thank you, Matteo," I say, tears in my eyes. I pick him up and hug him despite his protests. "If I live more than a week, I'll have you to thank, my *goodman*." He blushes when I set him down.

"Manage your temper," he reminds me, his small voice darkening. "Manners, manners, then burn their *bloodydamn* house to the ground."

I clutch the Pegasus in my hand as the shuttle crosses over the Martian countryside. Fingers of green stretch over the earth I've lived to dig. I wonder who the Helldiver of Lambda is now. Loran is too young. Barlow is too old. Kieran? He's too responsible. He's got children to love, and he's seen enough of our family die. There's no fire in his belly. Leanna's got enough, but women aren't allowed to dig. It is probably Dain, Eo's brother. Wild, but not bright. The typical Helldiver. He'll die fast. The thought makes me nauseous.

It's not just the thought. I'm nervous. I realize it slowly as I look around the shuttle's interior. Six other youths sit quietly. One, a slender boy with an open gaze and pretty smile, catches my eye. He's the sort who still laughs at butterflies.

"Julian," he declares properly, and takes my forearm. We have no data to offer each other through our datapads; they took them when we boarded the shuttle. So instead I offer him the seat across from me. "Darrow, a very interesting name."

"Have you ever been to Agea?" I ask Julian.

"Course," he says, smiling. He always smiles. "What, you mean you haven't? It's strange. I thought I knew so many Golds, but hardly any of them managed to get past the entrance exams. It's a brave new world of faces, I fear. Anyway, I envy you the fact you haven't been to Agea. It's a strange place. Beautiful, no doubt, but life there is fast, and cheap, so they say."

"But not for us."

He chuckles. "I suppose not. Not unless you play at politics."

"I don't much like playing." I notice his reaction, so I laugh my seriousness off with a wink. "Not unless there's a wager, man. You hear?"

"I hear! What's your game? Bloodchess? Gravcross?"

"Oh, bloodchess is all right. But fauxWar takes the prize," I say with a Golden grin.

"Especially if you're a Nortown fan!" he agrees.

"Oh . . . *Nortown.* I don't know if we'll get along," I say, wincing. I jab myself with a thumb. "Yorkton."

"*Yorkton!* I don't know if we'll *ever* get along!" he laughs.

And though I smile, he doesn't know how cold I am inside; the conversation, the jibes, the smiles, are all a pattern of sociality. Matteo's done me well, but to Julian's credit, he doesn't seem a monster.

He should be a monster.

"My brother must already have arrived at the Institute. He was already in Agea at our family's estate, causing trouble no doubt!" Julian shakes his head proudly. "Best man I know. He'll be the Primus, just you watch. Our father's pride and joy, and that's saying something with how many family members I have!" Not a flicker of jealousy in his voice, just love.

"Primus?" I ask.

"Oh, Institute talk; it means leader of his House."

The Houses. I know these. There are twelve loosely based on underlying personality traits. Each is named for one of the gods of the Roman pantheon. The SchoolHouses are networking tools and social clubs outside of school. Do well, and they'll find you a powerful family to serve. The families are the true powers in the Society. They have their own armies and fleets and contribute to the Sovereign's forces. Loyalty begins with them. There is little love for the denizens of one's own planet. If anything, they are the competition.

"You sobs done beating each other off yet?" an impish kid sneers from the corner of the shuttle. He's so drab he is khaki instead of Gold. His lips are thin and his face like a cruel hawk just as it spies a mouse. A Bronzie.

"Are we bothering you?" My sarcasm has a polite nip.

"Does two dogs humping bother me? Likely, yes. If they are noisy."

Julian stands. "Apologize, cur."

"Go slag yourself," the small kid says. In half a second, Julian has drawn a white glove from nowhere. "That to wipe my ass, you golden pricklick?"

"What? You little heathen!" Julian says in shock. "Who raised you?"

"Wolves, after your mother's cootch spat me out."

"You beast!"

Julian throws the glove at the small kid. I'm watching, thinking this is the height of comedy. The kid seems pulled straight from the Lykos crop, Beta maybe. He's like an ugly, tiny, irritable Loran. Julian doesn't know what to do, so he makes a challenge.

"A challenge, *goodman*."

"A duel? You're that offended?" The ugly kid snorts at the princeling. "Fine. I'll stitch your family pride together after the Passage, pricklick." He blows his nose into the glove.

"Why not now, coward?" Julian calls. His slender chest is puffed out just as his father must have taught him. No one insults his family.

"Are you stupid? Do you see razors about? Idiot. Go away. We'll duel after the Passage."

"Passage . . . ?" Julian finally asks what I'm thinking.

The scrawny kid grins wickedly. Even his teeth are khaki.

"It's the last test, idiot. And the best secret this side of the rings around Octavia au Lune's cootch."

"Then how do you know about it?" I ask.

"Inside track," the kid says. "And I don't know about it. I know *of* it, you giant pisshead."

His name is Sevro, and I like his angle.

But the talk of a Passage worries me. There is so little I know, I realize, as I listen in as Julian strikes up a conversation with the last member of our shuttle. They talk about their test scores. There is a severe disparity between their low scores and mine. I notice Sevro snort as they say theirs aloud. How did applicants with such low scores get in? I've got an ill feeling in my gut. And what did Sevro score?

We come to the Valles Marineris in darkness. It is a great scar of light across Mars's black surface, going as far as eyes can see. At the center of it, the capital city of my planet rises in the night like a garden of jewelswords. Nightclubs flicker on rooftops, dance floors made of condensed air. Scantily-dressed girls and foolish boys rise and fall as gravMixers play with physics. NoiseBubbles separate city blocks. We cut through them and hear worlds of different sounds.

The Institute is beyond Agea's night districts and is built into the side of the eight-kilometer-high walls of the Valles Marineris. The walls rise like tidal waves of green stone cradling civilization with flora. The Institute itself is made of white stone—a place of columns and sculpture, Roman to its core.

I have not been here before. But I have seen the columns. Seen the destination of our voyage. Bitterness wells in me like bile rising from stomach to throat as I think of his face. Think of his words. His eyes as they scanned the crowd. I watched on the HC as the ArchGovernor gave his speech time and again to the classes before my own. Soon I'll hear it from his lips myself. Soon I'll suffer the rage. Feel the fire lick over my heart as I see him in person once again.

We land on a drop pad and are shepherded into an open-air marble square looking over the vast valley. The night air is crisp. Agea sprawls behind and the gates of the Institute stretch before us. I stand with over a thousand Goldbrows, all glancing about with the cocksureness of their race. Many clump together, friends from beyond the white walls of the school. I did not think their classes so large.

A tall Golden man flanked by Obsidians and a coterie of Gold advisors rises on a pair of gravBoots before the gate. My heart goes cold as I recognize his face and hear his voice and see the glimmer in his ingot eyes.

"Welcome, children of Aureate," ArchGovernor Nero au Augustus says in a voice as smooth as Eo's skin. It is preternaturally loud. "I assume you understand the gravity of your presence here. Of the thousand cities of Mars. Of all the Great Families, you are the chosen few. You are the peak of the human pyramid. Today, you will begin your campaign to join the best caste of our race. Your fellows stand like you in the Institutes of Venus, of the Eastern and Western Hemispheres of Earth, of Luna, of the Gas Giant Moons, of Europa, of the Astrodian Greek Cluster and the Astrodian Trojan Cluster, of Mercury, of Callisto, of the joint venture Enceledas and Ceres, and of the farpioneers of Hildas."

It seems only a day ago that I knew I was a pioneer of Mars. Only a day ago that I suffered so that humanity, desperate to leave a dying Earth, could spread to the red planet. Oh, how well my rulers lied.

Behind Augustus, in the stars, there's movement, but it is not the stars that move. Nor is it asteroids or comets. It is the Sixth and Fifth Fleets. The Armada of Mars. My breath catches in my chest. The Sixth Fleet is commanded by Cassius's father, while the smaller Fifth Fleet is under the ArchGovernor's direct control. Most of the ships are owned by families who owe allegiance to either Augustus or Bellona.

Augustus shows us why we, they, rule. My flesh tingles. I am so small. A billion tons of durosteel and nanometal move through the heavens, and I have never been beyond Mars's atmosphere. They are like specks of silver in an ocean of ink. And I am so much less. But those specks could ravage Mars. They could destroy a moon. Those specks rule the ink. An Imperator commands each fleet; a Praetor commands squadrons within that fleet. What I could do with that power . . .

Augustus is haughty as he gives his speech. I swallow the bile in my throat. Because of the impossible distance of my enemies, my anger was once a cold, quiet sort. Now it burns in me.

"Society has three stages: Savagery, Ascendance, Decadence. The great rise because of Savagery. They rule in Ascendance. They fall because of their own Decadence."

He tells us how the Persians were felled, how the Romans collapsed because their rulers forgot how their parents gained them an empire. He prattles about Muslim dynasties and European effeminacy and Chinese regionalism and American self-loathing and self-neutering. All the ancient names.

"Our Savagery began when our capital, Luna, rebelled against the tyranny of Earth and freed herself from the shackles of Demokracy, from the Noble Lie—the idea that men are brothers and are created equal."

Augustus weaves lies of his own with that golden tongue of his. He tells of the Goldens' suffering. The Masses sat on the wagon and expected the great to pull, he reminds. They sat whipping the great until we could no longer take it.

I remember a different whipping.

"Men are not created equal; we all know this. There are averages. There are outliers. There are the ugly. There are the beautiful. This would not be if we were all equal. A Red can no more command a starship than a Green can serve as a doctor!"

There's more laughter across the square as he tells us to look at pathetic Athens, the birthplace of the cancer they call Demokracy. Look how it fell to Sparta. The Noble Lie made Athens weak. It made their citizens turn on their best general, Alcibiades, because of jealousy.

"Even the nations of Earth grew jealous of one another. The United States of America exacted this idea of equality through force. And when the nations united, the Americans were surprised to find that they were disliked! The Masses are jealous! How wonderful a dream it would be if all men were created equal! But we are not.

"It is against the Noble Lie that we fight. But as I said before, as I say to you now, there is another evil against which we war. It is a more pernicious evil. It is a subversive, slow evil. It is not a wildfire. It is a cancer. And that cancer is Decadence. Our Society has passed from Savagery to Ascendance. But like our spiritual ancestors, the Romans, we too can fall into Decadence."

He speaks of the Pixies.

"You are the best of humanity. But you have been coddled. You have been treated like children. Were you born to a different Color, you would have calluses. You would have scars. You would know pain."

He smiles as if he knows pain. I hate this man.

"You think you know pain. You think the Society is an inevitable force of history. You think Her the end of history. But many have thought that before. Many ruling classes have believed theirs to be the last, the pinnacle. They grew soft. Fat. They forgot that calluses, wounds, scars, hardship, preserve all those fine pleasure clubs you young boys love to frequent and all those fine silks and diamonds and unicorns you girls ask for on birthdays.

"Many Aureates have not sacrificed. That is why they do not wear this." He shows a long scar on his right cheek. Octavia au Lune has the same scar. "The Scar of a Peer. We are not the masters of the Solar System because we are born. We are the masters because we, the Peerless Scarred, the iron Golds, made it that way."

He touches the scar on his cheek. I'd give him another if I were closer. The children around me suck down this man's garbage like oxygen.

"Right now, the Colors who mine this planet are harder than you. They are born with calluses. Born with scars and hatred. They are tough as nanosteel. Fortunately, they are also very stupid. For instance, this *Persephone* you have no doubt heard of is nothing more than a dim girl who thought singing a song was worth a hanging."

I bite a bloody hole in my cheek. My skin shivers from rage as I find out that my wife is part of this bastard's speech.

"The girl did not even know the video would be leaked. Yet it is her willingness to suffer hardship that gave her power. Martyrs, you see, are like bees. Their only power comes in death. How many of you would sacrifice yourself to not kill, but merely hurt your enemy? Not one of you, I wager."

I taste blood in my mouth. I have the knifeRing Dancer gave me. But I breathe the fury down. I am no martyr. I am not vengeance. I am Eo's dream. Still, doing nothing while her murderer gloats feels like a betrayal.

"In time you will receive your Scars from my sword," Augustus closes. "But first you must earn them."

17

THE DRAFT

"Son of Linus and Lexus au Andromedus, both of the House Apollo. Would you prefer to mark yourself as requesting House Apollo preferentiality?" a tedious Aureate administrator asks me.

Goldbrows' first loyalty is to Color, then family, then planet, then House. Most Houses are dominated by one or two powerful families. On Mars, the Family Augustus, the Family Bellona, and the Family Arcos influence all others.

"No," I reply.

He shuffles over his datapad. "Very well. How do you believe you performed on the slangSmarts test? That is the extrapolational test," he clarifies.

"I think my results speak for themselves."

"You were not paying attention, Darrow. I shall mark that against you. I'm asking for *you* to speak for your results."

"I think I took a gory piss on your test, *sir*."

"Ah." He smiles. "Well, you did. You did. House Minerva for brains might be right for you. Perhaps Pluto, for the deviousness. Apollo for the pride. Yes. Hmm. Well, I have a test for you. Please complete it to the best of your ability. Interviews will commence when you have finished."

The test is quick and it is in the form of an immersion game. There is a goblet on a hill that I need to acquire. Many obstacles stand in my way. I pass them as rationally as possible, trying to hide my anger when a little elf steals a key I acquire. But every step of the way, there's some damn setback, some inconvenience. And it is always unforeseen. It is always something beyond the bounds of extrapolation. In the end, I reach the goblet, but only after killing an annoying wizard and cruelly enslaving the race of elves by means of said wizard's magic wand. I could have left the elves be. But they annoyed me.

Soon, the interviewers come in intervals. I learn they are called Proctors. Each one of them is a Peerless Scarred. They are chosen by the ArchGovernor to teach and represent the students of the House within the Institute.

All said, the Proctors are impressive. There's a huge Scarred man with hair like a lion and a lightning bolt on his collar for Jupiter, a matronly woman with gentle golden eyes, and a quick-witted man with winged feet on his collar. He can't sit still and his baby face seems immensely fascinated by my hands. He makes me play a game with him in which he puts out both hands flat and facing up and I put mine atop facing down. He tries slapping my hands, but never quite manages. He leaves after clapping his hands together in joy.

Another strange encounter comes when a beautiful man with coiled hair interviews me. A bow marks his collar. Apollo. He asks me how attractive I believe myself to be and is displeased when I undershoot his estimate. Still, I think he likes me, because he asks me what I would like to be one day.

"An Imperator of a fleet," I say.

"You could do great things with a fleet. But a lofty notion," he sighs, accenting every word with a feline purr. "Perhaps too lofty for your family. Maybe if you had a benefactor of better familial origin. Yes, maybe then." He looks at his datapad. "But unlikely due to your birth. Hm. Best of luck."

I sit alone for an hour or more till a sullen man comes to join me. His unfortunate face is pinched like a hatchet, but he has the Scar and a razor hilt hangs on his hip. His name is Fitchner. A wad of gum fills his mouth. The uniform he wears is black with gold, and it nearly conceals the slight belly paunch that sticks outward despite the faint smell of metabolizers. Like many of the others, he wears badges about his personage. A golden wolf with two heads decorates his collar. And a strange hand marks his cuff.

"They give me the mad dogs," he says. "They give me the killers of our race, the ones full of piss and napalm and vinegar." He sniffs the air. "You smell full of shit."

I say nothing. He leans against the door and frowns at it as though it offended him in some way. Then back to me, sniffing improperly.

"Problem is, we of House Mars always burn out. Kids rule the Institute at first. Then they find out that napalm lasts about . . ." He snaps his fingers. I have no reply. He sighs and plops down in a chair. After a while of watching me, he stands and punches me in the face. "If you punch me back, you will be sent home, Pixie."

I kick him in the shin.

He limps away, laughing like a drunk Uncle Narol.

I'm not sent home. Instead, I find myself escorted with one hundred others into a large room with floatChairs and a large wall dominated by ivory gridwork. The gridwork forms a checkerboard square on the wall, ten rows high, ten rows across. I'm taken on a lift to the middle row, some fifty feet off the ground. Ninety-nine other students are ushered in till each box is filled. This is the prime crop, the best of the students. I look out from my box, peering up above me. A girl's feet dangle out of the box above my head. Numbers and letters appear in front of my box. My statistics. Supposedly I am very rash and have upper-outlier characteristics in intuition and loyalty and, most noticeably, rage.

There are twelve groups in the audience. Each group sits close together in floatChairs around vertical golden standards. I see an archer, a lightning bolt, an owl, a wolf with two heads, an upside-down crown, and a trident, amongst others. One of the Proctors accompanies each group. They alone do not have their faces covered. The others wear ceremonial masks, featureless and golden and slightly like the animals of their Houses. If only I had known this was going to happen, I might have brought a nuke. These are the Drafters, the men and women of highest prestige. Praetors and Imperators and Tribunes and Adjudicators and Governors sit there watching me, trying to choose the new students for their House, trying to find young men and women they can test and offer apprenticeships. With one bomb, I could have destroyed the best and the brightest of their Golden rule. Maybe that's the rashness speaking.

The Draft begins when a titan of a genAlt boy is chosen first to the House of the lightning bolt. House Jupiter. Then go more girls and boys of unnatural beauty and physical prowess. I can only guess they are geniuses as well. The fifth pick comes. The baby-faced interviewer with the winged feet floats up to me on golden boots. Several of the Drafters of House Mercury float along with him. They speak quietly amongst themselves before asking me questions.

"Who are your parents? What are their family's accomplishments?"

I tell them about my modest false family. One of them seems to think highly of a relative of mine who has long since passed away. But despite the Proctor's objections, they pass me over for another student from a family with the ownership of ninety mines and a stake on one of Mars's southern continents.

The Mercury Proctor curses and shoots me a quick smile.

"Hope you're available next round," he says.

Next goes a delicate girl with a mocking smile. I can barely pay attention, and, at times, it is difficult to see who else is being selected. We're arrayed in an odd way. With the tenth pick, the Proctor who struck me in the interviews floats my way. There is disagreement amongst the Drafters. I have two ardent advocates: one is as tall as Augustus, but her hair flows down to her spine in three golden braids. And the second is broader, not very tall. He's old. Can tell by the scars and wrinkles on his thick hands. Hands that bear the signet ring of an Olympic Knight. I know him immediately even without seeing his face. Lorn au Arcos. The Rage Knight, the third-greatest man on Mars, who chose to serve the Society by safeguarding the Society's Compact, instead of reaching for crowns in politics. When he points to me, Fitchner grins.

I am chosen tenth. Tenth out of one thousand.

18

CLASSMATES

I feel a sinking in my stomach as I walk with the chattering mass into the dining hall. It is overgrand—white marble floors, columns, a holosky displaying birds in flight at sunset. The Institute is not what I expected. According to Augustus, the classes are to be hard on these little godlings. I snort down a laugh. Let the lot of them spend a year in a mine.

There are twelve tables, each with one hundred place settings. Our names float above the chairs in golden letters. Mine floats to the right of a table's head. It is a place of distinction. The firstDraft. A single bar floats to the right of my name. A -1 is to the left. The first to get five bars becomes Primus of his House. Each bar is bounty for an act of merit. Apparently my high score on the test was the first bit of merit.

"Wonderful, a cutter in the lead for Primus," a familiar voice says. The girl from the exam. I read her name. Antonia au Severus. She has cruel good looks—high cheekbones, a smirking smile, scorn in her eyes. Her hair is long, full, and golden as Midas's touch. She was born to be hated and to hate. A -5 floats beside her name. It is the second-closest score to mine at the table. Cassius, the boy I met at testing, sits diagonally across from me. A -6 shimmers by his broad smile. He runs a hand back through his curls.

Another boy sits directly across from me; -1 and a golden bar float by his name. While Cassius lounges, this other boy, Priam, sits as straight as a blade. His face is celestial. His eyes alert. His hair coiffed. He's tall as me, but broad in the shoulders. I don't think I've ever seen a more perfect human being. A bloodydamn statue. He wasn't in the Draft, I discover. He is what they call a Premier; they cannot be drafted. His parents choose his House. Then I discover why. His scandalous mother, a bannerwoman of the House Bellona, owns our planet's two moons.

"Fate brings us together again," Cassius chuckles to me. "And Antonia. My love! It seems our fathers conspired to place us side by side."

Antonia replies with a sneer, "Remind me to beam him a thank-you."

"Toni! No need for nastiness." He wags a finger. "Now toss me a smile like a good doll."

She flips him the crux with her fingers. "Rather toss you out a window, Cassi."

"Rawr." Cassius blows her a kiss. She ignores it. "So, Priam, I suppose you and I will have to play gently with these fools, eh?"

"Oh, they look like swell sorts to me," Priam replies primly. "I fancy we'll do very well as a group."

They talk in highLingo.

"If the dregs of the Draft don't weigh us down, my good man!" He gestures to the end of the table and starts naming them: "Screwface, for obvious reasons. Clown because of that ridiculous puffy hair. Weed because, well, he's thin. Oy! You, you're Thistle because your nose looks hooked as one. And . . . that itty-bitty one right there next to the Bronzie-looking fellow, that's little Pebble."

"I think they will rather surprise you," Priam says in defense of the far end of the table. "They may not be as tall or as athletic or even as intelligent as you or me, if intelligence really can be measured by *that* test, but I do not think it charity to say that they will be the spine of our group. Salt of the earth, if you will. Good sorts."

I see the small kid from the shuttle, Sevro, at the very foot of the table. The salt of the earth is not making friends. And neither am I. Cassius glances at my -1. I see him concede that Priam might have scored better than he, but Cassius makes a point in saying he's never heard of my parents.

"So, dear Darrow, how did you cheat?" he asks. Antonia glances over from her conversation with Arria, a small girl made of curling hair and dimples.

"Oh, come now, man." I laugh. "They sent Quality Control after me. How could I have cheated? Impossible. Did you cheat? Your score is high."

I speak the midLingo. It's more comfortable than that highLingo fartdust Priam jabbers on in.

"Me? Cheat! No. Just didn't try enough, apparently," Cassius replies. "If I had my wits, I'd have spent less time with the girls and more on studying, like you."

He's trying to tell me if he tried he could have done just as well. But he's too busy to put in as much effort. If I wanted him as a friend, I'd let him get away with it.

"You studied?" I ask. I feel a sudden urge to embarrass him. "I didn't study at all."

A chill goes through the air.

I shouldn't have said it. My stomach plummets. *Manners*.

Cassius's face sours and Antonia smirks. I've insulted him. Priam frowns. If I want a career in the fleet, then I will likely need Cassius au Bellona's father's patronage. Son of an Imperator. Matteo drilled this into me. How easy it is to forget. The fleet is where the power is. Fleet or government or army. And I don't like government, not to mention that this sort of insult is how duels begin. Fear trickles down my spine as I realize how thin a line there is to tread. Cassius knows how to duel. I, for all my new skills, do not. He would rip me to pieces, and he looks like he wants to do just that.

"I joke." I tilt my head to Cassius. "Come on, man. How could I score so high and not have studied till my eyes were bleeding? Wish I'd spent more time fooling off like you—we're in the same spot now, after all. Fat lot that studying did for me."

Priam nods his approval at the peace offering.

"I bet it was a slog!" Cassius crows, tipping his head to acknowledge my peculiar breed of apology. I expected the play to go over his head. Thought his pride would blind him to my sudden apology; the Gold may be proud, but he isn't stupid. None of them are. Have to remember that.

After that, I do Matteo proud. I flirt with a girl named Quinn, befriend and joke with Cassius and Priam—who has probably never sworn in his life—throw my hand out to a tall brute named Titus whose neck is as thick as my thigh. He squeezes too hard on purpose. He's surprised when I nearly break his hand, but damn is his grip strong. The boy is even taller than Cassius and I, and he's got a voice like a titan, but he grins when he realizes that my grip, if nothing else, is stronger than his. Something strange about his voice, though. Something decidedly disdainful. There's also a feather of a boy named Roque who looks and speaks like a poet. His smiles are slow, few, but genuine. Rare.

"Cassius!" Julian calls. Cassius stands and throws an arm around his thinner, prettier twin. I didn't piece it together before, but they are brothers. Twins. Not identical. Julian did say his brother was already in Agea.

"Darrow here is not what he seems," Julian tells the table with a very grave face. He has a knack for theatrics.

"You don't mean . . ." Cassius puts a hand to his mouth.

My finger grazes my steak knife.

"Yes." Julian nods solemnly.

"No." Cassius shakes his head. "He's not a *Yorkton* supporter? Julian, tell me it isn't so! Darrow! Darrow, how could you be? They never win a game! Priam, are you hearing this?"

I throw my hands up in apology. "A curse of birth, I suppose. I am a product of my upbringing. I cheer for the underdog." I manage not to sneer the words.

"He confessed it to me on the shuttle."

Julian is proud to know me. Proud his brother knows he knows me. He looks for Cassius's approval. Cassius isn't oblivious to this either; he gently doles out a compliment and Julian leaves the high-

Drafts and returns to his midDraft seat halfway down the table with a content smile and squared shoulders. I didn't think Cassius would be the kind sort.

Of those I meet, only Antonia openly dislikes me. She doesn't watch me like the others at the table. From her, I feel only a distant breed of contempt. One moment she is laughing, flirting with Roque, and then she feels my gaze and becomes ice. The feeling is mutual.

My dormitory is from a dream. Gold trim lines a window that looks out into the valley. A bed is laden with silks and quilts and satins. I lie in it when a Pink masseur comes in and stays for an hour kneading my muscles. Later, three lithe Pinks file through to tend to my needs. I send them to Cassius's room instead. To calm the temptation, I take a cold shower and immerse myself in a holoexperience of a digger in the mining colony Corinth. The Helldiver in the holoexperience is less talented than I was, but the rattling, the simulated heat, the darkness and the vipers, they comfort me so much that I wrap my old scarlet rag around my head.

More food comes. Augustus was all talk. Gob full of exaggerations. This is their version of hardship. I feel guilty as I fall asleep with a full stomach, clutching the locket with Eo's flower inside. My family will go to bed hungry tonight. I whisper her name. I take the wedding band from my pocket and kiss it. Feel the ache. They stole her. But she let them. She left me. She left me tears and pain and longing. She left me to give me anger, and I cannot help but hate her for a moment even though beyond that moment there is only love.

"Eo," I whisper, and the locket closes.

19

THE PASSAGE

I vomit as I wake. A second fist strikes my full stomach. Then a third. I'm empty and gasping for air. Drowning in my sick. Coughing. Hacking. I try to scramble away. A man's hand grabs me by the hair and throws me into the wall. God, he's bloody strong. And he's got extra fingers. I reach for my knifeRing, but they've already dragged me into the hall. I've never been so manhandled; even my new body can't recover from their strikes. There's four of them in black—Crows, the killers. They've discovered me. They know what I am. It's over. All over. Their faces are expressionless skulls. Masks. I pull the knife I took from dinner from my waist and am about to stab one of them in the groin. Then I see the flash of gold on their wrists and they hit me till I drop the knife. It's a test. Their strikes against a higher Color are sanctioned by the issuer of the bracelets. They haven't found me out at all. A test. That is what this is. It is a test.

They could have used stunners. There's a purpose to the beating. It's something most Golds have never experienced. So I wait. I curl up and let them beat me. When I don't resist, they think they've done their job. They sort of do; I'm raggedshit by the time they're satisfied.

I'm dragged through the hallway by men nearly three meters tall. A bag is shoved over my head. They're staying away from technology to scare me. I wonder how many of these kids have felt physical force like this? How many have been so dehumanized? The bag smells like death and piss as they drag me along. I start laughing. It's like my bloodydamn frysuit. Then a fist hits my chest and I crumple, gasping.

The hood also has a sound device installed. I'm not breathing hard, but my breaths come back louder than they should. There are over a thousand students. Dozens at a time must suffer this same fate, yet I hear nothing. They don't want me to hear the others. I'm supposed to think I'm alone, that my Color means nothing. Surprisingly, I find myself offended that they dare strike me. Don't they know I'm a bloodydamn Gold? Then I snort back a laugh. Effective tricks.

I'm lifted up and thrown hard onto a floor. I feel a vibration, the smell of exhaust. Soon we're in the air. Something in the bag covering my head disorients me. I can't tell which direction we're flying, how high we've risen. The sound of my own raspy breath has become terrible. I think the bag also filters out the oxygen, because I'm hyperventilating. Still, it's not worse than a frysuit.

Later. An hour? Two? We land. They drag me by my heels. Head bumps on stone, jarring me. It's not till much later that they take the bag off of my head in a barren stone room lit by a single light. Another person is already here. The Crows strip away my clothing, rip away the precious Pegasus pendant. They leave.

"Cold in here, Julian?" I chuckle as I stand, unclenching my left hand from the dirty red Helldiver sweat band. My voice echoes. We're both naked. I fake a limp with my right leg. I know what this is.

"Darrow, is that you?" Julian asks. "Are you well?"

"I'm prime. They busted up my right leg, though," I lie.

He stands too, pushing himself up with his left hand. That's his dominant one. He looks tall and feeble in the light. Like bent hay. I caught more kicks and punches than him, though, loads more. My ribs might be cracked.

"What do you think this is?" he asks.

"The Passage, obviously."

"But they lied. They said it would be tomorrow."

The thick wooden door squeals on rusted hinges and Proctor Fitchner saunters in popping a gumbubble.

"Proctor! Sir, you lied to us," Julian protests. He brushes his pretty hair back out of his eyes.

Fitchner's movement is sluggish but his eyes are like a cat's. "Lying takes too much effort," he grunts idly.

"Well . . . how dare you treat us like this!" Julian snaps. "You must know who my father is. And my mother is a Legate! I can have you up on charges for assault in a moment's notice. And you hurt Darrow's leg!"

"It's one A.M., dipstick. It's tomorrow." Fitchner pops another gumbubble. "There are also two of you. Alas, only one spot is available in your class." He tosses a golden ring emblazoned with the wolf of Mars and a star shield of the Institute onto the dirty stone ground. "I could make it ambiguous, but you look like rustyheaded lads. Only one comes out alive."

He leaves the way he came. The door squeals and then slams shut. Julian flinches at the sound. I do not. We both stare at the ring and I have a sick feeling in my gut that I'm the only one in the room who knows what just happened.

"What do they think they are doing?" Julian asks me. "Do they expect us to . . ."

"Kill each other?" I finish. "Yes. That's what they expect." Despite the knot in my throat. I ball my fists, Eo's wedding band tight on my finger. "I intend to wear that ring, Julian. Will you let me have it?"

I am bigger than he. Not quite as tall. But that doesn't matter. He doesn't stand a chance.

"I have to have it, Darrow," he murmurs. He looks up. "I am of the Family Bellona. I can't go home without it. Do you know who we are? You can go home without shame. I can't. I need it more than you!"

"We're not going home, Julian. One person comes out alive. You heard him."

"They wouldn't do that. . . ." he tries.

"No?"

"Please. Please, Darrow. Just go home. You don't need it like I do. You don't. Cassius . . . he would be so ashamed if I didn't make it. I wouldn't be able to look at him. Every member of my family is Scarred. My father is an Imperator. An Imperator! If his son did not even make it through the Passage . . . what would his soldiers think?"

"He would still love you. Mine would."

Julian shakes his head. He takes a breath and stands tall.

"I am Julian au Bellona of the Family Bellona, my goodman."

I don't want to do this. I can't explain how badly I don't want to hurt Julian. But when has what I wanted ever mattered? My people need this. Eo sacrificed happiness and her life. I can sacrifice my wants. I can sacrifice this slender princeling. I can even sacrifice my soul.

I make the first move toward Julian.

"Darrow . . . ," he murmurs.

Darrow was kind in Lykos.

I am not. I hate myself for it. I think I'm crying, because my vision is unclear.

The rules and manners and morals of society are pulled away. All it takes is a stone room and two people needing the same scarce thing. Yet the shift isn't instantaneous. Even when I punch Julian in the face and his blood smears my knuckles, it doesn't seem a fight. The room is quiet. Awkward. I feel rude punching him. Like I'm acting. The stone is cold on my feet. My skin prickles. Breath echoes.

They want me to kill him because he didn't do well on their tests. This is a mismatch. I am Darwin's scythe. Nature scraping away the chaff. I don't know how to kill. I've never killed a man. I have no blade, no thumper, no scorcher. It seems impossible that I could make this boy of meat and muscle bleed dry just with my hands. I want to laugh and Julian does. I am a naked child slapping at another naked child in a cold room. His hesitancy is obvious. His feet move like he's trying to remember a dance. But when his elbows come to eye level, I panic. I don't know how he is fighting. He strikes halfheartedly at me in a foreign, artistic way. He's tentative, slow, but his timid fist gets my nose.

Rage overtakes me.

My face goes numb. My heart thunders. It's in my throat. My veins prickle.

I break his nose with a straight. God, my hands are strong.

He wails and ducks into me, grappling my arm into an odd angle. It pops. I use my forehead. It takes him just at the bridge of his nose. I grab the back of his neck and hit him again with my forehead. He can't break away. I do it again. Something cracks. Blood and spit lather my hair. His teeth cut my scalp. I drop back like I'm dancing, reverse off my left foot, weave forward and hit him with all my weight behind my right fist in his chest. My Helldiver knuckles shatter his reinforced sternum.

There's a great wheezing gasp. And a crackling noise like snapping twigs.

He tips backward onto the ground. I'm dazed from striking him with my forehead. Seeing red. Seeing double. I stumble toward him. Tears stream down my cheeks. He's twitching. When I grab his golden hair, I find him already limp. Like a wet golden feather. Blood pulses from his nose. He is quiet. He no longer moves. No longer smiles.

I mutter my wife's name as I fall to cradle his head. His face has become like a blood blossom.

PART III

GOLD

"This is your slingBlade, son. It will scrape the earth's veins for you. It will kill pitvipers. Keep it sharp and if you get stuck in the drills, it will save your life for the price of a limb."
So said my uncle.

20

THE HOUSE MARS

There's stillness in my soul as I look at the broken boy. Even Cassius would not recognize Julian now. A cavity is carved into my heart. My hands tremble as the blood dribbles off them onto cold stone. Rivers along the golden Sigils upon my hands. I am a Helldiver, but the sobs come even as the tears are gone. His blood trickles from my knee down my hairless shin. It's red. Not golden. My knees feel the stone and my forehead touches it as I sob till exhaustion fills my chest.

When I look up, he is still dead.

This wasn't right.

I thought the Society only played games with its slaves. Wrong. Julian didn't score like I did on the tests. He wasn't as physically capable as I. So he was a sacrificial lamb. One hundred students per House and the bottom fifty are only here to be killed by the top fifty. This is just a bloodydamn test . . . for me. Even the Family Bellona, powerful as they are, could not protect their less capable son. And *that* is the point.

I hate myself.

I know they made me do this, yet it still feels like a choice. Like when I pulled Eo's legs and felt the snap of her small spine. My choice. But what other choice was there with her? With Julian? They do this to make us wear the guilt.

There's nowhere to wipe the blood, only stone and two naked bodies. This is not who I am, who I want to be. I want to be a father, a husband, a dancer. Let me dig in the earth. Let me sing the songs of my people and leap and spin and run along the walls. I would never sing the forbidden song. I would work. I would bow. Let me wash dirt from my hands instead of blood. I want only to live with my family. We were happy enough.

Freedom costs too much.

But Eo disagreed.

Damn her.

I wait, but no one comes to see the mess I've made. The door is unlocked. I slip the golden ring over my finger after I close Julian's eyes, and walk naked into the cold hall. It is empty. A soft light guides me up never-ending stairs. Water drips from the subterranean tunnel's ceiling. I use it to try to clean my body, but all I do is lather the blood into my skin, thinning it. I cannot escape it, what I've done, no matter how far I follow the tunnel. I am alone with my sin. This is why they rule. The Peerless Scarred know that dark deeds are carried through life. They cannot be outrun. They must be worn if one is to rule. This is their first lesson. Or was it that the weak do not deserve life?

I hate them, but I hear them.

Win. Bear the guilt. Reign.

They want me pitiless. They want my memory short.

But I was raised differently.

All my people sing of are memories. And so I will remember this death. It will burden me as it does not burden my fellow students—I must not let that change. I must not become like them. I'll remember that every sin, every death, every sacrifice, is for freedom.

Yet now I'm afraid.

Can I bear the next lesson?

Can I pretend to be as cold as Augustus? I now know why he did not flinch in hanging my wife. And I am beginning to understand why Golds rule. They can do what I cannot.

Though I am alone, I know I will soon find others. They want me to soak in the guilt for now. They want me lonely, mournful, so that when I meet the others, the winners, I will be relieved. The murders will bind us, and I'll find the company of the winners a salve to my guilt. I do not love my fellow students, but I will think I do. I will want their comfort, their reassurances that I am not evil. And they will want the same. This is meant to make us a family—one with cruel secrets.

I am right.

My tunnel leads me to the others. I see Roque, the poet, first. He bleeds from the back of his head. Blood is slick on his right elbow. I didn't think him capable of killing. Whose blood? His eyes are red from crying. We find Antonia next. Like us, she is naked; she moves like a golden ship, drifting along, quiet and aloof. Her feet leave bloody footprints where she walks.

I dread finding Cassius. I hope he is dead, because I'm afraid of him. He reminds me of Dancer—handsome, laughing, yet a dragon just beneath the surface. But that's not why I'm afraid. I'm afraid because he has a reason to hate me, to want to kill me. No one in my life has had just cause before. No one has ever *hated* me. He will if he finds out. Then I realize it. How could the House ever be knit tightly with such secrets? It can't. Cassius will know someone here killed his brother. Others will have lost friends, and so the House will devour itself. The Society did this on purpose; they want chaos. It will be our second test. Tribal strife.

The three of us find the other survivors in a cavernous stone dining hall dominated by a long wooden table. Torches light the room. Night's mist slithers through open windows. It is like something from the old tales. The times they call Medieval. Toward the far end of the long room is a plinth. A giant stone towers there; embedded in its center is a golden Primus hand. Golden and black tapestries flank the stone. A wolf howls upon the tapestries, as though calling out a warning. It is the Primus hand that will tear this House apart. Each one of these little princes and princesses will think themselves deserved of the honor of leading the House. Yet only one can.

I move like a ghost with the other students, drifting around the stone halls of what seems to be a giant castle. There is a room in which we are to clean ourselves.

A trough runs icy water along the cold floor. Now blood runs with the water to the right and disappears into the stone. I feel like some sort of specter in a land of fog and rock.

Black and gold fatigues are laid out for us in a relatively barren armory. Each student finds the fatigue bundle tagged with his or her name. A golden symbol of a howling wolf marks the high collars and sleeves of our clothing. I take my clothing with me and dress alone in some storage room. There, I fall into the corner and sit, silent. This place is so cold and quiet. So far from home.

Roque finds me. He's striking in his uniform—lean like a strand of golden summer wheat, with high cheekbones and warm eyes, but his face is pale. He sits on his haunches across from me for several minutes before he reaches over to clasp my hands. I draw back, but he holds on till I look at him.

"If you are thrown into the deep and do not swim, you will drown," he says, and raises his thin eyebrows. "So keep swimming, right?"

I force a chuckle.

"A poet's logic."

He shrugs. "Doesn't count for much. So I'll give you facts, brotherman. This is the system. The lower Colors have their children by use of catalysts. Fast births, sometimes only five months of gestation before labor is induced. Except for the Obsidians, only *we* wait nine months to be born. Our mothers receive no catalysts, no sedatives, no nucleics. Have you asked yourself why?"

"So the product can be pure."

"And so that nature is given a chance to kill us. The Board of Quality Control is firmly convinced that 13.6213 percent of all Gold children should die before one year of age. Sometimes they make reality fit this number." He splays out his thin hands. "Why? Because they believe civilization weakens natural selection. They do nature's work so that we do not become a soft race. The Passage, it seems, is a continuation of that policy. Only we were the tools they used. My . . . *victim* . . . was, bless his soul, a fool. He was from a family of no worth, and he had no *wits,* no *intelligence,* no *ambition,*" he frowns at the words before sighing, "he had nothing the Board values. There is a reason he was to die."

Was there a reason Julian was to die?

Roque knows what he does because his mother is on the Board. He loathes his mother, and only then do I realize I should like him. Not only that, I take refuge in his words. He disagrees with the rules, but he follows them. It is possible. I can do the same until I have power enough to change them.

"We should join the others." I say, standing.

In the dining hall, our names float above the chairs in golden letters. Our test scores are gone. Our names have also appeared beneath the Primus hand in the black stone. They float, golden, upward toward the golden hand. I'm closest, though there's still much distance to cover.

Some of the students cry together in small groups by the long wooden table. Others sit against the wall, heads in their hands. A limping girl looks for her friend. Antonia glares over at the table where small Sevro sits eating. Of course he's the only one with an appetite. Frankly, I'm surprised he survived. He is tiny and was our ninety-ninth and last draft pick. By Roque's proposed rules, he should be dead.

Titus, the giant, is alive and bruised. Those knuckles of his look like a dirty butcher's block. He stands arrogantly apart from the rest, grinning like this is all splendid fun. Roque speaks quietly with the limping girl, Lea. She falls down crying and throws her ring. She looks like a deer, eyes wide and glistening. He sits with her and holds her hand. There's a peacefulness to him that is unique in the room. Wonder how peaceful he seemed when strangling some other kid to death. I roll my ring on and off my finger.

Someone smacks my head lightly from behind.

"*Oy,* brotherman."

"Cassius." I nod.

"Cheers to your victory. I was worried you were all brains," Cassius laughs. His golden curls are not even tousled. He throws an arm around me and surveys the room with a wrinkled nose. He feigns this nonchalance; I can tell he's worried.

"Ah. Is there anything more ugly than self-pity? All this crying." He smirks and points at a girl with a busted nose. "And she just became aggressively unpleasant. *Not that she was ever much to sniff at. Eh? Eh?*"

I forget to speak.

"Shell-shocked, man? They get your windpipe?"

"Just not much for joking about right now," I say. "Took some knocks to the head. Shoulder is a bit slagged too. This isn't my usual scene."

"Shoulder can be fixed straight off. Let's get it back in the socket." He casually grips my dislocated shoulder and jerks it into its socket before I can protest. I gasp in pain. He chuckles. "Prime. Prime." He slaps me on the same shoulder. "Help me out, won't you?"

He extends his left hand. His dislocated fingers look like lightning bolts. I pull them straight. He laughs with the pain, not knowing his brother's blood is under my fingernails. I'm trying not to hyperventilate.

"Spotted Julian yet, man?" he finally asks. He speaks in midLingo now that Priam is nowhere to be seen.

"Not a sight."

"Meh, the kid is probably trying to be gentle with his fight. Father taught us the Silent Art, Kravat. Julian is a prodigy at it. He thinks I'm better." Cassius frowns. "Thinks I'm better at everything—which is understandable. Just got to get him going. Speaking of it, who'd you slag?"

My insides knot.

I make up a lie, and it is a good one. Vague and boring. He only wants to talk about himself now anyway. After all, this is what Cassius was bred for. There are roughly fifteen kids who have that same quiet gleam in their eye. Not evil. Just excited. And those are the ones to watch, because they're the born killers.

Looking around, it's easy to see that Roque was right. There weren't many tough fights. This was forced natural selection. Bottom of the heap getting slaughtered by the top. Hardly anyone is severely injured except a couple of small lowDrafts. Natural selection sometimes has its surprises.

Cassius's fight was easy, he says. He did it right and fair and quick. Crushed the windpipe with a bladejab ten seconds into squaring up. Caught his fingers oddly, though. *Prime.* I've made a corpse of the best killer's brother. Dread creeps into me to make a home.

Cassius grows quieter when Fitchner saunters in and orders us to the table. One by one, the fifty seats fill. And bit by bit, his face darkens as each chance for Julian to join the table disappears. When the last seat fills, he does not move. It is a cold anger that radiates. Not hot as I thought it would be. Antonia sits across from us, opposite me, and watches him. Her mouth works but she says nothing. You don't comfort his sort. And I didn't think her the kind to try.

Julian isn't the only one missing. Arria, all curls and dimples, is lying limp on a cold floor somewhere. And Priam is gone. Perfect Priam the Premier, heir of Mars's moons. I heard he was the First Sword in the Solar System for his birthyear. A duelist without peer. I guess he wasn't too lethal with his fists. I look around the tired faces. Who the hell killed him? The Board messed that one up, and I wager his mother will cause hell, because he certainly wasn't meant to die.

"We're wasting the best of us," Cassius murmurs measuredly.

"Hello, you little shiteaters." Fitchner yawns and kicks his feet up onto the table. "Now, it might have dawned on you that the Passage may as well be called the Culling." Fitchner scratches his groin with his razor's hilt.

His manners are worse than mine.

"And you may think it a waste of good Golds, but you're an idiot if you think fifty children make a dent in our numbers. There are more than one million Golds on Mars. More than one hundred million in the Solar System. Not all get to be Peerless Scarred, though, eh?

"Now if you still think this was vile, consider that the Spartans would kill more than ten percent of all children born to them; nature would kill another thirty. We are gory humanitarians in comparison. Of the six hundred students that are left, most were in the top one percent of applicants. Of the six hundred that are dead, most were in the bottom one percent of applicants. There was no waste." He chuckles and looks around the table with a suprising amount of pride. "Except for that idiot, Priam. Yeah. There's a lesson for you lot. He was a brilliant boy—beautiful, strong, fast, a genius who studied day and night with a dozen tutors. But he was pampered. And someone, I won't say who, because that'd undermine the fun of this whole curriculum, but someone knocked him down onto the stone and then stomped on his trachea till he died."

He puts his hands behind his head.

"*Now!* This is your new family. House Mars—one of twelve Houses. No, you are not special because you live on Mars and are in House Mars. Those in House Venus on Venus are not special. They merely fit the House. You get the flow. After the Institute, you're looking for apprenticeships—hopefully with the families Bellona, Augustus, or Arcos, if you want to do me proud. Prior graduates from House Mars may help you find these apprenticeships, may offer you apprenticeships of their own, or maybe you'll be so successful that you don't need anyone's help.

"But let us make it crystal. Right now you are babies. Stupid little babies. Your parents handed you everything. Others wiped your little asses. Cooked your food. Fought your wars. Tucked your little shiny noses in at night. Rusters dig before they get a chance to screw; they build your cities and find your fuel and pick up your shit. Pinks learn the art of getting someone's jollies off before they even need to shave. Obsidians have the worst gory life you could imagine—nothing but frost and steel and pain. They were bred for their work, trained early for it. All you little princelings and princesses have had to do was look like little versions of Mommy and Daddy and learn your manners and play piano and equestrian and sport. But now you belong to the Institute, to House Mars, to the Prefecture of Mars, to your Color, to the Society. Blah. Blah."

Fitchner's smirk is lazy. His veiny hand rests on his paunch.

"Tonight you finally did something yourselves. You beat a baby just like you. But that's worth about as much as a Pinkwhore's fart. Our little Society balances on the tip of a needle. The other Colors would rip your gorydamn hearts out given the chance. And then there's the Silvers. The Coppers. The Blues. You think they'd be loyal to a bunch of babies? You think the Obsidians will follow little turds like you? Those babystranglers would make you their little cuddleslaves if they saw weakness. So you must show none."

"So, what, the Institute is supposed to make us tough?" huge Titus grunts.

"No, you colossal oaf. It's supposed to make you smart, cruel, wise, hard. It's supposed to age you fifty years in ten months and show you what your ancestors did to give you this empire. May I continue?"

He blows a gumbubble.

"Now, House Mars." His thin hand scratches his belly. "Yeah. We've got a proud House that could maybe even match some of the Elder Families. We've got Politicos, Praetors, and Justiciars. The current ArchGovernors of Mercury and Europa, a Tribune, dozens of Praetors, two Justices, an Imperator of a fleet. Even Lorn au Arcos of the Family Arcos, third most powerful family on Mars, for those not keeping track, maintains his bonds with us.

"All of those highUps are looking for new talent. They picked you from the other candidates to fill the roster. Impress these important men and women and you'll have an apprenticeship after this. Win and you'll have your pick of apprenticeships within the House or an Elder Family; maybe even Arcos himself will want you. If that happens, you'll be on the fast track to position, fame, and power."

I lean forward.

"But win?" I ask. "What is there to win?"

He smiles.

"At this moment, you are in a remote terraformed valley in the southernmost part of Valles Marineris. In this valley, there are twelve Houses in twelve castles. After orientation tomorrow, you will go to war with your fellow students to dominate the valley by any means at your disposal. Consider it a case study in gaining and ruling an empire."

There are murmurs of excitement. It is a game. And here I thought I would have to study something in a classroom.

"And what if you are Primus of the winning House?" Antonia asks. She twirls a finger through her golden curls.

"Then welcome to glory, darling. Welcome to fame and power."

So, I must be Primus.

We eat a plain dinner. When Fitchner leaves, Cassius stirs, his voice coming cold and filled with dark humor.

"Let us all play a game, my friends. We will each say whom we killed. I will start. Nexus au Celintus. I knew him when we were children, as I know some of you. I broke his trachea with my fingers." No one speaks. "Come now. Families should not keep secrets."

Still, no one answers.

Sevro is the first to leave, making his derision for Cassius's game clear. First to eat. First to sleep. I want to follow. Instead, I make small talk with peaceful Roque and massive Titus after Cassius gives up on his game and retires as well. Titus is impossible to like. He's not funny, but everything is a joke to him. It's like he's sneering at me, at everyone, even though he is smiling. I want to hit him, but he doesn't give me a reason. Everything he says is perfectly innocuous. Yet I hate him. It's like he doesn't think me a human; instead I'm just a chess piece and he's waiting to move me around. No. Shove me around. He somehow forgot to be seventeen or eighteen like the rest. He is a man. Taller than two meters, easy. Maybe nearing two and a half meters. Lithe Roque, on the other hand, reminds me so much of my brother Kieran, if Kieran could kill. His smiles are kind. His words patient and wistful and wise, just as they had been earlier. Lea, the girl who looks like a limping baby deer, follows him everywhere. He's patient with her in a way I couldn't be.

Late in the night, I look for the places where the students died. I cannot find them. The stairs no longer exist. The castle has swallowed them. I find rest in a long dormitory filled with thin matresses. Wolves howl from the shifting mists that cloak the highlands beyond our castle. I find sleep quickly.

21

OUR DOMINION

Fitchner wakes us from the long dormitories in the dark of morning. Grumbling, we roll out of double bunk beds and set out from the keep to the castle's square, where we stretch, then set off at a run. We lope easily in the .37grav.

Clouds drop soft showers. The canyon walls fifty kilometers west and forty kilometers east of our little valley tower six kilometers high. Between them is an ecosystem of mountains, forests, rivers, and plains. Our battlefield.

Ours is a highland territory. There rise mossy hills and craggy peaks that dip into U-shaped, grassy glens. Mist blankets all, even the thick forests that lie like homespun quilts over the foothills. Our castle stands on a hill just north of a river in the middle of a bowl-like glen—half grass, half woods. Greater hills cup the glen in a semicircle to the north and south. I should like it here. Eo would have. But without her, I feel as lonely as our castle looks on its high, removed hill. I reach for the locket, for our haemanthus. Neither is with me. I feel empty in this paradise.

Three walls of our hill castle stand atop eighty-meter stone cliffs. The castle itself is huge. Its walls rise thirty meters. The gatehouse swells out from the walls as a fortress with turrets. Inside the walls, our square keep is part of the northwestern wall and rises fifty meters. A gentle slope leads up from the glen's floor to the castle's western gate, opposite the keep. We run down this slope along a lonely dirt road. Mist embraces us. I relish the cold air. It purifies me after hours of fitful sleep.

The mist burns away as the summer day dawns. Deerling, thinner and faster than the creatures of Earth, graze in the fir woods. Birds circle above. A single raven promises eerie things. Sheep litter the field and goats wander the high rocky hills we run up in a line of fifty and one. Others of my House may see animals of Earth, or curious creatures the Carvers decided to make for fun. But I see only food and clothing.

The sacred animals of Mars make their home in our territory. Woodpeckers hammer oak and fir. At night, wolves howl across the highlands and stalk during the day through the woodlands. There are snakes near the river. Vultures in the quiet gulches. Killers running beside me. What friends I have. If only Loran or Kieran or Matteo were here to watch my back. Someone I could trust. I'm a sheep wearing wolves' clothing in a pack of wolves.

As Fitchner runs us up the rocky heights, Lea, the girl with the limp, falls. He lazily nudges at her with his foot till we carry her on our shoulders. Roque and I bear the load. Titus smirks, and only Cassius helps when Roque tires. Then Pollux, a lean, craggy-voiced boy with buzzed hair, takes over for me. He sounds like he's been smoking burners since he was two.

We trudge through a summer valley of forests and fields. Bugs nip at us there. The Goldbrows drip with sweat, but I do not. This is an icy bath compared to the rigors of my old frysuit. All about me are trim and fit, but Cassius, Sevro, Antonia, Quinn (the bloodydamn fastest girl or thing I've ever seen on two feet), Titus, three of his new friends, and I could leave the rest behind. Only Fitchner with his gravBoots would outpace us. He bounds along like a deerling, then he chases one down and his razor whips out. It encircles the deerling's throat, and he contracts the blade to kill the animal.

"Supper," he says, grinning. "Drag it."

"You could have killed it closer to the castle," Sevro mutters.

Fitchner scratches his head and looks around. "Did anyone else hear a squat ugly little Goblin go . . . well, whatever sound Goblins make? Drag it."

Sevro grabs the deer's leg. "*Dickwit*."

We reach the summit of a rocky height five kilometers southwest of our castle. A stone tower dominates the peak. From the top, we survey the battlefield. Somewhere out there, our enemies do the same. The theater of war stretches to the south farther than we can see. A snowy mountain range fills the western horizon. To the southeast, a primordial wood knots the landscape. Dividing the two is a lush plain split by a massive southbound river, the Argos, and its tributaries. Farther south, past the plains and rivers, the ground dips away into marshes. I cannot see beyond. A great floating mountain hovers two kilometers up in the bluish sky. It is Olympus, Fitchner explains, an artificial mountain where the Proctors watch each year's class. Its peak shimmers with a fairy-tale castle. Lea shuffles closer to stand beside me.

"How does it float?" she asks sweetly.

I haven't the faintest clue.

I look north.

Two rivers in a forested valley split our northern territory, which is at the edge of a vast wilderness. They form a V pointing southwest to the lowlands, where they eventually form one tributary to the Argos. Surrounding the valley are the highlands—dramatic hills and dwarf mountains scarred with gulches where mist still clings.

"This is Phobos Tower," Fitchner says. The tower lies in the far southwest of our territory. He drinks from a canteen while we go thirsty, and points northwest where the two rivers meet in the valley to form their V. A massive tower crowns a distant dwarf mountain range just beyond the junction. "And that is Deimos." He traces an imaginary line to show us the bounds of House Mars's territory.

The eastern river is called the Furor. The western, which runs just south of our castle, is the Metas. A single bridge spans the Metas. An enemy would have to cross it to enter between the V into the valley and strike northeast across easy, wooded ground to reach our castle.

"This is a slaggin' joke, isn't it?" Sevro asks Fitchner.

"Whatever do you mean, Goblin?" Fitchner pops a gumbubble.

"Our legs are as wide as a Pinkwhore's. All these mountains and hills and anyone can just walk right in the front door. It's a perfect flat passage from the lowlands right to our gate. Just one stinking river to cross."

"Pointing out the obvious, eh? You know, I really do not like you. You foul little Goblin." Fitchner stares at Sevro for a purposeful moment and then shrugs. "Anyway, I'll be on Olympus."

"What does that mean, Proctor?" Cassius asks sourly. He doesn't like the look of things either. Though his eyes are red from weeping through the night for his dead brother, it hasn't dulled his impressiveness.

"I mean it's your problem, little prince. Not mine. No one's going to fix anything for you. I am your Proctor. Not your mommy. You're in school, remember? So if your legs are open, well, make a chastity belt to protect the softspot."

There's general grumbling.

"Could be worse," I say. I point past Antonia's head toward the southern plains where an enemy fortress spans a great river. "We could be exposed like those poor bastards."

"Those poor bastards have crops and orchards," Fitchner muses. "You have . . ." He looks over the ledge to find the deer he killed. "Well, Goblin here left the deer behind, so you have nothing. The wolves will eat what you do not."

"Unless we eat the wolves," Sevro mutters, drawing strange looks from the rest of our House.

So we have to get our own food.

Antonia points to the lowlands.

"What are they doing?"

A black dropship slides down from the clouds. It settles in the center of the grassy plain between us and the distant enemy river fortress of Ceres. Three Obsidians and a dozen Tinpots stand guard as Browns hustle out to set hams, steaks, biscuits, wine, milk, honey, and cheeses onto a disposable table eight kilometers from Phobos Tower.

"A trap, obviously," Sevro snorts.

"Thank you, Goblin." Cassius sighs. "But I haven't had breakfast." Circles ring his reckless eyes. He glances over at me through the crowd of our fellows and offers a smile. "Up for a race, Darrow?"

I start with surprise. Then I smile. "On your mark."

And he's off.

I've done dumber things to feed my family. I did dumber things when someone I loved died. Cassius is owed the company as he races down the steep hillside.

Forty-eight kids watch us scamper to fill our bellies; none follow.

"Bring me a slice of honeyed ham!" Fitchner shouts. Antonia calls us idiots. The dropship floats away as we leave the highlands behind for gentler terrain. Eight kilometers in .376grav (Earth standard) is a cinch. We scramble down rocky hillsides, then hit the lowland plains at full tilt through ankle-high grass. Cassius beats me to the tables by a body length. He's fast. We each take a pint of the ice water on the table. I drink mine faster. He laughs.

"Looks like the House Ceres's mark on their flagpole. The Harvest Goddess." Cassius points over across the green plains to the fortress. A few trees dot the several kilometers between us and the castle. Pennants flap from their ramparts. He pops a grape into his mouth. "We should take a closer look before chowin' down. A little scouting."

"Agreed . . . but something isn't right here," I say quietly.

Cassius laughs at the open plain. "Nonsense. We'd see trouble if it was coming. And I don't think any one of them is going to be faster than us two. We can strut up to their gates and take a shit if we so like."

"I do have something brewing." I touch my stomach.

Yet still, something is wrong. And not just in my belly.

It's six kilometers of open ground between the river fortress and us. The river gurgles in the distance to the right. Forest to the far left. Plains in front. Mountains beyond the river. Wind rustles the long grass and a sparrow coasts in with the breeze. It swoops low to the ground before flinching up and away. I laugh loudly and lean against the table.

"They are in the grass," I whisper. *"A trap."*

"We can steal sacks from them and carry more of this back," he says loudly. *"Run?"*

"Pixie."

He grins, though neither of us is sure if we're allowed to start the fighting during orientation day. Whatever.

On three, we kick apart the disposable table's legs till we each have a meter of duroplastic as a weapon. I scream like a madman and sprint toward the spot where the sparrow fled, Cassius at my side. Five House Ceres Golds rise from the grass. They're startled by our mad rush. Cassius catches the first in the face with a proper fencer's lunge. I'm less graceful. My shoulder is stiff and sore. I scream and break my weapon across one of their knees. He goes down howling. Duck someone's swing. Cassius deflects it. We dance as two. There's three of them left. One squares up with me. He doesn't have a knife or a bat. No, he has something I'm far more interested in. A question mark of a sword. A slingBlade for reaping grain. He faces me with his back hand on his hip and the crooked blade out like a razor. If it were a razor, I'd be dead. But it's not. I make him miss, block one of Cassius's attackers' blows. Lurch forward at my attacker. I'm much quicker than he and my grip is like durosteel to his. So I take his slingBlade and his knife before I punch him down.

When he sees how I twirl the slingBlade in my hand, the last uninjured boy knows it's time to surrender. Cassius jumps high in the .376grav and executes an unnecessary twirling sideways kick to the boy's face. Reminds me of the dancers and leapers of Lykos.

Kravat. The Silent Dance. Eerily similar to the boast dancing of young Reds.

Nothing is silent about the boys' curses. I feel no pity for these students. They all murdered someone the night before, just like me. There are no innocents in this game. The only thing that worries me is seeing how Cassius dispatched his victims. He is grace and finesse. I am rage and momentum. He could kill me in a second, if he knew my secret.

"What a lark!" he croons. "You were gory terrifying! You just took his weapon! Gory fast! Glad we weren't paired earlier. Prime stuff! What have you to say for yourselves, you sneaking fools?"

The captured Golds just swear at us.

I stand over them and cock my head. "Is this the first time you've lost at something?" No answer. I frown. "Well, that must be embarrassing."

Cassius's face shines—for a moment he's forgotten his brother's death. I haven't. I feel darkness. Hollow. Evil when the adrenaline fades. Is this what Eo wanted? For me to play games? Fitchner arrives in the air above us, clapping his hands. His gravBoots glimmer golden. He's got his ham slice between his teeth.

"Reinforcements come!" he laughs.

Titus and a half dozen of the faster boys and girls run toward us from the highlands. Opposite, a golden shape rises from the distant river fortress and flies toward us. A beautiful woman with short-cropped hair settles next to Fitchner in the air. The Proctor of House Ceres. She carries a bottle of wine and two glasses.

"Mars! A picnic!" she calls, referring to him by his House's deity.

"So who arranged for this drama, Ceres?" Fitchner asks.

"Oh, Apollo, I suppose. He's lonely up in his mountain estates. Here, this is zinfandel from his vines. Much better than last year's varietal."

"Delicious!" Fitchner proclaims. "But your boys were squatting in the grass. Almost as if they expected the picnic to spontaneously manifest. Suspicious, no?"

"Details!" Proctor Ceres laughs. "Pedantic details!"

"Well, here's a detail. It seems two of mine are worth five of yours this year, my dear."

"These pretty boys?" Ceres snickers. "I thought the vain ones went to Apollo and Venus."

"Oho! Well, yours certainly fight like housewives and farmers. Well placed, they were."

"Don't judge them yet, you cad. They are midDraft picks. My highDrafts are elsewhere, earning their first calluses!"

"Learning the ovens? Huzzah," Fitchner declares ironically. "Bakers do make the best rulers, so I've heard."

She nudges him. "Oh, you *devil.* No wonder you interviewed for the Rage Knight post. Such a scoundrel!"

They clink their glasses together as we watch from the ground.

"How I love orientation day," Ceres titters. "Mercury just let a hundred thousand rats loose in Jupiter's citadel. But Jupiter was ready because Diana tattled and arranged the delivery of a thousand cats. Jupiter's boys won't go hungry like last year. Cats will be as fat as Bacchus."

"Diana is a harlot," Fitchner declares.

"Be kind!"

"I was. I sent her a great phallic cake filled with live woodpeckers."

"You didn't."

"I did."

"You beast!" Ceres caresses his arm and I note the free-loving demeanor these people have. I wonder if other Proctors are lovers as well. "Her fortress will be riddled with holes. Oh, the sound must be horrible. Well played, Mars. They say Mercury is the trickster, but your japes always have a certain . . . *flair*!"

"Flair, eh? Well, I'm sure I could rustle up some tricks for you on Olympus . . ."

"Huzzah," she coos suggestively.

They toast again, floating above their sweating and bloody students. I can't help but laugh. These people are mad. Bloodydamn crazy in their empty Golden heads. How are they my rulers?

"*Oy!* Fitch! If you don't mind. What are we supposed to do with these farmers?" Cassius calls up. He pokes one of our injured captives on the nose. "What are the rules?"

"Eat them!" Fitchner cries. "And Darrow, put down that gory scythe. You look like a grain reaper."

I don't drop it. It is close to the shape of my slingBlade from home. Not as sharp, because it isn't meant to kill, but the balance is no different.

"You know you *could* let my children go and give them back the reaping scythe," Ceres suggests to us.

"Give me a kiss and you have a deal," Cassius calls up.

"The Imperator's boy?" she asks Fitchner. He nods. "Come ask for one when you're Scarred, little prince." She looks over her shoulder. "Until then, I would advise you and the reaper to run."

We hear the hooves before we see the painted horses galloping at us across the plain. They come from the opened gates of House Ceres's castle. The girls on the horses' backs carry nets.

"They gave you horses! Horses!" Fitchner complains. "That is so unfair!"

We run and barely make it to the woods. I didn't like my first encounter with horses. They still scare the piss out of me. All snorting and stomping. Cassius and I gasp for breath. My shoulder aches. Two of Titus's reinforcements are captured as they find themselves stranded in open ground. Bold Titus knocks a horse over and is laughing as he's about to lay waste to one of the girls with his boot. Ceres zaps him with a stunfist and makes peace with Fitchner. The stunfist causes Titus to piss himself. Only Sevro is careless enough to laugh. Cassius says something about bad manners, but he snickers quietly. Titus notices.

"Are we allowed to kill them or not?" Titus growls that night at dinner. We eat the leftovers from Bacchus's feast. "Or am I going to get stunned every time?"

"Well, the point isn't to kill them," Fitchner says. "So no. Let's not go around massacring your classmates, you mad ape."

"But we did before!" Titus protests.

"What is wrong with you?" Fitchner asks. "The Passage was where the culling is done. It's no longer survival of the fittest, you mad, stupid, colossal sack of muscle. What would be the point if we now had the fittest just murder each other till only a few are left? There are new tests to pass now."

"Ruthlessness." Antonia crosses her arms. "So now it's not acceptable? Is that what you're saying?"

"Oh, it better be acceptable." Titus grins broadly. He's been boasting all night about knocking over the horse, as if it'd make everyone forget the piss that stained his pants. Some have. He's already gathered a pack of hounds. Only Cassius and I seem to have an ounce of his respect, but even we're smirked at. So is Fitchner.

Fitchner sets down his honeyed ham.

"Let us clarify, children, so this water buffalo doesn't go around stomping on skulls. Ruthlessness *is* acceptable, dear Antonia. If someone dies by accident, that is understandable. Accidents happen to the best of us. But you will not murder each other with scorchers. You will not hang people from your ramparts unless they're already dead. MedBots are on standby in case any medical attention is direly needed. They are fast enough to save lives, most of the time."

"*Remember, though*, the point is not to kill. We don't care if you're as ruthless as Vlad Dracula. He still lost. The point is to win. That's what we want."

And that simple test of cruelty is already past.

"We want you to show us your brilliance. Like Alexander. Like Caesar, Napoleon, and Merrywater. We want you to manage an army, distribute justice, arrange for provisions of food and armor. Any fool can stick a blade into another's belly. The school's role is to find the *leaders* of men, not the *killers* of men. So the point, you silly little children, is not to kill, but to conquer. And how do you conquer in a game where there are eleven enemy tribes?"

"Take them out one at a time," Titus answers knowingly.

"No, ogre."

"*Dumbass,*" Sevro snickers to himself. Titus's pack quietly watches the smallest boy in the Institute. No threats are snarled. No faces twitch. Just a silent promise. It's hard to remember that they are all geniuses. They look too pretty. Too athletic. Too cruel to be geniuses.

"Anyone besides Ogre have a guess?" Fitchner asks.

No one answers.

"You make one tribe out of twelve," I finally say. "By taking slaves."

Just like the Society. Build on the backs of others. It isn't cruel. It is practical.

Fitchner claps mockingly. "Prime, Reaper. Prime. Looks like someone is bucking for Primus." Everyone shifts in agitation at that last bit. Fitchner pulls a long box from under the table. "Now, ladies and gentlemen, this is what you use to make the slaves." He pulls out our standard. "Protect this. Protect your castle. And conquer all the others."

22

THE TRIBES

Fitchner is gone in the morning. In his chair lies the standard. It is a one-foot length of iron tipped with our howling wolf; a serpent coils beneath the wolf's feet, the star-tipped pyramid of the Society beneath that. A five-foot oak pole connects to the iron end. If the castle is our home, the standard is our honor. With it, we are able to turn enemies into our slaves by pressing it to their foreheads. There a wolf sigil will appear until another standard is pressed to the forehead. Slaves must obey our express commands or forever be Shamed.

I sit across from the standard in the morning dark, eating Apollo's leftovers. A wolf calls out in the mist. Its howl comes through the keep's high window. Tall Antonia is the first to join me. She glides in like a lonely tower or a beautiful golden spider. I haven't decided which way her personality runs. We exchange glances but no greetings. She wants Primus.

Cassius and raspy Pollux saunter in next. Pollux grumbles about having to go to bed without having Pinks to tuck him in.

"A positively hideous standard, don't you think?" Antonia complains. "They could at least have given it a splash of color. I think it should be draped with red for rage and blood."

"It's not too heavy." Cassius hefts the standard by its pole. "Reckoned it'd be gold." He admires the golden Primus hand within the block of black stone. He wants it too. "And they gave us a map. Swell."

A new stone map dominates one of the walls. The detail near our castle is remarkable. The rest less so. The fog of war. Cassius claps me on the back and joins in eating. He doesn't know I heard him weep again in the night. We shared a new bunk in a barracks in the keep's high tower. Many others still sleep in the main tower. Titus and his friends have taken the low tower even though they don't have enough bodies to fill it.

Most of the House has woken by the time Sevro drags in a dead wolf by its legs. It's already gutted and skinned.

"Goblin has brought victuals!" Cassius applauds daintily. "Hmm. We will need firewood. Does anyone know how to make a fire?" Sevro does. Cassius grins. "Of course you do, Goblin."

"Found the sheep too easy to kill?" I ask. "Where'd you get the weapon?"

"Born with them." His fingernails are bloody.

Antonia wrinkles her nose. "Where in the hell were you raised?"

Sevro presents his middle finger to her, the crux.

"Ah," Antonia sniffs. "Hell, then."

"So, as I'm sure you've all noticed, it will be some time before anyone has enough bars of merit to become Primus," Cassius declares when we've all gathered around the table. "Naturally, I was thinking that we need a leader before Primus is chosen." He stands and scoots away from Sevro so that his fingers rest on the edge of the standard. "In order for us to function, we must have immediate and coordinated decisions."

"And which of you two fools do you think it should be?" Antonia asks dryly. Her large eyes glance from him to me. She turns to regard the others, voice sweet like thick syrup. "At this point, what makes any of us better suited to lead than anyone else?"

"They got us dinner . . . and breakfast," Lea says meekly from beside Roque. She gestures to the leftover picnic victuals.

"While running right into a trap—" Roque reminds everyone.

Antonia nods sagely. "Yes, yes. A wise point. Rashness can hurt us."

"—but they did fight free," Roque finishes, earning a glare from Antonia.

"With table legs against real weapons," Titus rumbles his approval, with a qualification. "*But* then they fled and left the food behind. So it was Fitchner who gave us the food. They would have given it to the enemy, delivering food like Browns."

"Yeah, that's a twist on what happened," Cassius says.

Titus shrugs. "I only saw you running like a little Pixie."

Cassius goes cold.

"Watch your manners, *goodman*."

Titus holds up his hands. "Merely observing; why so angry, little prince?"

"You watch your manners, *goodman,* or we'll have to trade our words for blades." Cassius wields his looted pitchfork and points it at Titus. "You heed, Titus au Ladros?"

Titus holds gaze with him, then glances over at me, grouping me with Cassius. Suddenly Cassius and I form a tribe in everyone's eyes. The paradigm shifts that quickly. Politics. I take my time twirling my looted knife between my fingers. The whole table watches the knife. Sevro especially. My Red right hand has collected a million metric tones of helium-3 with its dexterity. My left, half a million. The dexterity of an average lowRed would startle these Golds. I dazzle them. The knife is like a hummingbird's wings in my nimble fingers. I look calm but my mind is racing.

We have all killed. Those were the stakes. What are they now? Titus has already made it clear that he wants to kill. I could stop him now, I wager. Drive my knife into his neck. But the thought almost makes me drop my blade. I feel Eo's death in my hands. I hear the wet thump of Julian dying. I can't bear the blood, especially when it doesn't seem necessary. I can back this huge puppy down.

I level my eyes coldly at Titus. His smile is slow, the disdain barely noticeable. He's calling me out. I have to fight him or something if he doesn't look away—that's what wolves do, I think.

My knife spins and spins. And suddenly Titus is laughing. He looks away. My heart slows. I've won. I hate politics. Especially in a room full of alphas.

"Of course I hear you, Cassius. You're standing ten feet away," Titus chuckles.

Titus doesn't think he's strong enough to challenge Cassius and me openly, even with his pack. He saw what we did to the Ceres boys. But just like that the lines are drawn. I stand suddenly, confirming that I am with Cassius. It strips Titus of any momentum.

"Is there anyone who wouldn't want either of us to lead?" I ask.

"I wouldn't want Antonia to lead. She's a bitch," Sevro says.

Antonia shrugs her agreement but cocks her head.

"Cassi, why are you in such a rush to find us a leader?" she asks.

"If we do not have one leader, then we will fracture and do as we each think is best," Cassius says. "That's how we lose."

"Instead of what *you* think is best," she says with a soft smile and a nod. "I see."

"Don't give me that condescension, Antonia. Priam even agreed we needed one leader."

"Who is Priam?" Titus laughs. He's trying to get attention back on himself once more. Every Gold kid on the planet knew Priam. Now Titus tries to make it clear who killed him, and the others take note. Momentum regained. Except I know Titus didn't kill Priam. They wouldn't put someone like him in with Priam. They would have put a weakling in there. So Titus is a liar as well as a bully.

"Ah, I see. Because you plotted with Priam, you know what needs to be done, Cassius? You know better than all of us?" Antonia waves at the table. "You're telling us we're helpless without your guidance?"

She's trapped him, and me too.

"Listen, boys, I know you're eager to lead," she continues, "I get that. We are all leaders by nature. Each person in this room is a born genius, a born captain. But that is why the Primus merit system exists. When someone has earned five fingers of merit and is ready to be Primus, then we will have a leader.

"Until then, I say we hold out. If Cassius or Darrow earns it, then so be it. I'll do whatever they command, obedient as a Pink, simple as a Red." She gestures to the others. "Until then, I think one of you should also have a chance to earn it. . . . After all, it may decide your career!"

She's clever. And she's sunk us. Every brat in the room was no doubt wishing they'd been more assertive from the get-go, wishing they could have another chance to make people notice them. Now Antonia gives it to them. This will be chaos. And she may end up as Primus. Definitely a spider.

"Look!" Lea says from Roque's side.

A horn bellows beyond the castle.

The standard chooses that moment to shimmer. Snake and wolf shed iron for gleaming gold. Not only that, but the stone map on the wall comes alive. Our wolf banner ripples over a miniature of our castle. Ceres's banner does the same. No other castles mark the map, but the banners of the undiscovered Houses flap off in the map's key. No doubt they'll find a home as soon as we scout the surrounding territory.

The game has begun. And now everyone wants to be the Primus.

I see why Demokracy is illegal. First comes yelling. Frustration. Indecision. Disagreements. Ideas. Scout. Fortify. Gather food. Lay traps. Blitz. Raid. Defense. Offense. Pollux spits. Titus knocks him out cold. Antonia leaves. Sevro says something snide to Titus and drags his wolf off to God knows where, never having lit a fire. It's like my Lambda drillteam whenever a headTalk would take an hour sick. That's how I learned I could drill. Barlow snuck off to take a smoke and I hopped on the rig and did as I thought was best. I do the same now as the children bicker.

Cassius, Roque, and Lea—who follows Roque everywhere—come with me, though Cassius likely thinks we follow him. We agree that the others will not know what to do and so will inevitably do nothing today. They will guard the castle or seek out wood for a fire or cluster around the standard for fear of it walking off.

I don't know what to do. I don't know if our enemies are slinking through the hills toward us. I don't know if they are making alliance against Mars. I don't know how the damn game is even played. But for some reason, I assume that not all of the other Houses will fall to discord like this. We of Mars seem more prone to disagreement.

I ask Cassius what he thinks we should do.

"Once, I challenged this prancing oaf to a duel for disrespecting my family—an Augustus fop. He was very methodical—tightened his gloves, tied back his pretty hair, swished his razor as he did before every gory practice bout he's ever had at the Agea Martial Club."

"And?"

"And I hooked him and stabbed him through the kneecap while he was still swishing his razor in preparation." He catches Lea's disapproval. "*What?* The duel *had* begun. I'm foxy, but I'm not a beast. I just win."

"I feel like you all think that," I say. "*We* all, I mean."

They don't notice my slipup.

His point stands. Our House can't attack an enemy in our state, but an enemy could attack us as we run about preparing, and ruin all my hopes of rising within the Society. So, information. We need to know if our enemies are in a glen half a kilometer to the north or if they are fifteen kilometers south. Are we at a corner of the playing field or in the center? Are there enemies in the highlands? North of the highlands?

Cassius and I agree. We must scout.

We split up. Cassius and I head to Phobos and then move counterclockwise. Lea and Roque strike to Deimos and scout clockwise. We're to meet at dusk.

We don't see a soul from the top of Phobos. The lowlands are empty of horses and Ceres's fighters, and the highland range to the south is full of lochs and goats. Southeast, atop a high dwarf mountain, we glimpse part of the Greatwoods to the south and southeast. An army of giants could be hiding there for all we know, and we can't investigate; it would take half a day to cover the distance to even make it close to the tree line.

Some ten kilometers from our castle, we find a weatherworn stone fort upon a low hill guarding a pass. Inside is a rustic survival box of iodine, food, a compass, rope, six durobags, a toothbrush, sulfur matches, and simple bandages. We store the items in a clear durobag.

So supplies have been hidden about the valley. Something tells me there are more important items hidden in the countryside than little survivor kits. Weapons? Transportation? Armor? Technology? They can't mean for us to make war with sticks and stones and metal tools. And if they don't want us to kill each other, stun weapons must soon replace our metal ones.

We earn nasty sunburns that first day. The mist chills them as we return. Titus and his pack, six now, have just returned from a fruitless incursion to the plains. They've killed two goats but don't have a fire to cook with, since Sevro slipped off somewhere. I don't tell them about my matches. Cassius and I agree that Titus, if he wants to be the big man, should at least be able to conquer fire. Sevro, wherever he is, must agree as well. Titus's boys hit metal on stone trying to create sparks, but the stones of the castle don't spark. Clever Proctors.

Titus's pack makes the dregs, the lowDrafts, fetch wood despite the fact that they have no fires. They all go hungry that night. Only Roque and Lea don't. They get some of our survival bars. I like the pair even if they are Golds, and I excuse befriending them by telling myself that I do it only to build my own tribe. Cassius seems to think that fast midDraft girl, Quinn, will be useful. But he can make himself think that about most pretty girls.

The tribes grow, and the first lesson is already under way.

Antonia finds friends with a squat, sour, curlyheaded fellow named Cipio, and she manages to send groups armed with shovels and axes found in the castle to garrison Deimos and Phobos. The girl may be a spoiled witch, but at least she isn't stupid. Then Titus's pack steals their axes as they sleep and I revise my opinion.

Cassius and I scout together. On the third day, we see smoke rising in the distance, maybe some twenty kilometers to the east. It is like a beacon in the dusk. Enemy scouting parties would be out like us. If it were closer or we had horses, we would investigate. Or if we had more men, we might set out overnight and plan a raid for slaves. The distance and our lack of coherence make all the difference. Between us and the smoke are ravines and gulches that could hide warbands. Then there's many kilometers of plains to walk exposed. We won't make the trek. Not when some Houses have horses. I don't tell Cassius this, but I am afraid. The highlands feel safe, but just out there in the landscape beyond are roving bands of psychotic godlings. Godlings I do not want to run across quite yet.

The thought of meeting other Houses is made all the more terrifying by the idea that even home is not safe. It's like Octavia au Lune always says: no man can pursue any endeavor in the face of tribal warfare. We can't afford to leave Titus alone for too long. He's already stolen berries Lea and Quinn collected. And this morning he tried to use the standard on Quinn to see if it could make slaves for his raiding parties out of the House's own members. It couldn't.

"We have to bind the House together somehow," Cassius tells me as we scout the northern highlands. "The Institute is with us for the rest of our lives. If we lose, we may never gain position, ever."

"And if we're enslaved during the course of the game?" I ask.

He looks worriedly over at me. "What worse loss could there be?"

As if I needed more motivation.

"Your father won his year, I wager. He was Primus?" I ask. To be an Imperator, he'd have to have won his year.

"Right. Always knew he won his year, though I had no slagging idea what that meant till we got here."

We both agree that in order to bind our House back together, Titus must go. But it is futile to fight him outright; that chance passed after the first day. His tribe has grown too large.

"I say we kill him in his sleep," Cassius suggests. "You and I could do it."

His words chill me. We make no decision, yet the proposition serves to remind me that he and I are different creatures. Or are we really? His wrath is a cruel, cold thing. Yet I never see the anger again, not even around Titus. He's all smiles and laughter and challenging members of Titus's pack to races and wrestling when they aren't going out on raids—just as I am around my enemies.

Yet while I'm regarded warily by most, Cassius is loved by all except Titus's pack. He's even started sneaking off with Quinn. I like her. She killed a deer with a trap, then told a story about how she killed the thing with her teeth. Even showed us evidence—hair between her teeth and gums along with bitemarks on the deer. We thought we had a prettier Sevro on our hands till she laughed too hard to go on with the tall tale. Cassius helped her get the deer hair out of her teeth. I like a committed liar.

Conditions worsen in the first few days. People remain hungry because we've yet to build a fire in the castle, and hygiene is quickly forgotten when two of our girls are snatched up by Ceres horsemen as they bathe in the river just beneath our gate. The Golds are confused when even their fine pores begin clogging and they gain pimples.

"Looks like a beesting!" Roque laughs to Cassius and me. "Or a radial, distant sun!"

I pretend to be fascinated by it, as though I didn't have them all my Red life.

Cassius leans forward to inspect it. "Brotherman, that is just—" Then Roque pops the pimple right into Cassius's face, causing him to reel back and gag from disgust. Quinn falls over giggling.

"I do wonder sometimes," Roque begins after Cassius has recovered, "as to the purpose of all this. How can this be the most efficient method of testing our merit, of making us into beings who can rule the Society?"

"And do you ever come to a conclusion?" Cassius asks warily. He keeps his distance now.

"Poets never do," I say.

Roque chuckles. "Unlike most poets, I sometimes manage. And I have our answer to this."

"Spit it out," Cassius urges.

"As though I wasn't going to without instruction from our resident primadonna." Roque sighs. "They have us here because this valley was humanity before Gold ruled. Fractured. Disunited even in our very own tribe. They want us to go through the process that our forefathers went through. Step by step, this game will evolve to teach us new lessons. Hierarchies within the game will develop. We'll have Reds, Golds, Coppers."

"Pinks?" Cassius asks hopefully.

"Makes sense," I say.

"Oh, that would be ripe strange," Cassius laughs, twisting his wolf ring on his finger. "Mothers and fathers would be throwing fits if that went on. Probably why Titus leers at the girls. He likely wants a toy. Speaking of toys, where did he send Vixus?"

I laugh. Vixus, likely the most dangerous of Titus's followers, and the others departed nearly two hours ago on Titus's orders to use Phobos Tower's height advantage to scout the plains in preparation for a raid on House Ceres.

"It'd be best to have Vixus on our side if we make a play," I say. "He's Titus's right hand."

Roque continues on a different train of thought.

"I . . . don't know about Pinks," Roque says. The idea of a Gold being a Pink offends him. "But . . . the rest is simple. This is a microcosm of the Solar System."

"Seems to me like capture the flag with swords, if you recall that game," I reply. I never played the sport, but my studying with Matteo brought me up to speed on the games these children played in their parents' gardens.

"Mhm." Cassius nods. He shoves a mock-serious finger in Roque's chest. "Agreed. So you can take your quick talk and put it where the sun dare not shine, Roque. We two great minds have decided. It's a game of capture the flag."

"I see." Roque laughs. "Not all men can understand metaphor and subtlety like me. But do not fear, muscular friends, I will be here to guide you through the mind-bending things. For instance, I can tell you that our first test will be to piece the House back together again before an enemy comes a-knocking."

"Hell," I mutter, looking out over the edge of the parapet.

"Something in your bum?" Cassius asks.

"Looks like the game just started." I point downward.

Across the glen, just where the forest meets the grass plain, Vixus drags a girl by her hair. The first slave of House Mars. And far from being revolted, I'm jealous. Jealous that I did not capture her. Titus's minion did, and that means that Titus now wields credibility.

23

FRACTURE

Though we all still sleep under the same roof, it took only four days for the House to dissolve into four tribes. Antonia, apparently the scion of a family that owns a sizable asteroid belt, gets the midDrafters: the talkers, the whiners, the brains, the dependents, the wimps, the snobs, and the Politicos.

Titus draws mostly highDrafts or midDrafts—the physical specimens, the violent, the fast, the intrepid, the prototypically intelligent, the ambitious, the opportunists, the obvious selection for House Mars. The prodigy pianist, quiet Cassandra, is his. So is raspy Pollux and the psychotic Vixus, who shivers with pleasure at the mere idea of putting metal into flesh.

If Cassius and I had been more political, we might have managed to steal the highDrafts from Titus. Hell, we might have had everyone ready to follow if we just told them they had to obey. After all, Cassius and I were the strongest for a brief moment, but then we gave Titus time to intimidate and Antonia time to manipulate.

"Damned Antonia," I say.

Cassius laughs and shakes his golden head as we bound east along the highlands in search of more hidden caches of supplies. My long legs can cover a kilometer in just over a minute.

"Oh, you come to expect these things from her. If our families hadn't spent holidays together when we were little things, I might have called her out as a demokrat on the first day. But she's hardly that. More like Caesar or . . . what did they call them, Presidents?—a tyrant in necessity's clothing."

"She's a turd in the swillbowl," I say.

"What the gory slag does that mean?" Cassius laughs.

Uncle Narol could have told him.

"Sorry? Oh. Heard it in Yorkton once from a highRed. Means she's a fly in the wine."

"A highRed?" Cassius snorts. "One of my nannies was a highRed. I know. Odd. Should have been a Brown. But the woman would tell me stories as I tried to go to sleep."

"That's nice," I say.

"I thought her an uppity bugger. Tried to tell Mother to make her shut up and leave me alone, because all she wanted to do was talk about vales and dreary romances that always end in some sort of sadness. Depressing creature."

"What did your mother do when you complained?"

"Mother? Ha! She clapped me on the head and said there's always something to learn from anybody. Even a highRed. She and Father like to pretend they're progressives. Confuses me." He shakes his head. "But *Yorkton.* Julian couldn't believe *you* were from Yorkton."

The darkness returns in me. Even thinking of Eo doesn't dispel it. Even thinking of my noble mission and all the license it gives me doesn't banish the guilt. I'm the only one who shouldn't feel guilty for the Passage, yet besides Roque, I think I am the only one who does. I look at my hands and remember Julian's blood.

Cassius points up suddenly to the sky southwest of us. "What the gory hell?"

Dozens of blinking medBots pour from floating Olympus's castle. We hear their distant whine. Proctors flicker after them like flaming arrows toward the distant southern mountains. Whatever has happened, one thing is certain: chaos reigns in the South.

Although my tribe continues to sleep in the castle, we've moved from the high tower to the gatehouse so we don't have to rub shoulders with Titus's lot. To keep safe, we leave our cooking a secret.

We meet our tribe for supper by a loch in the northern highlands. They are not all highDrafts. We have some—Cassius and Roque. But then no one above seventeenth pick. We've some midDrafts—Quinn and Lea—but the rest are the dregs, the lowDrafts—Clown, Screwface, Weed, Pebble, and Thistle. This bothers Cassius even though the dregs of the Institute are still certifiably superhuman compared with the rest of the Colors. They are athletic. They are resilient. They never ask you to repeat yourself unless they are making a point. And they accept my orders, even anticipating what next I'll ask them to do. I credit their less privileged upbringings.

Most are smarter than I. But I have that unique thing they call slangsmarts, proven by my high score in the extrapolational intelligence test. Not that it matters, I have sulfur matches and that makes me the god Prometheus. Neither Antonia nor Titus have fire as far as I know. So I'm the only one who can fill bellies. I make each of my tribe kill goats or sheep. No one is allowed to freeload, even though Screwface tries his best. They don't notice my hands trembling when I cut my first goat's throat with a knife. There's so much trust in the beast's eyes, followed by confusion as it dies, still thinking me its friend. The blood is warm, like Julian's. The neck muscle tough. I have to saw with the dull knife, just as Lea does when she kills her first sheep, squealing as she does it. I make her skin it too with Thistle's help. And when she cannot, I take her hands into my own and guide her along, giving her my strength.

"Daddy gonna have to cut up your meat for you too?" Thistle taunts.

"Shut it," Roque says.

"She can fight her own battles, Roque. Lea, Thistle asked you a question." Lea blinks over at me, wide eyes confused. "Ask her another, Thistle."

"What's gonna happen when we get in a tight spot with Titus, will you squeal then too? Child." Thistle knows what I want her to do. I asked her to do it thirty minutes ago, before I brought the goat to Lea.

I motion my head at Lea to Thistle.

"You going to cry?" Thistle asks. "Wipe your eyes in—"

Lea snarls and jumps at her. The two roll around punching each other in the face. It's not long before Thistle's got Lea in a chokehold. Roque stirs beside me. Quinn pulls him back down. Lea's face goes purple. Her hands slap at Thistle's. Then she passes out. I give Thistle a nod of thanks. The darkfaced girl gives a slow nod.

Lea's shoulders are squarer the next morning. She even musters enough courage to hold Roque's hand. She also claimed to be a better cook than the rest of us; she isn't. Roque tries his hand but he's hardly any better. Eating their grub is like taking down stringy, dry sponges. Even Quinn, with all her stories, can't muster up a recipe.

We cook goat and deer meat over our camp kitchen six kilometers from the castle, and we do it at night in the gulches so the light and smoke cannot be seen. We do not kill the sheep; instead we collect and deposit them in a northern fort for safekeeping. I could bring more over to my tribe with the food, but the food is as big a danger as it is a boon. What Titus and his killers would do if he found that we had fire, food, clean water . . .

I am returning to the castle with Roque from a scouting trip to the south when we hear noises coming from a small grove of trees. Creeping closer, we hear grunts and hacking sounds. Expecting to see a wolfpack ravaging a goat, we peer through the brush and find four of Titus's soldiers squatting around a deer corpse. Their faces are bloody, eyes dark and ravenous as they tear strips out of the dead deer with their knives. Five days without fire, five days of bad berries, and they have already turned into savages.

"We have to give them matches," Roque tells me afterward. "The stones here don't spark with flint."

"No. If we give them matches, then Titus will have even more power."

"Does it matter at this point? They are going to get sick if they keep eating raw meat. They already are sick!"

"So they shit their pants," I grunt. "There are worse things."

"Tell me, Darrow. Would it be worse to have Titus in power and have Mars strong or for Darrow to be in power with Mars weak?"

"Better for whom?" I ask petulantly.

He only shakes his head.

"Let them rot their gory bellies," is Cassius's opinion. "They made their beds. Now let them shit in them."

My army agrees.

I am fond of my army, the dregs, the lowDrafts. They aren't *as* entitled or well-bred as the highDrafts. Most remember to thank me when I give them food—at first they didn't. They don't prance off after Titus on midnight axe-raids simply because it gets their jollies off. No, they follow us because Cassius is as charismatic as the sun and, in his light, the shadow I cast looks like it knows what it's doing. It doesn't. It, like me, was born in a mine.

Still, it does seem like I have some strategy. I have us make maps of our territory on digislates we found in a waterlogged cellar at the bottom of a ravine, but we still have no weapons other than my slingBlade and several knives and sharpened sticks. So whatever strategy we have is based in acquiring information.

Funny thing is, only one tribe has a silvershit's idea what is going on. And it's not ours. It's not Antonia's. And it sure as hell isn't Titus's. It's Sevro's, and I'm nearly certain he's the only member in that tribe, unless he's adopted wolves by now. It is hard to say if he has or hasn't. Our House does not have family dinners. Though occasionally we'll see him running along the hillsides at night in his wolfskin, looking, as Cassius put it best, "like some sort of hairy demonchild on hallucinogens." And once Roque even heard something, not a wolf, howling in the shrouded highlands. Some days Sevro walks around all normalish—insulting everything that moves, except for Quinn. He makes an exception for her, delivering meats and edible mushrooms instead of insults. I think he's sweet on her even though she's sweet on Cassius.

We ask her to tell us stories about him, but she won't. She's loyal, and maybe that's why she reminds me of home. She's always telling good stories, most all of them certainly gilded lies. A life spark is in her, just like the one that was in my wife. She is the last of us to call Goblin "Sevro." She's also the only one who knows where he lives. Even with all our scouting, we can't find a trace of where he sleeps. For all I know, he's out taking scalps beyond the highlands. I know Titus has sent scouts to stalk him, but I don't think they are successful. They can't even follow me. I know that rubs Titus raw.

"I think he's wanking off in the bushes," Cassius chuckles. "Just waiting for us to all kill each other."

It's when Lea comes limping back to the castle that Roque seeks Cassius and me out.

"They beat her," he says. "Not bad, but they kicked her in the stomach and took her day's labor."

"Who?" Cassius bristles. "Who's the slagger?"

"Doesn't matter. What matters is they are hungry. So stop playing at an eye for an eye. This can't go on," Roque says. "Titus's boys are starving. What do you expect they'd do? Hell, the big brute is hunting Goblin because he needs fire and food. If we just give that to him, we can unite the House, maintain civility. Maybe even Antonia will bring her tribe to reason."

"Antonia? Reason?" Cassius asks, guffawing.

"Even if that happens, Titus will still be the most powerful," I say. "And that's not the cure for anything."

"Ah. Yes. That's something you can't abide, someone else having power. Fine then." Roque tugs at his long hair. "Talk to Vixus or Pollux. Take away his captains if you must. But heal the House, Darrow. Otherwise, we'll lose when another House comes knocking."

On the sixth day I take his advice. Knowing Titus is out raiding, I risk seeking Vixus in the keep. Unfortunately, Titus returns earlier than expected.

"You're looking lively and spry," he says to me before I can find Vixus in the keep's stone halls. He blocks my path with his large body—shoulders nearly spanning the width of the wall. I feel another in the hallway behind me. Vixus and two others. My stomach sinks a little. It was stupid to do this. "Where are you going, if I may ask?"

"I wanted to compare our scouting maps to the main map in the command room," I lie, knowing I have a digislate in my pocket.

"Oh, you wanted to compare scouting maps to the main map . . . for the good of Mars, noble Darrow?"

"What other good is there?" I ask. "We are all on the same side, no?"

"Oh, we are on the same side," he says. Titus booms an insincere laugh. "Vixus, if we are on the same side, don't you think it would be best if we shared his little maps with one another?"

"It would be for the very best," Vixus agrees. "Mushrooms. Maps. All the same." So he assaulted little Lea. His eyes are dead. Like raven eyes.

"Yes. So I'll take a look *for* you, Darrow." Titus snatches the scouting maps from me. There's nothing I can do to stop him.

"You're welcome to them," I say. "So long as you know there are enemy fires to the far east and likely enemies in the Greatwoods to the south. Raid all you like. Just don't get caught with your pants down."

Titus sniffs the air. He wasn't listening to me.

"Since we are sharing, Darrow." He sniffs again, closer to my neck. "Perhaps you'll share with us why you smell like woodsmoke."

I stiffen, not knowing what to do.

"Look at him squirm. Look at him weave a lie." Titus's voice is all disgust. "I can smell your deceit. Smell the lies dripping from you like sweat."

"Like a woman in heat," Pollux says sardonically. He shrugs apologetically at me.

"Disgusting," Vixus sneers. "He's a vile thing. A wretched, womanish thing." I don't know why I thought I'd be able to turn him on Titus.

"You're a little parasite," Titus continues. "Nibbling away at morale because you will not come to heel; waiting for my noble boys and girls to starve." They're closing in on me from behind, from the sides. Titus is huge. Pollux and Vixus are cruel, nearly as big as I. "You're a wretched creature. A worm in our spine."

I shrug casually, trying to let them think I'm not worried.

"We can fix this," I say.

"Oh?" Titus asks.

"The solution is simple, big man," I counsel. "Bring your boys and girls home. Stop raiding Ceres every day before some other House comes in and slaughters you all. Then we'll talk about fire. About food."

"You think you can tell us what to do, Darrow? That the thrust of it?" Vixus asks. "Think you're better because you scored higher on a stupid little test? Because the Proctors chose you first?"

"He does," Titus chuckles. "He thinks he *deserves* Primus."

Vixus's hawkish face leans close to mine, lips sneering each word. Handsome in repose, his lips peel back cruelly now, and his breath stinks as he looks me over, measuring me and trying to make me think he's not impressed. He snorts a contemptuous laugh. I see him shifting his head to spit on my face. I let him. The glob of phlegm hits and drips slowly down my cheek toward my lips.

Titus watches with a wolfish smile. His eyes glimmer; Vixus looks to him for encouragement. Pollux comes closer.

"You're a pampered little prick," Vixus says. His nose nearly brushes mine. "So that's what I'm gonna take from you, goodman—your little prick."

"Or you could let me leave," I say. "You seem to be blocking the door."

"Oho!" he laughs, looking at his master. "He's trying to show he's not afraid, Titus. Trying to avoid a fight." He looks as me with those golden, dead eyes. "I've broken uppity boys like you in the dueling clubs a thousand times."

"You have?" I ask incredulously.

"Broken them like twigs. And then taken their girls for sport. What embarrassments I've made them in front of their fathers. What weeping messes I make of boys like you."

"Oh, Vixus," I say with a sigh, keeping the tremble of anger and fear out of my voice. "Vixus, *Vixus*, *Vixus*. There are no boys like me."

I look back at Titus to make sure our eyes are joined when I casually, as if I were dancing, loop my Helldiver hand around and slam it into the side of Vixus's neck at the jugular with the force of a sledgehammer strike. It ruins him, yet I hit him with an elbow, a knee, my other hand, as he falls. Had his legs been anchored better, the first strike might have snapped his neck in half. Instead, he cartwheels sideways in the low gravity, going horizontal and shuddering from my raining blows as he hits the ground. His eyes go blank. Fear rises in my belly. My body is so strong.

Titus and the others are too startled by the sudden violence to stop me as I spin past their outstretched hands and run down the halls.

I did not kill him.

I did not kill him.

24

TITUS'S WAR

I did not kill Vixus. But I killed the chance of uniting the House. I sprint down the keep's winding stairwells. Shouts behind me. I pass Titus's lounging students; they're sharing bits of raw fish they managed to spear from the river. They could trip me if they knew what I've done. Two girls watch me go by and, hearing their leaders shouts, are too late in moving. I'm past their hands, past the keep's lower gatehouse and into the main square of the castle.

"Cassius!" I call up at the gatehouse to the castle where my men sleep. "Cassius!" He peeks his head out the window and sees my face.

"Oh. Shit. *Roque*!" he shouts. "It happened! Raise the Dregs!"

Three of Titus's boys and one of his girls chase after me across the courtyard. They're slower than I, but another is coming from her post on the wall to cut me off, Cassandra. Her short hair jingles with bits of metal she's woven in. Effortlessly, she hops down the eight meters from the parapet, an axe in hand, and races to intersect my path before I reach the stairs. Her golden wolf ring glimmers in the ebbing light. She's a beautiful sight.

Then my entire tribe pours out of the gatehouse. They bring their makeshift packs, their knives and the beating sticks we carved from felled branches taken from our woods. But they do not set toward me. They are bright, so they crank open the huge double gates that separate the castle from the long sloping path leading down to the glen. Mist seeps through the open gate and they disappear into the murk. Only Quinn is left behind.

Quinn, the fastest of Mars. She bounds along the cobblestone like a gazelle, coming to my aid. Her beating stick twirls in the air. Cassandra doesn't see her. A long golden ponytail flops in the chill night air as Quinn winds up, a smile on her face, and blindsides Cassandra from the flank, hitting her full-force in the knee with her beating stick. The crack of wood on strong Gold bone is loud. So is Cassandra's scream. Her leg doesn't break, but she flips onto the cobblestone. Quinn does not slow her stride. She swoops in beside me, and together we leave Titus's pack behind.

We catch up with the others in the bowl of the glen. Setting across the rugged hills, we aim toward our northern fort in the deep mist-shrouded highlands. Vapor clings to our hair, dripping off in pearls. We reach the fort well past midnight. It is a cavernous, barren tower that leans over a ravine like a drunken wizard. Lichen covers the thick gray stone. Mist swaddles its parapets and we make our first meal of the birds in the eaves of the single tower. Some escape. I hear their wings in the dark night. Our civil war has begun.

Unfortunately, Titus is not a stupid enemy. He does not come for us as we thought he would. I had hoped he would come try and lay siege to our northfort, that his army would see our fires inside the stone walls and smell the meat as it sizzled in fat. The sheep we gathered earlier would have lasted us weeks, months if we had water. We could have feasted every night. They would have broken then. They would have left Titus behind. But Titus knows of my weapon, fire, so he avoids us so that his boys and girls cannot see what luxuries we have.

He does not let his tribe alone long enough to think. Frenzy, war, numb the sense in man. So they raid House Ceres from the sixth day on, and he creates trophies for acts of bravery and violence, giving boys and girls marks in blood on their cheeks that they bear proudly. We slink along watching their war parties from the brush and the tall grasses of the plains. Sometimes we gain a vantage on the southern highland peaks near Phobos. From there we witness the siege of House Ceres.

Around House Ceres, the smoke rises in a sullen crown. Apple trees are hewn down. Horses stolen. Titus's raiders even lasso a torch from one of the Ceres ramparts in an attempt to bring fire to Mars's castle. Ceres horsemen ride them down with pails of water before they reach home. Titus shrieks in rage when this happens and the Ceres horses fly by, dashing the flame with water before circling home. With his best soldier, Vixus, he upends one of the horses with a tree branch fashioned like a pike. The rider spills from the saddle and Pollux is on her. They take two more slaves that day and Titus takes the horse for himself.

It is on our eighth day in the Institute that I watch the siege with Cassius and Roque from the highlands. Today, Titus rides the captured horse beneath the wall of House Ceres with a lasso, daring their archers to shoot their arrows at him and his horse. One poor girl leans her head out to get a better angle with her bow. She draws the arrow back to her ear, aims, and just before she is about to loose the arrow, Titus hurls his lasso upward. It flails through the air. She jerks back. Not fast enough. The lasso loops her neck and Titus kicks his horse away from the wall, tightening the lasso. Her friends scramble to grab her. They hold tight but are forced to let go before her neck snaps.

Her friends' screams echo across the plains as she's jerked violently down from the top of the wall and dragged by Titus back to his cheering followers. There, Cassandra kicks the girl to her knees and enslaves her with our standard. The flames from the burning crops lick up into the twilight where several Proctors hover with flagons of wine and a tray of some rare delicacy.

"And violent hearts set harshest flame," Roque murmurs from his knee.

"He's bold," I say deferentially, "and he likes this." His eyes sparkled when I struck Vixus in the throat. Cassius nods along. "Too much."

"He is lethal," Cassius agrees, but he means something different. I look over at him. There's a raw edge to his voice. "And he's a liar."

"Is he?" I ask

"He didn't kill Priam."

Roque becomes quiet. Smaller than us, he seems a child as he remains on a knee. His long hair is held in a ponytail. Dirt crusts his nails, which scrabble in tying his shoes as he looks up.

"He didn't kill Priam," Cassius repeats. The wind moans over the hills behind us. Night comes slow today. Cassius's cheeks sink into shadow; still, he's handsome. "They wouldn't have put Priam with a monster like Titus. Priam's a leader, not a warlord. They'd put Priam with someone easy like one of our Dregs."

I know where Cassius is going with this. It's in the way he watches Titus; the coldness in his eyes reminds me of a pitviper's gaze as it follows its prey. My insides turn sour as I do it, but I lead Cassius in the direction he seems to want to go, inviting him to bite. Roque tilts his head at me, noticing something strange in my interaction with Cassius.

"And they would give Titus someone else," I say.

"Someone else," Cassius repeats, nodding.

Julian, he is thinking. He doesn't say it. Neither do I. Better to let it fester in his mind. Let my friend think our enemy killed his brother. This is a way out.

"Blood begets blood begets blood begets blood . . ." Roque's words into the wind, which carries west toward the long plain and toward the flames that dance in the low horizon. Beyond, the mountains hunker cold and dark. Snow already gathers on their peaks. It's a sight to steal one's breath, yet Roque's eyes never leave my face.

I find it a small pleasure that Titus's slaves are not very effective allies for him. Far from being indoctrinated as thoroughly as a Red might be, these newly made slaves are stubborn creatures. They follow orders or risk being labeled Shamed after graduation. But they purposefully never do more or less than he demands; it is their act of rebellion. They fight where he tells them to fight, whom he tells them to fight, even when they should retreat. They gather the berries he shows them, even if they know they are poisonous, and pile stones till the pile falls over. But if there is an open gate leading to the enemy's fortress and Titus doesn't tell them to go into it, they'll stand there and pick their butts.

Despite the addition of slaves and the razing of Ceres's crops and orchards, Titus's force, which is quite sound at violence, is pitiful when they attempt to do anything else. His men empty their bowels in shallow latrines or behind trees or in the river in an attempt to poison the students of House Ceres. One of his girls even falls in after emptying her bowels into the water. She flails around in her own waste. It's a scene of comedy, but laughter has become seldom except from the students of Ceres. They sit behind their high walls and catch fish from the river and eat breads from their ovens and honey from their apiaries.

In response to the laughter, Titus drags one of the male slaves up in front of the gate. The slave is a tall one with a long nose and a mischievous smile meant for the ladies. He thinks this is all a game till Titus cuts off one of his ears. Then he cries for his mother like a young child. He will never command warships.

The Proctors, even House Ceres's, do not stop the violence. They watch from the sky in twos and threes, floating about as medBots whine down from Olympus to cauterize a wound or treat severe head trauma.

On the twentieth morning of the Institute, the defenders throw a basket of bread loaves down as Titus's men attempt to batter in the tall gate with a felled tree. The besiegers end up fighting each other for the food only to find that the bread was baked around razor blades. The screams last till the afternoon.

Titus's reply comes just before night falls. With five newly minted slaves, including the male with the missing ear, he approaches the gate till he's near a mile off. He parades in front of the slaves, holding four long sticks in his hand. These he gives to each of the slaves except the girl he pulled down from the ramparts with a lasso.

With a low bow to the Ceres gate, he waves a hand and orders the slaves to commence beating the girl. Like Titus, she is tall and powerful, so it is difficult to pity her. At first.

The slaves hit the girl gingerly with the initial swings. Then Titus reminds them of the shame that will forever mark their names if they do not obey; they swing harder; they aim for the girl's golden head. They hit her and hit her till her shouts have long faded and blood mats her blonde hair. When Titus grows bored, he drags the wounded girl back to his camp by her hair. She slides limply over the earth.

We watch from our place in the highlands, and it takes Lea and Quinn both to stop Cassius from sprinting down into the plains. The girl will live, I tell him. The sticks are all show. Roque spits bitterly into the grass and reaches for Lea's hand. It's odd seeing her give him strength.

The next morning, we discover that Titus's reply did not stop with the beating. After we retired to our castle, Titus snuck back in the dead of night to hide the girl directly in front of the Ceres gate underneath a thick blanket of grass, gagged and tied. Then he had one of his female followers shriek during the night to pretend she was the slave at the camp. She screamed of rape and violations.

Maybe the captured Ceres girl thought she was safe under the grass. Maybe she thought the Proctors would save her and she would go home to mother and father, home to her equestrian lessons, home to her puppies and her books. But in the early dark of morning she is trampled as riders, enraged by the fake screams, gallop from the Ceres fortress to rescue her from Titus's makeshift camp. They only learn of their folly when they hear the medBots descending behind them to carry her broken body up to Olympus.

She never returns. Still the Proctors do not interfere. I'm not sure why they even exist.

I miss home. Lykos, of course, but also the place where I was safe with Dancer, Matteo, and Harmony.

Soon there are no more slaves to take. House Ceres does not come out after dark anymore, and their high walls are guarded. The trees outside the wall have all been cut down, but there are crops and more orchards inside their long walls. Bread still bakes and the river still flows within their ramparts. Titus can do nothing but savage their land and steal what remains of their apples. Most have been sown with needles and stingers from wasps. Titus has failed. And so, as do those of any tyrant after a failed war, his eyes turn inward.

25

TRIBAL WAR

Thirty days into the Institute and I've not seen evidence of another enemy House except for the smoke signs of distant fires. House Ceres's soldiers roam the eastern fringes of our land. They ride with impunity now that Titus's tribe has retreated into our castle. Castle. No. It has become a hovel.

I come upon it with Roque in the early morning. Fog still clings to the four spires and light struggles to penetrate the dreary sky of our highland climate. Sounds from inside the stone walls echo into the quiet morning like coins rattling about in a tin can. Titus's voice. He's cursing at his tribesmen to get up. Apparently few do. Someone tells him to go slag himself, and it's little wonder. The bunk beds are the only real amenity the castle has, no doubt put there to encourage slothfulness. My tribe has no such amenities; we sleep on stone curled next to one another around our crackling fires. Oh, what I'd give for a bed again.

Cassius and I slink along the slanted dirt road that leads to the gatehouse. We can hardly even see it, the fog is so thick. More sounds from inside. It seems like the slaves are up. I hear coughs, grumbling, and a few shouts. A long creak and the clatter of chains means the gate is opening. Cassius pulls me off to the side of the road, tucking us into the mist as the slaves shuffle past. Their faces are pallid in the low light. Hollows make homes in their sunken cheeks, and their hair has been dirtied. Mud-caked skin around their Sigils. He passes near enough to me that I smell his body odor. I stiffen suddenly, worried he will again smell the smoke on me, but he doesn't. Beside me, Cassius is quiet, yet I feel his anger.

We sneak back down the path and watch the slaves toil from the relative safety of the woods. They are not Aureates as they scrub shit and scavenge for berries in the sharp thistlebushes. One or two are missing ears. Vixus, recovered from my attack except for a huge purple bruise on his neck, walks around slapping at them with a long stick. If the test is to unite a fractious House, I am failing.

As early morning fades and appetites change with the arrival of warm sunshine, Cassius and I hear a sound that makes our skin prickle. Screams. Screams from the high tower of Mars. They are a particular sort, a kind to darken the spirits.

When I was a boy in Lykos, my mother was serving me soup at our stone family table the night of a Laureltide. It was a year after my father died. Kieran and Leanna sat with me, neither yet older than ten. A single light unit flickered on and off above the table, so Mum was shrouded in darkness except her arm from the elbow down. Then came the scream, muffled by distance and the twists of our cavern township. I still see how the broth quivered in the ladle, how my mother's hand shook when she heard it. Screams. Not of pain, but of horror.

"What he's doing to the girls . . . ," Cassius hisses to me as we slink away from the castle as night descends. "He's a beast."

"This is war," I say, though the words sound hollow even in my own ears.

"It's school!" he reminds me. "What if Titus did this to our girls? To Lea . . . to Quinn?"

I say nothing.

"We would kill him," Cassius answers for me. "We would kill him, cut his prick off and shove it in his mouth." And I know he's also thinking of what Titus must have done to Julian.

Despite Cassius's mutterings, I take his arm and pull him away from the castle. The gates are locked against the night. There is nothing we can do. I feel helpless again. Helpless as when Ugly Dan took Eo from me. But I am different now. My hands turn to fists. I am more than I was then.

On our way back to our northfort, we see a glimmer in the air. Golden gravBoots shimmer as Fitchner descends. He's chewing gum and holds his heart when he sees our evil glances.

"Whatever did I do, young friends, to earn such glares?"

"He's treating the girls like animals!" Cassius seethes. Veins in his neck stand out. "They are Golds and he is treating them like dogs, like Pinks."

"If he is treating them like Pinks, then it is because they merited no better in this little world than Pinks do in our big world."

"You're joking." Cassius can't understand. "They are Golds, not Pinks. He's a monster."

"Then prove you're a man and stop him," Fitchner says. "As long as he's not murdering them one by one, it is not our concern. All wounds heal. Even these."

"That's a lie," I tell him. I'll never be healed of Eo. That pain will last forever. "Some things do not fade. Some things can never be made right."

"Yet we do nothing because he has more *fighters,*" Cassius spits.

An idea sweeps over me. "We can fix that."

Cassius turns to me. He hears the deadness in my voice just as I see it in his eyes when he speaks of Titus. That's a peculiar thing we share. We're made of fire and ice—though I am not sure which of us is ice and which is fire. Nevertheless, extremes rule us more than we'd like; that is why we are of Mars.

"You have a plan," Cassius says.

I nod coldly.

Fitchner watches us two and he grins. "About gorydamn time."

IIIIIIIIII

The plan starts with a concession only someone once a husband could make. Cassius cannot stop laughing when I tell him the details. Even Quinn snorts a laugh the next morning. Then she's off, running like a deer to Deimos Tower to bring my formal apology to Antonia. She's to meet me with Antonia's response at one of our supply caches near the Furor River, north of the castle.

Cassius guards our new fort with the remainder of our tribe, in case Titus tries to attack while Roque and I go to the supply cache during the day. Quinn does not come. Dusk does. Despite the dark, we trace the path she would have taken from Deimos Tower. We go till we reach the tower itself, which sits in the low hills surrounded by thick woods. Five of Titus's men lounge around its base. Roque grabs me and pulls me down into the woods' brush. He points to a tree fifty meters distant where Vixus sits hidden in wait on a high branch. Did they catch Quinn? No, she's too fast to be caught. Did someone betray us?

We return to our fort by early morning. I'm sure I've been more tired, but I can't remember when. Blisters ruin my feet despite the fitted shoes, and my neck peels from long days in the sun. Something is wrong.

Lea meets me by the fort's gate. She hugs Roque and looks up at me like I'm her father or something. She is not her usual timid self. Her birdlike body shakes not from fear, but anger.

"You have to kill that piece of filth, Darrow. You have to cut his slagging balls off."

Titus. "What happened?" I look around. "Lea. Where is Cassius?"

She tells me.

Titus captured Quinn as she was on her way back from the tower. They beat her. Then Titus sent one of her ears here. It was meant for me. They thought Quinn was *my* girl, and Titus thinks he knows my temper. They got the reaction they wanted, just not from me.

Cassius was on watch and as the others slept he snuck away to the castle to challenge Titus. Somehow the brilliant young man was arrogant enough to think hundreds of years of Aureate honor and tradition would survive the sickness that has consumed Titus's tribe in only a few weeks. The Imperator's son was wrong. And he is also unused to having his heritage be of such little consequence. In the real world, he would have been safe. In this small one, he is not.

"But he's alive," I say.

"Yeah, I'm alive, you Pixie!" Cassius stumbles shirtless out of the fort.

"Cassius!" Roque gasps. His face pales suddenly.

Cassius's left eye is swollen shut. Lips are split. Ribs purple as grapes. His other eye is bloody. Three dislocated fingers shoot out like tree roots, and his shoulder is odd. The others stare at him with such sadness. Cassius was the Imperator's boy—their shining knight. And now his body is a ruin, and the looks upon their faces, the pallid cast to their skin, tell me that they have never before seen someone beautiful mutilated.

I have.

He smells like piss.

He tries to play it off as some lark. "They beat the slag out of me when I challenged him. Hit me with a shovel on the side of the head. Then stood around and had themselves a circle piss. Then they tied me up in that stinkhole keep, but Pollux set me free, like a good lad, and he's agreed to open the gate if we need it done."

"I didn't think you were so stupid," I say.

"Of course he is, he wants to be one of the Sovereign's knights," Roque mutters. "And all they do is duel." He shakes his long hair. Dirt crusts the leather band that holds it in a ponytail. "You should have waited for us."

"What's done is done," I say. "We go ahead with the plan."

"Fine," Cassius snorts. "But when the time comes, Titus is mine."

26

MUSTANG

Part of Cassius is gone. That invincible boy I first met is somehow different. The humiliation changed him. I can't decide how, though, as I straighten his fingers and help him fix his shoulder. He falls down from the pain.

"Thank you, brother," he says to me, and cups the side of my head to help himself up. It is the first time he says it. "I failed the test." I don't disagree with him. "I went in there like a plum fool. If this were anywhere else, they would have killed me."

"Least it didn't cost you your life," I say.

Cassius chuckles. "Just my pride."

"Good. Something you have in abundance," Roque says with a smile.

"We have to get her back." Cassius's own grimace fades as he looks at Roque, then at me. "Quinn. We have to get her back before he takes her up to his tower."

"We will." We bloody will.

Cassius and I go east according to my plan, farther than we have gone before. We stay to the northern highlands, but we make sure we walk along the high crests visible to the open plains below. East and east, our long legs taking us fast and far.

"A rider to the southeast," I say. Cassius doesn't look.

We pass through a humid glen where a dark loch offers us the chance to catch a drink across from a family of deerling. Mud covers our legs. Bugs flit over the cold water. The earth feels good between my fingers as I bend to drink. I dunk my head and join Cassius in eating some of our aging lamb. It needs salt. My belly cramps from all the protein.

"How far east of the castle do you reckon we are?" I ask Cassius, pointing behind him.

"Maybe twenty klicks. Hard to peg it. Feels farther but my legs are just tired." He straightens and looks where I point. "Ah. Got it."

A girl on a dappled mustang watches us from the edge of the glen. She has a long covered bar tied to her saddle. Can't make out her House, but I have seen her before. I remember her like it was yesterday. The girl who called me a Pixie when I fell off that pony Matteo put me on.

"I want her horse to ride back," Cassius tells me. He can't see out his left eye but his bravado is back, a little too forcefully. "Hey, darling!" he calls. "*Shit, that hurts the ribs.* Prime ride! What House are you?"

I'm worried about this.

The girl rides to within ten meters, but she has the sigils on sleeve and neck covered with two lengths of sewn cloth. Her face is streaked with three diagonal lines of blue berry juice mixed with animal fat. We don't know if she is from Ceres. I hope not. She could be from the southern woods, from the east, from the far northeastern highlands even.

"Lo, Mars," she says smugly, looking at the sigil on our jackets.

Cassius bows pathetically. I don't bother.

"Well, this is swell." I kick a stone with my shoe. "Lo . . . Mustang. Nice sigil. And horse." I let her know having a horse is something rare.

She is small, delicate. Her smile is not. It mocks us. "What are you boys about in the hinterlands? Reaping grain?"

I pat my slingBlade. "We have enough back home." I gesture south of our castle.

She suppresses a laugh at my feeble lie.

"Sure you do."

"I will be even with you." Cassius forces his battered face into a smile. "You are stunningly beautiful. You must be from Venus. Hit me with whatever is under that cloth on your saddle and take me back to your fortress. I'll be your Pink if you promise not to share me and to keep me warm every night." He takes an unsteady step forward. "And every morning." Her mustang takes four back till he gives up trying to steal her horse.

"Well, aren't you the charmer, handsome. And by that pitchfork in your hand, you must be a prime fighter too." She bats her eyelashes.

Cassius puffs out his chest in agreement.

She waits for him to understand.

Then he frowns.

"Yup. Uh-oh. You see, we didn't have any tools in our stronghold except those pertaining to our deity, soooo you must have encountered House Ceres already." She leans forward in the saddle sardonically. "You don't have crops. You just fought those who do, and you don't have any better weapons, clearly, or you would be carrying them with you. So Ceres is in these parts as well. Likely in the lowlands near the woods for crops. Or near that big river everyone is talking about."

She's all laughing eyes and a smirking mouth in a face shaped like a heart. Hair so golden it sparkles in the sun and flows down her back in braids.

"So you are in the woods?" she asks. "North in the highlands, probably. Oh, this is fun! How bad *are* your weapons? You clearly don't have horses. What a poor House."

"Slag," Cassius makes a point of saying.

"You seem pretty proud of yourself." I put my slingBlade on my shoulder.

She raises a hand and wiggles it back and forth. "Sort of. Sort of. More proud than Handsome there should be. He's full of tells." I shift my weight on my toes to see if she notices. She moves her horse back. "Now, now, Reaper, are you going to try and get in my saddle too?"

"Just trying to knock you out of it, Mustang."

"Fancy a roll in the mud, do we? Well, how about I promise to let you up here with me if you give me more clues as to where your castle squats? Towers? Sprawls? I can be a kind master."

She looks me up and down playfully. Her eyes sparkle like a fox's might. This is still a game to her, which means her House is a civil place. I'm envious as I examine her in kind. Cassius didn't lie; she is something to look at. But I'd rather knock her off her mustang. My feet are tired and we're playing a dangerous game.

"What Draft number were you?" I ask, wishing I'd paid more attention.

"Higher than you, Reaper. I remember Mercury wanted you something awful, but his Drafters wouldn't let him pick you in the first round. Something about your rage metric."

"You were higher than me? So you're not Mercury then, because they chose a boy instead of me, and you're not a Jupiter, because they took a gorydamn monstrous kid." I try to remember who else was chosen before me, but I can't, so I smile. "Maybe you shouldn't be so vain. Then I wouldn't know what Draft you were."

I notice the knife under her black tunic, but I still can't remember her from the Draft. Wasn't paying attention. Cassius should have remembered her the way he looks at girls, but maybe he can only think of Quinn and her missing ear.

Our job is done. We can leave Mustang. She's smart enough to figure out the rest. But leaving might be a problem without a horse, and I don't think Mustang really needs hers.

I feign boredom. Cassius keeps an eye on the hills around. Then I start suddenly as if I've noticed something. I whisper "Snake" into his ear while looking at the horse's front hooves. He looks too, and at this point, the girl's movement is involuntary. Even as she realizes it's a trick, she leans forward to peer at the hooves. I lunge to close the ten-meter gap. I'm fast. So is she, but she's just a hair off balance and has to lean back in order to jerk her horse away. It scrambles back in the mud. I dive for her and my strong right hand grips her long braids just as the horse darts away. I try to jerk her out of the saddle, but she's all hellfire.

I'm left with a handful of coiled gold. The mustang is off and the girl laughs and curses about her hair. Then Cassius's pitchfork wobbles through the air and trips the horse. Girl and beast go down in the muddy grass.

"Dammit, Cassius!" I shout.

"Sorry!"

"You might have killed her!"

"I know! I know! Sorry!"

I run to see if she's broken her neck. That would ruin everything. She's not moving. I lean in to feel her pulse and sense a blade graze my groin. My hand is already there to twist her wrist away. I take the knife and pin her down.

"I knew you wanted to roll me in the mud." Her lips smirk. Then they purse as if she wants a kiss. I recoil. Instead, she whistles and the plan becomes a bit more complicated.

I hear hooves.

Everyone has bloodydamn horses but us.

The girl winks and I force the cloth from her sigil. House Minerva. Greeks would have called it Athena. Of course. Seventeen horses tear down the glen from the crest of the hill. Their riders have stunpikes. Where the hell did they get stunpikes?

"Time to run, Reaper," Mustang taunts. "My army comes."

There's no running. Cassius dives into the loch. I jump off Mustang, run after him through the mud, and throw myself over the bank to join him in the water. I cannot swim, but I learn quickly.

The horsemen of House Minerva taunt Cassius and me as we tread water in the center of the small loch. It's summer but the water is cold and deep. Dusk is coming. My limbs are numb. The Minervans still circle the lake, waiting for us to tire. We won't. I had three of the durobags in my pockets. I blow them full of air and give two to Cassius, keeping one for myself. They help us float, and since none of the Minervans seem intent on swimming to meet us, we're safe for the time being.

"*Roque should have lit it by now,*" I tell Cassius some hours into our swim. He's in bad shape from his wounds and the cold.

"*Roque will light it. Faith . . . goodman . . . faith.*"

"*We're also supposed to be almost home.*"

"*Well, it's still going better than my plan did.*"

"*You look bored, Mustang!*" I shout out with chattering teeth. "Come in for a swim."

"And get hypothermia? I'm not stupid. I'm in Minerva, not Mars, remember!" She laughs from the shore. "I'd rather warm myself by your castle's hearth. See?" She points behind us and speaks quickly to three tall boys, one of whom looks as big as an Obsidian—shoulders like a huge thunderhead.

A thick column of smoke rises in the distance.

Finally.

"How the slag did those pricks pass the test?" I ask loudly. "They've given our castle away."

"If we get back, I'm going to drown them in their own piss," Cassius replies even louder. "Except for Antonia. She's too pretty for that."

Our teeth chatter.

The eighteen raiders think House Mars is stupid, horseless, and unprepared.

"Reaper, Handsome, I must leave you now!" Mustang calls to us. "Try not to drown before I return with your standard. You can be my pretty bodyguards. And you can have matching hats! But we'll have to teach you to think better!"

She gallops away with fifteen riders, the huge Gold reining his horse in beside hers like some sort of colossal shadow. Her followers whoop as they ride. She also leaves us company. Two horsemen with stunpikes. Our farming tools lie in the mud on the shore.

"M-mustang is a s-sexp-p-pot," Cassius manages to shiver out.

"She's s-s-scary."

"R-r-reminds m-m-me of my m-mother."

"S-s-something is wrong w-with y-ou."

He nods in agreement. "So . . . the p-plan is sort of w-w-working."

If we can get out of the loch without being captured.

Night falls in earnest, and with the darkness come the howls of the wolves in the misty highlands. We begin to sink as our durobags leak air from small stress holes. We might have had a chance to slink away in the night, but the remaining Minervans are not lazily sitting around a fire. They stalk through the darkness so that we never even know where they are. Why can't they be stupidly sitting in their castle infighting like our fellows?

I'm going to be a slave again. Maybe not a real slave, but it doesn't matter. I won't lose. I cannot lose. Eo will have died for nothing if I let myself sink here, if I let my plan fail. Yet I do not know how to beat my enemies. They are clever and the odds are stacked heavily against me. Eo's dream sinks with me into the darkness of the loch, and I'm about to swim to shore, regardless the outcome, when something spooks the horses.

Then a scream slices across the water.

Fear trickles down my spine as something howls. It is not a wolf. It can't be what I think it is. Blue light flashes as a stunpike flails in the air. The boy screams another curse. A knife got him. Someone runs to his aid and electricity flares blue again. I see a black wolf standing over one body as another falls. Darkness again. Silence, then the mournful whine of medBots descending from Olympus.

I hear a familiar voice.

"Clear now. Come out of the water, fishies."

We paddle to shore and pant in the mud. Mild hypothermia has set in. It won't kill us but my fingers are still slow as mud squishes between them. My body shakes like a drillBoy at work.

"Goblin, you psychopath. Is that you?" I call.

The fourth tribe slides out of the darkness. He's wearing the pelt of the wolf he killed. It covers his head to his shins. Damn small kid. The gold of his black fatigues is coated in mud. So's his face.

Cassius crawls from his knees to clasp Sevro in a hug. "Oh, y-you are b-beautiful, Goblin. B-beautiful, beautiful b-b-oy. And smelly."

"He been nibbling on mushrooms?" Goblin asks over Cassius's shoulders. "Stop touching me, you Pixie." He pushes Cassius away, looking embarrassed.

"Did you k-kill these t-two?" I ask, shivering. I bend over them and take off their dry clothing to exchange for my own. I feel pulses.

"No." Sevro cocks his head at me. "Should I have?"

"W-w-why are you asking m-me like I'm your P-praetor?" I laugh. "You know what's what."

Sevro shrugs. "You're like me." He looks at Cassius with disdain. "And somehow still like him. So, should I kill them?" he asks casually.

Cassius and I share startled glances.

"N-n-no," we agree just as the medBots arrive to take the Minervans away. He hurt them badly enough to end their time in the game.

"So what, p-p-pray tell, are you doing w-w-wandering ab-b-bout in a wolfsk-k-kin all the way out h-here?" Cassius asks.

"Roque said you lot would be out east," Sevro replies curtly. "Plan is still a go, says he."

"Hav-v-ve the Minervans arrived at the castle?" I ask.

Sevro spits in the grass. The twin moons cast eerie shadows over his dark face. "How the piss should I know? They passed me on the way. But you have no leverage, you know. It is a dead-end plan." Is Sevro actually helping us? Of course his help begins with listing out our inadequacies. "If the Minervans get to the keep, they will destroy Titus and take our territory."

"Yes. That is the point," I say.

"They will also take our standard—"

"That's a r-risk we have to take."

"—so I stole the standard from the keep and buried it in the woods."

I should have thought of that.

"You just stole it. Just like that." Cassius starts laughing. "Crazy little sod. You're prime mad. One hundredth pick. Prime mad."

Sevro looks annoyed. Pleased. But annoyed. "Even then, we cannot guarantee they leave our territory."

"Your sug-g-g-gestion?" I ask, still shivering but impatient. He could have helped us before.

"Get leverage to get them out after they do their job of taking Titus down, *obviously*."

"Yes. Y-yes. I get it." I shake off the last of my shivers. "But how?"

Sevro shrugs. "We'll take Minerva's standard."

"W-wait," Cassius says. "You know how to do that?"

Sevro snorts. "What do you think I've been doing this whole time, you silky turd? Wanking off in the bushes?"

Cassius and I look at each other.

"Kind of," I say.

"Yeah, actually," Cassius agrees.

We ride the Minervan horses east of the highlands. I'm not a sound equestrian. Of course Cassius is, so I learn to clutch his bruised ribs very well. Our faces are painted with mud. It will look like shadow in the night, so they will see our horses, our pikes, our sigils, and will think us their own.

The Minervan castle lies in rolling country quilted with wildflowers and olive trees. The moons glimmer bright over the pitching landscape. Owls hoot in the gnarled branches above. As we reach their sprawling sandstone fortress, a voice challenges us from the rampart above the gate. Sevro is not very presentable in his wolfcloak, so he guards the escape.

"We found Mars," I call up. "Oy! Open the damn gate."

"Password," the sentry demands lazily from the battlements.

"Bosombutthead!" I shout up. Sevro heard it last time he was here.

"Prime. Where's Virginia and the raiders?" the sentry calls down.

Mustang?

"Took their standard, man! The pissers didn't even have horses. We might still manage to take the castle!"

The sentry bites.

"Prime news! Virginia is a devil. June's made supper. Fetch some in the kitchen and then join me, if you like. I'm bored and need to be entertained."

The gate creaks open very, very slowly. I laugh when it finally parts enough for us to ride in abreast. Cassius and I aren't even met by guards. Their castle is different— drier, cleaner, and less oppressive. They have gardens and olive trees that wend between the sandstone columns of the bottom level.

We hide in the shadows as two girls pass with cups of milk. They have no torches or fires an enemy can spot from the distance, only small candles. It makes it easy to slink about. Apparently the girls are pretty, because Cassius makes a face and pretends to follow them up the stairs.

After flashing me a smile, he sneaks toward the sounds of the kitchen as I look for their command room. I find it on the third level. Windows overlook the dark plain. In front of the windows lies Minerva's atlas. A burning flag floats above my House's castle. I don't know what it means, but it can't be good. Another fortress, House Diana's, lies south of Minerva's in the Greatwoods. Those are all that have been discovered.

They have their own score sheets to keep track of accomplishments. Someone named Pax seems a bloody nightmare. He's taken eight slaves personally, and caused medBots to come down to fetch nine students, so I assume he's the one that stood as tall as an Obsidian.

I don't find their standard anywhere in the command room. Like us, they weren't stupid enough to leave it just lying about. No problem, we'll find it our own way. On cue, I smell Cassius's smokefires seeping through the windows. What a pretty war room they have. Much prettier than Mars's.

I break everything.

And when I have ruined their map and am finished defacing a statue of Minerva, I use the axe I found to chop the name of Mars into their long, beautiful war table. I'm tempted to etch another House's name into the debris to confuse them, but I want them to know who did this. This House is too put together, too ordered and level headed. They have a leader, raiders, sentries (naïve ones), cooks, olive trees, warm milk, stunpikes, horses, honey, strategy. Minervans. Proud piggers. Let them feel a bit more like House Mars. Let them feel rage. Chaos.

Shouts come. Cassius's fire spreads. A girl runs into the warroom. I nearly make her faint as I lift my axe. There's no point in hurting her. We can't take prisoners, not easily. So I pull out both the sling-Blade and the stunpike. Mud on my face. My golden hair wild. I look a terror.

"Are you June?" I growl.

"N-no . . . why?"

"Can *you* cook?"

She laughs despite her fear. Three boys turn the corner. Two are thicker but shorter than me. I scream like a rage god. Oh, how they run.

"Enemies!" they scream. "Enemies!"

"They're in the towers!" I roar to confuse them again and again as I descend the stairs. "The top levels! Everywhere! Too many! Dozens! Dozens! Mars is here! *Mars* has come!" Smoke spreads. So do their cries.

"Mars!" they shout. "Mars has come!"

A young man flashes past me. I grab his collar and throw him out a window into the courtyard below, scattering the Minervans massed there. I go to the kitchen. Cassius's fire is not bad. Mostly grease and brush. A howling girl beats at it.

"June!" I call out. She turns into my stunpike and shudders as the electricity dumbs down her muscles. That's how I steal their cook.

Cassius finds me running with June over my shoulder through their gardens.

"What the hell?"

"She's a cook!" I explain.

He laughs so hard he can barely breathe.

Minervans fall into chaos, running from their barracks. They think the enemy is in their towers. They think their citadel is burning down. They think Mars has come in full force. Cassius pulls me along into their stables. Seven horses have been left behind. We steal six after tossing a candle into their hay stores and ride out the main gate as smoke and panic consumes the fortress. I don't have the standard. Just as we planned. Sevro said there was a hidden back gate to the fortress. We wagered that someone very desperate to flee a fallen fortress would use it to escape, someone trying to protect the standard. We were right.

Sevro joins us two minutes later. He howls out from under his wolfcloak as he comes. Far behind, the enemy chases him on foot with stunpikes. Now they're the ones without horses. And they've no chance to get back the owl standard that glitters in his muddy hands. The cook unconscious across my saddle, we ride under the starry night back to our battle-torn highlands, the three of us laughing, cheering, howling.

27

THE HOUSE OF RAGE

We find Roque at Phobos Tower with Lea, Screwface, Clown, Thistle, Weed, and Pebble. We have eight horses—two stolen at the lake, six stolen in the castle. We add them to our plan. Cassius, Sevro, and I cross the bridge that spans the river Metas. An enemy scout bolts north to warn Mustang. Our other stolen horses, led by Antonia, follow once the scout is away, looping north. Roque, horseless, loops south.

My horse alone is not covered with mud. She is a bright mare. And I am a bright sight. I carry Minerva's golden standard in my left hand. We could have hidden it. Could have kept it safe. But they need to know we have it, and even though Sevro stole it, he doesn't want to carry it. He likes his curved knives too much. I think he whispers to them. And Cassius we need for other things besides carrying the standard. Plus, if he carried it, then he would look the leader. And that will not do.

Dead silence as we ride through our lowlands. Fog seeps around the trees. I cut through it. Cassius and Sevro ride to either side. I cannot see or hear them now, but wolves howl somewhere. Sevro howls back. I struggle to keep my seat as the mare spooks. I fall off twice. Cassius's laughs come from the darkness. It's hard to remember I'm doing all this for Eo, all this to start a rebellion. It feels like a game this night; in a way it is, because I'm finally beginning to have fun.

Our castle is taken. Firelight along its ramparts tells me this. The castle stands high above the glen on its hill, its torches making strange halos in the fog-quilted darkness. My horse's hooves thump softly on wet grass as to my right the Metas gurgles like a sick child in the night. Cassius rides there but I cannot see him.

"Reaper!" Mustang shouts through the mist. Her voice is not playful. She's forty meters off, near the base of the sloped road that leads to the castle. She leans forward, arms crossed over the pommel of her saddle. Six riders flank her. The rest must be garrisoning the castle. Otherwise I'd hear about it. I look at the boys behind her. Pax is so large that his pike looks like a scepter in his huge mitts.

"Lo, Mustang."

"So, you didn't drown. That would have been easier." Her quick face is dark. "You are a vile breed, you know that?" She's been inside the keep and she doesn't have words for her anger. "Rape? Mutilation? Murder?" She spits.

"I did nothing," I say. "And neither did the Proctors."

"Yes. You did *nothing*. Yet now you have our standard and what? Handsome somewhere out there in the mist? Go ahead, pretend like you're not their leader. Like you're not responsible."

"Titus is responsible."

"The big bastard? Yes, Pax laid him low." She gestures to the monster of a boy beside her. Pax's hair is shorn short, his eyes small, chin like a heel with a dent in it. Beneath him, his horse looks like a dog. His bare arms are flesh stretched over boulders.

"I didn't come to talk, Mustang."

"Come to cut my ear off?" she sneers.

"No. Goblin did."

Then one of her men slips screaming from his saddle.

"What the . . . ," a rider murmurs.

Behind them, knives already dripping, Sevro howls like a maniac. A half dozen other howls join his as Antonia and half her Phobos garrison ride from the north hills on the stolen mudblack steeds. They howl like mentals in the mist. Mustang's soldiers wheel about.

Sevro takes another one down. He doesn't use stunpikes. MedBots scream through the sky, which is suddenly filled with Proctors. All of them have come to watch. Mercury trails behind the rest, carrying an armful of spirits, which he tosses to his fellows. Each of us peers up to watch their strange appearance; the horses continue to run. Time pauses.

"To the fray!" dark Apollo mocks from on high. His golden robes show he's just risen from bed. "To the fray."

Then chaos hits as Mustang shouts orders, strategy. Four more horsemen ride down the sloped road from the gate to support her troop. My turn. I slam Minerva's standard upright into the earth and scream bloody murder. I kick my heels into my mare. She lurches forward, almost losing me. My body shudders as she pounds the moist earth with her hooves. My strong left hand grips the reins and I draw my slingBlade. I feel a Helldiver again when I howl.

The enemy scatters as they see me raging toward them. It is the rage that confuses them. It is the insanity of Sevro, the manic brutality of Mars. The horsemen scatter, except one. Pax jumps from his horse and sprints at me.

"*Pax au Telemanus*" he screams, a titan possessed, foaming at the mouth. I dig my heels into my horse and howl. Then Pax tackles my horse. His shoulder hits my horse's sternum. The beast screams. My world flips. I fly out of my saddle, over my horse's head, and crash to the ground.

Dazed, I stumble to my knee in the hoof-churned field.

Madness consumes the field. Antonia's force crashes into Mustang's flank. They have primitive weapons, but their horses are shock enough. Several Minervans fly from the saddle. Others kick their mounts toward their abandoned standard, but Cassius appears out of the fog at a gallop and swipes the standard away to the south. Two enemies give chase, dividing their force. The other six soldiers from Antonia's tower garrisons are waiting to ambush them in the woods, where the horses cannot gallop.

Reflexes make me duck as a pike sweeps toward my skull. I'm up with my slingBlade. I slash it at a wrist. Too slow. I move as if in a dance, remembering the thumping pattern my uncle taught me in the abandoned mines. The Reaping Dance carries my motions into one another like flowing water. I swoop the slingBlade into a kneecap. The Aureate bone does not break, but the force knocks the rider from the saddle. I spin sideways and strike again, and again, and sweep the hoof of a horse away, breaking a fetlock. The animal falls.

A different stunpike stabs at me. I avoid the point and rip it free with my Red hands and jam the electrocuting tip into another assailant. The boy falls. A mountain pushes it aside and runs at me. Pax. In case I am an idiot, he roars his name at me. His parents bred him to lead Obsidian landing parties into hull breaches.

"Pax au Telemanus!" He beats his huge pike against his chest and hits puffy-haired Clown so hard, my friend flies back four meters. *"Pax au Telemanus."*

"Is a pricklicker!" I mock.

Then a horse's flank thumps into my back and I stumble toward the monstrous boy. I'm doomed. He could have gotten me with his pike. Instead, he hugs me. It's like being embraced by a golden bear that keeps screaming its own damn name. My back cracks. Mothermercy. He's squeezing my skull. My shoulder aches. Bloodyhell. I can't breathe. I've never met a force like this. Dear God. He's a bloodydamn ogre. But someone is howling. Dozens of howls. Back popping.

Pax roars his personal victory. "I have your captain! I piss on you, Mars! Pax au Telemanus has slagged your captain! Pax au Telemanus!"

My vision flickers black and fades. But the rage in me does not.

I roar out one last bit of wrath before I faint. It's cheap. Pax is honorable. I still mash his grapes flat with my knee. I make sure to get both as many times as I can. One. Two. Three. Four. He gawps and collapses. I faint atop him in the mud to the sound of Proctors cheering.

Sevro tells me the story as he picks through the pockets of our prisoners after the battle. After Pax and I finished one another off, Roque sallied into the glen with Lea and my tribe. Mustang, the crafty girl, escaped into the castle and manages yet to hold it with six fighters. All the prisoners of Mars she captured won't be hers until she touches them with the tip of her standard. Fat chance. We have eleven of her men and Roque digs up our standard to make them our slaves. We could besiege our own castle—there's no storming its high walls—but Ceres or the rest of Minerva could come at any time. If they do, Cassius is supposed to ride to give Ceres Minerva's standard. It also keeps him away while I cement my position as leader.

Roque and Antonia come with me to negotiate with Mustang at the gate. I limp up and favor a cracked rib. It hurts to breathe. Roque takes a step back so that I am most prominent when we reach the gate itself. Antonia wrinkles her nose and eventually does the same. Mustang is bloody from the skirmish and I can't find a smile on her pretty face.

"The Proctors have been watching all of this," she says scathingly. "They've seen what happened in that . . . place. Everything—"

"Was done by Titus," Antonia drawls tiredly.

"And no one else?" Mustang looks at me. "The girls won't stop crying."

"No one died," Antonia says in annoyance. "Weak as they are, they will repair themselves. Despite what happened, there's been no depletion of Golden stock."

"The Golden stock . . . ," Mustang murmurs. "How can you be so cold?"

"Little girl," Antonia sighs, "Gold is a cold metal."

Mustang looks up at Antonia incredulously and then shakes her head. "*Mars*. A gruesome deity. You're fit for this, aren't you lot? Barbarity? Past centuries. Dark ages."

I don't have a mind to be lectured by an Aureate about morality.

"We would like you to leave the castle," I tell her. "Do so with your men and you may have those we captured. We won't turn them into slaves."

Down the hill, Sevro stands beside the captives with our standard in hand; he's tickling a disgruntled Pax with a horse hair.

Mustang jams a finger into my face.

"This is a school. You realize that, yes? No matter the rules your House decides to play by. Be ruthless all you gorywell like. But there are limits. There are slagging limits to what you can do in this school, in the game. The more brutal you are, the more foolish you look to the Proctors, to the adults who will know what you've done—what you're capable of doing. You think they want monsters to lead the Society? Who would want a monster for an apprentice?"

I see a vision of Augustus watching my wife dangle, eyes dead as a pitviper's. A monster would want a student in his own image.

"They want visionaries. Leaders of men. Not reapers of them. There are limits," she continues.

I snap. "There are no goddamned limits."

Mustang's jaw tightens. She understands how this will play out. In the end, giving us back our horrible castle won't cost her anything; trying to keep it would. She might even end up like one of the girls in the high tower. She never thought of that before. I can tell she wants to leave. It's her sense of justice that is killing her. Somehow she thinks we should pay, that the Proctors should come down and interfere. Most of the kids think that about this game; hell, Cassius said it a hundred times as we scouted together. But the game isn't like that, because life isn't like that. Gods don't come down in life to mete out justice. The powerful do it. That's what they are teaching us, not only the pain in gaining power, but the desperation that comes from not having it, the desperation that comes when you are not a Gold.

"We will keep the Ceres slaves," Mustang demands.

"No, they are ours," I drawl. "And we will do with them what we like."

She watches me for a long moment, thinking.

"Then we get Titus."

"No."

Mustang snaps. "We *will* keep Titus or there are no terms."

"You will keep no one."

She's not used to being told no.

"I want assurances they are safe. I want Titus to pay."

"It doesn't matter a flying piss what you want. Here you get what you take. That's part of the lesson plan." I pull out my slingBlade and set its tip into the soil. "Titus is of House Mars. He is ours. So please, try and take him."

"He'll be brought to justice," Roque says to Mustang to reassure her.

I turn to him, eyes blazing. "Shut up."

He looks down, knowing he should not have spoken. It doesn't matter. Mustang's eyes don't look to Antonia or Roque. They don't look down the slope where Lea and Cipio have her warband on their knees in the glen, and Thistle sits on Pax's back with Weed, taking their turn tickling him now. Her eyes don't look at the blade. They are only for me. I lean in.

"If Titus raped a little girl who happened to be a Red, how would you feel?" I ask.

She doesn't know how to answer. The Law does. Nothing would happen. It isn't rape unless she wears the sigil of an elder House like Augustus. Even then, the crime is against her master.

"Now look around," I say quietly. "There are no Golds here. I'm a Red. You're a Red. We are all Reds till one of us gets enough power. Then we get rights. Then we make our own law." I lean back and raise my voice. "That is the point of all this. To make you terrified of a world where you do not rule. Security and justice aren't given. They are made by the strong."

"You should hope that is not true," Mustang says quietly to me.

"Why?"

"Because there is a boy here like you." Her face takes on a gloomy aspect, as though she regrets what she must say. "My Proctor calls him the Jackal. He is smarter and crueler and stronger than you, and he will win this game and make us his slaves if the rest of us go about acting like animals." Her eyes implore me. "So please, hurry up and evolve."

28

MY BROTHER

I pretend the matches came from one of the Minervans when I light our first fire inside castle Mars. June is fetched from her makeshift prison, and soon she has prepared us a feast from the meat of goats and sheep and herbs gathered by my tribe. My tribe pretends it's the first meal they've had in weeks. The others of the House are hungry enough to believe the lie. Minerva and her warband have long since slunk on home.

"What now?" I ask Roque as the others eat in the square. The keep is a place of squalor still, and the light of the fire does nothing but illuminate the filth. Cassius has gone to see Quinn, so I am alone for the moment with Roque.

Titus's tribe sits in quiet groups. The girls will not speak to the boys because of what they've seen some of them do. All eat with their heads down. There's shame there. Antonia's people sit with mine and glare at Titus's. Disgust fills their eyes. Betrayal too, even as they fill their bellies. Several scuffles have already escalated from minor words to thrown fists. I thought the victory might bring them together. But it did not. The division is worse than ever, only now I cannot define it and I think there is only one way to mend it.

Roque doesn't have the answer I want to hear.

"The Proctors aren't interfering, because they want to see how and if we handle justice, Darrow. It is the deeper trait that this situation probes. How do we manage Law?"

"Brilliant," I say. "So what? We're supposed to whip Titus? Kill him? That would be Law."

"Would it? Or would it just be vengeance?"

"You're the poet. You figure it out." I kick a stone off the ramparts.

"He can't stay tied up in the cellars. You know this. We will never move on from this torpor if he does, and it has to be you who decides what to do with him."

"Not Cassius?" I ask. "I think he's earned a say. After all, he did claim him." I don't want Cassius to share leadership, but I don't want him to come out of the Institute without any prospects. I owe him.

"Claim him?" Roque coughs. "And how barbaric does *that* sound?"

"So Cassius should play no role?"

"I love him like a brother, but no." Roque's narrow face tenses as he sets a hand on my arm. "Cassius cannot lead this House. Not after what happened. Titus's boys and girls might obey him, but they won't respect him. They won't think him stronger than them, even if he is. Darrow, they *pissed* on him. We are Golds. We do not forget."

He's right.

I pull my hair in frustration and glare at Roque as though he were being difficult.

"You don't understand how much this means to Cassius. After Julian's death . . . He has to succeed. He cannot be remembered solely for what happened. He can't."

Why do I care so much?

"Doesn't matter a flying piss how much it means to him," Roque echoes my words with a smile. His fingers are thin like hay on my bicep. "They'll never fear him."

Fear is necessary here. And Cassius knows it. Why else is he absent in victory? Antonia has not left my side. Pollux, the gate opener, hasn't either. They linger several meters away to associate with my power. Sevro and Thistle watch them with sly grins.

"Is that why you're here too, you scheming weasel?" I ask Roque. "Sharing the glory?"

He shrugs and gnaws on the leg of mutton Lea brings him.

"Slag that. I'm here for the food."

I find Titus in the cellar. The Minervans tied him and beat him bloody after they saw the slave girls in his tower. That's their justice. He smiles as I stand over him.

"How many of House Ceres did you kill in your raids?" I ask.

"Suck my balls." He spits bloody phlegm. I dodge.

I resist kicking him there, barely. Already got Pax for the day. Titus has the gall to ask what has happened.

"I rule House Mars now."

"Outsourced your dirty work to the Minervans, eh? Didn't want to face me? Typical Golden coward."

I am afraid of him. I don't know why. Yet I bend on a knee and stare him in the eye.

"You are a pissing fool, Titus. You never evolved. Never got past the first test. You thought this whole thing is about violence and killing. Idiot. It's about civilization, not war. To have an army, you must first have a civilization—you went straight to violence like they wanted us to. Why do you think they gave us of Mars nothing and the other Houses have so many resources? We're meant to fight like mad, but we're meant to burn out like you did. But I beat that test. Now I'm the hero. Not the usurper. And you're just the ogre in the dungeon."

"Oh, huzzah. Huzzah!" He tries clapping his bound hands. "I don't give a piss."

"How many did you kill?" I ask.

"Not enough." He tilts his large head. His hair is greasy and dark with dirt, almost as though he's tried to black out the gold. He seems to like the dirt. It's under his fingernails, coats his burnished skin. "I tried to bash their heads in. Kill them before the medBots came. But they were always so fast."

"Why did you want to kill them? I don't understand what the point is. They are your own people."

He smirks at this. "You could have changed things, you bastard." His large eyes are calmer, sadder than I remember. He does not like himself, I realize. Something about him is too mournful. The pride I thought he had is not pride; it is just scorn. "You say I'm cruel, but you had matches and iodine. Don't think I didn't know even before I smelled you. We starved, and you used what you found to become leader. So do not lecture me on morality, you backstabbing piss-sucker."

"Then why didn't you do something about it?"

"Pollux and Vixus were frightened of you. So the rest were too. And they thought Goblin would kill them in their sleep. What could I do if I was the only one who wasn't scared?"

"Why aren't you?"

He laughs hard. "You're just a boy with a slingBlade. First I thought you were hard. Thought we saw things similarly." He licks a bloody lip. "Thought you were like me, only worse because of that coldness in your eyes. But you're not cold. You care about these piss-pricks."

My eyebrows pinch together. "How's that?"

"Simple. You made friends. Roque. Cassius. Lea. Quinn."

"So did you. Pollux, Cassandra, Vixus."

Titus's face contorts horribly. *"Friends?"* he spits. "Friends with *them*? Those Goldbrows? They are monsters, soulless bastards. Nothing but a bunch of cannibals, all of them. They did the same as I did, but . . . *pfah*."

"I still don't understand why you did what you did to the slaves," I say. "Rape, Titus. Rape."

His face is quiet and cruel. "They did it first."

"Who?"

But he's not listening. Suddenly he's telling me about how they took "her" and raped "her" in front of him. Then the slaggers came back a week later to do it some more. So he killed them; bashed their heads in. "I killed the bloodydamn monsters. Now their daughters bloodywell get what she got."

It's like I've been punched in the face.

Oh hell.

A chill spreads through me.

Bloodydamn.

I stumble back.

"What the hell is the matter with you?" Titus asks. If I were a Gold, I might have not noticed, might've just been befuddled by the odd word. I'm no Gold. "Darrow?"

I pull my way into the hall. I move in a haze. It all makes sense. The hate. The disgust. The vengeance. Cannibals eat their own. He called them cannibals. Pollux, Cassandra, Vixus—who are their own? *Their* own. Golden. *Bloodydamn.* Not *gory.* Titus said *bloodydamn.* No Gold says that. Ever. And he called it a slingBlade, not a reaper's scythe.

Oh hell.

Titus is a Red.

29

UNITY

Titus is what Dancer did not want me to become. He is like Harmony. He is a creature of vengeance. A rebellion with Titus at the helm would fail in weeks. Worse, if Titus continues this way, continues unstably, he puts me at risk. Dancer lied, or else he did not know that there are other Reds who've been carved, other Reds who have donned the mask of the Golds. How many more are there? How many has Ares planted here, in the Society? In the Institute? It doesn't matter if it is a thousand or just one. Titus's instability puts every Red ever carved into a Gold at risk. He puts Eo's dream at risk. And that is something I cannot abide. Eo did not die so that Titus can kill a few kids.

I sob in the armory as I resolve what must be done.

More blood will stain these hands, because Titus is a mad dog and must be put down.

In the morning, I pull him into the square in front of the House. They clear away the remnants of the night's feast. I even have the slaves there to watch. A few Proctors flicker high above. There is no medBot floating beside them, which must stand as their silent consent.

I push Titus down on the ground in front of his former tribe. They watch quietly, mist hanging in the air above them, nervous feet scraping the cold cobblestones of the courtyard. A chill seeps into my hands through the durosteel of my slingBlade.

"For crimes of rape, mutilation, and attempted murder of fellow House members, I sentence Titus au Ladros to death." I list the reasons. "Does anyone contest my right to do so?" First, I glance to the Proctors above. Not one makes a sound.

I stare at cruel Vixus. His bruise is not yet gone. My eyes go to Cassandra next. I even look at craggy Pollux, the one who saved Cassius and opened the gates for us. He stands by Roque. How loyalties shift here.

How my own shift. I will make a Red die because he killed Golds. He dug the earth like me. He has a soul like mine. In death, it will go to the vale, but in life he was stupid and selfish with his grief. He should have been better than this. Reds are better than him, aren't we?

Titus's tribe stays silent; their guilt is bound up with their leader. When he goes, it'll go. That is what I tell myself. Everything will be well.

"I contest the sentence," Titus says. "And issue a challenge to you, turdlicker."

"I accept, *goodman*." I bow curtly.

"Then a duel per custom of the Order of the Sword," Roque announces.

"I choose then," Titus says, eyeing my slingBlade. "Straight blades. Nothing curved."

"As you have it," I say, but as I step forward, I feel a hand at my elbow and feel my friend come close behind.

"Darrow, he is mine," Cassius whispers coldly. "*Remember?*" I make no sign of acknowledgment. "Please, Darrow. Let me honor House Bellona."

I look to Roque; he shakes his head "No." As does Quinn, who stands behind Cassius. But I am leader here. And I did promise my friend, who now recognizes my ascendance. He requests instead of demands, and so I make a show of considering and then accepting his request. I stand aside as Cassius steps forward with a straight blade held in his fencer's grip. It is an ugly weapon, but he's sharpened it on stones.

"The little prince," Titus snickers. "Wonderful. I'll be happy to drench your corpse with piss again when we're through."

Titus is meant for brawls. Meant for muddy battlefields and civil wars. I wonder if he knows how easily he will die today.

Roque draws a circle in ash around the two combatants. Clown and Screwface walk out with arms full of weapons. Titus picks a long broadsword he took from a Ceres soldier five days before. The metal scrapes over stone. Echoes around the courtyard. He swings it once, twice to test the metal. Cassius does not move.

"Pissing your pants already?" Titus asks. "No fretting, I'll be quick about it."

Roque performs the necessities and commences the fight.

Cassius is not quick about it.

The ugly blades sound brittle against each other. The clangs are harsh. The blades chip. They grind. But how silent they are when they find flesh.

The only sound is Titus's gasp.

"You killed Julian," Cassius says quietly. "Julian au Bellona of House Bellona."

He pulls his blade free of Titus's leg and slides it in somewhere else. He rips it out.

Titus laughs and swings feebly. It is pathetic at this point.

"You killed Julian." A thrust accompanies the words, words he repeats until I no longer watch. "You killed Julian." But Titus is long dead. Tears stream down Quinn's face. Roque takes her and Lea away. My army is silent. Thistle spits on the cobbles and puts her arm over Pebble's shoulders. Clown looks even more dejected than usual. Even the Proctors make no comment. It is Cassius's rage that fills the courtyard, a cruel lament for a kind brother. He said he did it for justice, for the honor of his family and House. But this is revenge, and how hollow it seems.

I grow cold.

This was meant for me. Not for my poor brother, Titus—if that was ever really his name. He deserved better than this.

I'm going to cry. The anger and sadness well in my chest as I push through the army. Roque looks at me when I pass him. His face is like a corpse's.

"That wasn't justice," he murmurs without looking me in the eyes.

I failed the test. He's right. It wasn't justice. Justice is dispassionate; it is fair. I am the leader. I passed the sentence. I should have done it. Instead, I gave license to vengeance and vendetta. The cancer will not be cut away; I made it worse.

"At least Cassius is feared again," Roque mutters. "But that's the only thing you got right."

Poor Titus. I bury him in a grove near the river. I hope it speeds him on his way to the vale.

That night I do not sleep.

I don't know if it was his wife or his sister or his mother they hurt. I do not know what mine he came from. His pain is my own. His pain broke him as mine broke me on the scaffold. But I was given a second chance. Where was his?

I hope his pain fades in death. I did not love him till he was dead; and he should be dead, but he is still my brother. So I pray he finds peace in the vale and that I will see him again one day and we'll embrace as brothers as he forgives me for what I did to him, because I did it for a dream, for our people.

My name, three bars beside it now, floats nearer the Primus hand.

Cassius has risen too.

But there can be only one Primus.

Since I cannot sleep, I take the guard shift from Cassandra. Mist curls around the battlements, so we tie sheep around the walls. They will bleat if an enemy comes. I smell something strange, rich and smoky.

"Roast duck?" I turn and find Fitchner standing beside me. His hair is messy over his narrow brow and he wears no golden armor today, only a black tunic striped with gold. He hands me a piece of duck. The smell makes my stomach rumble.

"We should all be pissed at you," I say.

His face is one of surprise. "Tots who say that usually mean to explain why they are not pissed."

"You and the Proctors can see everything, yes?"

"Even when you wipe your ass."

"And you didn't stop Titus, because it's all part of the curriculum."

"The real question is why we did not stop you."

"From killing him."

"Yes, little one. He would have been valuable in the military, don't you think? Perhaps not as a Praetor with ships in the ink. But what a Legate he would have made, leading men in starShells through enemy gates as fire rained down against their pulseShields. Have you ever seen an Iron Rain? Where men are launched from orbit to take cities? He was meant for that."

I do not answer.

Fitchner wipes grease from his lips with the black sleeve of his tunic.

"Life is the most effective school ever created. Once upon a time they made children bow their heads and read books. It would take ages to get anything across." He taps his head. "But we have widgets and datapads now, and we Golds have the lower Colors to do our research. We need not study chemistry or physics. We have computers and others to do that. What we must study is humanity. In order to rule, ours must be the study of political, psychological, and behavioral science—how desperate human beings react to one another, how packs form, how armies function, how things fall apart and why. You could learn this nowhere else but here."

"No, I understand the purpose," I murmur. "I learn more when I make mistakes, so long as they don't kill me." How well I learned from trying to be a martyr.

"Good. You make plenty of them. You're an impulsive little turd. But this is the place to frag up. To learn. This is life . . . but with medBots, second chances, artificial scenarios. You might have guessed that the first test, the Passage, was the measurement of necessity versus emotion. The second was tribal strife. Then there was a bit of justice. Now there will be more tests. More second chances, more lessons learned."

"How many of us can die?" I ask suddenly.

"Don't worry about that."

"How many."

"There is a limit set each year by the Board of Quality Control, but we're well within the bounds despite what happened with the Jackal." Fitchner smiles.

"The Jackal . . . ," I say. "Is that what happened the other night when the medBots blitzed south?"

"Did I say his name? Oops." He grins. "I mean to say that the medBots are very effective. They heal nearly all wounds. But will they be so effective when Cassius finds out who really killed his brother?"

My stomach tightens.

"He already killed Julian's murderer. Apparently you weren't watching."

"Of course. Of course. Mercury thinks you brilliant. Apollo thinks you're uppity. He really does not like you, you know."

"I could give a piss."

"Oh, you should care much more than that. Apollo's a peach."

"Right. So what do you think? You are my Proctor."

"I think you are an ancient soul." He watches me and leans against the rampart. The night is misty beyond the castle. From its depths, a wolf howls. "I think you're like that beast out there. Part of a pack but deeply sad, deeply alone. And I can't puzzle out why, my dear boy. This is all so much fun! Enjoy it! Life doesn't get better."

"You're the same," I say. "Lonely. You're all japes and snide comments, just like Sevro, but it's just a mask. It's because you don't look like the others, isn't it? Or are you poor? Somehow you're an outsider."

"My looks?" He barks a laugh. "What does that matter? Think

I'm a *Bronzie* because I'm not an Adonis?" He leans forward, because he really does care about what I'm going to say.

"You are ugly and you eat like a pig, Fitchner, but you chew metabolizers when you could just go to a Carver and fix yourself to look like the others. They could take care of that paunch in a second."

Fitchner's jaw muscle flickers. Is it anger?

"Why should I have to visit a Carver?" he hisses suddenly. "I can kill an Obsidian with my bare hands. An Obsidian. I can outwit a Silver in parlance and negotiation. I can do math Greens only dream of. Why should I make myself look any different?"

"Because it is what holds you back."

"Despite my low birth, I am of note. I am important." His hatchet face dares me to contradict. "I am Gold. I am a king of man. I do not change to suit others."

"If that's true, why do you chew metabolizers?" He does not answer. "And why are you only a Proctor?"

"Becoming a Proctor is a position of prestige, boy," Fitchner snaps. "The Drafters voted me to represent the House."

"Yet you're no Imperator. You lead no fleets. You're not even a Praetor in command of a squadron. Nor are you any sort of Governor. How many men can do the things you say you can do?"

"Few," he says very quietly, face all anger. "Very few." He looks up. "What is the bounty you desire for capturing the Minervan standard?"

"Isn't that Sevro's deal?" I say, understanding the conversation is nearing its end.

"He has passed it to you."

I ask for horses and weapons and matches. He agrees curtly and turns to leave before I can ask him one last question. I grab his arm as he starts to ascend. Something happens. My nerves fry. Like needles in acid through my hand and arm. I gasp. My lungs can't function for a second.

"Goryhell," I cough out, and fall to the ground. He wears pulseArmor. I can't even see the generator. It's like a pulseShield, but inlaid in the armor itself.

He waits without a smile.

"The Jackal," I say. "You mentioned him. The Minervan girl mentioned him. Who is he?"

"He's the ArchGovernor's son, Darrow. And he makes Titus look like a blubbering child."

Large horses graze in the fields the next morning. Wolves try to take down a small mare. A pale stallion trots up and kicks one of the wolves to death. I claim him. The others call him Quietus. It means "the final stroke."

He reminds me of the Pegasus that saved Andromeda. The songs we sang in Lykos spoke of horses. I know Eo would have liked a chance to ride one.

I do not realize till days later that when they named my horse Quietus, they were mocking me for my part in Titus's death.

30

HOUSE DIANA

A month passes. In the wake of Titus's death, House Mars becomes stronger. The strength comes not from the highDrafts but from the dregs, from my tribe and the midDrafts. I have outlawed the abuse of slaves. The Ceres slaves, though still skittish around Vixus and a few of the others, provide our food and fires; they are good for little else. Fifty goats and sheep have been gathered in the castle in case of a siege; so too has firewood been stockpiled. But we have no water. The pumps to the washroom shut off after the first day, and we have no buckets to store water inside in case of a siege. I doubt it was an accident.

We hammer shields into basins and use helmets to bring water from the river glen below our high castle. We cut down trees and carve them hollow to make troughs in which to store the water. Stones are pulled up and a well is dug, but we cannot dig far enough to get past the mud. Instead, we line the well with stone and timber and try to use it as a tank for water. It always leaks. So we have our troughs, and that is it. We cannot let ourselves be besieged.

The keep is cleaner.

After seeing what happened to Titus, I ask Cassius to teach me the blade. I'm an unreasonably fast study. I learn with a straight. I never use my slingBlade; it already is like part of my body. And the point is not to learn how to use the straight blade, which is much like the razors, but to learn how it will be used against me. I also do not want Cassius to learn how to fight the curved blade. If he ever finds out about Julian, the curve is my only hope.

I am not as proficient in Kravat. I can't do the kicks. I learn how to break tracheas, though. And I learn how to properly use my hands. No more windmill punches. No more foolish defense. I am deadly and fast, but I do not like the discipline Kravat requires. I want to be an efficient fighter. That is all. Kravat seems intent on teaching me inner peace. That is a lost cause.

Yet now I hold my hands like Cassius, like Julian, in the air, elbows at eye level so I am always striking or blocking downward. Sometimes Cassius will mention Julian and I will feel the darkness rise. I think of the Proctors watching and laughing about this; I must look like an evil, manipulative thing.

I forget that Cassius, Roque, Sevro, and I are enemies. Red and Gold. I forget that one day I might have to kill them all. They call me brother, and I cannot but think of them in the same way.

The battle with House Minerva has broken down into a series of warband skirmishes, neither side gaining enough advantage over the other to ever score a decisive victory. Mustang will not risk the pitched battle that I want, nor can they really be goaded. They are not so easily tempted as my soldiers are to bouts of glory or violence.

Still the Minervans are desperate to capture me. Pax turns into a madman when he sees me. Mustang even tried offering Antonia, or so Antonia claims, a mutual defense compact, a dozen horses, six stunpikes, and seven slaves in exchange for me. I don't know if she is lying when she tells me this.

"You would betray me in a heartbeat if it got you to Primus," I tell her.

"Yes," she says irritably, as I interrupt her fastidious nail maintenance. "But since you expect it, it shan't really be a betrayal, darling."

"Then why didn't you accept the offer?"

"Oh, the dregs look up to you. It would be disastrous at this point. Maybe after you have failed at something, yes, maybe then when momentum is against you."

"Or you're waiting for a higher price."

"Exactly, darling."

Neither of us mentions Sevro. I know she's still afraid he'll cut her throat if she touches me. He follows me now, wearing his wolfskin. Sometimes he walks. Sometimes he rides a small black mare. He does not like armor. Wolves approach him at random, as though he were one of their own pack. They come to eat deer he kills because they've grown hungry as we lock away the goats and sheep. Pebble always leaves them food at the walls whenever we slaughter a beast. She watches them like a child as they come in fours and threes.

"I killed their pack leader," Sevro says when I ask why the wolves follow him. He looks me up and down and flashes me an impish grin from beneath the wolf pelt. "Don't worry, I wouldn't fit in your skin."

I've given Sevro the dregs to command because I know they might be the only people he'll ever like. At first he ignores them. Then slowly, I begin noticing that more unearthly howls fill the night than before. The others call them the Howlers, and after a few nights under Sevro's tutelage, each wears a black wolfcloak. There are six: Sevro, Thistle, Screwface, Clown, Pebble, and Weed. When you look at them, it seems as though each of their passive faces stares out from the open, fanged maw of a wolf. I use them for quiet tasks. Without them, I'm not sure I would still be leader. My soldiers whisper slurs about me as I pass. The old wounds have not healed.

I need a victory, but Mustang will not meet in combat, and the thirty-meter walls of House Minerva are not as easy to pass as they were initially. In our warroom, Sevro paces back and forth and calls the game stupidly designed.

"They had to know we couldn't gorywell get past each other's walls. And no one is dumb enough to send out a force they can't afford to lose. Especially not Mustang. Pax might. He's an idiot, built like a god, but an idiot and he wants your balls. I hear you popped one of his."

"Both."

"Should just put Pebble or Goblin in a catapult and launch them over the wall," Cassius suggests. "Course we'd have to find a catapult . . ."

I'm tired of this war with Mustang. Somewhere in the south or west, the Jackal is building his strength. Somewhere my enemy, the ArchGovernor's son, is readying to destroy me.

"We are looking at this the wrong way," I tell Sevro, Quinn, Roque, and Cassius. They're alone with me in the warroom. An autumn breeze brings in the smell of dying leaves.

"Oh, do share your wisdom," Cassius says with a laugh. He's lying on several chairs, his head in Quinn's lap. She plays with his hair. "We're dying to hear."

"This is a school that has existed for, what, more than three hundred years? So every permutation has been seen. Every problem we face has been designed to be overcome. Sevro, you say the fortresses cannot be taken? Well, the Proctors have to know that. So that means we have to change the paradigm. We need an alliance."

"Against whom?" Sevro asks. "Hypothetically."

"Against Minerva," Roque answers.

"Stupid idea," Sevro grunts, and cleans a knife and slides it into his black sleeve. "Their castle is tactically inconsequential. No value. None. The land we need is near the river."

"Think we need Ceres's ovens?" Quinn asks. "I could do with some bread."

We all could. A diet of meat and berries has made us muscle and bones.

"If the game lasts through winter, yeah." Sevro pops his knuckles. "But these fortresses don't break. Stupid game. So we need their bread and their access to the water."

"We have water," Cassius reminds him.

Sevro sighs in frustration. "We have to leave the castle to get it, Sir Numbnuts. A real siege? We'd last five days without replenishing our water. Seven if we drank the animals' blood like Morgdy. We need Ceres's fortress. Also, the harvest pricks can't fight to save their lives, but they have something in there."

"Harvest pricks? Hahaha," Cassius crows.

"Stop talking, everyone," I say. They don't. To them this is fun. It is a game. They have no urgency, no desperate need. Every moment we waste is a moment the Jackal builds his strength. Something in the way Mustang and Fitchner talked about him scares me. Or is it the fact that he is the son of my enemy? I should want to kill him; instead, I want to run and hide at the thought of his name.

It's a sign of my fading leadership that I have to stand up.

"Quiet!" I say, and finally they are.

"We've seen fires on the horizon. War consumes the South where the Jackal roams."

Cassius chuckles at the idea of the Jackal. He thinks him a ghost I conjured up.

"Will you stop laughing at everything?" I snap at Cassius. "It's not a gorydamn joke, unless you think your brother died for amusement."

That shuts him up.

"Before we do anything else," I stress, "we must eliminate House Minerva and Mustang."

"Mustang. Mustang. Mustang. I think you just want to snake Mustang," Sevro sneers. Quinn makes a sound of objection.

I snatch Sevro's collar and lift him up into the air with one hand. He tries to dart away, but he's not as fast as me, so he dangles from my grip, two feet off the ground.

"Not again," I say, lowering him nearer my face.

"Registers, Reap." His beady eyes are inches from my own. "Off limits." I set him down and he straightens his collar. "So, it's to the Greatwoods for this alliance, right?"

"Yes."

"Then it's to be a merry quest!" Cassius declares, sitting up. "We'll be a troop!"

"No. Just me and Goblin. You aren't going," I say.

"I'm bored, I think I'll come with."

"You're staying," I say. "I need you here."

"Is that an order?" he asks.

"Yes," Sevro says.

Cassius stares at me. "*You* giving *me* orders?" he says in a strange way. "Perhaps you've forgotten that I go where I want."

"So you'll leave control to Antonia while we both go risk our necks?" I ask.

Quinn's hand tightens on his forearm. She thinks I don't notice. Cassius looks back at her and smiles. "Of course, Reaper. Of course I'll stay here. Just as you've *suggested*."

Sevro and I make camp in the southern highlands within view of the Greatwoods. We do not light a fire. Our scouts and others roam these hills at night. I see two horses on a far hill, silhouetted against the setting sun behind the bubbleroof. The way the sun catches on the roof makes sunsets of purples and reds and pinks; it reminds me of the streets in Yorkton as seen from the sky. Then it is gone and Sevro and I sit in darkness.

Sevro thinks this is a stupid game.

"Then why do you play it?" I ask.

"How was I to know what it'd be like? Think I got a pamphlet? Did you get a slagging pamphlet?" he asks irritably. He's picking his teeth with a bone. "Stupid."

Yet he seemed to know on the shuttle what the Passage was. I tell him that.

"I didn't."

"And you seem to have every gory skill required for this school."

"So? If your mother was good in bed, you suppose she's a Pink? Everyone adapts."

"Lovely," I mutter.

He tells me to cut to the point of it.

"You snuck into the keep and stole our standard and buried it. Saving it. And then you managed to steal Minerva's piece. Yet you don't get a single bar of merit for Primus. Doesn't strike you as odd?"

"No."

"Be serious."

"What should I say? I've never been liked." He shrugs. "I wasn't born pretty and tall like you and your buttboy, Cassius. I had to fight for what I want. That doesn't make me likeable. Just makes me a nasty little Goblin."

I tell him what I've heard. He was the last one drafted. Fitchner didn't want him, but the Drafters insisted. Sevro watches me in the dark. He doesn't speak.

"You were picked because you were the smallest boy. The weakest-looking. Terrible scores and so small. They drafted you like they drafted all the other lowDrafts, because you'd be easy to kill in the Passage. A sacrificial lamb for someone they had plans for, big plans. You killed Priam, Sevro. That's why they won't let you be Primus. Am I on target?"

"You're on target. I killed him like I'd kill a pretty dog. Quick. Easy." He spits the bone onto the ground. "And you killed Julian. *Am I on target?*"

We never speak of the Passage again.

In the morning, we leave the highlands behind for the foothills. Trees intersperse with grass. We move at a gallop in case Minerva's warbands are near. I see one in the distance as we reach the trees. They didn't see us. Far to the south, the sky is smoke. Crows gather over the Jackal's domain.

I would like to say more to Sevro, ask about his life. But his gaze penetrates too deep. I don't want him to ask about me, to see through me as easily as I saw through Titus. It is strange. This boy likes me. He insults me, but he likes me. Even stranger, I desperately want him to like me. Why? I think it is because I feel as though he is the only one, including Roque and Cassius, who understands life. He is ugly in a world where he should be beautiful, and because of his deficiencies, he was chosen to die. He, in many ways, is no better than a Red.

I want to tell him I'm a Red. Some part of me thinks he is too. And some other part of me thinks he'll respect me more if he knows I am a Red. I was not born privileged. I am like him. But I guard my tongue; there's no doubt the Proctors watch us.

Quietus does not like the woods. At first the shrubbery is so thick that we must cut our way forward with our swords. But soon the shrubbery thins and we enter the realm of godTrees. Little else can exist here. The colossuses block the light, their roots stretching up like tentacles to sap the energy from the soil as they grow tall as buildings. I am in a city again, one where animals bustle and tree trunks instead of metal and concrete obstruct my view. Then, as we venture deeper into the woods, I'm reminded of my mine—dark and cramped beneath the boughs, as though there is no sky or sun.

Autumn leaves the size of my chest crinkle underfoot. I know we are being watched. Sevro does not like this. He wants to slink away to find the eyes at our backs.

"That would defeat the purpose," I tell him.

"That would defeat the purpose," he mocks.

We break for a lunch of pillaged olives and goat meat. The eyes in the trees think I'm too stupid to shift my paradigm, as though I would never suppose they'd hide above me instead of on the ground. Yet I don't look up. No need to frighten the idiots or let them know I know their game; I'll have to conquer them soon, if I still am the leader of my House. I wonder if they have ropes to traverse the trees. Or are the limbs wide enough?

Sevro still itches to pull out his knives and scale one of the trees. I shouldn't have brought him. He's not meant for diplomacy.

At last someone chooses to speak at me.

"Hello, Mars," one says. Other voices echo it to my right. Stupid children. Should have saved their tricks for the night. It would be miserable in these woods in the dark, voices coming from all around. Something startles the horses. The goddess Diana's animals are the bear, the boar, and the deer. We brought spears for the first two. There are supposed to be huge bloodbacks in these woods—monstrous bears made by Carvers because, most likely, the Carvers grew bored of making deerlings. We hear the bloodbacks roaring in the deeper parts of the wood. I settle Quietus.

"My name is Darrow, leader of House Mars. I'm here to meet with your Primus, if you have one. If you don't, your leader will suffice. And if you don't have one of those either, take me to whoever has the biggest balls."

Silence.

"Thank you for your assistance," Sevro calls out.

I raise an eyebrow at him, and he just shrugs. The silence is silly. It is to make me think they aren't taking orders from me. They do things on their own schedule. What big boys and girls they are. Then two tall girls come from behind a distant tree. They wear fatigues the color of the woods. Bows hang from their backs. Knives in their boots. I think one has a knife in her coiled hair. They've used the berries of the woods to paint the hunting moon on their faces. Animal pelts dangle from their belts.

I do not look like war. I have washed my hair till it shines. My face is clean, wounds covered, the tears in my black fatigues stitched. I even washed out the sweat stains with sand and animal fat. I look, as Quinn and Lea both confirmed, devilishly handsome. I do not want House Diana intimidated. That's why I let Sevro come. He looks ridiculous and childish, so long as his knives are kept away.

These two girls smirk at Sevro and can't help but soften their eyes when they see me. More come down. They take most of our weapons—those they can find. And they throw furs over our faces so we cannot know the way to their fortress. I count the steps. Sevro counts too. The furs stink of rot. I hear woodpeckers and I remember Fitchner's prank. We must be close, so I stumble and fall to the ground. No shrubbery. We're spun around again, then led away from the woodpeckers. At first I'm worried that these hunters are smarter than I gave them credit for. Then I realize they are not. Woodpeckers again.

"Hey, Tamara, we got him down here!"

"Don't bring them up, you chowderheads!" a girl shouts. "We're not letting them have a free scouting party. *How many times do I* . . . Just wait. I'll come down."

They walk me somewhere and shove me against a tree.

A boy speaks over my shoulder. His voice is slow and languid, like a drifting knife blade. "I say we peel their balls off."

"Shut up, Tactus. Just make them slaves, Tamara. There isn't diplomacy here."

"Look at his blade. Fragging reaper scythe."

"Ah, so that's him," someone says.

"I claim his blade when we decide spoils. I'd also like his scalp, if no one else has intentions on it." Tactus sounds like a very unpleasant boy.

"Shut up. All of you," a girl snaps. "Tactus, put that knife away."

They take the fur from my head. I stand with Sevro in a small grove of trees. I see no castle but I can hear the woodpeckers. I look around and receive a sharp strike to the head from a lean, wiry youth with bored eyes and bronze hair spiked up with sap and red berry juice. His skin is dark like oak honey and his high cheekbones and deep-set eyes give him a look of permanent derision.

"So, you're who they call the *Reaper,*" Tactus drawls. He swings my blade experimentally. "Well, you just look too pretty to be much damage at all."

"Is he flirting with me?" I ask the Tamara girl.

"Tactus, go away! Thank you, but now go away," says the thin, hawkish girl. Her hair is shorter than mine. Three large boys flank her. The way they glare at Tactus confirms my judgment of his character.

"Reaper, why are you with a pygmy?" Tactus asks, gesturing to Sevro. "Does he shine your shoes? Pick things out of your hair?" He chuckles to the other boys. "Maybe a butler?"

"Go away, Tactus!" Tamara snarls.

"Of course," Tactus bows. "I shall go play with the other children, Mother." He tosses the blade to the ground and winks at me like we alone know the joke that's about to be played.

"Sorry about that," Tamara says. "He's not quite polite."

"It's fine," I say.

"I am Tamara of . . . I almost said my real family," she laughs. "Of Diana."

"And they are?" I ask about the boys.

"My bodyguard. And you are . . ." She holds up a finger. "Let me guess. Let me guess. *Reaper*. Oh, we've heard of you. House Minerva doesn't like you at all."

Sevro snorts at my infamy.

"And he is?" she asks with raised eyebrows.

"*My* bodyguard."

"*Bodyguard?* But he is so very short!"

"And you look like—" Sevro growls.

"So are wolves," I reply, interrupting Sevro midcurse.

"We're more afraid of Jackals here than wolves."

Maybe Cassius should have come along, just to know I'm not making the bastard up. I ask her about the Jackal, but she ignores my question.

"Help me out here," Tamara says cordially. "If someone were to say that Reaper of the butcher House would come to my glade and ask for diplomacy, I would think it a Proctor's joke. So, what do you really want?"

"House Minerva off my back."

"So you can come here and fight us instead?" one of her bodyguards growls.

I turn to Tamara with a reasonable smile and tell her the truth. "I want Minerva off my back so I can come here and beat you, sure." And then win the stupid game and destroy your civilization, please.

They laugh.

"Well, you're honest. But not too bright, so it seems. Fitting. Let me tell you something, Reaper. Our Proctor says your House has not won in years. Why? Because you butchers are like a wildfire. In the early stages of the game, you burn everything you touch. You destroy. You consume. You ruin Houses because you can't sustain yourselves. But then you starve because there is nothing more to burn. The sieges. The winter. The advance in technology. It kills your bloodlust, your famous rage. So tell me, why would I shake hands with a wildfire when I can just sit back and watch it run out of things to consume?"

I nod and dangle the bait.

"Fire can be useful."

"Explain."

"We may starve while you watch, but will you watch as a slave of some other House? Or will you watch from your strong fortress, your armies twice as large and ready to sweep up the ashes?"

"Not enough."

"I will personally promise that House Mars will brook no aggression toward House Diana so long as our agreement is not violated. If you help me take Minerva, I will help you take Ceres."

"House Ceres . . . ," she says, looking over to her bodyguards.

"Don't be greedy," I say. "If you go after Ceres on your own, both Mars and Minerva will set upon you."

"Yes. Yes." She waves an annoyed hand. "Ceres is near?"

"Very. And they have bread." I look at the pelts her men wear. "Which I imagine would be a nice change from all that meat."

Her weight shifts on her toes and I know I have her. Always negotiate with food. I make a note.

Tamara clears her throat. "So you were saying I could make my army twice as large?"

31

THE FALL OF MUSTANG

I ride dressed for war. All in black. Hair wild and bound by goatgut. Forearms covered with durosteel vambraces looted in battle. My durosteel cuirass is black and light; it will deflect any edge less than an ionBlade or a razor. My boots are muddy. Streaks of black and red go across my face. SlingBlade on my back. Knives everywhere. Nine red crossbones and ten wolves cover Quietus's flank. Lea painted them. Each crossbone is an incapacitated opponent, who are often healed by medBots and then thrown back into the fray. Each wolf a slave. Cassius rides at my side. He shimmers. The durosteel he received as a bounty is polished as bright as his glimmering sword and his hair, which bounces like coiled golden springs about his regal head. It's as though he's never been stood around and pissed on.

"Well, I do believe I am the lightning," Cassius declares. "And you, my brooding friend, are the thunder."

"Then what am I?" Roque asks, kicking his horse up beside us. Mud flies. "The wind?"

"You're full enough of it," I snort. "The hot sort."

The House rides behind us. All of it except Quinn and June, who stay behind as our castle's garrison. It is a gamble. We ride slowly so that Minerva knows we are coming. What they do not know is that I was there in the night just hours before and that Sevro is there now. Mud still sticks underneath my fingernails.

Minerva's scouts dart across their rocky hilltops. They make a show of mocking us, but really they count our number to better know our strategy. Yet they seem confused when we ride into their country of high grass and olive trees. So confused that they withdraw their scouts behind their walls. We've never come in full force like this. The Howlers, our scouts, ride in full view on their black horses, black cloaks fluttering like crow wings. Our highDraft killers move as the vanguard of the main body—cruel Vixus, craggy Pollux, spiteful Cassandra, many of Titus's band. The slaves jog about their owners, those who captured them.

I ride forward with Cassius and Antonia flanking me. She carries the standard today. Only a few archers man the walls, so I tell Cassius to make sure we are not ambushed from the flanks in case any of Minerva are about. He gallops away.

Minerva's fortress is ringed by a hundred meters of barren earth made mud from the torrential rains of the last week. It is the killing field. Step into the ring and the archers will try to kill your horse. If you still do not retreat, they will try to kill you. Nearly twenty horses of both Houses litter the field. Cassius led a bloody assault on a Minervan warband up to the very gates of the castle itself just two days before.

Beyond the killing field is grass. Oceans of grass so high in some places that Sevro could stand tall and still not be seen. We stand at the edge of the mud ring amidst a meadow of autumn wildflowers. The ground squishes underfoot and Quietus whinnies beneath me.

"Pax!" I then shout. *"Pax."*

I hurl the name against the walls until their main gate opens ponderously, as ponderously as it once opened that night when Cassius and I snuck inside. Mustang rides out. She trots slowly through the mud and pulls short of us. Her eyes take in everything.

"Is it to be a duel?" she asks with a grin. "Pax of Wise and Noble Minerva versus the Reaper of the Bloody Butcher House?"

"You make it sound so exciting," Antonia yawns. She's not got a spot of dirt on her.

Mustang ignores her.

"And you're sure you've no one hiding in that grass waiting to ambush us when we come out to support our champion?" Mustang asks me. "Should we burn it and find out?"

"We've brought everyone," Antonia says. "You know our numbers."

"Yes. I can count. Thank you." Mustang doesn't look at her. Just at me. She seems worried; her voice lowers. "Pax will hurt you."

"Pax, how are your balls?" I shout over her head. She winces as a drum beats suddenly from inside the fortress. Except it's not a drum. Pax comes out of the gate. His war axe thumps his shield. Mustang shouts him back and he obeys like a dog, but the beating of the axe on the shield does not cease. We agree that the stakes should be all the remaining slaves between the two of us. A hefty bounty.

"I thought Handsome was the duelist?" Mustang says, then shrugs. Her eyes keep going to the grass. "Where is that mad fellow? Your shadow—the one who leads that wolfpack? Is he hiding in the grass? I don't want him popping up behind me again."

I shout for Sevro. A hand rises amongst the Howlers. Mud covers the faces that peer out from beneath the black wolfcloaks. Mustang counts. All five Howlers accounted for. In fact, all our forces save one, Quinn, are accounted for. Still Mustang isn't satisfied. We are to remove our army six hundred meters from the edge of the mud ring. She will burn away all the grass within one hundred meters of where we now stand. When the grass is done burning, the scorched earth will be the duel field. Ten men of her choosing will join ten of my choosing in creating a circle in which to fight. The rest of hers will stay inside the city, and mine will stay six hundred meters removed.

"Don't trust me?" I ask. "I don't have men in the grass."

"Good. Then no one will burn."

No one burns. When the fire dwindles and the ground is all ash and smoke and mud within the killing field, I leave my army. Ten of mine accompany me. Pax thumps his war axe on a shield emblazoned with a woman's head, her hair all of snakes. Medusa. I've never fought a man with a shield before. His armor is tight and covers everything but his joints. I heft a stunpike in the hand I've painted red and my slingBlade in the hand I've painted black.

My heart rattles as the circle forms around us. Cassius motions me over. Even in the muted light, he glows with color. He shares an ironic smile.

"Never stop moving. It's like Kravat, this." He eyes Pax. "And you're faster than this gory bastard. Right?" I get a wink. He thumps me on the shoulder. "Right, brother?"

"Damn right." I return his wink.

"Thunder and lightning, brother. Thunder and lightning!"

Pax is built like an Obsidian. He's over seven feet tall, easliy, and he moves like a bloodydamn panther. In this .37grav, he could throw me thirty meters or more. I wonder how high he can jump. I jump to stretch my legs. Nearly three meters. I can easily clear his head. The ground still smokes.

"Jump. Jump, little grasshopper," he grumbles. "It'll be the last time you use your legs."

"What's that?" I ask.

"I said it'll be the last time you use your legs."

"Odd," I murmur.

He blinks at me and frowns. "What's . . . odd?"

"You sound like a girl. Did something happen to your balls?"

"You little . . ."

Mustang trots up with their standard and says something about girls never challenging each other to stupid duels. "The duel is to—"

"Yielding," Pax says impatiently.

"To the death," I correct. Really it doesn't matter. I'm just screwing with them at this point. All I have to do is give the signal.

"To yielding," Mustang confirms. She finishes necessaries and the duel begins. Almost. A series of pops in the sky above signal sonic booms as the Proctors come to join us from Olympus. They spin down from their high-floating mountain, coming from several different towers. Each wears his or her sign today, great headpieces of glittering gold. Their armor is a spectacle. They do not need it, but they love to dress up. Today they've brought a table with them. It floats on its own gravLift, supporting huge flagons of wine and trays of food as they set to having a dinner party.

"I hope we're sufficient entertainment," I cry up. "Mind dropping some wine? It's been a while!"

"Good luck against the titan, little mortal!" Mercury cries down. His baby face laughs jovially and he showily brings a flagon of wine to his lips. Some of it tumbles the quarter mile from the sky to fall on my armor. It drips down like blood.

"I suppose we ought to give them a show," Pax booms.

Pax and I share a real grin. It's a compliment, of sorts, that they would all come to watch. Then Neptune, her trident headdress wobbling as she swallows a quail egg, shouts for us to get on with it, and Pax's axe sweeps at my legs like an evil broom. I know he wants me to jump, because he's about to charge forward with his shield to swat me from the air like a fly. So I step back, then spring forward as his arm finishes its stroke. He's moving too, but upward in anticipation, so I shoot right past his right arm and jam the stunpike into his armpit with all of my strength. It snaps in half. But he doesn't fall even as electricity courses through him. Instead, he backhands me so hard that I fly through the circle and into the mud. Broken molar. Mouthful of mud and blood. Whiplash. I'm already rolling.

I stumble to my feet with my slingBlade. Mud covers me. I glance at the walls. Their army rings the parapet—couldn't help but watch the champions fight. This is the point. I could give the signal. The gates are open in case they have to send aid. Our nearest horseman is six hundred meters away, much too far. I planned for that. Yet I do not signal. I want my own victory today, even if it's a selfish one. My army has to know why I lead.

I come back into the circle. I have nothing clever to say. He's stronger. I'm faster. That's all we've learned about one another. This is not like Cassius's fight. There is no pretty form. Only brutality. He bashes me with his shield. I stay close so he can't swing his axe. The shield is ruining my shoulder. Every strike shoots agony into my molar. He lunges with it again and I jump, pull on the shield with my left hand and launch myself over him. A knife flickers from my wrist and I stab it at his eyes as I pass. I miss and scrape his helmet's visor.

Putting a little distance between us, I reach for a knife and try a familiar trick. He bats the flying blade away contemptuously with his shield. But when he lowers it to look at me, I'm in the air, landing on his shield with all my weight. The suddenness of it pulls the shield down just a hair. I slam mud into his helmet with my off hand.

He's blind. One hand holds the axe. One holds the shield. Neither can wipe his visor clean. It'd be a simple matter if he could just do that. But he can't. I hit him a dozen times on his wrist till he drops his axe. Then I take the monstrous thing and hit him on the helmet with it. The armor still doesn't break. He almost knocks me unconscious with his shield. I swing the heavy axe again and finally Pax crumples. I fall to a knee, panting.

Then I howl.

They all howl.

Howls fill the lands of Minerva. Howls from my far-distant army. Howls from my ten highDraft killers who help make this dueling circle. Howls from the killing field. Mustang hears the dread sound behind her and she wheels her horse. Her face is one of terror. Howls from the laughing Proctors, except Minerva, Apollo, and Jupiter. Howls from the bellies of the dead horses in the middle of the killing field. The ones near her open gate.

"They're in the mud!" Mustang shouts.

She's almost right. But she thinks like a Gold. Someone screams as they see Sevro and his Howlers cutting their way out of the stitched-up bellies of the dead and bloated horses that litter the mud up to the gate. Like demons being born, they slither from swollen guts and parted stomachs. A half-score of House Diana's best soldiers exit with them. Tactus and his spiked hair burst from the belly of a pale mare. He runs with Weed and Thistle and Clown. All within fifty meters of the ponderously slow gates.

The Minervan guards all stand upon the ramparts watching the duel. They cannot repel the sudden blitz of demon soldiers by closing their slow gates. They hardly manage to nock and draw their bows before Sevro, the Howlers, and our allies slip through the closing gate. On the other side of the city, the House Diana's soldiers will be slowly scaling the walls with the ropes they use to climb their silly trees. Yes. The whistle sounds now from the other side. A guard there has seen them. No one will come to help him. My army moves forward, even the fake Howlers we borrowed from Diana and dressed up to look like Sevro and his band.

We destroy House Minerva in minutes. High above, the Proctors still howl and laugh. I think they are drunk. It is over before Mustang can do anything except gallop away across the muddy field through the still-smoldering grass. A dozen horses set off in pursuit, Vixus and Cassandra amongst them. She'll be caught before nightfall, and I've seen what Vixus does to prisoners and their ears, so I mount Quietus and set off in pursuit.

Mustang abandons her horse at the edge of a small wood to the south. We dismount and leave three men to guard the horses in case she doubles back. Cassandra plunges into the woods. Vixus follows me, purposefully stalking as though I might know where Mustang is hiding. I do not like this. I do not like being in the woods with Vixus and Cassandra. All it would take is a blade in the spine. Either would do it. Unlike Pollux, they still hate me, and my Howlers and Cassius are far away. Yet no knife comes.

I find Mustang by mistake. Two golden eyes peer out from a pit of mud. They meet mine. Vixus is with me. He swears something about how excited he is to break the gorydamn mare, see what she looks like with a bridle on. Standing there, leering into the brush, he looks bent and twisted and evil—like a withered tree after a fire. He has less bodyfat than anyone I've ever seen, so each of his veins and tendons ripple beneath his tight skin. His tongue flits over his perfect teeth. I know he's goading me, so I lead him away from the mud pit.

Eo didn't deserve to die a slave to the Society. And despite her Color, Mustang doesn't deserve any sort of bridle.

32

ANTONIA

I passed this test. The interminable war with House Minerva is done. And I've also trapped House Diana.

House Diana had three choices before the battle. They could have betrayed me to Minerva and taken my House as slaves, but I had Cassius send pickets to intercept any rider. They could have accepted my proposal. Or they could have gone to our castle and tried to take it. I couldn't care less if they chose that option; it was a trap. We left no water inside and could have besieged them easily.

Now they have the Minervan fortress and we are outside in the plains. They could honor their agreement. We would get the standard; they would get the city and all its inhabitants. But I know they'll become greedy. And they do. The gates close and they think they've a strategic bastion. Good. That's why I have Sevro inside with them.

Smoke plumes soon rise. He destroys the food stores as they enslave the Minervans and guard the walls from my army. Then he fouls the wells with feces and hides with his Howlers in the cellars.

House Diana is not used to this sort of warfare. They have never really left their woods behind. It is hardly an effort to wait them out. Three days in and they are apparently still surprised we do not leave.

Instead, we camp north and south of the city with our horses and light bonfires all around so they cannot slip away in the night. They are thirsty. Their leader, Tamara, does not receive me. She is too embarrassed at being caught in her betrayal.

Eventually, on the fourth day, Tamara offers me ten Minervan slaves and all our enslaved soldiers if I allow her passage home. I send Lea to tell her to go slag herself. Lea giggles like a child when she returns. She flips her hair, grabs my arm, and leans in close to mock Tamara's desperateness.

"Have decency!" she cries. *"Are you not a man of your word?"*

When they try to break out the fifth night, we capture every last one of them. Except Tamara. She fell from her horse and was trampled to death in the mud.

"Her saddle was cut through underneath." Sevro shows me the cleanly severed strip of leather. "Tactus?"

"Probably."

"His mother's a Senator, Father's a Praetor." Sevro spits. "Met him when we were children. Beat a girl half to death when she wouldn't kiss him on the cheek. Mad bastard."

"Let it slide," I say. "We can't prove anything." Tactus is our slave, as is all of Diana and Minerva. Even Pax. I sit with Cassius and Roque atop our horses as we watch our new slaves labor in stacking wood and hay throughout the Minervan fortress. They set a massive blaze and we three toast each other in victory.

"This will be your last bar of merit," Cassius tells me. "That makes you Primus, brother." He pats my shoulder, and I see only a twinge of jealousy in his eyes. "Couldn't be a better pick."

"Lord on high, I never thought I would see this side of our handsome friend," Roque says. "Humility! Cassius, is that truly you?"

Cassius shrugs. "This game is but a year of our lives, maybe less. After that, we have our apprenticeships or academies. After that, we have our lives. I'm only glad that we three were in the same House—just rewards will be there eventually for all of us."

I squeeze his shoulder. "Agreed."

He's still looking down, unable to meet our eyes till he finds his voice again.

"I . . . may have lost a brother here. That pain won't fade. But I feel like I've gained two more." He looks up fiercely. "And I mean that, lads. I gorywell mean that. We'll have to do ourselves proud here. Beat some more Houses, win the whole damn thing; but my father will need officers for the ships in his armada . . . if you are interested, that is. The House Bellona always needs Praetors to make us stronger."

He says that last part timidly, as though we'd have something better to do.

I grip his shoulder once more and nod even as Roque says something smartass about being a politician because he'd rather send people to their deaths than go to his own. The Sons of Ares would drool if I became a Praetor to House Bellona.

"And don't worry, Roque, I'll mention your poetry to Father," Cassius laughs. "He's always wanted a warrior bard."

"Of course," Roque embellishes. "Be sure to let dear Imperator Bellona know that I am a master with metaphor and a rogue with assonance."

"Roque a rogue . . . oh God," I laugh as Sevro rides up with Quinn and a girl on a type of horse I have not seen before. The girl wears a bag over her head. Quinn announces her as an emissary from House Pluto.

Her name is Lilath and they found her waiting near the edge of the woods. She wishes to speak with Cassius.

Lilath was once a moonfaced girl with cheeks that did smile but now don't. They are drawn and newly burned, pocked and cruel. She's seen hunger, and there's a coldness to her that I don't recognize. I'm frightened. I feel like Mickey when he looked at me. I was a cold, quiet thing he didn't understand. So is she. It's like looking at a fish from an underground river.

Lilath's words come slow and linger in the air.

"I come from the Jackal."

"Call him by his real name, if you will," I suggest.

"I did not come to speak with you," she says without a hint of emotion. "I came for Cassius."

Her horse is small and lean. Its hooves nicked. Extra clothing makes her saddle fat. I see no weapons other than a crossbow. They are a mountain House—more clothing for colder climates, smaller horses for harder rides. Unless it is deception. I make her show me her ring. It is a mourning tree—the cypress of Pluto. Its roots leak into the ground. Two of her fingers are gone. Burns seal the stumps, so they have ion weapons. Her hair clatters when she moves. I don't know why.

She looks me over quietly, as though judging me against her master.

Apparently I am lacking.

"Cassius au Bellona, my master desires the Reaper." She goes on before either of us can say a word. We're too surprised. "Alive. Dead. We don't care. In return for him, you will receive fifty of these for your . . . army."

She tosses him two ionBlades.

"You can tell your master he should come face me himself," I say.

"I make no words with dead boys," Lilath says to the air. "My master has put the mark on the Reaper. Before winter comes, he will be dead. By one hand or another."

"You can go slag yourself," Cassius replies.

She tosses Cassius a small pouch. "To help you make your decision."

She does not speak again. Quinn raises her eyebrows and shrugs her confusion as she leads Lilath away.

I look at the small pouch Cassius holds in his hands. Paranoia overwhelms me. What is inside?

"Open it," I say.

"Nah. She's mad as a Violet, that one," Cassius laughs. "Don't need her to infect us." Yet he tucks the pouch in his boot. I want to scream at him to open it, but I smile as though there is nothing to worry about.

"Something was wrong in her. Didn't seem human," I say casually.

"Looked like one of our starved wolves." Cassius gives the ion-

Blade a swing. The air shrieks. "At least we got these two. Now I can teach you how to duel properly. These'll go straight through duro-Armor. Dangerous things, really."

The Jackal knows about me. The thought makes me shiver. Roque's words are worse.

"Did you notice how her hair clattered?" he asks. His face is white. "Her braids were laced with teeth."

We must prepare to meet the Jackal's army. That means consolidating my forces and eliminating lingering threats. I need the remainder of House Diana in the Greatwoods destroyed. And I need House Ceres. I send Cassius with the Howlers and a dozen horsemen to destroy the remainder of Diana. The rest of my army and slaves I take back to our castle to prepare for the Jackal. I've not yet devised a plan, but I'll be ready for him if he rears his head.

"After sleeping in dead horses, our Howlers will probably stink them out of the Greatwoods!" Cassius laughs as he spurs his horse away from the main column. "I'll sic Goblin on them and be back before you're even in bed."

Sevro does not want to go without me. He does not understand why Cassius needs his help to mop up the remainders of Diana. I tell him the truth.

"Cassius has a pouch in his boot, the one Lilath gave him. I need you to steal it."

His eyes do not judge. Not even now. There are times when I wonder what I did to earn such loyalty, then others when I try not to press my luck by looking the gift horse in the mouth.

That night as Cassius lays siege to Diana in the Greatwoods, the rest of my army feasts behind our tall highland walls in Mars Castle. The keep is clean and the square merry. Even the slaves are given June's thyme-roasted goat and venison drizzled with olive oil. I watch over it all. The slaves look down out of embarrassment as I pass, even Pax. The howling wolf on his forehead has crushed his pride. Tactus alone meets my eyes. His dark honey skin is like Quinn's, but his eyes remind me of a pitviper's.

He winks at me.

After my victory over Pax, my highDrafts seem to have finally fully embraced my leadership, even Antonia. It reminds me of how I was treated on the streets after Mickey carved me. I am the Gold here. I am the power. It's the first time I've felt this way since sentencing Titus to death. Soon Fitchner will come down and give me the Primus hand from the stone and all will be well.

Roque, Quinn, Lea, and now Pollux eat with me. Even Vixus and Cassandra, who normally sit in commune with Antonia, have come to give their congratulations on the victory. They laugh and clap me on the shoulder. Cipio, Antonia's plaything, is counting the many slaves. Antonia herself does not venture my way, but she does tilt her golden head in approval. Miracles do happen.

I am Primus. I have five golden bars. Soon Fitchner will come to bestow the honorifics. In the morning, House Ceres will fall. They have less than one-third our number. With their grain to feed my army and their fortress to use as a base of operations, I will have the power of four Houses. We will sweep away whatever is left in the North and then descend upon the South before the first snow even falls. Then I will face the Jackal.

Roque comes to stand beside me as we watch the feast.

"I've been thinking of kissing Lea," he says suddenly to me. I see her laughing with several midDrafts near one of the fires. She's cut her hair short, and she spares us a glance, coquettishly ducking her head when Roque holds her gaze. He blushes too and looks away.

"I thought you didn't like her. She follows you about like a puppy." I laugh.

"Well, yes. At first she didn't intrigue me because I thought she was attaching herself to me as one would to a . . . life raft to stop from sinking. But . . . she's grown . . ."

I look over at him and laugh. I can't stop laughing.

We look like blond wolves. We're leaner than when the Institute began. Dirtier. Our hair is long. We have scars. Me more than most. I'm likely too dependent on red meat. One of my molars is split. But I laugh. I laugh till my molar can't take it anymore. I'd forgotten that we are people, kids who have crushes.

"Well, don't waste the first kiss," I say. "That's my only advice."

I tell him to take her somewhere special. Take her somewhere here that means something to him, or them. I took Eo to my drill—Loran and Barlow made jokes about that. The thing was off and in a ventilated tunnel, so we didn't have to wear frysuit lids, just had to watch for pitvipers. Still she sweated from excitement. Hair clinging to her face, to the nape of her neck. She gripped my wrist so hard, and only let go when she knew she had me. When I kissed her.

I grin and slap Roque on the butt for luck. Uncle Narol says it's tradition. He used the flat of a slingBlade on me. I think he was lying.

I dream of Eo in the night. I do not often sleep without dreaming of her. The castle's high tower bunk beds are empty. Roque, Lea, Cassius, Sevro, the Howlers, are gone. Except for Quinn, all my friends are off. I am Primus, yet I feel so alone. The fire crackles. Cold autumn wind comes in. It moans like a wind from the abandoned mine tunnels and makes me think of my wife.

Eo. I miss her warmth in the bed beside me. I miss her neck. I miss kissing her soft skin, smelling her hair, tasting her mouth as she whispered how she loved me.

Then I hear feet and she fades.

Lea bursts through the dormitory door. She talks frantically. I can barely understand her. I stand, towering over her, and put a hand on her shoulder to calm her. It's impossible. Manic eyes look at me from behind her short-cut hair.

"Roque!" she wails. "Roque has fallen into a crevice. His legs are broken. I can't reach him!"

I follow her so fast I don't even bring my cloak or slingBlade. The castle is asleep except for the guards. We fly through the gate, forgetting the horses. I shout for one of the guards to come help me. I don't watch to see if she does. Lea runs ahead, guiding me down into the glen and then up over the northern hills to the highland gulch where we made our first fires as a tribe. The mists are thick. The night is dark. And I realize how stupid I am.

It's a trap.

I stop following Lea. I don't tell her. I don't know if they'll come from behind me, so I dive to my belly and shuffle to a gully so that I am lost in the mist. I put ferns over myself. I hear them now. The sound of swords. Of feet and stunpikes. Curses. How many are there? Lea calls my name frantically. She is not alone now. She's led me to them. I hear crooked Vixus. I smell Cassandra's flowers. She's always rubbing them on her skin to cover her body odor.

Their voices call to each other in the mist. They know I discovered their trap. How can I get back to my army? I dare not move. How many are there? They look for me. If I run, would I make it? Or would I end up on the end of a sword? I have two knives in my boots. That is it. I pull them out.

"Oh, Reaper!" Antonia calls from the mist. She's somewhere above me. "Fearless leader? Oh, Reaper. There's no need to hide, darling. We're not mad at you ordering us about like you're our king. We're not indignant enough to bury knives in your eyes. Not at all. Darling?"

They call taunts, playing on my vanity. I've never had much, but they can't understand that. A boot steps near my head. Green eyes peer through the darkness. I think they see me. They don't. NightOptics. Someone gave them nightOptics. I hear Vixus and Cassandra. Antonia grows frustrated.

"Reaper, if you do not come out to play, there shall be consequences." She sighs. "What consequences, you ask? Why, I will cut little Lea's throat to the bone." I hear a yelp as Lea's hair is seized. "Roque's lover. . . ."

I don't come out. Goddammit. I don't come out. My life is more than my own. It is Eo's, my family's. I cannot throw it away, not for my pride, not for Lea, not to avoid the pain of losing another friend. Do they have Roque too?

My jaw aches. I clench my teeth. My molar screams. Antonia won't do it.

She can't.

"Last chance, my darling. No?" There's a meaty sound followed by a gurgle and a thump as a body crumples to the ground. "Pity."

I loose a silent scream as I see the medBot whine through the night's mist. For all the power in my hands, in my body, I'm powerless to stop this, them.

I do not move until the early morning, when I am sure they are gone. The medBots did not take Lea's body away. The Proctors left it so I would know she died, so I could not hold on to hope that somehow she lived. The bastards. Her body is fragile in death. Like a little bird that has fallen from the nest. I build a cairn over her. The stones are high but they will not keep the wolves away.

I do not find Roque's body, so I do not know what has become of him. Is my friend dead?

I feel a ghost as I pick my way along the highlands, circling around the castle to avoid Antonia's henchmen. I put myself in the path Cassius will take in returning from the Greatwoods, hiding beneath shrubs to stay from sight. It is midday when he returns at the head of a small column of horse and slaves. He kicks his horse forward to greet me as I come from the shrubs.

"Brother!" he calls. "I brought you a gift!" He hops off and gives me a hug before pulling out one of Diana's tapestries and wrapping it about my shoulders. He pulls back from me. "You're as pale as a ghost. What's the matter?" He picks a leaf out of my hair. Maybe that's when he sees the sadness in my eyes.

Sevro rides up behind him as I tell them what has happened.

"The bitch," Cassius murmurs. Sevro is silent. "Poor Lea. Poor Lea. She was a sweetheart. Do you think Roque is dead?"

"I don't know." I say. "I just don't know."

"Gorydamn." Cassius shakes his head.

"A Proctor must have given Antonia nightOptics," Sevro speculates. "Or the Jackal bribed her. It fits."

"Who cares about that?" Cassius cries, flinging out his arm. "Roque may be wounded or dead out there, man. Don't you register?" He grips the back of my neck and brings my forehead to his. "We'll find him, Darrow. We'll find our brother."

I nod, feeling a numbness spreading in my chest.

Antonia never returned to our castle. Neither did her henchmen,

Vixus and Cassandra. They failed to kill me and must have fled. But to where?

Quinn flings her hands up in the air and shouts at us as we come through the gate.

"I didn't know where the goryblazes anyone was! The slaves outnumbered us four to one till you got back. But it's fine. It's fine." She grips Cassius's hand when we tell her what's happened. The tears well in her eyes for Lea, but she refuses to believe Roque is dead. She keeps shaking her head. "We can use the slaves to search for Roque. Probably wounded and hiding out there. That's it. That has to be it."

We do not find him. The entire army searches. Not a sign. We convene in our warroom around the long table.

"He's probably dead at the bottom of a ditch," Sevro says that night. I almost hit him. But he's right.

"The Jackal did this," I mutter.

"Tough shit," he says.

"Come again?"

"Doesn't matter if he did it, is what Sevro means. We can't do anything against the Jackal now. Even if he tried to take your life, we're not in a position to hurt him," Quinn declares. "Let's deal with our neighbors first."

"*Stupid*," Sevro mutters.

"What a surprise. It looks like Goblin disagrees," Cassius snaps. "Speak up if you got something in your craw, pygmy."

"Don't talk down to me," Sevro sneers.

Cassius chuckles. "Don't piss on my foot because you only come to my knees."

"I'm every bit your equal." The look on Sevro's face is such that I lean forward suddenly, frightened a knife will suddenly appear in Cassius's eye.

"My equal? At what? Birth?" Cassius grins. "Oh, wait, I meant height, looks, intelligence, money? Shall I stop?"

Quinn kicks his chair hard with her foot.

"What the hell is your problem?" she snaps at him. "Never mind. Just shut the hell up."

Sevro looks at the ground. I have the sudden urge to put a hand on his shoulder.

"What were you saying, Sevro?" Quinn asks.

"Nothing."

"Come on."

"He said nothing." Cassius chuckles.

"Cassius." My voice alone shuts him up. "Sevro, please."

Sevro sighs and looks up at me, cheeks flushed with anger. "Just thought we should not pick our butts here while the Jackal does whatever he wants." He shrugs. "Send me south. And let me cause trouble."

"Trouble?" Cassius asks. "What you going to do, kill the Jackal?"

"Yes." Sevro looks quietly at Cassius. "I'll put a dagger in his throat and then carve a hole till I see his spine."

The tension is enough to make me uneasy.

"You can't be serious," Quinn says quietly.

"He's serious." Cassius's forehead creases. "And he's wrong. We're not monsters. Not you and I, at least, Darrow. Bellona Praetors aren't knives in the night. We have five hundred years of honor to guard."

"Piss and lies." Sevro dismisses him with a wave.

"It's in the breeding." Cassius elevates his nose ever so slightly.

Sevro's mouth twists cruelly. "You're a Pixie if you buy all that. Think your papa cut his way up to Imperator by being honorable?"

"Call it chivalry, *Goblin,*" Cassius sneers. "It wouldn't be right trying to murder someone in cold blood, particularly not at a *school*."

"I agree with Cassius," I say, breaking my silence.

"Small wonder." Sevro stands to leave very suddenly. I ask him where he is going.

"You obviously don't need me. Have all the advice you can handle."

"Sevro."

"I'm gonna search the ditches. *Again*. Bet Bellona wouldn't do that. Wouldn't get his precious knees dirty." He bows mockingly to Cassius before leaving.

Quinn, Cassius, and I remain in the warroom until Cassius yawns something about catching a bit of REM before the dawn hits in six hours. Quinn and I are left alone. Her hair has been cut short and jagged, though the bangs hang just over her narrow eyes. She slouches boyishly in her chair and picks at her nails.

"What are you thinking on?" she asks me.

"Roque . . . and Lea." I hear the gurgle in my mind. With it echoes all the sounds of death. Eo's *pop.* Julian's silence as he twitched in his own blood. I am the Reaper and death is my shadow.

"Is that all?" she asks.

"I think we should grab some sleep," I reply.

She says nothing as she watches me leave.

33

APOLOGIES

Cassius wakes me in the middle of the night.

"Sevro found Roque," he says quietly. "He's a mess. Come."

"Where?"

"North. They can't move him."

We gallop away from the castle under the light of twin moons. An early winter snow fills the air with dancing flurries. Sucking sounds come from the mud as we head toward the north Metas. No sounds but the gurgling of the water and the wind in the trees. Wiping sleep from my eyes, I look over to Cassius. He has our two ionSwords, and suddenly a pit opens in my stomach as I realize what's what. He doesn't know where Roque is. But he knows something else.

He knows what I've done.

This is a trap I cannot ride away from. I guess there are those times in life. It's like staring at the ground as you fall from a height. Seeing the end coming doesn't mean you can dodge it, fix it, stop it.

We ride for twenty more minutes.

"It was no surprise," Cassius says suddenly.

"What's that?"

"I've known for over a year that Julian was meant to die." The snow falls silently as we move together through the mud. The hot horse moves between my legs. Step by step through the mud. "He made a mess of his test. He was never the brightest, not in the way they wanted. Oh, he was kind and bright with emotions—he could sense sadness or anger a klick away. But empathy is a lowColor thing."

I say nothing.

"There are feuds that do not change, Darrow. Cats and dogs. Ice and fire. Augustus and Bellona. My family and the ArchGovernor's."

Cassius's eyes are fixed ahead even as his horse stumbles and his breath makes fog in the air.

"But despite what it portended, Julian was excited when he received the acceptance letter stamped with the ArchGovernor's personal seal. Didn't seem right to me or my other brothers. Never thought Julian would be the sort to make it in. I loved him, all my brothers and cousins did; but you met him. Oh, you've met him—he wasn't the keenest of mind, but he wasn't the dullest; he wouldn't have been the bottom one percent. No need to cull him from the stock. But he had the name Bellona. A name which our enemy loathes. And so our enemy used bureaucracy, used his title, his duly appointed powers, to murder a kind boy.

"To turn down an invitation to the Institute is an illegal act. And he was so delighted, and we—my mother and father and brothers and sisters and cousins and loved ones—were so hopeful for him. He trained so hard." His voice takes a mocking tone. "But in the end, Julian was fed to the wolves. Or should I say wolf?"

He pulls his horse to a halt, eyes burning into me.

"How did you find out?" I ask, staring ahead over the dark water. Flakes of snow disappear into the black surface. The mountains are but shadowed mounds in the distance. The river gurgles. I do not dismount.

"That you did Augustus's dirty work?" He laughs scornfully. "I trusted you, Darrow. So I did not need to see what the Jackal sent me. But when Sevro tried to steal it from me as I slept in the Greatwoods, I knew something was the matter." He notices my reaction. "What? You thought you consorted with dullards?"

"Sometimes. Yes."

"Well, I watched it tonight."

A holo.

With Roque and Lea, I had forgotten about the package. Better that I had. Better that I had trusted him and not sent Sevro to steal it. Maybe he would have discarded it then. Maybe things would be different.

"Watched what?" I ask.

"A holo that shows you killing Julian, *brother*."

"The Jackal got a holo," I snort. "His Proctor gave it to him then. Guess that means the game is rigged. Suppose it doesn't matter to you that the Jackal is the ArchGovernor's son and that he's manipulating you into getting rid of me."

He flinches.

"Didn't know the Jackal was his son, eh? I reckon you'd recognize him if you saw him and that's why he sent Lilath."

"I wouldn't recognize him. I've never met the bastard's spawn. He kept them hidden from us before the Institute. And my family kept me from him after . . ." His voice fades as his eyes sink into a distant memory.

"We can beat him, together, Cassius. We needn't be divided—"

"Because you killed my brother?" He spits. "There is no *we,* you feckless quim. Get off your gorydamn horse."

I dismount and Cassius throws me one of the ionSwords. I stand facing my friend in the mud. No one to watch but the crows and the moons. And the Proctors. My slingBlade is on the saddle; it at least has a curve, but it's useless against an ionBlade. Cassius is going to kill me.

"I didn't have a choice," I tell him. "I hope you know that."

"You will rot in hell, you manipulative son of a bitch," he cries. "You allowed me to call you *brother*!"

"So what would you have had me do? Should I have let Julian kill me in the Passage? Would you?"

That freezes him.

"It's how you killed him." He's quiet for a moment. "We come as princes and this school is supposed to teach us to become beasts. But you came a beast."

I laugh bitterly. "And what were you when you ripped apart Titus?"

"I was not like you!" Cassius shouts.

"I let you kill him, Cassius, so the House wouldn't remember that a dozen boys took a good long piss on your face. So don't treat me as though I'm some monster."

"You are," he sneers.

"Oh, shut your goddamned gob and let's just cut to it. Hypocrite."

The duel is not long. I have been practicing with him for months. He has played at duels his entire life. The blades echo across the moving river. Snow falls. Mud sticks and sloshes. We pant. Breath billows. My arms rattle as the blades clang and scrape. I'm faster than him, more fluid. Almost get his thigh, but he knows the mathematics of this game. With a little flick of his wrists to move my sword sideways, he steps in and drives his ionBlade through my armor into my belly. It should cauterize instantly and destroy the nerves, leaving me damaged though alive, but he has the ion charge off, so I only feel a horrible tightness as alien metal slides into my body and warmth gushes out.

I forget to breathe. Then I gasp. My body shivers. Hugs the sword. I smell Cassius's neck. He's close. Close as when he used to cup my head and call me brother. His hair is oily.

Dignity leaves me and I begin to whimper like a dog.

Throbbing pain blossoms—begins like a pressure, a fullness of metal in my stomach, becomes an aching horror. I shudder for breaths, gulp at them. Can't breathe. It's like a black hole in my gut. I fall back moaning. There is pain. That is one thing. This is different. It is terror and fear. My body knows this is how life ends. Then the sword is gone and the misery begins. Cassius leaves me bleeding and sniveling in the mud. Everything that I am goes away and I am a slave to my body. I cry.

I become a child again. I curl around the wound. Oh God, it is horrible. I don't understand the pain. It consumes me. I'm no man; I'm a child. Let me die faster. I sink in the cold, cold mud. I shiver and weep. I can't help it. My body does things. It betrays me. The metal went through my guts.

My blood goes out. With it go Dancer's hopes, my father's sacrifice, Eo's dream. I can hardly think of them. The mud is dark and cold. This hurts so much. Eo. I miss her. I miss home. What was her second gift? I never found out. Her sister never told me. Now I know pain. Nothing is worth this. Nothing. Let me be a slave again, let me see Eo, let me die. Just not this.

PART IV

REAPER

The Elderwomen of Lykos say that when a man is bitten by a pitviper, all the poison must be drawn out of the bite, for the poison is wicked. When I was bitten, Uncle Narol left some in on purpose.

34

THE NORTHWOODS

There is agony.

And claustrophobia.

I am sick and wounded.

The pain is in dreams.

It is in darkness. In the pit of my stomach.

I wake up and scream into a gentle hand.

I glimpse someone.

Eo? I whisper her name and reach up. My muddy hand smears her face. Her angel's face. She's come to take me to the vale. Her hair has turned Golden. I always thought she could be Golden. Her Colors are golden wings. No Red sigil on her hands. It took death.

I sweat despite the rains and snows that come. Something shelters me. I shiver. Clutch my scarlet headband. Lost the haemanthus. When was that again? Mud in my hair. Eo washes it away. Tenderly strokes my brow. I love her. Something inside me bleeds. I hear Eo speak to herself, to someone. I haven't long. Have I time at all? Am I in the vale? There is mist. There is sky and a great tree. Fire. Smoke.

I shiver and sweat. Rot in hell, Cassius. I was your friend. I might have killed your brother, but I had no choice. You did. You arrogant slag. I hate him. I hate Augustus. I see them hanging Eo together.

They mock me. They laugh at me. I hate Antonia. I hate Fitchner. I hate Titus. I hate. I hate. I am burning and mad and sweating. I hate the Jackal. The Proctors. I hate. I hate myself for all I've done. All I've done. For what? To win a game. To win a game for someone who will never know about anything I do. Eo is dead. It isn't as if she will ever be coming back to see all I have done for her.

Dead.

Then I wake. The pain is there in my gut. It goes through me. But I no longer sweat. The fever is gone, and the angry red lines of infection have faded. I'm in a cave's mouth. There's a small fire and a sleeping girl just inches away. Furs cover her. She breathes softly the smoky air. Her hair is tousled and gold. She isn't Eo. Mustang.

I cry silently. I want Eo. Why can't I have her? Why can't I will her back to life? I want Eo. I don't want this girl beside me. It aches worse than the wound. I can never fix what happened to Eo. I couldn't even run my army. I couldn't win. I couldn't beat Cassius, not to mention the Jackal. I was the best Helldiver; I'm nothing here. The world is too big and cold. I am too small. The world has forgotten Eo. It has already forgotten her sacrifice. There's nothing left.

I sleep again.

When I wake, Mustang sits by the fire. She knows I'm awake but lets me pretend otherwise. I lie there with my eyes closed, listening to her hum. It's a song I know. It is a song I hear in dreams. The echo of my love's death. The song sung by the one they call Persephone. Hummed by an Aureate, an echo of Eo's dream.

I weep. If ever I've felt there was a God, it is now as I listen to the mournful chords. My wife is dead, but something of hers lingers still.

I speak to Mustang the next morning.

"Where did you hear that song?" I ask her without sitting up.

"From the HC," she says, blushing. "A little girl sang it. It's soothing."

"It's sad."

"Most things are."

It has been four weeks, Mustang tells me. Cassius is Primus. Winter has come. Ceres is no longer under siege. Jupiter's soldiers sometimes come into the woods. There are sounds of battle between the two superpowers of the North, Jupiter and Mars. Jupiter to the west, Mars to the east. Since the river froze, they've been able to cross and raid one another. Our buzzards have risen out of their winter gulches. Hungry wolves howl at night. Crows flock from the south. But Mustang really knows very little, and I grow impatient with her.

"Keeping you breathing was a little distracting," she reminds me. Her standard lies underneath a blanket near my feet. She's the last of House Minerva. Yet unbridled. And she didn't enslave me.

"Slaves are stupid," she says. "And you're already a gimp. Why make you stupid too?"

It is days before I'm able to walk. I wonder where those nifty medBots are now. Tending someone the Proctors like, no doubt. I won Primus and they never gave it to me. Now I know why the Jackal will win. They are getting rid of his competition.

Mustang stalks with me through the woods during the next weeks. I move stiffly through the thick snow but my strength is returning. She credits medicine she found lying conspicuously under a bush. A friendly Proctor placed it there. We pause when we spot the deer. I draw the bow, but I can't get the string to my ear. My wound aches. Mustang watches me. I try again. Pain deep inside. I let the arrow fly. I miss. We eat leftover rabbit that night. It tastes funny and gives me cramps. I always have cramps now. It's the water too. We have nothing to boil it in. No iodine. Just snow and a little creek to drink from. Sometimes we can't have fire.

"You should have killed Cassius or sent him away," Mustang tells me.

"Would have thought you nobler than that," I say.

"I like to win. Family trait. And sometimes cheating is in the rulebook." She smiles. "You get a merit bar every time you recapture your standard. So I arranged for it to be lost to House Diana by someone else several times. Then rode out to capture it. Got to Primus in a week."

"Tricky. Yet your army liked you," I say.

"Everyone likes me. Now eat your damn rabbit. You're skinny as a razor."

The winter grows colder. We live in the deep north woods, far north of Ceres, northwest of my former highlands. I have not yet seen a soldier of Mars. I don't know what I would do if I did.

"I've hidden from everyone but you," Mustang says. "It keeps me alive and ticking."

"What's your plan?" I ask.

She laughs at herself. "To be alive and ticking."

"You're better at it than I am."

"How do you mean?"

"No one in your House would have betrayed you."

"Because I didn't rule like you," she says. "You have to remember, people don't like being told what to do. You can treat your friends like servants and they'll love you, but you tell them they're servants and they'll kill you. Anyway, you put too much stock in hierarchy and fear."

"Me?"

"Who else? I could spot it a mile away. All you cared about was your mission, whatever it is. You're like a driven arrow with a very depressing shadow. First time I met you, I knew you'd cut my throat to get whatever it is you want." She waits for a moment. "What is it that you want, by the way?"

"To win," I say.

"Oh, please. You're not that simple."

"You think you know me?" The coals crackle in our small fire.

"I know you cry in your sleep for a girl named Eo. Sister? Or a girl you loved? It is a very offColor name. Like yours."

"I'm a farplanet hayseed. Didn't they tell you?"

"They wouldn't tell me anything. I don't get out much. Strict father." She waves a hand. "Anyway, doesn't matter. All that matters is that no one trusts you because it's obvious you care more about your goal than you do about them."

"And you're something different?"

"Oh, very much so, Sir Reaper. I like people more than you do.

You are the wolf that howls and bites. I am the mustang that nuzzles the hand. People know they can work with me. With you? Hell, kill or be killed."

She's right.

When I had a tribe, I did it right. I made every boy and every girl love me. Made them earn their keep. I taught them how to kill a goat as if I knew how. I gave them fire as if I had created the matches. I shared a secret with them—that we had food and Titus didn't. They saw me as their father. I remember it in their eyes. When Titus was alive, I was a symbol of goodness and hope. Then when he died . . . I became him.

"Sometimes I forget that the Institute is meant to teach me things," I say to Mustang.

The golden girl tilts her head at me. "Like how we must live for more?"

Her words strike my heart. They echo through time from another's lips. Live for more. More than power. More than vengeance. More than what we're given.

I must learn better than them, not simply *beat* them. *That* is how I will help Reds. I am a boy. I am foolish. But if I learn to become a leader, I can be more than an agent of the Sons of Ares. I can give my people a future. That is what Eo wanted.

Deep winter. The wolves are hungry now. They howl in the night. When Mustang and I make a kill, we sometimes have to scare them off. But when we kill a caribou at dusk, a pack descends from the northlands. They come from the trees like dark specters. Shadows. The biggest of them is my size. His fur is white. The fur of the others is gray, no longer black. These wolves change with the season. I watch how they surround us. Each moves with individual cunning. Yet each moves as part of the pack.

"This is how we should fight," I whisper to Mustang as we watch the wolves approach.

"Could we talk about this later?"

We take down the pack leader with three arrows. The rest flee.

Mustang and I set to skinning the big white brute. As she slips her knife along beneath the fur, she looks up, nose red from the cold.

"Slaves aren't part of the pack, so we can't fight like them. Not that it matters. The wolves don't have it right either. They take too much from their pack leader. Cut off the head, the body retreats."

"So the answer is autonomy," I say.

"Maybe." She bites her lip.

Later that night, she elaborates. "It's like a hand." She sits close and cozy, leg touching mine. Close enough for guilt to crawl along my spine. The caribou roasts, filling the cave with a cozy, thick aroma. A blizzard rages outside and the wolf fur dries over the fire.

"Give me your hand," she says. "Which is your best finger?"

"They are all better at different things."

"Don't be obstinate."

I tell her my thumb. She has me try to hold a stick with only my thumb. She easily pulls it from my grasp. Then she has me hold it without my thumb and only the other fingers. With a twist, the stick is free.

"Imagine that your thumb is your Housemembers. The fingers are all the slaves you have conquered. The Primus or whoever is the brain. It all works pretty gory seamlessly. Yeah?"

She can't pull the stick from my grip. I set it down and ask her the point.

"Now try to do something beyond simply grabbing the standard. Just move your thumb counterclockwise and your fingers clockwise except your middle."

I do it. She stares at my hands and laughs incredulously. "Ass." I ruined her demonstration. Helldivers are dexterous. I watch her hands as she tries to do it too. Of course she fails. I understand.

"A hand is like the Society," I say.

It is the structure of the armies at the Institute. The hierarchy is good for simple tasks. Some fingers are more important than others. Some are better at certain things. All fingers are controlled by the highest order, the brain. The brain's control is effective. It makes your thumb and fingers work together. But the single brain's control is limited. Imagine each one of the fingers had a brain of its own that interacted with the main brain. The fingers obey, but they function independently. What could the hand do then? What could an army do? I twirl the stick along my fingers in intricate patterns. Exactly.

Her eyes linger on mine, and her fingers trace along my palm as she explains. I know she wants me to react to her touch, but I force my mind to be lost on other things.

This idea of hers isn't part of the Proctors' lesson.

Their lesson is about the evolution from anarchy to order. It is about control. About the systematic accumulation of power, the structure of that power, and then its preservation. It is a model to show that the Rule of Hierarchies is the best. The Society is the final evolution, the only answer. She just slagged that rule, or at least showed its limitations.

If I could earn the voluntary allegiance of the slaves, the army created would look nothing like the Society. It would be better. Like if the Reds of Lykos thought they could actually win the Laurel, they would be so much more productive. Or if a Praetor on board his starcruiser could utilize not only his own genius, but that of his crew of Blues.

Mustang's strategy is Eo's dream.

It's like an electric shock jolts through me.

"Why didn't you try it with the slaves you captured?"

She pulls her hand away from mine after I don't respond to her touch.

"I tried."

She's quiet the rest of the night. Near morning, she develops a cough.

Mustang takes sick over the next few days. I hear fluid in her lungs and feed her broth made from marrow and wolf and leaves boiled in a helmet I found. She looks like she will die. I don't know what to do. We're low on food, so I hunt. But the game is scarce and the wolves are hungry. Prey has fled these woods, so we survive on small hares. All I can do is keep her warm and pray a medBot descends from the clouds. The Proctors know where we are. They always know where we are.

I find human tracks in the woods the next week. A set of two. I follow them to an abandoned campsite, hoping they might have food I can steal. There are animal bones and embers still hot. No horses, though. Probably not scouts then. Oathbreakers, the Shamed who have broken their vows after being enslaved. There's plenty of them now.

I follow their tracks through the woods for an hour before I grow worried. They circle back around, leading somewhere familiar, leading to our cave. It is night by the time I return. I hear laughter from the home I share with Mustang. The arrow feels thin in my fingers as I nock it on the bowstring. I should kneel to gather my breath. My wound aches. I pant. But I can't give them more time. Not if they have Mustang.

They cannot see me as I stand at the edge of the frozen caribou skin and hardpacked snow that walls off our cave from sight and elements. The fire crackles inside. Smoke seeps out through vents Mustang and I took a day in making. Two boys sit together eating what's left of our meat, drinking our water.

They are dirty and ragged. Hair like greased weeds. Stained complexions. Blackheads. Once beautiful, I'm sure. One boy sits on Mustang's chest. The girl who saved my life is gagged and in her undergarments. She shivers from the cold. One of the boys bleeds from a bite wound on his neck. They are planning on making her pay for that wound. Knives heat till red in the fire. One boy obviously enjoys the sight of her nakedness. He reaches to touch her skin as though she's a toy meant for his pleasure.

My thoughts are primal, wolflike. A terrifying emotion sweeps over me, one that I did not know I had for this girl. Not till now. It takes a moment to calm myself and stop my hands from shaking. His hand is on the inside of her thigh.

I shoot the first boy in the kneecap. The second I shoot as he reaches for a knife. I'm a bad aim. I get his shoulder instead of his eye socket. I slide into the shelter with my skinning knife, ready to finish the boys off as they howl in pain. Something in me, the human part, has turned off, and it's only when I see Mustang's eyes that I stop.

"Darrow," she says softly.

Even shivering, she is beautiful—the small, quick-smiling girl who brought me back to life. The bright-eyed soul who keeps Eo's song alive. I shudder with anger. If I had been ten minutes later in returning, this night could have broken me forever. I cannot bear another death. Especially not Mustang's.

"Darrow, let them live," she says again, whispering it to me as Eo would whisper she loved me. It cuts to my core. I can't take the sound of her voice, the anger inside me.

My mouth doesn't work. My face is numb; I can't lose the grimace of rage that controls it. I drag the two boys out by their hair and kick them till Mustang joins us. I leave them moaning in the snow and return to help her dress. She feels so fragile as I pull her animal skins around her bony shoulders.

"Knife or snow," she asks the boys when she's dressed. She holds the knives heated in the fire in her trembling hands. She coughs. I know what she's thinking. Let them go and they kill us as we sleep. Neither will die from their wounds. The medBots would come if that were the case. Or maybe they won't for Oathbreakers.

They choose snow.

I'm glad. Mustang didn't want to use the knife.

We tie them to a tree at the edge of the woods and light a signal fire so that some House will find them. Mustang insisted on coming along, coughing all the way, as if she were worried I wouldn't do as she asked. She was right to think that.

In the night, after Mustang has gone to sleep, I get up to go back and kill the Oathbreakers. If Jupiter or Mars finds them, then they will spill where we are and we will be taken.

"Don't, Darrow," she says as I pull back the caribou skin. I turn. Her face peers out from our blankets.

"We will have to move if they live," I say. "And you're already sick. You'll die."

We have warmth here. Shelter.

"Then we will move in the morning," she says. "I'm tougher than I look."

Sometimes that is true. This time it is not.

I wake in the morning to find that she shifted in the night to curl into me for warmth. Her body is so frail. It trembles like a leaf in the wind. I smell her hair. She breathes softly. Salt tracks mark her face. I want Eo. I wish it were her hair, her warmth. But I don't push Mustang away. There's pain when I hold her, but it comes from the past, not from Mustang. She is something new, something hopeful. Like spring to my deep winter.

When morning comes, we move deeper into the woods and make a lean-to shelter against a rock face with fallen trees and packed snow. We never find out what happened to the Oathbreakers or our cave.

Mustang can barely sleep, she coughs so much. When she sleeps curled into me, I kiss the nape of her neck softly, softly so that she will not wake; though I secretly wish she would if just to know that I'm here. Her skin is hot. I hum the Song of Persephone.

"I can never remember the words," she whispers to me. Her head lies in my lap tonight. "I wish I did."

I have not sung since Lykos. My voice is raspy and raw. Slowly the song comes.

Listen, listen
Remember the wane
Of sun's fury and waving grain
We fell and fell
And danced along
To croon a knell
Of rights and wrongs

And

My son, my son
Remember the burn
When leaves were fire and seasons turned
We fell and fell
And sang a song
To weave a cell
All autumn long

And
Down in the vale
Hear the reaper swing, the reaper swing
the reaper swing
Down in the vale
Hear the reaper sing
A tale of winter long

My girl, my girl
Remember the chill
When rains froze and snows did kill
We fell and fell
And danced along
Through icy hell
To their winter song

My love, my love
Remember the cries
When winter died for spring skies
They roared and roared
But we grabbed our seed
And sowed a song
Against their greed

My son, my son
Remember the chains
When gold ruled with iron reins
We roared and roared
And twisted and screamed
For ours, a vale
of better dreams

And
Down in the vale
Hear the reaper swing, the reaper swing
the reaper swing

Down in the vale
Hear the reaper sing
A tale of winter done

"It is strange," she says.

"What is?"

"Father told me that there would be riots because of that song. That people would die. But it is such a soft melody." She coughs blood into a pelt. "We used to sing songs by the campfire, out in the country, where he kept us out of . . ." coughs again ". . . of the public . . . eye. When . . . my brother died . . . Father never sang with me again."

She will soon die. It's only a matter of time. Her face is pale, her smiles feeble. There's only one thing I can do, since the medBots haven't come. I will have to leave her to seek out medicine. One of the Houses might have found some or received injectables as a bounty. I'll have to go soon, but I need to get her food first.

Someone follows me that day as I hunt alone in the winter woods. I wear my new white wolfcloak. They are camouflaged as well. I do not see whoever it is, but he is there. I pretend my bowstring needs fixing and steal a glance back. Nothing. Quiet. Snow. The sound of wind on brittle branches. They still follow as I move along.

I feel them behind me. It's like the ache in my body from my wound. I pretend to see a deer and pass quickly through a thicket only to scramble up a tall pine on the other side.

I hear a *pop*.

They pass beneath me. I feel it on my skin, in my bones. So I shake the branches under my legs. Gathered snow tumbles down. A distorted hollow in the shape of a man forms in the snowfall. It is looking at me.

"Fitchner?" I call down.

His bubblegum pops again.

"You may come down now, boyo," Fitchner barks up. He deactivates his ghostCloak and gravBoots and sinks into the snow. He's wearing a thin black thermal. My layered fatigues and stinking animal skins don't keep me half as warm.

It's been weeks since I last saw him. He looks tired.

"Going to finish what Cassius started?" I ask as I hop down.

He looks me over and smirks. "You look horrible."

"You do too. The soft bed, warm food, and wine giving you trouble?" I point up. We can just barely see Olympus between the skeletal branches of the winter trees.

He smiles. "Readout says you've lost twenty pounds."

"Baby fat," I tell him. "Cassius's ionSword carved it off." I pull up my bow and point it at him. I wonder if he's wearing a pulseShield. It'll stop anything short of pulseWeapons and razors. Only recoilPlate can gird off those weapons—and even then, not well. "I should shoot you."

"You wouldn't dare. I'm a Proctor, boyo."

I shoot him in the thigh. Except the arrow loses velocity before it hits the invisible pulseShield, which flickers iridescent, and the arrow bounces to the ground. So they wear it at all times, even when they don't wear recoilArmor.

"Well, that was petulant." He yawns.

PulseShield, gravBoots, ghostCloak, looks like he has a pulseFist too, and those famous razors. Snow melts as it touches his skin. He saw me in the tree, so I'm guessing his eyes have injected optics. Certainly thermal scopes and night vision. He has a widget and an analyzerMod too. He knew my weight. Probably knows my white blood cell count. What about spectrum analysis?

He yawns again. "Little sleep these days on Olympus. Busy days."

"Who gave the Jackal the holo of me killing Julian?" I ask.

"Well, you don't dally away time."

He did something just as I spoke, and the sound around us localizes. I can't hear anything beyond an invisible five-meter bubble. Didn't know they had toys like that.

"The Proctors gave it to the Jackal," he tells me.

"Which ones?"

"Apollo. All of us. Doesn't matter."

I don't understand. "I assume it's because they favor the Jackal. Am I right?"

"As usual." His gum pops. "Unfortunately, you're just not allowed to win, and you were gaining momentum. Sooo . . ."

I ask him to explain. He says he just did. His eyes are ringed and tired despite the collagen and cosmetics he now wears to cover his fatigue. His stomach has grown. Arms are still skinny. Something worries him, and it isn't just his appearance.

"Allowed to?" I echo. "Allowed to. No one can be *allowed* to win. I thought the gorydamn point was to carve our own ladder to the top. So if I'm not *allowed* to win, that means the Jackal is."

"Pegged it." He doesn't sound very happy.

"Then that doesn't make any lick of sense. It corrupts the entire thing," I say hotly. "You broke the rules."

The best of Gold is supposed to rise, yet they already have chosen a winner. Not only does this ruin the Institute, it ruins the Society. The fittest reign. That's what they say. Now they've betrayed their own principles by taking sides in a schoolyard fight. This is the Laurel all over again. Hypocrisy.

"So this kid is what? A predestined Alexander? A Caesar? A Genghis? A Wiggin?" I ask. "This is slagging nonsense."

"Adrius is the son of our *dear* ArchGovernor Augustus. That's all that matters."

"Yes, you've told me that, but why is he supposed to win? Simply because his father is important?"

"Unfortunately, yes."

"Be more specific."

He sighs. "The ArchGovernor has secretly threatened and bribed and cajoled all twelve of us till we came to agree upon the fact that his son should win. But we have to be careful in our cheating. The Drafters, my real bosses, watch every move from their palaces, ships, et cetera. They are very important people as well. And then there's the Board of Quality Control to worry about, and the Sovereign and Senators and all the other Governors themselves. Because, though there are many schools, any of them can watch you whenever they like."

"What? How?"

He taps my wolf ring.

"Biometric nanoCam. Don't worry, it's showing them something else right now. I threw down a jamField, and anyway, there's a half-day delay for editing purposes. All other times, any Drafter, any Scarred, can watch you to see if they would like to offer you an apprenticeship when this is over. Oh, do they like you."

Thousands of Aureates have been watching me.

My insides, already cold, tighten.

Tiberius au Bellona, Imperator of the Sixth Fleet, father of Cassius and Julian, Drafter of House Mars, has watched me kill one son and deceive the other. It takes the wind out of me. What if I had told Titus that I knew he was a Red because I was a Red? Did they notice him say "bloodydamn"? Did I say he was a Red out loud or was that just in my head?

"What if I take the ring off?"

"Then you disappear, except for the cameras we have hidden in the battlefield." He winks. "Don't tell anyone. Now, if the Drafters discover the ArchGovernor's scheme . . . there will be hell to pay. Tension between the school Houses, certainly. But more importantly, there could be a Blood War between the Augustuses and Bellonas."

"And you'll be in trouble if they find out about the bribery?"

"I'll be dead." He fails in trying a smile.

"That's why you look like hell. You're in the middle of a shit storm. So how do I fit into this?"

He chuckles dryly.

"Many Drafters like you. Those of House Mars get to offer you your first apprenticeships, but you can entertain offers outside the House. If you die, they will be very unhappy. Especially the Sword of House Mars. His name is Lorn au Arcos; no doubt you've heard of him. He is prime good with his razor."

"How. Do. I. Fit. In?" I repeat.

"You don't. Stay alive. Stay out of the Jackal's path. Otherwise, Jupiter or Apollo will kill you and there will be nothing I can do to stop it."

"So they're his guard dogs, eh?"

"Amongst others, yes."

"Well, if they kill me, the Drafters would know something is wrong."

"They won't. Apollo will use other Houses to do it or we'll do it ourselves and edit out the footage from the nanoCams. Apollo and Jupiter are not stupid. So don't fiddle with them. Let the Jackal play and you'll have a future."

"And so will you."

"And so will I."

"I understand," I say.

"Good. Good. I knew you'd see sense. You know, many of the Proctors like you. Minerva even does. She hated you at first, but since you let Mustang go, she's been able to stay around on Olympus. Much less embarrassing that way."

"She's allowed to stay around on Olympus?" I ask innocently.

"Naturally. It's the rules of the Institute. Once your House is defeated, the Proctor heads home to face the music and explain what went wrong to the Drafters." Fitchner's smile contorts when he sees the sudden glimmer in my eyes.

"So if their House is destroyed, they have to leave? And it was Apollo and Jupiter who want me dead, you say?"

"No . . . ," he begs, suddenly hearing the menace in my voice.

I tilt my head. "No?"

"You . . . can't!" he sputters, confused. "I just told you, the Sword of the damn House Mars wants you as an apprentice. And there are others—Senators, Politicos, Praetors. Don't you want a future?"

"I want to rip the Jackal's balls off. That's all. Then I will find my apprenticeship. I imagine it will be an impressive one if I do that."

"Darrow! Be reasonable, man."

"Fitchner, my friends Roque and Lea died because of the ArchGovernor's meddling. Let's see how he likes it when I make his son, the Jackal, my slave."

"You're mad as a Red!" he says with a shake of his head. "You're screwing with the Proctors' livelihoods. None are content with their current station. They are all looking to ascend as well. If you threaten their futures, Apollo and Jupiter will come down and they will cut off your head!"

"Not if I destroy their Houses first." I frown. "Because don't they have to leave if I do that? Someone reliable told me those were the rules." I clap my hands together. "*Now,* I have another friend who is dying and I'd like some antibiotics. It'd be prime if you could give me some."

He gawps at me. "After this, why would I?"

"Because you've been a piss-poor Proctor up until now. You owe me bounties. And you have your own future to look after."

He snorts a defeated laugh. "Fair enough."

He takes an injectable from a medcase on his leg and hands it to me. I notice how the pulseShield doesn't hurt me when his hand touches mine. So they can turn it off. I thank him by clapping his shoulder affectionately. He rolls his eyes. The armor is turned off over the entire body. Then it's back. I hear the microhum at his waist where the contraption sits. Now that I've got Proctors for enemies, it's a good thing to know.

"So what will you do?" Fitchner asks.

"Who is more dangerous? Apollo or Jupiter? Be honest, Fitchner."

"Both are monsters of men. Apollo is more ambitious. Jupiter is simple—he just enjoys playing god here."

"Then House Apollo first. After that, I'll crush Jupiter. And when they are gone, who will protect the Jackal?"

"The Jackal," he says dryly.

"Then we'll see if he really does deserve to win."

Before I go, Fitchner tosses a small package to the ground.

"Not that it matters now, but this was given to me. I was told to say that you're to know that your friends have not forsaken you."

"Who?"

"I cannot say."

Whoever gave it to him is a friend, because inside the box is my Pegasus, and inside that is Eo's haemanthus blossom. I put the Pegasus necklace about my neck.

35

OATHBREAKERS

My friends are with me. What would they mean by that? Which friends? The Sons of Ares? Or was the mystery friend being more general, alluding to those who support my chances at the Institute? Do they know the significance of the Pegasus? Or were they simply reuniting me with something they thought I might miss?

So many questions; none of them matter. They are outside the game. The game. What else is there but the game? All the true things in the world, all my relationships, all my aspirations and needs, are wrapped up in this game, wrapped up in me winning. To win, I'll need an army, but it cannot be made of slaves. Not again. I now need, as I'll need at the head of a rebellion, followers, not slaves.

Man cannot be freed by the same injustice that enslaved it.

A week after I inject Mustang and her fever fades, we set off to the north. Her strength grows the more we move. Her cough is gone and her quick smile returns. Sometimes she needs a rest, but soon she comes close to outpacing me. She lets me know it too. We make as much noise as possible when we move to draw our prey to us. On the sixth night of setting obnoxiously large fires, we get our first nibble.

The Oathbreakers come along a stream, using its sounds to mask their approach. I like them immediately. Were our fire not a trap, they would have caught us unawares. But it is a trap, and when two step into the light, we almost spring it. Yet if they are smart enough to come along the stream, they are smart enough to leave someone in the dark. I hear an arrow nock on a bowstring. Then there's a yelp. Mustang takes the one in the dark. I take the other two. I stand up from my snowpile, my wolfcloak shedding snow, and knock them down from behind with the flat of my bow.

Afterward, the one Mustang struck nurses his swollen eye by our fire as I speak with their leader. Her name is Milia. She's a tall willow with a long horseface and a slight hunch to her shoulders. Rags and stolen furs cover her bony frame. The other uninjured one is Dax. Short, comely, with three frostbitten fingers. We give them extra furs and I think that makes all the difference in the conversation.

"You understand we could make you slaves, yes?" Mustang asks, brandishing her standard. "So you'd be twice Oathbreakers and twice shunned once this game is over."

Milia doesn't seem to care. Dax does. The other just follows Milia.

"Could give a rat's prick. No difference between once and twice," Milia says. They all bear the slave mark of Mars. I don't recognize them but their rings say they are from Juno. "Rather bear shame than bruise my knees. Do you know my father?"

"I don't care about your father."

"My father," she persists, "is Gauis au Trachus, Justiciar of the southern Martian hemisphere."

"I still don't care."

"And his father was—"

"I don't care."

"Then you are a fool," she drawls. "Twice a fool if you think to make me *your* slave. I will cut you in the night."

I nod to Mustang. She stands suddenly with the standard and puts it to Milia's head. The mark of Mars becomes that of Minerva. Then she erases the Minerva mark. Dax's eyes widen.

"Even if I free you?" I ask Milia. "You're still going to cut me?"

She doesn't know what to say.

"*Mily,*" Dax says quietly. "What are you thinking?"

"No slavery," I elaborate. "No beatings. If you dig a shit pit, I dig two shit pits for the camp. If someone cuts you, I rip them apart. So, will you join our army?"

"*His* army," Mustang corrects. I look over at her with a frown.

"And who's he?" Milia asks, her eyes not leaving my face.

"He's the Reaper."

It takes a week to gather ten Oathbreakers. The way I look at it is those ten already made it clear they don't want to be slaves. So they might like the first person who will give them purpose, food, furs, who is not demanding that they lick a bootheel. Most of them have heard of me, but all are disappointed that I don't have the famous slingBlade I used to beat Pax. Apparently he's become quite the legend. They say he picked up and threw a horse and rider into the Argos as Mars's slaves fought Jupiter's.

As we grow, we hide from the larger armies. Mars may be my House, but with Roque dead and Cassius an enemy, only Quinn and Sevro are left as friends. Pollux perhaps, but he'll go whatever way the wind blows. Rat bastard.

I cannot be with my House. There's no place for me there. I may have been their leader, but I remember how they looked at me. And now it is crucial they know I am alive.

Despite the war between Mars and Jupiter, stalwart Ceres stands unconquered by the riverside. Behind their high walls, bread smoke still rises. Mounted warbands from both armies roam the plains around Ceres, crossing the frozen Argos at will. They carry low-charged ionSwords now, so they can electrocute and maim one another with a brush of metal. MedBots scream over the battlefield when skirmishes break into pitched frays, healing wounded students as they bleed or moan from broken bones. The champions of each army wear ionArmor to protect themselves against the new weapons. Horses smash together. IonArrows fly. Slaves mill about hitting each other with older, simple weapons across the wide plain that separates the highlands from the great river Argos. It is a spectacular thing to see—but foolish, so foolish.

I watch with Mustang and Milia as two armored warbands of Mars and Jupiter streak toward each other across the plains in front of Phobos Tower. Pennants flap. Horses trample the deep snow. It's a clash of armored glory when the two metal tides collapse into one another. Lances spark with stunning electricity on broad shields and armor. Dazzling swords slam other blades like their own. HighDrafts battling highDrafts. Slaves run in scores to smash into each other, pawns in this giant chess match.

I see Pax in a rusty bulk of crimson armor so ancient it looks like a frysuit. I laugh as he tackles a horse and rider. But if ever there was a picture of a perfect knight, it would not be Pax. No, it'd be Cassius. I see him now. His armor glows as he stuns opponent after opponent, galloping through the enemy, his sword humming left and right, flickering like a tongue of fire. He can fight, but I'm shocked at how foolishly he chooses to—diving nobly into the enemy's gut with a force of lancers, capturing enemies. And then the surviving troops regroup and do the same to him. Over and over, neither side taking substantial advantage.

"What idiots," I say to Mustang. "All that pretty armor and swords blind them. I know. Maybe if they slam into one another three or four more times, it may just work."

"They've got tactics," she says. "Look, a wedge formation there. And a feint there that'll turn into a flank sweep."

"Yet I'm right."

"Yet you're not wrong." She watches for a moment. "Like our little war all over again, except you're not running around howling at people like a moontouched wolf." Mustang sighs and puts a hand on my shoulder. "Ah, the good old days."

Milia watches us with a wrinkled nose.

"Tactics win battles. Strategy wins wars," I say.

"Oooo. I am Reaper. God of wolves. King of strategy." Mustang pinches my cheek. "You are just too adorable."

I swat her away. Milia rolls her eyes.

"So, what is our strategy, milord?" Mustang asks me.

The longer I draw out any conflict with an enemy, the more chances the Proctors will get to ruin me. My rise must be meteoric. I don't tell her this.

"Speed is our strategy," I say. "Speed and extreme predjudice."

The next morning, House Mars's warband finds their bridge across the Metas blocked by trees felled in the night. As expected, the warband turns around and rides back to the castle, fearing some sort of trap. Their watchmen in Phobos and Deimos cannot see us; they peer down and send smoke signals that there is no enemy in the barren deciduous woods around the bridge. They do not see us because we have been bellydown in the same position in the woods fifty yards from the bridge since black dawn. Each of my Oathbreakers has a white or gray wolfcloak now. It took a week to find the wolves, but perhaps that was for the better. The hunt created a bond. My ten soldiers are a scrappy lot. Liars, wicked cheats who would rather ruin their futures than be slaves in this game. So a proud, practical but not very honorable lot. Just the sort I need. Their faces are painted white with bird dung and gray clay, so we've the look of spectral winter beasts as breath billows from our grinning maws.

"They like being valued by someone fearsome," Milia told me the night before, her voice as cold and brittle as the icicles hanging from the aspen trees. "As do I."

"Mars'll take the bait," Mustang whispers to me now. "Not so much brainpower left in the House." Not with Roque gone. She chose a place close to me in the snow. So close that her legs stretch along mine, and her face, twisted sideways as she lies on her belly, is only inches from my own underneath our white cloaks. When I inhale, the air is already warm from her breath. I think this is the first time I've thought of kissing her. I chase the thought away, and summon the sight of Eo's mischievous lips.

It is midday when Cassius sends troops—mostly slaves, for fear of an ambush—to clear the felled trees from the bridge. In fact,

Cassius plays too clever a game. Since he believes he is fighting Jupiter, his assumption is that the ambush will be a sudden cavalry charge once the bridge is clear. So he has his horses go around the river, south through the highlands, and loop around on the far side of the bridge near Phobos to spring an ambush on the cavalry he assumes will come from the Greatwoods or the plains. Milia, the shifty girl, brings me news of this movement of horse in the form of a howl from her perch nearly a mile off, where she serves as lookout in the high pines. It is time to move.

We do not howl or shout as we ten sprint through the leafless woods toward the toiling slaves. Four highDrafts sit on horses watching the work. One is Cipio. We sprint faster. Faster through the barren trees, coming from their flank. They do not see us. We fan out. Racing one another to make the first strike.

I win.

Jumping five meters forward in the lowGrav, I fly out of the woods like a demon possessed and take Cipio at the shoulder with a blunted sword. He spills from the saddle. Horses whinny. Mustang takes down another highDraft with her standard. My troops swarm forward, silent and shadowed with white and gray. Two more of my Oathbreakers leap onto the highDrafts' horses and bludgeon the riders with clubs and blunted axes. I ordered no killing; it's over in four seconds. The horses don't even know where their riders went. My troops flow past the horses into the slaves as they clear the bridge of the felled logs. Half don't even hear us till Mustang has turned six into Minerva slaves and ordered them to help us subdue the rest. Then there's shouting and the Mars slaves turn their axes against my troops.

Those from Minerva recognize Mustang and are set free when she clears away the mark of Mars. It's like a shifting tide. Six slaves are ours. They tackle Mars's other slaves and pin them down as Mustang runs over and converts them. Eight, by the same process. Ten. Eleven, till only one offers trouble. And he's the prize. Pax. He doesn't have his armor, thank God. He's here for labor, but it still takes seven of us to take him to the ground. He's roaring and screaming his name. I dive at him and take a fist to the face. I'm spitting and laughing as we pile on till there's twelve of us holding the genetic monster down. Mustang frees him of the mark of Mars and his roars become laughter so high pitched, it sounds like a girl's.

"Freeeeeedom!" he roars. He jumps up, looking for someone to maim. "Darrow au Andromedus!" he shouts at me, ready to break my face till Mustang shouts him down.

"He's on our side," Mustang says.

"The truth?" Pax asks. His giant face splits into a smile. "What news!" And he's got me in a bear hug. "*Freeeedom,* brothers . . . and sisters! Sweet freedom!" We leave Cipio and the other highDrafts moaning on the ground.

The smoke signals plume up from Phobos and Deimos as we sprint through the vale's woods into the dwarf mountains to the north before the horsemen of Mars can loop back around the blocked bridge to assail us. The watchmen saw it all. And they must be horrified. It happened in less than a minute. Pax won't stop laughing like a girl.

House Mars will be confused by the sudden depletion of their ranks. But I need more than that. I need them to replace the vision they have of me, one of a flawed leader, with something supernatural, something beyond their understanding. I need to be like the Jackal—nameless and superhuman.

That night, I slither through the snow north of Castle Mars. Riders patrol the glen. Their hooves are soft on the grass in the night. I hear their bridles clinking in the darkness. I do not see them. My wolfcloak is white as the falling snow. I've pulled its head up, so I look like a guardian creature from the colder levels of hell. The rock face is steeper than I remember. I nearly fall as I pull myself along the snowy vertical. I reach the castle wall. Torches flicker on the ramparts. Wind whips the flames about. Mustang should be about to light the blaze.

I strip away my cloak and ball it up. My skin is coated in charcoal. I push the metal tongs into the spaces between the stones. It is like climbing my drill again except I'm stronger and I'm not wearing a frysuit. Easy. The Pegasus bounces against my chest as I pull myself up. I'm not even panting when I reach the top six minutes later.

My fingers cling to the stone just beneath the ramparts. I hang, listening to the passing sentry. Of course it is a slave. And she's not stupid. She sees me as I pull myself over the rampart and shoves a spear against my throat. I flash my Mars ring and hold my finger to my lips.

"Why should I not call out?" she asks. She was once of Minerva.

"Did they tell you to guard the wall for enemies? I'm sure they did. But I'm of House Mars. The ring says so. I can't be an enemy then, yes?"

She frowns. "The Primus told me to watch the walls for intruders and to kill or call out . . ."

"This is my home. I am rightful Primus of House Mars. I am your master and I *demand* you continue to watch the wall for intruders. It is imperative." I wink. "I swear Virginia would be happy if you followed your orders to the letter."

She cocks her head at Mustang's real name and looks me over.

"My Primus is alive?"

"House Minerva has not yet fallen," I say.

The girl's face almost breaks she smiles so hard. "Well . . . then . . . I suppose this is your home. Can't stop you from entering it. Bound by oath to obey, I am. Wait . . . I know you. They said you were dead."

"Thank your Primus that I draw breath."

I learn from her that the Housemembers sleep while the slaves guard the fortress at night. That is the problem with slaves. They are so willing to find a way around their duty, and so excited to share secrets. I leave her behind and steal into the keep using a key she accidentally dropped into my hand.

Sneaking through my home, I am tempted to pay Cassius a visit. But I'm not here to kill him. Violence is the fool's way out. Sometimes I'm the fool, but tonight I'm feeling smart. I'm also not there to steal the standard. They will be guarding that. No. I'm there to remind them that they once were afraid of me. That I am the best of them all. I can go where I please. Do what I please.

I stay in the shadows even though I could use the same argument on every slave guard they have. Instead, I carve a slingBlade on every door in the keep. I slip into the warroom and carve a slingBlade into the huge table there to create the myth. Then I carve a skull into Cassius's chair and slab a knife deep into the back of the wood chair to create the rumor.

As I leave the way I came, I see the hillside north of the castle erupt in flame. The brush stacked in the shape of the Reaper's sling-Blade burns hot in the night.

Sevro, if he is still with Mars, will find me. And I could use the little bastard's help.

36

A SECOND TEST

In order to have an army, I must be able to feed it. So I will take the ovens of Ceres that Jupiter and Mars both lust over.

The new members of our band from House Minerva find it perfectly reasonable to accept my authority. I don't fool myself. Yes, they were impressed by me hiding my Howlers inside dead horses months ago, and they remember me defeating Pax. But it's only because Mustang trusts me that they obey. We leave those of House Diana as slaves for now. I need to earn their trust. Tactus, oddly, is the only one who seems to trust me. Then again, the laconic youth was all smiles when I told him I'd be sewing him inside of a dead horse over a month ago. There are two more of Diana that I sewed away. The others call them the DeadHorses, and they each wear braids of white horsehair. I think they're a bit mental.

If there is anything in the woods and highlands, it is an abundance of wolves. We hunt them to train our new recruits in my way of fighting. No glamorous cavalry charges. No damn lances. And certainly no stupid rules of engagement. Everyone gets cloaks, which are smelly things as they dry and we peel away the rot. Everyone except Pax. They haven't yet made a wolf big enough for him.

"House Ceres is no stranger to siege," Mustang says. She's right.

At night, they seem to have more soldiers awake than in the day. They watch for sneak assaults. Blazing bundles of tinder light the base of their walls at night. Somehow, they have dogs now. Those prowl along the battlements. The way from the water is guarded ever since I tried sending Sevro in through the latrines long ago during a sneak attack I arranged when we were at war with Minerva. He barely forgave me for that one. The Ceres students come out no longer. They've learned the risks of battling stronger Houses on open ground. They'll hole up for winter, and when the cold and hunger have weakened the other Houses, they'll emerge from their fortress in the spring—strong, prepared, and organized.

But they'll never make it to the spring.

"So we attack during the day?" Mustang guesses.

"Naturally," I say. Sometimes I wonder why we even bother speaking. She knows my thoughts. Even the mad ones.

This idea is an especially mad one. We practiced it in a clearing in the Northwoods for a whole day after flattening out the wood with axes. Pax makes the plan possible. We hold competitions to see who has the best balance on the wood. Mustang wins. Horsefaced Milia is second, and she's spitting bitter that she doesn't beat Mustang. I'm third.

As we did when springing the trap on House Mars, we sneak as close as we dare the night before and bury ourselves in the deep snow. Again, Mustang and I pair off, huddling tight with one another under the snow. Tactus tries pairing with Milia, but she tells him to go slag himself.

"If you look at it properly, I was trying to do you a favor," he mutters over at Milia as he huddles down under Pax's smelly armpit. "You're about as pretty as a gargoyle's wart. So when else would you get a chance to snuggle with the likes of me? Ungrateful sow."

Mustang and the other girls snort their derision. Then the quiet of night and the chill of the open ice plain bite into us and we grow silent.

Come morning, Mustang and I shiver into one another, and a new snowfall threatens to ruin our plan, burying us even deeper in the plain. But the wind is manageable and the flakes do not bury us too deep as they spin through the air. I'm first up, though I do not move. And soon after I yawn away the last vestige of sleep, my army wakes organically, one student stirring and grumbling into another till there's a snake of sniffing and coughing Golds buried together in a shallow tunnel beneath the snow's surface. I can't see them, but I hear their waking despite the sound of the snowstorm's wind.

Ice formed around me in the night outside my thick cloaks. Mustang's hands are inside my pelts, warm against my side. Her breath heats my neck. As I stir, she yawns and straightens, pulling a little away as she stretches, catlike, under the snow. Snow crumbles in between us.

"Gory hell, this is miserable," Dax, Milia's companion, mutters. I can't see him in our snow tunnel.

Mustang nudges me. We can just barely see Tactus curled into the hollow of Pax's armpit. The two men snuggle together and wake like lovers, only to flinch away from one another when their ice-crusted eyelids flutter open.

"Wonder which is Romeo," Mustang whispers, her throat raspy.

I chuckle and carve a hole in the roof of our tunnel to see that my band of twenty-four is alone in the plains except for early morning horse scouts in the distance. They will not be a problem. Wind rolls in from the north river, biting deep into my face.

"You ready for this?" Mustang asks me with a grin as I bring my head back into our shelter. "Or are you too cold?"

"It was colder in the loch when I first tricked you," I say, smiling. "Ah, the old days."

"All part of my master plan to win your trust, little man." She smirks mischievously. She sees the worry in my eyes, so she grips my thigh and comes close so the others can't hear. "Think I'd be squatting here with you in the snow if this plan could go belly up? Negative. But I'm freezing my balls off and the wind is dying, so let's go, Reaper."

I give the countdown and we're up, snow crumbling around us, wind stinging our faces, and sprinting the hundred meters across the plains to the walls. All twenty-four of us. Silent again. The wind comes in fits. We carry the long tree between us, huddling tight to it as we did in the night when it shared our tunnel with us. It's heavy, but we're twenty-four and Pax's parents gave him the genes to knock over bloodydamn horses. Panting. Legs burning. Gritting as the wood weighs down our shoulders in the deep snow. It's a trudge. A shout comes from the wall. A lonely, hollow call that echoes over the still winter morning. More shouts. Still few. Barks. Confusion. An arrow whistles past. Then another. It's amazing how quiet the world is as the arrows sail, carrying death. The wind has faded again. Sun peeks from behind a cloudlayer and we're bathed with morning warmth.

We're at the wall. Shouts spread beyond the stone fortification, from their towers. A signal horn. Barking of dogs. Snow falls from the parapets as archers lean over the stone battlements. An arrow shivers in the wood by my hand. Someone goes down bloodylike, Dax. Then Pax roars the word and he, Tactus, and five more of our strongest take the long wood beam we cut from the tree trunk and shove the tip as hard as they can into the wall. They hold it there at an angle. They are roaring from the burden. It's still five meters short of the top of the wall, but I'm already sprinting up the thin slope. Pax grunts like a boar as he heaves against the angled strain. He's shouting, roaring. Mustang is right behind me, then Milia. I almost slip. My balance and Helldiver hands keep me scrabbling up the knotted wood. In our fur, we look like squirrels, not wolves. An arrow hisses through my cloak. I'm against the wall at the top of the wobbling beam. Pax and his boys roar gutturally from the exertion. Mustang is coming. I cup my hands. She stirrups her foot at the run and I hurl her up the last five meters to clear the battlements. Her sword slashes and she screams like a banshee. Then Milia launches the same way off my hands, and the rope she has tied to her waist dangles after her. She anchors up top as I use it to pull myself up the last five meters. The wooden beam crashes to the ground behind me. My sword is out. It's mayhem. House Ceres was caught unaware. They've never had an enemy on the battlements. And there are three of us, screaming and slashing. Rage and excitement fill me and I begin my dance.

They only have bows. It's been months since they've used swords.

Ours aren't sharp or fused with electricity, but cold durosteel is nasty to take in any form. The dogs are the hardest to manage. I kick one in the head. Throw another one off the battlements. Milia is down. She bites a dog in the neck and punches it in the balls till it whimpers off.

Mustang tackles someone off the battlements. I slidetackle one of the archers as he levels his bow at her. Outside, Pax shouts for me to open the gates. He's actually crying for combat.

I follow Mustang down into their courtyard, jumping from the parapets down to where she fights a big Ceres student. I end the boy with my elbow and take my first glimpse of the bread fortress. The castle is an unfamiliar design, a courtyard leading to several buildings and a huge keep where the bread bakes, making my stomach rumble; but all that matters to me is the gate. We rush to it. Shouts from behind us. Too many for us to fight. We get to the gate just as three dozen House Ceres students run at us across the courtyard from their keep.

"Hurry!" Mustang shouts. "Uh, *hurry!*"

Milia shoots arrows at the enemy from the parapets.

Then I open the gate.

"PAX AU TELEMANUS! PAX AU TELEMANUS!"

He shoves me aside. He's shirtless, massive, muscled, screaming. His hair is painted white and spiked with sap to form two horns. A piece of wood as long as my body serves as his club. The House Ceres students flinch back. Some fall. Some stumble. A boy screams as Pax thunders close.

"PAX AU TELEMANUS! PAX AU TELEMANUS!"

He wants no nickname as he charges forward like a minotaur possessed. When he hits the mass of House Ceres students, it is ruin. Boys and girls fly through the air like chaff on reaping day.

The rest of my army sprints in behind the mad bastard. They begin to howl, not because I told them to, not because they think they are Sevro's Howlers, but because it was the sound they heard when my soldiers cut their way out of horses' bellies, the sound that made their hearts sink as they were conquered. Now it's their turn to howl as they turn the battle into a mad melee. Pax screams his name, and he screams mine as he conquers the citadel almost single-handedly. He picks a boy up by the leg and uses him as a club. Mustang drifts about the battlefield like some Valkyrie, enslaving those who lie stunned on the ground.

In five minutes, the ovens and citadel are ours. We shut their gates, howl, and eat some bloodydamn bread.

I free the House Diana slaves who helped me capture the fortress and take a moment with each to share a laugh. Tactus sits on some poor boy's back, braiding the prisoner's hair in girlish pigtails, till I nudge him to get off. He slaps at my hand.

"Don't touch me," he snaps.

"What did you say?" I growl.

He stands fast, his nose coming only to my chin, and speaks very quietly so only we can hear. "*Listen, big man. I am of the gens Valii. My pure blood goes back to the Conquering. I could buy and sell you with my weekly allowance. So you don't demean me in this little game like all the others, you schoolyard king.*" Then louder so others can hear: "I do as I like, because I took this castle for you and slept in a dead horse so we could take Minerva! I deserve to have *some* fun."

I lean close. "*Three pints.*"

He rolls his eyes. "Whatever are you growling about?"

"*That's how much blood I'm about to make you swallow.*"

"Well, might makes right," he chuckles, and turns his back on me.

Then, mastering my anger, I tell the members of my army that they will never be slaves in this game again, so long as they wear my wolfskin. If they don't like that notion, they can clear out. None do, but that's expected. They want to win, but to follow my orders, to understand that I don't think I'm some high and mighty emperor, their proud hearts need to feel valued. So I make sure they know they are. I pay each student a specific compliment. One they remember forever.

Even when I am ruining their Society at the vanguard of a billion screaming Reds, they will tell their children that Darrow of Mars once clapped them on the shoulder and paid them a compliment.

The defeated students from House Ceres watch me free my army's slaves and they gape. They don't understand. They recognize me, but they don't comprehend why there isn't a single other Mars student, or why I'm in power, or why I think it is allowed to free slaves. While they are still gaping, Mustang enslaves them with the symbol of House Minerva, and they become doubly confused.

"Win me a fortress, and you get your freedom too," I tell them. Their bodies are different from ours. Softer from much bread and little meat. "But you must be starving for some venison and wild meat. Some protein is missing in your diets, I think." We brought plenty to share.

We free several slaves taken by House Ceres months prior. There are few, but most are House Mars or Juno. They find this new alliance strange, but it is an easy pill to swallow after months of toiling in the ovens.

The night ends on a sour note as I am woken an hour into sleep. Mustang sits on the edge of my bed as my eyes flutter open. When I see her, I feel a spike of terror in me, assuming she's come for a different reason, that her hand on my leg means something simple, something human. Instead, she brings me news I wished never to hear again.

Tactus flouted my authority and tried to rape a Ceres slave during the night. Milia caught him, and Mustang barely stopped her from cutting Tactus a thousand different ways. Everyone is up in arms.

"It's bad," Mustang says. "The Diana students are in their wargear and are about to try and take him back from Milia and Pax."

"They're mad enough to fight *Pax?*"

"Yeah."

"I'll get dressed."

"Please."

I meet her in the Ceres warroom two minutes later. The table is already carved with my slingBlade. I didn't do it, and it's much better work than I could have managed.

"Thoughts?" I fall into the seat opposite Mustang. We're a council of two. It's times like this when I miss Cassius, Roque, Quinn, all of them. Especially Sevro.

"When Titus did this, you said we make our own law, if I remember right. You sentenced him to death. So are we still doing that? Or are we doing something more convenient?" she asks me as though she already thinks I'm letting Tactus off the hook.

I nod, surprising her. "He'll pay," I say.

"This . . . it just *pisses* me off." She takes her feet off the table and leans forward to shake her head. "We're meant to be better than this. That's all Peerless are supposed to be—transcendent of the urges that"—she holds up ironic airquotes—"*enslave* the weaker Colors."

"It isn't about urges." I tap the table in frustration. "It's about power."

"Tactus is of House Valii!" Mustang exclaims. "His family is ancient. How much power does that asshole want?"

"Power over *me,* I mean. I told him he couldn't do something. Now he's trying to prove he can do whatever he wants."

"So he's not another heathen like Titus."

"You've met him. Of course he's a heathen. But no. This was tactical."

"Well, the clever shit has put you in a tight spot."

I slap the table. "I don't like this—someone else picking the battles or the battlefield. That's how we will lose."

"It's a no-win, really. We can't come out ahead. Someone is going to hate you either way. So we just have to figure out which way is the least damaging. Prime?"

"What about justice?" I ask.

Her eyebrows float upward. "What about winning? Isn't that what matters?"

"You trying to trap me?"

She grins. "Just testing you."

I frown. "Tactus killed Tamara, his Primus. Cut her saddle and then rode over her. He's wicked. He deserves any punishment we give him."

Mustang raises her eyebrows as if this is all to be expected. "He sees what he wants, and he takes it."

"How admirable," I mutter.

She tilts her head at me, lively eyes going over my face. "Rare."

"What's that?"

"I was wrong, about you. That's rare."

"Am I wrong about Tactus?" I ask. "Is he wicked, really? Or is he just ahead of the curve? Does he just grasp the game better?"

"No one grasps the game."

Mustang puts her muddy boots on the table again and leans back. Her golden hair falls past her shoulders in a long braid. The fire crackles in the hearth, her eyes dance over my face. I don't miss my old friends when she smiles like that. I ask her to explain.

"No one grasps the game, because no one knows the rules. No one follows the same set of rules. It is like life. Some think honor universal. Some think laws binding. Others know better. But in the end, don't those who rise by poison die by poison?"

I shrug. "In the storybooks. In life there's no one left to poison them, often."

"They expect an eye for an eye, the House Ceres slaves. Punish Tactus, you piss off the Diana kids. They get you a fortress and you spit on them for it. Remember, as far as they are concerned, Tactus hid in a horse's belly half a day for *you* when you took my castle. Resentment will swell like a Copper bureaucracy. But if you don't punish him, you'll lose all of Ceres."

"Can't do that." I sigh. "I failed this test before. I put Titus to death and thought I was meting out justice. I was wrong."

"Tactus is an Iron Gold. His blood is as old as the Society. They look at compassion, at reform, as a disease. He is his family. He will not change. He will not learn. He believes in power. Other Colors are not people to him. Lesser Golds are not people to him. He is bound to his fate."

Yet I'm a Red acting like a Gold. No man is bound to his fate. I can change him. I know I can. But how?

"What do you think I should do?" I ask.

"Ha! The great Reaper." She slaps her thigh. "When have you ever cared what anyone thinks?"

"You're not just *anyone*."

She nods and, after a moment, speaks. "I was once told a story by Pliny, my tutor—a ghastly fellow, really. And a Politico now, so take this all with a shipload of salt. Anyway: On Earth, there was a man and his camel." I laugh. She keeps going. "They were traveling across this grand desert full of all sorts of nasties. One day, as the man prepared camp, the camel kicked him for no reason. So the man whipped the camel. The camel's wounds grew infected. It died and left the man stranded."

"Hands. Camels. You and metaphors . . ."

She shrugs. "Without your army, you're a man stranded in a desert. So tread carefully, Reaper."

I speak with Nyla, the Ceres girl, in private. She's a quiet one. Smart as a whip, but not physical in any way. Like a shuddering songbird, like Lea. She has a bloody swollen lip. It makes me want to castrate Tactus. She didn't come in wicked like the rest. Then again, she got through the Passage.

"He told me he wanted me to rub his shoulders. Told me to do what he said because he was my master because he spent blood taking the castle. Then he tried . . . well . . . you know."

A hundred generations of men have used that inhuman logic. The sadness her words create in me makes me miss home. But that happened there too. I remember the screams that made the soup ladle tremble in my mother's hand. Remember how my cousin earned antibiotics from that Gamma.

Nyla blinks and stares for a moment at the floor.

"I told him I was Mustang's slave. House Minerva's. It's her standard. I didn't have to obey him. He just kept pushing me down. I screamed. He punched me, then he just held my throat till things started to fade and I barely smelled his wolfcloak anymore. Then that tall girl, Milia, knocked him off, I guess."

She didn't mention that there were other Diana soldiers in the room. Others watched. My army. I gave them power and this is how they use it. It's my fault. They are mine but they are wicked. That will not be fixed by punishing one of them. They have to want to be good.

"What would you like for me to do to him?" I ask her. I don't reach out to comfort her. She doesn't need it, even though I think I do. She reminds me of Evey too.

Nyla touches her dirty curls and shrugs.

"Nothing."

"Nothing isn't enough."

"To fix what he tried to do to me? To make it right?" She shakes her head and her hands clutch her sides. "Nothing is enough."

The next morning, I assemble my army in the Ceres square. A dozen limp; few Aureate bones can really be broken because of their strength, so most of the injuries suffered in the assault were superficial. I smell the resentment from Ceres students, from Diana students. It's a cancer that'll eat away at the body of this army, no matter who it is focused on. Pax brings Tactus out and shoves him to his knees.

I ask him if he tried to rape Nyla.

"Laws are silent in times of war," Tactus drawls.

"Don't quote Cicero to me," I say. "You are held to a higher standard than a marauding centurion."

"In that, you're hitting the mark at least. I am a superior creature descended from proud stock and glorious heritage. Might makes right, Darrow. If I can take, I may take. If I do take, I deserve to have. This is what Peerless believe."

"The measure of a man is what he does when he has power," I say loudly.

"Just come off it, Reaper," Tactus replies, confident in himself as all like him are. "She's a spoil of war. My power took her. And before the strong, bend the weak."

"I'm stronger than you, Tactus," I say. "So I can do with you as I wish. No?"

He's silent, realizing he's fallen into a trap.

"You are from a superior family to mine, Tactus. My parents are dead. I am the sole member of my family. *But* I am a superior creature to you."

He smirks at that.

"Do you disagree?" I toss a knife at his feet and pull my own out. "I beg you to voice your concerns." He does not pick his blade up. "So, by right of power, I can do with you as I like."

I announce that rape will never be permitted, and then I ask Nyla the punishment she would give. As she told me before, she says she wants no punishment. I make sure they know this, so there are no recriminations against her. Tactus and his armed supporters stare at her in surprise. They don't understand why she would not take vengeance, but that doesn't stop them from smiling wolfishly at one another, thinking their chief has dodged punishment. Then I speak.

"But I say you get twenty lashes from a leather switch, Tactus. You tried to take something beyond the bounds of the game. You gave in to your pathetic animal instincts. Here that is less forgivable than murder; I hope you feel shame when you look back at this moment fifty years from now and realize your weakness. I hope you fear your sons and daughters knowing what you did to a fellow Gold. Until then, twenty lashes will serve."

Some of the Diana soldiers step forward in anger, but Pax hefts his axe on his shoulder and they shrink back, glaring at me. They gave me a fortress and I'm going to whip their favorite warrior. I see my army dying as Mustang pulls off Tactus's shirt. He stares at me like a snake. I know what evil thoughts he's thinking. I thought them of my floggers too.

I whip him twenty brutal times, holding nothing back. Blood runs down his back. Pax nearly has to hack down one of the Diana soldiers to keep them from charging to stop the punishment.

Tactus barely manages to stagger to his feet, wrath burning in his eyes.

"A mistake," he whispers to me. "Such a mistake."

Then I surprise him. I shove the switch into his hand and bring him close by cupping my hand around the back of his head.

"*You deserve to have your balls off, you selfish bastard,*" I whisper to him. "This is my army," I say more loudly. "This is *my* army.

Its evils are mine as much as yours, as much as they are Tactus's. Every time any of you commit a crime like this, something gratuitous and perverse, you will own it and I will own it with you, because when you do something wicked, it hurts all of us."

Tactus stands there like a fool. He's confused.

I shove him hard in the chest. He stumbles back. I follow him, shoving.

"What were you going to do?" I push his hand holding the leather switch back toward his chest.

"I don't know what you mean . . ." he murmurs as I shove him.

"Come on, man! You were going to shove your prick inside someone in *my* army. Why not whip me while you're at it? Why not hurt me too? It'll be easier. Milia won't even try to stab you. I promise."

I shove him again. He looks around. No one speaks. I strip off my shirt and go to my knees. The air is cold. Knees on stone and snow. My eyes lock with Mustang's. She winks at me and I feel like I can do anything. I tell Tactus to give me twenty-five lashes. I've taken worse. His arms are weak and so is his will to do it. It still stings, but I stand up after five lashes and give the lash to Pax.

They start the count at six.

"Start over!" I shout. "A little rapist cur can't swing hard enough to hurt me."

But Pax bloodywell can.

My army cries in protest. They don't understand. Golds don't do this. Golds don't sacrifice for one another. Leaders take; they do not give. My army cries out again. I ask them, how is this worse than the rape they were all so comfortable with? Is not Nyla now one of us? Is she not part of the body?

Like Reds are. Like Obsidians are. Like all the Colors are.

Pax tries to go light. But it's Pax, so when he's done, my back looks like chewed goatmeat. I stand up. Do everything I can to prevent myself from wobbling. I'm seeing stars. I want to wail. Want to cry. Instead, I tell them that anyone who does anything vile—they know what I mean—will have to whip me like this in front of the entire army. I see how they look at Tactus now, how they look at Pax, how they look at my back.

"You do not follow me because I am the strongest. Pax is. You do not follow me because I am the brightest. Mustang is. You follow me because you do not know where you are going. I do."

I motion Tactus to come toward me. He wavers, pale, confused as a newborn lamb. Fear marks his face. Fear of the unknown. Fear of the pain I willingly bore. Fear when he realizes how different he is from me.

"Don't be afraid," I tell him. I pull him forward into a hug. "We are blood brothers, you little shit. Blood brothers."

I'm learning.

37

SOUTH

"Shit on a pike!" I yelp as Mustang puts salve on my back in the warroom. She flicks my back with a finger. "Why?" I moan.

"The measure of a man is what he does when he has power." She laughs. "You mock him for Cicero and then spit out Plato."

"Plato is older. He trumps Cicero. Ow!"

"And what was that about blood brothers? That means absolutely nothing. You might as well have said you were pinecone cousins."

"Nothing binds like pain shared."

"Well, here's some more of that." She pulls a bit of leather out of a wound. I yelp.

"Pain shared . . ." I shudder. "Not inflicted. Psychotic . . . *ow!*"

"You sound like a girl. Thought martyrs were tough. Then again, you could be barking mad. Fever when you were stabbed, probably. You traumatized Pax, by the way. He's crying. Good work."

I actually hear Pax's sniffles from the armory.

"But it did work, eh?"

"Sure, Messiah. You made yourself a cult," she mocks dryly. "They're building idols to you in the square. Kneeling in supplication of your wisdom. O mighty lord. I will laugh when they find out they don't like you and can have you flogged anytime they do a naughty. Now hold still, you Pixie. And stop talking. You annoy me."

"You know, when we graduate, maybe you should look into being a Pink. Your touch is so tender."

She smirks. "Send me to a Rose Garden? Hah! Now, that would tickle my father pink. Oh, stop squealing. The pun wasn't that bad."

The next day, I organize my army. I give Mustang the duty of choosing six squads of three scouts each. I have fifty-six soldiers; more than half are slaves. I make her put a Ceres in each group, the most ambitious. They get six of the eight commUnits I found in Ceres's warroom. The things are primitive, crackling earpieces, but they give my army something I've never had—an evolution beyond smoke signals.

"So I'm assuming you have a plan besides just going south like some Mongol horde . . . ," Mustang says.

"Of course. We're going to find the House Apollo." True to my promise to Fitchner.

The scouts strike out that night from House Ceres, fanning out to the south in six directions. My army follows at dawn, just before the winter sun rises. I will not squander this opportunity. Winter has forced the Houses into fortresses. Deep snows and hidden ravines make heavy cavalry sluggish, less useful. The game has slowed, but I won't. Mars and Jupiter can battle it out for all I care. I'll come back for both later.

At nightfall on the second day of our move south, we see the fortress of Juno, already conquered by Jupiter. It lies to the west on a tributary of the Argos. Mountains frame it. Beyond that are the wintry six-kilometer-high walls of the Valles Marineris. My scouts bring me news of three enemy scouts, cavalry, in the fringes of the woods to the east. They think it is Pluto, the Jackal's men. The horses are black, and the hair of the riders is dyed the same. They wear bones in their hair. I hear that they rattle like bamboo wind chimes as they ride.

Whoever the riders are, they never come close. Never fall into my traps. A girl is said to lead them. She rides a silver horse draped with a leather mantle sewn with unbleached bones—apparently the medBots are not so good in the South. Lilath, I think. She and her scouts disappear south as a larger warband appears from the southeast and skirts along the Greatwoods.

These are now real armies of heavy horse.

A single rider comes forward from the larger warband. He carries the archer pennant of Apollo. His hair is long and unbraided, his face hard from the winter winds that roll in from the southern sea. A cut on his forehead nearly claimed both his eyes, eyes that stare now at me like two burning coals set in a face of hammered bronze.

I walk forward to meet him after telling my army to look as weathered and pathetic as humanly possible. Pax manages poorly. Mustang makes him go to his knees so he looks relatively normal. She stands on his shoulders for comic relief, and starts a snowball fight as the emissary comes near. It's a rowdy, foolish affair, and it makes my army look wonderfully vulnerable.

I fake a limp. Toss away my wolfcloak. Fake a shiver. Make sure my pathetic durosteel sword looks more a cane than a weapon. Bend my long body as he approaches and I spare a look back at my playing army. My look of embarrassment is almost split in half with a laugh. I swallow it down.

His voice is like steel dragged over rough stone. No humor to him, no recognition that we're all teenagers playing a game and that the real world still flows on outside this valley. In the South, things have happened to make them forget. So when I offer him a self-effacing smile, he does not return it. He is a man. Not a boy. I think it is the first time I've seen someone fully transformed.

"And you are but a ragged remnant from the North," the Apollo Primus, Novas, scoffs. He tries guessing the House we hail from. I've made sure the Ceres standard is the one he sees. His eyes flicker. He wants it for his own glory. He also happily notices that more than half my army of fifty-six is enslaved. "You will not last long in the South. Perhaps you would like shelter from the cold? Warm food and bed? The South is harsh."

"I can't wager it will be worse than the North, man," I say. "They have razors and pulseArmor there. Proctors turned their favor from us."

"They are not there to favor you, weakling," he says. "They help those who help themselves."

"We helped ourselves as best we could," I say meekly.

He spits on the ground. "Little child. Do not whine here. The South does not listen to tears."

"But . . . but the South cannot be worse than the North." I shudder and tell him of the Reaper from the highlands. A monster. A brute. A killer. Evil, evil things.

He nods when I speak of the Reaper. So he has heard of me.

"The Reaper of yours is dead. A shame. I would have liked to test myself against him."

"He was a demon!" I protest.

"We have our own demons here. A one-eyed monster in the woods and a worse monster in the mountains to the west. The Jackal," he confides as he continues with his pitch. I would be allowed to join Apollo as a mercenary, not a slave, never a slave. He would help me defeat the Jackal, then retake the North. We would be allies. He thinks me weak and stupid.

I look at my ring. The Proctor of Apollo will know what I say here. I want him to know I am going to ruin his House. If he wants to try to stop me, this is his invitation.

"No," I say to Novas. "My family would shame me. I would be nothing to them if I joined you. No. I'm sorry." I smile inside. "We have enough food to march through your lands. If you let us, we will brook no—"

He slaps me across the face.

"You are a Pixie," he says. "Stiffen your quivering lip. You embarrass your Color." He leans toward me over his saddle pommel. "You are caught between giants, and you will be crushed. But make a man of yourself before we come for you. I do not fight children."

It is then that Mustang throws a snowball at his head; naturally, her aim is true and her laugh is loud.

Novas does not react. All that moves is his horse beneath him as it wheels to take him back to his roving warband. I watch the man go, and feel disquiet seep into me.

"Ride on home, little archer!" Tactus calls out. "Ride home to your mommy!"

Novas rejoins his thirty heavy horse. Our only cavalry is our scouts. They cannot stand against ionBlades and ionLances at full tilt, even with the deep snowbanks to muddle the heavier horses. Our weapons are still durosteel. Armor no better than duroplate or wolfskin. I don't even wear armor. I don't plan on fighting a battle where I need to for a while. We've not had a bounty after capturing Ceres's fortress and their standard. The Proctors have forsaken me, but the weather has not. Normally, infantry falls like dry wheat to cavalry, but the snow and its treacherous depths protect us.

We camp on the western bank of the river that night, nearer the mountains, away from the open plains in front of the dark Greatwoods. Apollo's heavy cavalry now has to cross the frozen river in the darkness if they want to raid our camp as we sleep. I knew they'd try when they thought us weak, ripe for the taking. They fail miserably. Arrogants. As dusk settled, I had Pax and his strongmen take axes out to soften the thick ice of the river bordering our camp. We hear horse screams and plunging bodies in the night. MedBots whine down to save lives. Those boys and girls are out of the game.

We continue south, aiming for where my scouts guess Apollo's castle lies. At night we eat well. Soups are made from the meat and bones of animals my scouts bring back. Bread is kept stored in makeshift packs. It is the food that keeps my army content. As the great Corsican once said, "An army marches on its stomach." Then again, he didn't fare so well in the winter.

Mustang walks beside me as I lead the column. Though she's swaddled with wolfcloaks as thick as my own, she hardly comes up to my shoulder. And when we walk through deep snow, it's almost a laugh to see her try to keep apace with me. But if I slow, I earn a scowl. Her braid bounces as she keeps up. When we reach easier ground, she glances over at me. Her pert nose is red as a cherry in the cold, but her eyes look like hot honey.

"You haven't been sleeping well," she says.

"When do I ever?"

"When you slept next to me. You cried out the first week in the woods. After that, you slept like a little baby."

"Is this you inviting me back?" I ask.

"I never told you to leave." She waits. "So why did you?"

"You distract me," I say.

She laughs lightly before drifting back to walk beside Pax. I'm left confused both by my response and by her words. I never thought she'd care one way or the other if I left. A stupid smile spreads on my face. Tactus catches it.

"Smitten as a lovebird," he hums.

I hurl a handful of snow at his head. "Not a word more."

"But I need another word, *a serious word*." He steps closer, takes a deep breath. "Does the pain in your back give you a hard-on like it gives me?" He laughs.

"Are you ever serious?"

His sharp eyes sparkle. "Oh, you don't want me serious."

"How about obedient?"

He claps his hands together. "Well, you know I'm not prime fond of the idea of a leash."

"Do you see a leash?" I ask, pointing to his forehead, where his slave mark could be.

"And since you know I don't need a leash, it may do to tell me where we are bound. I would be more . . . *effective* that way."

He's not challenging me, because he speaks quietly. After the whipping we both received, he's taken to me in a frighteningly loyal way. Despite all the smiles and sneers and laughs, I have his obedience. And his question is sincere.

"We're going to ruin Apollo," I tell him.

"But why Apollo?" he asks. "Are we merely checking off the Houses at random, or should I know something?"

The tone in his voice makes me cock my head. He's always reminded me of some kind of giant cat. Maybe it's the frighteningly casual way in which he lopes along. Like he'd kill something without even tensing his muscles. Or maybe it's because I can imagine him coiling up on a couch and licking himself clean.

"I've seen things in the snow, Reaper," he says quietly. "Impressions in the snow, to be specific. And these impressions are not made by feet."

"Paws? Hooves?"

"No, dear leader." He steps closer. "Linear impressions." I get his meaning. "GravBoots flying very low. Do tell me, why are the Proctors following us? And why are they wearing ghostCloaks?"

All his whispers mean nothing because of our rings. Yet he doesn't know that.

"Because they are afraid of us," I tell him.

"Afraid of you, you mean." He watches me. "What do you know that I don't? What do you tell Mustang that you don't tell us?"

"You want to know, Tactus?" I've not forgotten his crimes, but I take his shoulder and bring him close like he's a brother. I know the power touch can have. "Then knock House Apollo off the gorydamned map and I will tell you."

His lips curl into a feral smile. "A pleasure, good Reaper."

We stay away from the open plains and cling to the river as we move farther south, listening to our scouts relay news of enemy holdings over the comms. Apollo seems to control everything. All we see of the Jackal are his small bands of scouts. There's something strange about his soldiers, something that chills the heart. For the thousandth time, I think of my enemy. What makes the faceless boy so frightening? Is he tall? Lean? Thick? Fast? Ugly? And what gives him his reputation, his name? No one seems to know.

The Pluto scouts never come near despite the temptation we offer them. I have Pax carry the banner of Ceres high, so that every Apollo cavalryman in the surrounding miles can see it glimmer. Each realizes the chance for glory. Parties of cavalry dash into us. Scouts think they can pry our pride away and gain themselves status in their House. They come stupidly in threes, in fours, and we ruin them with the Ceres archers or Minerva's spearmen or with buried pikes in the snow. Little by little, we gnaw at them as the wolf gnaws at the elk. Always we let them escape, though. I want them angry as hell when I arrive on their doorstep. Slaves like them would slow us down.

That night, Pax and Mustang sit with me by a small fire and tell me of their lives outside the school. Pax is a riot when you get him going—a surprisingly energetic talker with a penchant for complimenting everything in his stories, including the villains, so half the time you don't know who is good and who is bad. He tells us of a time he broke his father's scepter in half, and another time he was mistaken for an Obsidian and nearly shipped off to the Agoge, where they train in space combat.

"I notion you could say I always dreamt of being an Obsidian," he rumbles.

When he was a boy, he would sneak from his family's summer manor in New Zealand, Earth, and join the Obsidians as they performed the Nagoge, the nightly necessity of their training, in which they looted and stole in order to supplement the paltry diet they were given at the Agoge. He would scrap and fight with them for morsels of food. He says he would always win, that is until he met Helga. Mustang and I lock eyes and try not to bust out with laughs as he waxes grandiloquent on Helga's ample proportions, her thick fists, her ample thighs.

"Theirs was a large love," I tell Mustang.

"A love to shake the earth," she replies.

I'm woken the next morning by Tactus. His eyes are cold as the dawn's freeze.

"Our horses have decided to run away. All of them." He guides us to the Ceres boys and girls who were watching the horses. "None of them saw a thing. One minute the horses were there; the next they were gone."

"Poor horses must be confused," Pax says sorrowfully. "It was stormy last night. Perhaps they ran for safety to the woods."

Mustang holds up the ropes that held the horses during the night. Pulled in half.

"Stronger than they looked," she says dubiously.

"Tactus?" I nod my head to the scene.

He looks over at Pax and Mustang before answering. "There are foot tracks . . ."

"But."

"Why waste my breath?" He shrugs. "You know what I'm going to say."

Proctors pulled the ropes apart.

I do not tell my army what happened, but rumor spreads quickly when people huddle together for warmth. Mustang does not ask questions even though she knows I'm not telling her something. After all, I did not simply *find* the medicine I gave her in the Northwoods.

I try to look at this newest kink as a test. When the rebellion begins, things like this will happen. How do I react? Breathe the anger out. Breathe it out and move. Easier said than done for me.

We move to the woods to the east. Without horses, we've no more play to make in the plains near the river. My scouts tell me the castle of Apollo is near. How will I take it without horses? Without any element of speed?

As night falls, another kink reveals itself. The soup pots we brought from Ceres to cook over our fires are cracked through. All of them. And the bread which we kept so securely wrapped in paper in our packs is full of weevils. They crunch like juicy seeds as I eat a supper of bread. To the Drafters it will look an unfortunate turn of events. But I know it is something more.

The Proctors warn me to turn back.

"Why did Cassius betray you?" Mustang asks me that night as we sleep in a hollow beneath a snowdrift. Our Diana sentries watch the camp's perimeter from the trees. "Don't lie to me."

"I betrayed him, actually," I say. "I . . . it was his brother that I had to kill in the Passage."

Her eyes widen. And after a moment she nods. "I had a brother die. It's not . . . it wasn't the same thing. But . . . a death like that, it changes things."

"Did it change you?"

"No," she says, as though she just realized it. "But it changed my family. Made them into people I don't recognize sometimes. That's life, I suppose." She pulls back suddenly. "Why did you tell Cassius that you killed his brother? Are you that mad, Reaper?"

"I didn't tell him slag. The Proctors did through the Jackal. Gave him a holocube."

"I see." Her eyes go cold. "So they are cheating for the Arch-Governor's son."

I leave her and the warmth of the fire to piss in the woods. The air is cold and crisp. Owls hoot in the branches, making me feel watched in the night.

"Darrow?" Mustang says from the darkness. I wheel about.

"Mustang, did you follow me?" Darrow. Not Reaper. Something is amiss. Something in the way she says my name, that she says my name at all. It is like seeing a cat bark. But I can't see her in the darkness.

"I thought I saw something," she says, still in shadow, voice emanating from the deeper woods. "It's just over here. It'll blow your mind."

I follow the sound of her voice. "Mustang. Don't leave the camp. *Mustang.*"

"We've already left it, darling."

Around me, the trees stretch ominously upward. Their branches reach for me. The woods are silent. Dark. This is a trap. It is not Mustang.

The Proctors? The Jackal? Someone watches me.

When something watches you and you don't know where it is, there is only one sensible thing to do. Change the bloodydamn paradigm, try to even the playing field. Make it have to look for you.

I break into movement. I sprint back toward my army. Then I dash behind a tree, scramble up it and wait, watching. Knives out. Ready to throw. Cloak curled about me.

Silence.

Then the snapping of twigs. Something moves through the woods. Something huge.

"Pax?" I call down.

No response.

Then I feel a strong hand touch my shoulder. The branch I crouch in sinks with the new weight as a man deactivates his ghostCloak and appears from thin air. I've seen him before. His curly blond hair is cut tight to his head and frames his dusky, godlike face. His chin is carved from marble, and his eyes twinkle evilly, bright as his armor. Proctor Apollo. The huge thing moves again below us.

"Darrow, Darrow, Darrow," he clucks over at me in Mustang's voice. "You were a favorite puppet, but you're not dancing as you ought. Will you reform and go north?"

"I—"

"Refuse? No matter." He shoves me off the branch, hard. I hit another on the way down. Fall into the snow. I smell dander. Fur. And then the beast roars.

38

THE FALL OF APOLLO

The bear is huge—bigger than a horse, big as a wagon. White as a bloodless corpse. Eyes red and yellow. Razor black teeth long as my forearm. Nothing like the bears I've seen on the HC. A strip of red runs along its spine. Its paws are like fingers, eight on a hand. It's unnatural. Made by the Carvers for sport. It's been brought to these woods to kill, to kill me in particular. Sevro and I heard it roaring months back as we went to make peace with Diana. Now I feel its spittle.

I stand there stupid for a second. Then the bear roars again and lunges.

I roll, run. I sprint faster than I ever have in my life. I fly. But the bear is faster, if less agile; the woods shudder as it crashes through brush and trees.

I run beside a massive godTree and dive through bramble. There the ground creaks beneath my feet and I realize, as leaves and snow crumble under my feet, where I stand. I put the place between myself and the bear and wait for the bear to tear through the underbrush. It bursts clear and lunges for me. I jump back. Then it is gone, shrieking as it plummets through the trap floor onto a bed of wooden spikes. My joy would have been longer lived if I didn't dance back and step into a second trap.

The earth flips. Well, I do. My leg snaps upward and I fly into the air on the end of a rope. I dangle for hours, too frightened to call to my army for fear of Proctor Apollo. My face tingles and itches from the blood rushing to my head. Then a familiar voice cuts the night.

"Well, well, well," it sneers from below. "Looks like we've two pelts to skin."

Sevro smirks when I tell him I've allied with Mustang. At camp, where Mustang was preparing search parties to send out for me, his reputation precedes him amongst the northerners. The Minervans fear him. Tactus and the other DeadHorses, on the other hand, are delighted.

"Why, if it isn't my belly buddy!" Tactus drawls. "Why the limp, my friend?"

"Your mother rode me ragged," Sevro grunts.

"Bah, you'd have to stand on your tiptoes to even kiss her chin."

"Wasn't her chin I was trying to kiss."

Tactus claps his hands together in laughter and draws Sevro in for an obnoxious hug. They are two very peculiar people. But I suppose snuggling in horse corpses gives a bond—makes twins of a morbid sort.

"Where were you?" Mustang asks me quietly to the side.

"In a second," I say.

Sevro has only one eye now. So he is the one-eyed demon the Apollonian emissary warned me about.

"I always wondered what sort of mad little fellows you Howlers were," Mustang says.

"Little?" Sevro asks.

"I—didn't mean to offend."

He grins. "I am little."

"Well, we of Minerva thought you were ghosts." She pats his shoulder. "You're not. And I'm not a real mustang, if you were wondering. No tail, you see? And no," she interrupts Tactus. "I've never worn a saddle, since you were going to ask."

He was.

"She'll do," Sevro mutters sideways to me.

"I like them," Mustang says of the Howlers a few moments later. "Make me feel tall."

"Perrrfect!" Tactus picks up the bloodback pelt with a grunt. "Looky look. They found something in Pax's size."

Before we join the group at the large fire that Pax stokes, Sevro pulls me aside and produces a blanket. Inside is my slingBlade.

"Kept it safe for you after finding it in the mud," he says. "And I made it sharper; time for using a dull blade is over."

"You're a friend. I hope you know that." I clap him on the shoulder. "Not a game friend. A real friend now, when we're out of here. You know that, yes?"

"I'm not an idiot." He blushes all the same.

I learn from him around the campfire that he and the Howlers, Thistle, Screwface, Clown, Weed, and Pebble—the dregs of my old House—stayed no longer than a day after I disappeared.

"Cassius said the Jackal took you," Sevro says through a mouthful of weevily bread. "Delicious nuts." He eats like he hasn't seen food in weeks.

We sit fireside in the Greatwoods, bathed in the light of crackling logs. Mustang, Milia, Tactus, and Pax join us in leaning on a fallen tree in the snow. We're all bundled like animals. I sit close with Mustang. Her leg is entwined with mine beneath the furs. The bloodback fur stinks and crackles over the fire. Fat drips into the flames. Pax will wear it when it dries.

Sevro sought the Jackal after Cassius fed him the lie. My small friend doesn't get into details. He hates details. He just taps his empty eye socket and says, "The Jackal owes me."

"You saw him then?" I ask.

"It was dark. I saw his knife. Didn't even hear his voice. I had to jump off the mountain. It was a long fall back to the rest of the pack." He says it so plainly. Yet I did notice his limp. "We couldn't stay in the mountains. His men . . . everywhere."

"But we took some of the mountains with us," Thistle says. She pats the scalps on her waist with a motherly smile. Mustang shudders.

It's been chaos in the South. Apollo, Venus, Mercury, and Pluto are all that's left, but I hear Mercury has been reduced to a force of roving vagabonds. A pity. I was fond of their Proctor. He almost chose me in the Draft, would have if he could have. Wonder how things would have gone then.

"Sevro, with that leg, how fast can you run, say, two kilometers?" I ask.

The others are puzzled by the question, but Sevro just shrugs. "Doesn't slow me. Minute and a half in this lowGrav."

I make a note to tell him my idea later.

"We have more important things to discuss, Reaper." Tactus smiles. "Now, I heard you were dangling upside down in the woods from this one here's trap." He pats little Thistle on her thigh; she smiles as he lets his hand linger. It's the scalp collection that draws his affection. "You didn't think you'd sneak out of telling the tale, did you?"

It's not so funny a thing as he might suspect.

I finger my ring. Telling them would be signing their death warrants. Apollo and Jupiter listen to me now. I look at Mustang and feel hollow. I'll risk losing her just to win their rigged game. If I were a good person, I would keep the ring on. I would hold my tongue. But there are plans to make, gods to undo. I take my ring off and set it on the snow. "Let us for one moment pretend we are not from different Houses," I say. "Let's all of us talk as friends, ringless."

Without horses, without mobility, I have no advantage over my enemy in the surrounding lands. Another lesson to be learned. I make an advantage for myself, a new strategy. I make them fear me.

My tactics are ones of fragmentation. I split my army into six pieces of ten under myself, Pax, Mustang, Tactus, Milia, and, due to a surprising recommendation from Milia, Nyla. I would have given Sevro his own unit, but he and his Howlers will not leave my side again. They blame themselves for the scar on my belly.

My army sets into Apollo's holdings like starving wolves. We do not assail their castle, but we raid their forts. We bring fire to their supply stores. We shoot arrows at their legs. We foul their water supplies and tell prisoners false news and let them escape. We murder their goats and pigs. We hack their riverboats with axes. We steal weapons. I do not allow prisoners to be taken except if they are students from Venus, Juno, or Bacchus enslaved by Apollo. All others we let escape. The fear and legend must spread. This my army understands better than anything else. They are dogmatic. They tell each other tales of me around the campfires. Pax is their ringleader; he thinks I am myth made man. Many of my soldiers begin carving my slingBlade into trees and walls. Tactus and Thistle carve sling-Blades into flesh. And the more industrious members of my army make standards of stained wolfpelts that we take into battle on the end of spears.

I split the slaves of House Ceres and the other captured slaves from one another to integrate them into the various units. I know their allegiances are shifting. Bit by bit. They begin to refer to themselves not as Ceres or Minerva or Diana, but by their unit name. I place four Ceres soldiers, the smallest, with Sevro in the Howlers. I do not know if the bakers will make for elite warriors as Mars's dregs did, but if anyone can carve off their baby fat, it's Sevro.

Fear gnaws at Apollo for a week. Our ranks swell. Theirs diminish. Freed slaves tell us of the terror in the castle, the worry that I will appear from the shadows with my bloody wolfcloaks to burn and maim.

I do not fear House Apollo; they are lumbering fools who cannot adjust to my tactics. What I fear is the Proctors, and the Jackal. To me, they are one and the same. After Apollo's failed attempt on my life, I fear they will be more direct. When will I wake with a razor in my spine? This is their game. At any time, I could die. I must destroy House Apollo now, get Proctor Apollo out of the game before it is too late.

My lieutenants and I sit around our fire in the woods to discuss the tactics of the next day. We are less than two miles from House Apollo's castle, but they dare not attack us. We are in the deep woods. They huddle in fear of us. We also don't attack them. I know Proctor Apollo would ruin even the cleverest of night assaults.

Before we can begin, Nyla asks about the Jackal. Sevro's voice is quiet as he tells what he learned in the mountains. It grows louder as he realizes we are all listening.

"His castle is somewhere in the low mountains. Subterranean, not in the high peaks. Just near Vulcan. Vulcan got off to a prime start. Fastlike. They blitzed Pluto on the third day. Efficient turds. Pluto wasn't ready. So the Jackal took control, had them retreat into their deep tunnels. Vulcan came howling in with advanced weapons from their forges. It was all going to be over. The Jackal would have been a slave from the first week on. So he collapsed the tunnel—no plan, no way out—in order to preserve his chance to win the game. Killed ten of his own House, tons of highDrafts. MedBots couldn't save anyone. Stranded forty of the rest in the dark caves. Plenty of water, no food. They were there for nearly a month before they dug their way out." He smiles and I remember why Fitchner called him Goblin. "Guess what they ate?"

If a Jackal is caught in a trap, it will chew off its own leg. Who told me that?

The fire crackles between us. I would have expected Mustang to shift uncomfortably, but instead what I see from her is anger as the details are relayed. Pure anger. Her jaw flexes and her face loses a shade. I grip her hand beneath the blanket, but it does not grip back.

"How did you find all that out?" Pax rumbles.

Sevro taps one of his curved knives with a fingernail, allowing a soft ding into the night air. It echoes into the woods, bouncing off trees and returning to our ears like a lost phrase. Then I can hear nothing from the woods, nothing beyond the fire. My heart leaps into my throat and I catch Sevro's eye. He'll have to find Tactus.

A jamField envelopes us.

"Hello, children," a voice says from the darkness. "Such a bright fire is dangerous at night. And you're like little puppies, all snuggled together; no, don't get up." This voice is melodious. Frivolous. Eerie to hear after so many months of hardship. No one's voice sounds like that. He strolls in lightly and plops down beside Pax. Apollo. This time he brought no bear, only a grand spear that drips purple sparks along its business end.

"Proctor Apollo, welcome," I say. Sentinels perch above us in the trees, their arrows pointed at the Proctor. I wave the trap away and ask the Proctor why he is here, as if we've never met. His presence sends a very simple message: my friends are in danger.

"To tell you to return home, my dear nomads." He opens up a flagon of wine and passes it around. No one drinks, except Sevro. He holds on to the flagon.

"Proctors aren't supposed to interfere with things. It is in the rules," Pax says in confusion. "By what right do you come here? This is dirty play."

Mustang seconds his question.

The Aureate sighs, but before he can say anything, Sevro stands and belches. He begins walking off.

"Where are you going?" Apollo snaps. "Don't walk away from me."

"Going to piss. Drank all your wine. Rather I piss here?" He cocks his head and touches his small stomach. "Maybe shit, too."

Apollo wrinkles his nose and looks back to us, dismissing Sevro.

"Influencing is hardly dirty play, my giant friend," he explains. "I merely care for your well-being. I am here, after all, to guide you in your studies. It would be best for you all to return to the North, that is all. Better strategy, let's say. Finish your battle there, consolidate your power, then expand out. It is the rules of war: Do not expose yourself when weak. Do not push your enemy to fight when you are inferior. You have no cavalry. No shelter. Meager weapons. You are not learning as you ought."

His grin is welcoming. It slashes through his beautiful face like a crescent moon as he twirls the rings on his finger, waiting for our response.

"It is kind of you to consider our well-being," Mustang replies in mocking highLingo. "I do say, very kind! Warms my bones. Paying special attention, no less, to the fact that you're from another

House. But tell me, does my Proctor know you are here? Does Mars's?" She nods over to silent Milia. "Does Juno's? Are you doing a naughtynaughty, good sir? If you're not, then why the jamField? Or do others watch?"

Apollo's eyes harden, though his smile remains.

"To be quite frank, your Proctors don't know what you children are playing at. You had your chance, Virginia. You lost. Don't allow yourself to be bitter. Darrow here beat you fair and sound. Or did your winter together blind you to the fact that there can only be one winning House, only one victorious Primus? Were all of you truly so blinded? This . . . boy can give you nothing."

He looks around at each of them.

"I shall repeat, since you are a rusty lot: Darrow's win will not mean you win. No one will offer you an apprenticeship, because they see him being the key to your success. You merely follow—like General Ney or Ajax Minor, and who remembers them? This *Reaper* does not even have his own standard. He is using you. That is all. He is embarrassing you and ruining your chances for careers beyond this First Year."

"You're quite annoying, all due respect, Proctor," Nyla says without her usual kindness.

"And you're still a slave." Apollo points to her mark. "Fit for all sorts of abuse."

"Only till I earn the right to wear one of those." Nyla gestures to Mustang's wolfcloak.

"Your loyalty is touching, but—"

Pax interrupts. "Would you let me whip you bloody, Apollo? Darrow did. Let me whip you, and I'll obey like a Pink. Promise on the graves of my ancestors, those of Telemanus and the—"

"You're nothing more than a bureaucratic Pixie," Milia hisses. "Do us a favor and piss off."

My lieutenants are loyal, though I shudder to think what Tactus or Sevro would have said had they been around the fire with us. I lean forward to stare down Apollo. Still, I must provoke him.

"Do us solid, eh? Take your advice, shove it up your ass, and piss off."

Someone laughs in the air above us, a woman's laugh. Other Proctors watch from inside the jamField. I see silhouettes in the smoke. How many watch? Jupiter? Venus, maybe, by the laugh? That would be perfect.

The fire flickers over Apollo's face. He is angry.

"Here is the logic I know. The winter could get colder, children. When it gets cold outside, things die. Like wolves. Like bears. Like mustangs."

I have a reply and it is perfectly longwinded.

"I wonder, Apollo, what happens if the Drafters find out that you are arranging to have the ArchGovernor's son win? If you were, say, rigging the game like a bazaar crime lord."

Apollo freezes. I continue.

"When you tried killing me in the woods with that stupid bear, you failed. Now you come here like the desperate fool you are to threaten my friends when they do not slaver at the idea of betraying me. Will you really kill us all? I know you can edit what you like from the footage the Drafters see. But however will you explain to all our Drafters how we all died?"

My lieutenants feign their shock.

I go on.

"Say an Imperator of a fleet, say a Legate, say any of the Drafters of any of the other Houses, found out that the ArchGovernor was paying the Proctors to cheat, to eliminate the competition so that his son would win and their children would lose. Do you think there would be consequences for the Proctors being bribed? For the ArchGovernor? Do you think they might care that their children are dying in a rigged game? Or that you're getting paid to ruin the meritocratic system? The best shall rise. Or is it the best connected?"

Apollo's jaw tightens.

He looks up to the other Proctors. They wisely stay invisible. He must have drawn the short straw to come down here and be the face of their cheating. My lieutenants stay silent as he speaks.

"If they did find out, children, then there would be consequences for everyone," Apollo threatens. "So feel free to guard your tongues while you have them."

"Or what?" Mustang asks violently. "What do you think you're going to do?"

"You of all people should know," he says. I don't understand his point, but this charade has run its course. I've counted the seconds since Sevro left. The Proctors have not. I turn to Mustang.

"How fast can Sevro run two kilometers?"

"A minute and a half, in this gravity, I do believe. Though he's a little liar, so likely faster."

"And how far is Apollo's castle?"

"Oh, I'd say three kilometers, maybe a little more."

Apollo jumps to his feet, looking around for Sevro.

"Splendid," I say. "Say, Mustang, do you know what I like most about jamFields?"

"That no sound can get out?"

"No. That no sound can get in."

Apollo disengages the jamField and we hear the howls. They come from the distance, two miles away. From ramparts. From Apollo's castle. MedBots wail toward the cries, streaking across the distant sky.

"Venus! Were you not watching them? You stupid . . ." Apollo snarls at the empty air.

"The little one took off his ring," an invisible woman cries. "They all took off their rings! I can't see anything without their rings on, and not in a jamField!"

"But they're all back on by now," I say. "So pull up your datapad and tell me what you see."

"You little . . ." Apollo's hands clench. I flinch back. Mustang steps between us, as does Pax.

"Uh-oh," Pax booms, thumping his huge axe against his chest. The armor beneath his wolfcloak thumps rhythmically. "Uh-oh!"

Snow flies as Apollo soars out of the woods, the other Proctors on his heels. They will be too late. Edit all they like, interfere all they like, the battle for House Apollo has begun, and Sevro and Tactus have claimed the ramparts.

My lieutenants and I arrive at the battle in time to see Tactus climbing the highest tower, a knife in his teeth. There, standing on the edge of the hundred-meter parapet like some careless Greek champion, he pulls down his pants and pisses on the banner of House Apollo. He's crawled through shit to earn that banner. The slaves we captured throughout the week told us of the castle's weaknesses—large latrine holes—and so Tactus, Sevro, and the Howlers exploited them in dreadfully efficient time. House Apollo's soldiers woke to demons covered in dung. Oh, how terribly my conquering soldiers smell as they open the gates for me. Inside, it's a mass of chaos.

The castle is tall, white, ornate. Its plaza stands round and has six grand doorways that lead to six grand, spiraling towers. Sheep and cows crowd makeshift pens on the far side of the plaza. Apollo guards have retreated there. More of their allies stream from the tower doorways behind them. My men are outnumbered three to one. But mine are freemen, not slaves. They will fight better. Yet it is not numbers that threatens to turn the tide against my invading army. It's the Apollo Primus, Novas. The Proctor gave him his own pulseWeapon. A spear that glimmers with purple sparks. Its tip touches one of the DeadHorses from Diana, and the girl flips ten feet backward, like a broken toy convulsing on the ground as its gears fall off their tracks.

I gather my forces near the gatehouse, just inside the plaza. Many are still in the towers like Tactus. I've got Pax, Milia, Nyla, Mustang, and thirty others at my back. The enemy Primus marshals his own forces. His weapon alone could ruin us.

"Mustang, ready with that standard?" I ask. I feel her hand on the small of my back, just beneath my breastplate. I wear no helm. My hair is bound by leather. My face is dark with soot. My right hand carries my slingBlade. The left, a shortened stunpike. Nyla carries the standard of Ceres.

"Pax, we're the scythe. Girls, you're the pickers."

My men in the towers howl as they sprint and jump down from their perches to join the battle, streaming into the plaza from all angles. Their stained wolfcloaks reek. The cobblestones between my band and Apollo's lie thick with ankle-high drifts of snow. Proctors glint in the air above, waiting for the pulseSpear to make short work of my army.

"Take their Primus," Mustang whispers in my ear. She points to the tall, hard boy and smacks my butt. "Claim him."

"Twenty meters and stop, Pax." He nods at my command.

"The Primus is mine!" I roar to my army and to theirs. "Novas, you gorywhore. You are *mine.* You piss-eating snail. You foul piece of shit." As the tall, mad invader with the slingBlade screams at their Primus, Apollo's forces shirk instinctively away. "Enslave the rest!" I howl.

Then Pax and I charge.

The rest stream after, trying to catch my heels. I let Pax overtake me. He's screaming with his war axe and charging at Novas and his band of bodyguards—heavily armored boys and girls with crimson handprints on their helmets. They lead the charge of the enemy host, going straight at Pax, lowering their spears to stop his mad charge. These are the tall sort, the dashing killers who have long since grown too arrogant to understand they are in danger or to feel fear as they make plans to meet Pax in arms.

Then Pax stops.

And without breaking stride, I jump so his hand catches my foot; I push off and he launches me ten meters forward into the air. I'm howling the entire way, like a thing torn from bloodydamn nightmares, until I smash into the bodyguards. Three go down. A random spear catches my stomach and scrapes along my ribs, spinning me just as a trident pierces the air where my head had been. I gain my feet, swing horizontally, sweeping legs. I spin away from a thrust and hack down diagonally as I come from my spin, shattering someone tall at the collarbone. Another spear comes at me; I slap it to the side and run along its length, jumping to bury my knee into the face of an Apollo highDraft. He falls back, taking me with him, my knee stuck in his helmet's visor. I slash madly as I go from the high vantage, stunning three other highDrafts with looping blows till I teeter down to the ground.

We hit the snow. The highDraft's nose is broken and he's unconscious, but my knee is numb and bloody from the impact as I jerk it out of his helmet. I roll away, expecting spears to fillet me. They don't. I shattered the head of the Apollo army in one mad charge; Pax and my army sweep in like an iron curtain till I'm left with Novas in the center of the chaos. He's tall and strong. A sweeping arc from his spear shatters a Howler's shield. He blasts Milia backwards and catches Pax in the arm with the spear, knocking him to the ground like a toy. I'm taller and stronger.

"Novas, you little girl!" I shout. "You sniveling Pink."

His eyes flash when he sees me coming.

The battle takes a collective breath as he wheels toward me like an elk turning on the leader of a wolfpack. We stalk toward one another. He lunges first. I dodge and spin along the length of the spear till I'm behind him. Then with one massive swing, like I'm hacking down a tree with my slingBlade, I break his leg and take his spear.

He moans like a child. I sit on his chest, smug with the satisfaction that I did not moan like this when my legs were broken and rewoven in Mickey's carveshop. I make a show of yawning despite the chaos swirling around me.

Mustang takes the reins of battle.

Only one member of House Apollo escapes. A girl. A fast girl, but an unimportant member of their House. Somehow, she jumps from the highest tower and simply floats down to the ground with her House's standard. Almost like magic. But I see the distortion around her. Proctor Apollo preserves his position in the game. The girl finds a horse and rides away from my horseless army. Pax hurls a spear at her from a distance. His aim is true and would have pinned the horse to the turf through the neck, but a freakish wind miraculously knocks the spear wide. In the end, it's Mustang who takes a horse from the Apollo stables and chases the girl down with the Howlers Thistle and Pebble. She brings her back bent over her own horse's neck, spanking her butt with the standard as they gallop back.

My army roars as Mustang trots into the conquered castle square. We've already freed the House Ceres slaves; they've earned their place in my army. I wave down at Mustang from my perch beside Sevro and Tactus on the high ramparts; our feet dangle carelessly over the edge. House Apollo has fallen in less than thirty minutes despite Apollo's interference with the pulseSpear.

Proctor Apollo confers with Jupiter and Venus in the sky. They glitter in the dawn light as though nothing has happened. But I know he will have to leave the game; the standard and castle are taken. He cannot hurt me any longer.

"You're through!" I taunt Apollo. "Your House has fallen!" My army roars once more. I bask in the sound and the winter air as the sun peeks over the western lip of the Valles Marinerise. Most of those voices would be slaves. Instead, they follow willingly. Soon even those of House Apollo will follow me.

I laugh wildly; the fire of victory is hot in my veins. We have beaten one Proctor. But Jupiter can still hurt us. His House is unbent, unbroken far to the north. A quick rage overtakes me along with another, darker passion—one of arrogance, furious, mad arrogance. I grab the pulseSpear, cock my arm, and hurl the weapon as hard as I can at the gathered Proctors. My army watches this act of impudence. The three Proctors scatter after the pulseSpear goes through their shielding. They turn to look at me. Fire glitters in their eyes. But the passion in me was not quenched by a mere spear throw. I hate these scheming fools. I will ruin them.

"Jupiter! You are next. You are next, you piece of dog shit!"

Then Pax bellows my name. And then Tactus's voice echoes it, then Nyla from a far tower. And soon a hundred voices chant it throughout the conquered castle—from the courtyard to the high parapets and towers. They beat their swords and spears and shields, and then they throw them at the Proctors. A hundred missiles thump harmlessly into pulseShields and many of my army must scatter so that they are not impaled by the falling weapons, but it is a sweet sight, a sweet sound of metal rain on cobbled stone. And again they take up my name. They chant and chant the name of the Reaper at the Proctors, because they know whom we now fight.

39

THE PROCTOR'S BOUNTY

My army sleeps well into the morning. I have no need of rest, though I keep company with Sevro and half a dozen others on the ramparts. They stand close, as though any space might present the Proctors an opportunity to kill me.

Sevro has freed five Mercury students from the Apollo slave groups. They cluster around him on the ramparts playing games of speed, slapping each other's knuckles to see who can move the fastest. I don't play, because I win too easily; best to let the children have their fun. After the taking of the castle, even though Sevro and Tactus did the heavy lifting, my boys and girls think that makes me some sort of marvel. Mustang told me it is a rare thing.

"It's as if they think you're something out of time."

"I don't understand."

"Like you're one of the old conquerors. The ancient Golds who usurped Earth, destroyed her fleets, and all that. They use it as an excuse not to compete with you, because how could Hephaestus compete with Alexander, or Antonius with Caesar?"

My insides knot. This is but a game, and they love me this much.

When the rebellion comes, these boys and girls will be my enemies, and I will replace them with Reds. How fanatical then will those Reds be? And will that fanaticism matter a lick if they have to stand against creatures like Sevro, like Tactus, like Pax and Mustang?

I watch Mustang slink toward me along the rampart. She limps ever so slightly from a sprained ankle, yet she's all grace. Her hair is a nest of twigs; circles ring her eyes. She smiles at me. She is beautiful. Like Eo.

From the ramparts, we can see over the Greatwoods and glimpse the beginnings of Mars's highlands to the north. The mountains glower at us from the west, to our left. Mustang points to the sky.

"Proctor incoming."

My bodyguards tighten around me, but it's only Fitchner. Sevro spits over the ramparts. "Our prodigal parent returneth."

Fitchner descends with a smile that tells a tale of exhaustion, fear, and a little bit of pride.

"May we talk?" he asks me, looking about at my scowling friends.

Fitchner and I sit together in the Apollo warroom. Mustang stokes the fire. Fitchner eyes her skeptically, disliking her presence. He has an opinion on most things, like someone else I know.

"You've made such a mess of things, lad."

"Let's agree that you won't call me *lad,*" I say.

He nods. There's no gum in his mouth. He doesn't know how to say what he wants to tell me. It's the worry in his eyes that cues me in.

"Apollo has not left Olympus," I say.

He stiffens, surprised at my guess. "Correct. He is still there."

"And what does that mean, Fitchner?" Mustang comes to sit beside me.

"Just that," Fitchner answers, looking at me. "He has not left Olympus like he ought. It's all a mess. Apollo was getting a juicy appointment if the Jackal won. Same with Jupiter and some of the others. There was talk of one of the Praetor Knight positions opening up on Luna."

"And now that choice is slipping away," Mustang says. She glances over at me with a smirk. "Because of a boy."

"Yes."

I laugh. The jamField makes the sound echo. "So what is to be done?"

"You still want to win, yes?" Fitchner asks.

"Yes."

"And that is the point of all this?" he asks me, though it's clear there's something else in his head. "You'll get an apprenticeship no matter."

I lean forward and tap my finger on the table. "The point is to show them that they can't gorywell cheat in their own game. That the ArchGovernor can't just say his son is best and should beat me just because he was *born* lucky. This is about merit."

"No," Fitchner says, leaning forward. "It's about politics." He glances at Mustang. "Will you send her away already?"

"Mustang stays."

"Mustang," he mocks. "So, Mustang, what do you think about the ArchGovernor cheating for his son?"

Mustang shrugs. "Kill or be killed, cheat or be cheated? Those are the rules I've seen Aureates follow, especially Peerless Scarred."

"Cheat or be cheated." Fitchner taps his upper lip. *"Interesting."*

"You should know about the cheating part," she says.

"You need to let Darrow and me have a word, *Mustang.*"

"She stays."

"It's okay," she mutters cryptically. She squeezes my shoulder as she leaves. "I'm bored of your Proctor anyway."

When Mustang is gone, Fitchner stares at me. He reaches to his pocket, hesitates, then pulls something out. A small box. He tosses it on the table and gestures for me to open it. Somehow I know what is inside.

"Well, you bastards do owe me a few bounties," I laugh bitterly as I slip Dancer's knifeRing onto my finger. I flex the joint and a blade pops out, extending along the top of the finger eight inches. I flex the joint again and it slithers home.

"The Obsidians took it from you before you went through the Passage, yes? I was told it was your father's."

"Someone told you that?" I pick at the warroom table with the blade. "How very innaccurate of them."

"You don't need to be snide, *lad*." My eyes flick up to look into Fitchner's. "You came here to win an apprenticeship. You've done that. If you keep pushing the Proctors, they will kill you."

"I seem to rememember us already having this conversation."

"Darrow, there is no slagging point to what you are doing! It is reckless!"

"No point?" I echo.

"If you beat the ArchGovernor's boy, then what? What does that achieve?"

"Everything!" I snap. I shudder with anger and stare at the fire till my voice finds control again. "It proves I am the best Gold in this school. It shows that I can do whatever they can. Why should I even speak to you, Fitchner? I've done all this without your help. I don't need you. Apollo tried to kill me and you did nothing! Nothing! So what exactly do I owe you? Maybe this?" I let the blade slither out.

"Darrow."

"Fitchner." I roll my eyes.

He slaps the table. "Don't talk to me like I'm a fool. Look at me. Look at me, you condescending little twit."

I look at him. His stomach paunch has grown. His face is haggard for a Gold. His hair yellow and slicked back. He's never been handsome—less now than ever.

"Look at me, Darrow. Everything I have, I've had to fight for. I was not born to an ArchGovernor's household. This is as far as I could ever go, yet I should go so much further. My son should go further, but he can't and he won't. He'll die if he tries. Everyone has a limit, Darrow. A limit they can't skip past. Yours is higher than mine, but it's not as high as you'd gorywell like. If you go past it, they'll knock you down."

He stares away as if ashamed, glowering at the fire. *His son*. It's in their coloring, in the face, in the disposition and the way they speak to one another. I'm a fool for not saying it out loud sooner.

"You're Sevro's father," I say.

He does not respond for some time. When he does, his voice is pleading. "You make him think he can climb higher than he can. You'll kill him, boyo. And you'll kill yourself."

"Then help us!" I urge him. "Give me something I can use against Apollo. Or better, fight them with me. Gather the other Proctors and we will take the battle to them."

"I can't, boyo. I can't."

I sigh. "No, I thought you wouldn't."

"My career would be over in a pinch if I helped you. All I've slaved for, all the many things, would be risked. For what? Just to prove a point to the ArchGovernor."

"Everyone is so frightened of change," I say before smiling sincerely at the broken man. "You remind me of my uncle."

"There will be no change," Fitchner grumbles as he stands. "Never is. Know your damn place or you won't make it out of this, boyo." He looks like he wants to reach and touch my shoulder. He doesn't. "Hell, the trap's already set for you. You're walking right into it."

"I'm ready for the Jackal's traps, Fitchner. Or Apollo's. It makes no difference. They won't be able to stop what's coming for them."

"No," Fitchner says, hesitating for a moment. "Not their traps. The girl's."

I answer him in a way he will understand. "Fitchner. Do not play me for a fool with vague, annoying references to duplicity. My army is mine, won in heart and body and soul. They can no more betray me at this point than I can betray them. We are something you have not seen before. So stop."

He shakes his head. "This *is* your fight, boyo."

"Yes. It is my fight." I smile. Now is the time I've been waiting for. "Fitchner, hold up," I say before he reaches the door. He stops and looks back. I kick back my chair and stride over to him. He eyes me curiously. Then I stick out my hand. "Despite everything, thank you."

He clasps it. "Good luck, Darrow," he says. "But take care of Sevro. The little shit will follow you anywhere, no matter what I say."

"I'll take care of him. I promise." My Helldiver grip tightens on his hand.

For a moment, if only a moment, we are friends. Then he winces at the pressure my hand is putting on his. He laughs at first, then he understands and his eyes widen.

"Sorry," I say.

That's when I break his nose and slam my elbow into his temple till he no longer moves.

40

PARADIGM

"Fitchner left?" she asks me.

"Through the window," I say.

I watch Mustang across Apollo's white warroom table. A blizzard has risen outside, no doubt meant to keep my army inside the castle around their warm fires and hot pots of soup. Her hair coils about her shoulders, held by leather bands. She wears the wolfcloak like the others, though hers is streaked with crimson. Muddy boots with spurs are kicked up on the table. Her standard, the only weapon she really favors, leans on a chair beside her. Mustang's face is a quick one. Quick to mocking smiles. Quick to pleasant frowns. She gives me the smile and asks what is on my mind.

"I am wondering when you will betray me," I say.

Her eyebrows knit together. "You're expecting that?"

"Cheat or be cheated," I say. "Echoed by your own lips."

"Are you going to cheat me?" she said. "No. Because what advantage would you gain? You and I have beaten this game. They would have us believe one must win at the cost to all the rest. That isn't true, and we're proving it."

I say nothing.

"You have my trust, because when you saw me hiding in the mud after taking my castle, you let me escape," she explains thoughtfully. "And I have your trust, because I pulled you from the mud when Cassius left you for dead."

I do not respond.

"So there is the answer. You are going to do great things, Darrow." She never calls me Darrow. "Maybe you don't have to do them alone?"

Her words make me smile. Then I bolt upright, startling her.

"Get our men," I order.

I know she was looking forward to resting here. I was too. The smell of soup tempts me. So does the warmth and the bed and the thought of spending a quiet moment with her. But that is not how men conquer.

"We're going to surprise the Proctors. We're going to take Jupiter."

"We can't surprise them." She taps her ring. The jamField Fitchner had is gone. We'd ditch the rings completely, but they are our insurance. The Proctors may be able to edit out a few things here and there, but common sense dictates that they can't tamper with the footage too much or the Drafters will get suspicious.

"And even if we make it through this storm, what will taking Jupiter accomplish?" she asks. "If Apollo didn't leave when his House lost, Jupiter won't either. You're just going to provoke them into interfering. We should go after the Jackal now!"

I know the Proctors are watching me plan this. I want them to know where I'm going.

"I'm not ready for the Jackal," I tell her. "I need more allies."

She looks at me, eyebrows pinched together. She doesn't understand, but it doesn't matter. She will soon enough.

Despite the blizzard, my army moves swiftly. We bundle ourselves in cloaks and furs so thickly that we look like animals stumbling through the snow. At night, we follow the stars, moving despite the mounting winds and the piling snow. My army does not grumble. They know I will not lead them purposelessly. My new soldiers press themselves harder than I would have thought possible. They have heard of me. Pax makes sure of that. And they are desperate to impress me. It becomes problematic. Wherever I walk, the procession around me suddenly doubles their efforts so that they overtake those in front or outpace those behind.

The blizzard is vicious. Pax always stands close to me and Mustang, as though he means to block us from the wind. He and Sevro are always stepping on each other's toes to be nearest me, though Pax would likely want to light my fires and tuck me in bed at night if I let him, while Sevro would tell me to pick my own ass. I see his father in him every time I look at him now. He seems weaker now that I know his family. There's no reason that should be the case; I guess I just supposed he really did spring from the loins of a she-wolf.

Eventually, the snows cease and spring comes fast and hard, which confirms my suspicions. The Proctors are playing games. The Howlers make sure all eyes are to the sky in case Proctors decide to harass us as we make our way. None do. Tactus keeps an eye out for their tracks. But it is quiet. We see no enemy scouts, hear no war trumpets in the distance, see no smoke rising except to the north in Mars's highlands.

We raid provision stores in burnt and broken castles as we push toward Jupiter. There are jugs from Bacchus's castle that Sevro was disappointed to discover full of grape juice instead of wine, salted beef from Juno's deep cellars, molding cheeses, fish wrapped in leaves, and bags of the ever-present smoked horsemeat. They keep us full as we march.

In four rugged days, I have reached and besieged Jupiter's triple-walled castle in the low mountain passes. Snow melts swiftly enough to make the ground soggy for our horses. Streams flow through our camp. I do not bother devising a plan of action. I simply tell Pax's, Milia's, and Nyla's divisions that whoever gives me the fortress will win a prize. The defenders are very few and my army takes the outer fortifications in a day by making a series of wooden ramps under intermittent arrow barrages.

My other three divisions scout the surrounding territory *en force* in case the Jackal decides to stick his nose into this. Jupiter's main army, it seems, is stranded across the now-thawed Argos laying siege to Mars's castle. They did not expect the river to thaw so quickly. Still there is no sign of the Jackal's men or of the Proctors. I wonder if they have found Fitchner locked in one of the Apollo Castle cells yet. I left him food and water and a face full of bruises.

On the third day of the siege, a white flag is flown from Jupiter's ramparts. A thin boy of middling height and timid smiles slips out Jupiter Castle's postern gate. The castle lies on high, rocky ground. It is sandwiched between two huge rock faces, so its three-tiered walls bow outward. Soon I would have tried sending men down the rock faces. It would have been a job for the Howlers—but they've had enough glory. This siege belongs to the soldiers captured when we fought Apollo.

The boy walks tentatively in front of the main gate. I meet him there with Sevro, Milia, Nyla, and Pax. We are a fearsome lot even without Tactus and Mustang, though Mustang could never really be called fearsome in appearance—maybe spirited, at best. Milia looks like something out of a nightmare—she's taken to wearing trophies like Tactus and Thistle. And Pax has cut notches along his huge axe for each slave he has taken.

In front of my lieutenants, the boy shows his nervousness. His smiles are quick, almost as if he's worried we might disapprove of them. The ring on his finger is that of Jupiter. He looks hungry, because it barely fits on him any longer.

"Name is Lucian," the boy says, trying to sound manly. He seems to think Pax is in charge. Pax booms a laugh and points to me and my slingBlade. Lucian flinches when he looks at me. I think he well knew I was the leader.

"So we here to swap smiles?" I ask. "What's your word?"

"The word is hunger," he laughs piteously. "We've not eaten anything but rats and raw grain in water for three weeks."

I almost pity the boy. His hair is dirty, eyes teary. He knows he's giving up a chance at an apprenticeship. They'll shame him for surrendering for the rest of his life. But he is hungry. So are the seven other defenders. Oddly, all are of Jupiter, not slaves. Their Primus left their weak instead of the slaves behind.

The only condition they have in surrendering the castle is that they must not be enslaved. Only Pax grumbles something honorable about them needing to earn their freedom like all the rest of us, but I agree to the boy's request. I tell Milia to watch them. If they act seditious, she'll make trophies of their scalps. We tether our horses in the courtyard. The stone is cobbled and dirty. A tall, angular keep stretches up and into the cliff's wall.

Darkness seeps through the clouds. A storm is coming to the mountain pass, so I bring my force into the castle and bar the gates. Mustang and her troop stay beyond the walls and will return later in the evening from scouting with Tactus. We speak over the comm-Units and Tactus curses us for having a dry roof over our heads. The night's rain is heavy.

I make sure our veterans get the first beds in Jupiter's dormitories before we eat. My army may be disciplined, but they'll shiv their own mothers for a warm bed. It's the one thing most of them never got used to—sleeping on the ground. They miss their mattresses and silk sheets. I miss the small cot I used to share with Eo. She's been dead now longer than we were married. I'm surprised how much it hurts to realize that.

I think I'm eighteen now, Earth metric. Not rightly sure.

Our bread and meats are like heaven to the starved defenders of Jupiter. Lucian and his lot, all skinny, tired-looking souls, eat so fast that Nyla is fussing about them ripping their guts. She runs around telling them each that the smoked horsemeat isn't galloping off anywhere. Pax and his BloodBacks occasionally throw bones at the meek lot. Pax's laugh is infectious. It booms out of him and then turns into something feminine as it continues past two seconds. No one can keep a straight face when he gets rolling. He's talking about Helga again. I look for Mustang so we can laugh about it, but she'll be away for hours more. I miss her even then, and I swell a little inside my chest because I know she will curl into my bed this night and together we'll snore like Uncle Narol after Yuletide.

I call Milia to the head of the table. My army lounges around Jupiter's warroom; they are easy in conquest. Jupiter's map is destroyed. I cannot make out what they know.

"What do you think of our hosts?" I ask Milia.

"I say put them under the sigil."

I cluck my tongue. "You really don't like to keep promises, do you?"

She looks very much like a hawk, face all angles and cruelty. Her voice is of a similar breed. "Promises are just chains," she rasps. "Both meant for breaking."

I tell her to leave the Jupitareans alone, but then loudly command her to fetch the wine we scavenged on our trek to Jupiter. She takes some boys and brings up the barrels from Bacchus's store.

I stand foolishly on the table. "And I order you to get drunk!" I roar to my army. They look at me like I am mad.

"Get drunk?" one says.

"Yes!" I cut him off before he can say more. "Can you manage that? Act like fools, for once?"

"We'll try," Milia cries. "Won't we?" She's answered in cheers. Some time later, as we drink Bacchus's stores, I loudly offer some to the Jupitareans. Pax stumbles up in protest at the idea of sharing good wine. He's a good actor.

"Are you contradicting me?" I demand.

Pax hesitates but manages to nod his giant head.

I draw my slingBlade from its back scabbard. It rasps in the humid warroom air. A hundred eyes go to us. Thunder rolls outside. Pax wobbles forward with a giant inebriated step. His own hand is on his axe's hilt, but he does not draw it. After a moment, he shakes his head and goes to a knee—he's still almost my own height. I sheathe my sword and pull him up. I tell him he's to run patrols.

"Patrols? But . . . in the storm and rain?"

"You heard me, Pax."

With a grumble, the BloodBacks wobble after him to go about their punishment. They're all smart enough to have figured out their parts even if they don't know the play. "Discipline!" I brag to Lucian. "Discipline is the best of mankind's traits. Even in big brutes like that. But he is right. No wine for you tonight. That, you must earn."

In Pax's absence, I make a show of giving ceremonial wolfcloaks to the slaves of Venus and Bacchus who earned their freedom in taking this fortress—ceremonial because we don't have any time to find wolves. There is laughter and lightness. Merriment for once, though no one discards their weapons. Nyla is coaxed into singing a song. Her voice is like an angel's. She sings at the Mars Opera House and was scheduled to perform in Vienna until a better opportunity came along in the form of the Institute. The opportunity of a lifetime. What a lark.

Lucian sits in the corner of the warroom with the other seven defenders watching our soldiers make a show of falling asleep atop tables, in front of the fire, along the walls. Some slink away to steal beds. The sound of snores tickles my ears.

Sevro stays close to me, as though the Proctors could rush in and kill me at any moment. I tell Sevro to get drunk and leave me be. He obeys and is soon laughing, then snoring atop the long table. I stumble over my sleeping army to Lucian, a smile across my face. I have not been drunk since before my wife died.

Despite Lucian's meekness, I find him curious. His eyes rarely meet mine and his shoulders slump. But his hands never go to his trouser pockets, never fold to guard himself. I ask him about the war with Mars. As I thought, it's almost won. He says something about a girl betraying Mars. Sounds like Antonia to me.

I must move quickly. I don't know what will happen if my House's standard and castle are taken even though I have my independent army. I could technically lose.

Lucian's friends are tired, so I give them leave to go try to find beds. They won't be a problem. Lucian stays to talk. I invite him over to the warroom table. As Lucian's friends file out, I hear Mustang in the hall. She waltzes into the room. Thunder rolls outside. Her hair is damp and matted, wolfcloak soaked, boots tracking mud.

Her face is a model of confusion when she sees me with Lucian.

"Mustang, darling!" I cry. "I fear you're too late. Went straight through Bacchus's stores already!" I gesture to my snoring army and wink. Maybe fifty remain, sprawled out and in various states of sleep across the large warroom. All drunk as Narol on Yuletide.

"Getting shitfaced seems a prime idea at a time like this," she says strangely. She looks back to Lucian, then to me. She doesn't like something. I introduce her to Lucian. He mumbles how nice it is to meet her. She snorts a laugh.

"How did he convince you not to make him a slave, Darrow?"

I don't know if she understands what game I'm playing.

"He gave me his fortress!" I wave my clumsy hand to the half-destroyed stone map on the wall. Mustang says that she will join us. She begins to call some of her men in from the hall, but I cut her off. "No, no. Me and Lucian here were becoming prime friends. No girls. Take your men and go find Pax."

"But . . ."

"Go find Pax," I command.

I know she's confused, but she trusts me. She murmurs goodbye to me and Lucian and closes the door. The sound of her bootheels slowly fades.

"Thought she'd never leave!" I laugh to Lucian. He leans back in his chair. He really is very slim, nothing excess to him at all. His blond hair is clipped plainly. His hands thin and useful. He reminds me of someone.

"Most people don't want pretty girls to leave," Lucian says, smiling sincerely. He even blushes a little when I ask if he really thinks Mustang is pretty.

We talk for nearly an hour. Gradually, he lets himself relax. He lets his confidence grow and soon he is telling me of his childhood, of a demanding father, of family expectations. But he's not pitiful when he does this. He is realistic, a trait I admire. It's no longer necessary for him to avoid my eyes when we talk. His shoulders don't hunch quite so much, and he becomes pleasant, even funny. I laugh loudly half a dozen times. The night grows late, but still we talk and joke. He laughs at the boots I wear, which are swaddled in animal furs for warmth. They are hot now that the snows melt, but I need to wear the pelts.

"But what of you, Darrow? We gab and gab over me. I think it's your turn. So tell me, what is it that's taken you here? What pushes you? I don't think I've heard of your family . . ."

"Not people you would care to hear about, to tell it true. But I think it comes down to a girl, that's all. I am simple. So are my reasons."

"The pretty one?" Lucian blushes. "Mustang? She hardly seems simple."

I shrug.

"I told you everything!" Lucian protests. "Don't be a vague Purple on me. Cut to it, man!" He raps the table impatiently.

"Fine. Fine. The whole story." I sigh. "See that pack beside you? There's a bag inside it. Reach and grab it for me, will you?"

Lucian pulls the bag out and tosses it to me. It clinks on the table.

"Let me see your hand."

"My hand?" he asks with a laugh.

"Right, just put it out, please." I pat the table. He doesn't react. "Come on, man. There's this theory I've been working on." I pat the table impatiently. He puts his hand out.

"How does this tell your story or theory?" His smile is still on.

"It's a complicated one. Better to show you."

"Fair enough."

I open the bag and dump out its contents. A score of golden sigil rings roll across the table. Lucian watches them roll.

"These all come from the dead kids. The kids the medBots couldn't save. Let's see." I shuffle through the pile of rings. "We have Jupiter, Venus, Neptune, Bacchus, Juno, Mercury, Diana, Ceres . . . and we have a Minerva right here." I frown and rummage around. "Hmm. Odd. I can't find a Pluto."

I look up at him. His eyes are different. Dead. Quiet.

"Oh, there's one."

41

THE JACKAL

He jerks back his hand. He is fast.

I am faster.

I bury my dagger through his hand, pinning it to the table.

His mouth gasps open at the pain. Some weird sort of feral exhalation hisses from his mouth as he jerks at the dagger. But I am bigger than him and I drove the dagger four inches into the table. I hammer it down with a flagon. He can't pull it out. I lean back and watch him try. There's something primal to his initial frenzied panic. Then something decidedly human in his recovery, which seems more brutally cold than my act of violence. He calms himself faster than anyone I've ever seen. It takes a breath, maybe three, and he leans back in his chair as though we were at drinks.

"Well, shit," he says tightly.

"I thought we should become better acquainted," I say. I point to myself. "Jackal, I am Reaper."

"You've the better name," he replies. He takes a breath. Another. "How long have you known?"

"That you were the Jackal? A hopeful guess. That you were up to no good? Before I entered the castle. No one surrenders without a fight. One of your rings didn't fit. And hide your hands next time.

Insecure sobs always hide or fiddle with their hands. But really you had no chance. The Proctors knew I was coming here. They thought to make it a trap to ruin me by telling you I was coming. So you would sneak in here, try to catch me with my pants down. Their mistake. Your mistake."

He watches me, wincing as he turns to look at my sober-as-day soldiers rising from the ground. Nearly fifty of them. I wanted them to see the ruse.

"Ah." The Jackal sighs as he realizes how futile his trap has become. "My soldiers?"

"Which ones? The ones that were with you or the ones you hid in the castle? Maybe in the cellars? Maybe beneath the floor in a tunnel? I don't wager they're smiles and giggles right now, man. Pax is a beast and Mustang will be helping him just in case."

"So that's why you sent her away."

And so she wouldn't accidentally ask why we were pretending to be drunk on grape juice.

Pax will have found their hiding place. Thunder still rolls. I hope the Jackal sank a large size of his force into this ambush. If he didn't, it'll be a hassle, because if he has Jupiter's castle, he probably has Jupiter's army, which has Juno and much of Vulcan, and soon Mars's. But I have him here.

The Jackal is pinned, bleeding, and surrounded by my army. His ambush undone. He has lost, but he is not helpless. He is no longer Lucian. It's almost like his hand isn't impaled. His voice doesn't waver. He is not angry, just pissinyourboots scary. He reminds me of me before I go into a rage. Quiet. Unhurried. I wanted my soldiers to see him squirm. He doesn't, so I tell them to leave. Only the ten Howlers, old and new, stay.

"If we're to have a conversation, please take this dagger out of my hand," the Jackal says to me. "Believe it or not, it hurts." He is not as playful as his words suggest. Despite his resolve, his face is pale and his body has begun to tremble from shock.

I smile. "Where is the rest of your army? Where is that girl, Lilath? She owes my friend an eye."

"Let me go and I will give you her head on a platter, if you want.

If you lend me an apple, I'll even put that in her mouth so she looks like a pig at feast. Your choice."

"There! Now, that's how you got your name, isn't it?" I say with mocking applause.

The Jackal clicks his tongue regrettably. "Lilath liked the sound of it. It stuck. That's why I'll put the apple in her mouth. Wish I could have been something more . . . regal than *Jackal,* but reputations tend to make themselves." He nods to Sevro. "Like the Little Goblin there and his Toadstools."

"What do you mean, 'Toadstools'?" Thistle asks.

"That's what we call you. Toadstools for Reaper and Goblin to squat on. But if you would like a better name beyond this little game, you need simply kill big nasty Reaper here. Don't stun him. Kill him. Drive a sword into his spine, and you can become Imperators, Governors, whatever. Father will be happy to oblige. Very simple stuff. *Quid pro quo*."

Sevro pulls out his knives and glares at his Howlers. "Not so simple."

Thistle doesn't move.

"Worth a try," the Jackal sighs. "I confess, I am a Politico, not a fighter. So if we're to converse, you must say something, Reaper. You look like a statue. I don't speak statue." His charisma is cold. Calculating.

"Did you really eat your own Housemembers?"

"After months in darkness, you eat whatever your mouth finds. Even if it's still moving. It isn't very impressive, really. Less human than I would have liked, very much like animals. And anyone would have done it. But dredging up my foul memories is no way to negotiate."

"We aren't negotiating."

"Humans are always negotiating. That's what conversation is. Someone has something, knows something. Someone wants something." His smile is pleasant, but his eyes . . . There is something wrong with him. A different soul seems to have filled his body since the time he was Lucian. I have seen actors . . . but this is different. It is as though he is reasonable to the point of being inhuman.

"Reaper, I will have my father give you whatever you like. A fleet. An army of Pinks to screw, Crows to conquer with, whatever. You'll have prime placement if I win this little year of schooling. If you win, there's still more schooling. Still more tests. More hardship. I hear your family is dead and poor—it will be difficult for you to rise on your own."

Almost forgot I had a fake family.

"I will make my own laurels."

"Reaper. Reaper. Reaper. You think *this* is the end of the line?" He makes a clicking sound of disgust with his tongue. "Negative. Negative, *goodman*. But if you let me go, then hardship . . ." He makes a brushing motion with his free hand. "Gone. My father will become your patron. Hello, command. Hello, fame. Hello, power. Just say goodbye to this"—he gestures to the knife—"and let your future begin. We were enemies as children. Now let us be allies as men. You're the sword, I'm the pen."

Dancer would want me to accept the offer. It would guarantee my survival. Guarantee my meteoric rise. I would be inside the halls of the ArchGovernor's mansion. I would be near the man who killed Eo. Oh, I want to accept. But then I would have to let the Proctors beat me. I'd have to let this little whorefart win and let his father smile and feel pride. I'd have to watch that smug smile spread across his bloodydamn face. Slag that. They'll feel pain.

The door opens and Pax ducks into the room. A smile splits his face.

"Goryfine night, Reaper!" he laughs. "Caught the little turds in the well. Fifty. Seems they had long tunnels down there like rats. Must be how they took the castle." He slams the door and sits on the edge of the table to gnaw on a piece of leftover meat. "It was wet work! Ha! Ha! We let them come up and it was dandy fine carnage, I tell you. Dandy fine. Helga would have loved it. They are all slaves now. Mustang is making them as we speak. But ohhh, she's in an odd mood." He spits out a bone. "Ha! This him then? *The Jackal?* He looks pale as a Red's ass." He peers closer. "Shit. You nailed him down!"

"I think you've taken bigger shits than him, Pax," Sevro adds.

"Prime have. More colorful ones too. He's drab as a Brown."

"Guard your tongue, fool," the Jackal tells Pax. "It may not always be there."

"Neither will your prick if you keep sassin'! Ha! Is it as small as you?" Pax booms.

The Jackal does not like being mocked. He stares silently at Pax before flicking his eyes back to me as a serpent might flick its tongue.

"Did you know the Proctors are helping you?" I ask. "That they've tried to kill me?"

"Of course," he says with a shrug. "My bounties are . . . above average."

"And you don't mind cheating?" I ask.

"Cheat or be cheated, no?"

Familiar.

"Well, they're not helping you anymore. It's too late for that. Now it's time you help yourself." I stab another knife down into the table. He knows what it's for.

"I once heard that if a Jackal becomes trapped, it will chew off its own leg to free itself. That knife might be easier than using teeth."

His laugh is quick and short, like a bark. "So if I cut my hand off, I can leave? Is that really it?"

"There's the door. Pax, hold the knife down so that he doesn't cheat."

Even if he ate others, he won't do it. He can sacrifice friends and allies, but not himself. He will fail this test. He is an Aureate. He is no one to fear. He is small. He is weak. He is just like his father. I find his Pluto ring in his boot and put it around his finger so his Drafters and father can watch their pride and joy give up. They will know I am better.

"The Proctors may be nudging me, but I still have to earn it, Darrow."

"We're waiting."

He sighs. "I told you. I am something different than you. A hand is a peasant's tool. A Gold's tool is his mind. Were you of better breeding, you may have realized this sacrifice means so very little to me."

Then he starts to cut. Tears stream down his face as the blood first wells. He's sawing and Pax can't even watch. The Jackal is half-way done when he looks up at me with a sane smile that convinces me of his complete insanity. His teeth chatter. He is laughing, at me, at this, at the pain. I've not met anyone like him. Now I know how Mickey felt when he met me. This is a monster in the flesh of a man.

The Jackal is about to break his own wrist to make the job easier when Pax curses and gives him an ionBlade. It will go through in a single stroke.

"Thank you, Pax," the Jackal says.

I don't know what to do. Everything inside me is screaming sense. I should kill him now. Put a blade through his throat. This is some-one you do not let go. This is someone you do not piss on and then send back into the wild. He is so far beyond Cassius it makes me want to laugh. Yet I told him he could leave if he cut, and he's cut-ting. Dear God.

"You're gory mad," Pax breathes.

The Jackal mutters something about fools. It's just a hand, he says. My hands are my everything. To him, they are nothing.

When he has finished, he sits there with a mostly cauterized stump. His face is like snow, but his belt is fastened into a tourni-quet. There's a shared moment between us where he knows I am not going to let him leave.

Then I see a distortion move through an open window. The Proc-tors came as I hoped, but I am distracted, unprepared. And when I see a small sonic detonator clatter onto the table and the Jackal grab it with his one hand, I know I've made such a mistake. I gave the Proctors time to help him. Everything slows, yet I can only watch.

With the same hand that holds the tiny detonator, the Jackal lashes upward with Pax's ionBlade. He sticks the blade into my big friend's throat. I shout and lunge forward just as the Jackal presses the detonator's button.

A sonic blast rips out from the device, throwing me across the room. The Howlers slam into the walls. Pax flips into the door. Cups, food, chairs, scatter like rice in the wind. I'm on the floor. I shake my head, trying to gain my bearings as the Jackal comes toward me. Pax staggers to his feet, blood dripping from his ears, from his throat. The Jackal says something to me, holds up the blade. Then Pax launches himself forward, not onto the Jackal, but onto me. His weight crushes me, and his body covers mine. I can barely breathe. I do not see what happens, but I feel it through Pax's body. A shudder. A spasm. Ten impacts as the Jackal stabs at Pax trying furiously to get at me like some rabid animal digging in the dirt, digging through Pax to kill me while I'm down.

Then there is nothing.

Blood drips onto my face, warms my body. It is my friend's.

I try to move Pax. I manage to squeeze out from under him. The Jackal has fled and Pax is bleeding to death. A banshee wails in my ears. The Proctors are gone as well. The Howlers stumble to their feet. When I look back to Pax, he is dead, his mouth pulled into a quiet smile. Blood slithers along the stone. My own chest tightens and I fall to a knee sobbing.

He had no last words. He had no goodbye.

He threw himself upon me. And was savaged.

Dead.

Loyal Pax. I clutch his huge head. It hurts to see my titan fallen. He was meant for more. Such a soft heart in such a hard form. He will never laugh again. Never stand on the bridge of a destroyer. Never wear the cape of a knight or carry the scepter of an Imperator. Dead. It shouldn't have been this way. It is my fault. I should have just ended things quickly.

What a future he could have had.

Sevro stands behind me, face pale. The Howlers are up and seething. Four weep silent tears. Blood trickles from their ears. The world is soundless. We cannot hear, but a pack of wolves does not need words to know that it is time to hunt.

He killed Pax. Now we kill him.

The Jackal's trail of blood leads to one of the keep's short spires. From there, it disappears into the courtyard. Rain has washed it away. We jump in a pack of eleven from the spire to a lower wall, rolling as we hit. Then we're down in the courtyard and Sevro, our tracker, leads the way through a postern gate into the rugged low mountains.

The night is hard. Rain and snow sweep sideways. Lightning flashes. Thunder rumbles, but I hear it as though in a dream. I run with the Howlers in a staggered line. We roll over dark crags, along precipitous drops in search of our quarry. My swaddled boots slow me, but they must be covered. My plan can still work, even after all this.

I do not know how Sevro guides us. I'm lost in the chaos. My mind is on Pax. He shouldn't have died. I cornered a Jackal and let him chew his way out. I remember how Mustang looked at him. She knew who he was. She knew and she wanted to talk to me in private. Whatever their connection, her loyalty was mine. But how does she know him?

Sevro takes us into the high mountain passes where snow still stacks kneehigh. Tracks here. Snow flurries around us. I'm chilled. My cloak is soaked. The slingBlade bounces on my back. My shoes squish. And blood dots the snow. We sprint uphill through a snowy pass between two rugged peaks. I see the Jackal. He's stumbling one hundred meters distant. He goes down in the snow, then he's up again. He's iron to have made it this far. We will catch him and we will kill him for what he did to Pax. He didn't have to stab my titan. My pack begins to howl sorrowfully. The Jackal looks back and stumbles on. He will not escape.

We sprint up the snowy incline. Night and darkness. Wind sweeps sideways. I howl, but it is muffled after the sonic blast, like the sound has been swaddled in cotton. Then something strange distorts the flurries in front of us. A shape. An invisible, intangible shape outlined by the falling snow. A Proctor. A stone sinks down into my stomach. This is where they kill me. This is what Fitchner warned me about.

Apollo deactivates his cloak. He smiles at me through his helmet and calls something. I cannot hear what he says. Then he waves a pulseFist and Sevro and the Howlers scatter as a tiny sonic boom blows five of our pack back down the hill. My eardrums wail. They may never be the same. PulseFist again. I dive away. Pain lances my foot. Spins me. Then the pain is gone. I'm up and sprinting at Apollo. His fist flickers a distortion of force at me. I dodge three blasts. Spinning, turning like a top. I jump. My sword comes down on his head and stops cold. PulseShield, when activated, cannot be penetrated by anything but a razor. I knew this. But there has to be some showmanship.

Apollo watches me, impervious in his armor. My pack has been blasted back down the hill. I see the Jackal struggling on the mountainside. He seems stronger now. A distortion follows him. Some other Proctor giving him strength. Venus, I think.

I scream out the rage that's been building in me since I went under Mickey's knife.

Apollo says something I can't hear. I curse him and swing my blade again. He catches it and tosses it into the snow. The invisible layer of pulseShield around his fist strikes my face—never touching, yet sending agony into the nerves. I scream and fall. Then he picks me up by my hair and we rise into the storm. He soars on gravBoots till we're three hundred meters up; I dangle from his hand. The snow swirls around us. He speaks again, adjusting some frequency so my damaged ears can hear.

"I will use small words so that you are sure to understand. We have your little Mustang. If you do not lose in your next encounter with the ArchGovernor's son so all the Drafters can bear witness, then I will ruin her."

Mustang.

First Pax. Now the girl who sang Eo's song by the fire. The girl who pulled me from the mud. The girl who curled beside me as the smoke swirled in our little cave. Brilliant Mustang, who would follow me out of choice. And this is where I led her. I did not expect this. I did not plan for this. They have her.

My stomach sinks. Not again. Not like Father. Not like Eo. Not like Lea. Not like Roque. Not like Pax. They will not kill her too. This son of a bitch will not kill anyone.

"I'm going to rip out *your bloodydamn heart*!"

He punches me in the belly, still holding me by my hair. His face is strange as he tries to place the word. *Bloodydamn*. We're floating in the air now, high. Very high. I dangle like a hanging man as he hits me again. I moan. But as I do, I remember one thing I learned from Fitchner as I clapped his shoulder in the woods. If Apollo is holding my hair and I do not feel his pulseShield, then it is turned off. And it is turned off over his entire body. He has physical recoil-Armor everywhere else, except one place.

"You are a stupid little puppet, I realize now," he says idly. "A mad, angry little puppet. You won't do as I say, will you?" He sighs. "I'll find another way. Time to cut your strings."

He drops me.

And I float there, inches from his outstretched hand.

I go nowhere, because beneath fur and cloth, I'm wearing the gravBoots I stole from Fitchner when I assaulted him in Apollo's warroom. And Apollo's shield is down. And he's pissed me off. He gawks at me, confused. I flex the knifeRing's blade out and punch him in the face, jamming the blade through his visor into his eye socket four times, jerking upward so that he dies.

"You reap what you sow!" I scream at him as he fades. All the rage I've felt swells in me, blinding me, and fills me with a pulsing, tangible hatred that seeps away only as Apollo's boots deactivate and he tumbles down through the swirling storm.

I find my Howlers around his body. The snow is red. They stare at me as I descend, my knifeRing wet with the blood of a Peerless Scarred. I had not intended to kill him. But he should not have taken her. And he should not have called me a puppet.

"They took Mustang," I tell my pack.

They look on silently. The Jackal no longer matters.

"So now we take Olympus."

The smiles they give one another are as chilling as the snow.

Sevro cackles.

42

WAR ON HEAVEN

There is no time to waste in going back to the fortress. I have the boys and girls I need. I have the hardest of all the armies. The small, the wicked, the loyal and quick. I steal Apollo's recoilArmor. The golden plate coils around my limbs like liquid. I give his gravBoots to Sevro, but they are ludicrously large on him. I strip off my own boots, his father's, so he can wear them; they jammed my toes something awful. I put on Apollo's boots instead.

"Whose are these?" Sevro asks me.

"Daddy's," I tell him.

"So you guessed." Sevro laughs.

"He's locked in Apollo's dungeons."

"The stupid Pixie!" He laughs again. They have an odd relationship.

I keep Apollo's razor, his helmet, his pulseFist, and his pulseShield along with his recoilArmor. Sevro gets the ghostCloak. I tell him to be my shadow. And then I tell my Howlers to tie their belts together.

GravBoots can lift a man in starShell as he carries an elephant in each arm. They are easily strong enough to lift me and my Howlers, who hang from my arms and legs on belt harnesses as I carry us through the swirling snowstorm up and up to Olympus. Sevro carries the others.

The Proctors have played their games. They pushed and pushed for so long. They knew I was something dangerous, something different. Sooner or later, they had to know I would snap and come to cut them down. Or perhaps they think I'm still a child. The fools. Alexander was a child when he ruined his first nation.

We rise through the storm and fly over the slopes of Olympus. It floats nearly a mile above the Argos. There are no doors. No dock. Snow covers the slopes. Clouds mask its glittering peak. I lead the Howlers to that bone-pale citadel at the top of the steep incline. It strikes up out of the mountain like a marble sword. Howlers unfasten their belts in pairs, dropping down on the highest balcony.

We crouch on the stone terrace. From here we can see the misty lands of Mars, the rocky hills and fields of Minerva, the Greatwoods of Diana, the mountains where my army garrisons Jupiter. I would be down there. The fools should have left well enough alone.

They shouldn't have taken Mustang.

I wear recoilArmor of gold. It is a second skin. My face alone is exposed. I take ash from one of the Howlers and streak it across my cheeks and mouth. My eyes burn with anger. Blond hair is wild to the shoulders, unbound. I pull my slingBlade and clench the shortwave pulseFist in my left. A razor hangs from my waist; I don't know how to use it. Dirt under my nails. Frostbite on my pinkie and middle finger of the left hand. I stink. My cloak stinks like the dead thing it is. It hangs limp behind me. White stained with a Proctor's blood. I pull up the hood. We all do. We look like wolves. And we smell blood.

The Drafters better enjoy this or I'm a dead man.

"We want Jupiter," I tell my Howlers. "Find me him. Neutralize the others if we come across any. Thistle, you take my gravBoots and fetch reinforcements. Go."

Barefoot, I blow open the doors with my pulseFist. We find Venus lying in bed in a silk shift, her armor dripping snow from its stand by the fire; she's only just returned from helping the Jackal. Grapes, cheesecake, and wine are on a nightstand. The Howlers pin her down. Four, just for effect. We tie Venus to the bedposts. Her golden eyes are wide with shock. She can hardly speak.

"You cannot! I am Scarred! I am Scarred!" is all she can manage. She says this is illegal, says she is a Proctor, says we're not allowed to assault them. How did we get here? How? Who helped us? Whose armor am I wearing? Oh, it's Apollo's. It's Apollo's. Where is Apollo? A man's gentle clothing is in the corner. They are lovers. "Who helped you?"

"I helped myself," I tell her, and pat her shining hand with a dagger. "How many other Proctors are left?" She has no words. This is not supposed to happen. It has never happened. Children do not take Olympus, not in history on all the planets was this even thought of. We gag her anyway and leave her tied, half naked, window open so she gets a taste of the chill.

The Howlers and I slink through the spire. I hear Thistle bringing reinforcements. Tactus will be here to bring his own breed of wrath. And Milia will come. Nyla soon. My army rises for Mustang. For me. For the Proctors who cheated us and poisoned our food and water and cut free our horses. We go room to room. Searching frigidariums, calderiums, steam rooms, ice rooms, baths, pleasure chambers filled with Pinks, holoImmersion tanks, for the Proctors. We take down Juno in the baths. Howlers splash in to wrestle her out. She has no weapons, but cloaked Sevro has to stun her with a stolen scorcher after she breaks Clown's arm and starts drowning him with her legs. Apparently she did not leave like she ought to have either. All these rule breakers.

Vulcan we find in a holoImmersion room, a fire crackling in the corner. He doesn't even see us come in till we turn off the machines. Vulcan was watching Cassius stand at the edge of a battlement as flaming missiles etch a smoky sky. They gave them fragging catapults. There was another screen showing the Jackal stumble through the snow into a mountain cavern's mouth. Lilath greets him there with a thermal cloak and a medBot.

I ask the Proctors where Mustang has been taken. They say to ask

Apollo or Jupiter. It isn't their concern. And it shouldn't be mine. Apparently my head is going to roll. I ask them what they will swing. "I have all the axes."

My army binds the Proctors and we take them with us as we descend, flowing down to the next level and the level after that like a flood of mad half-wolves. We run across highReds and Brown servants and housePinks. I pay them no mind, but my army in their rabid excitement sets upon any they see. They knock down Reds and absolutely obliterate any Grays that make the mistake of trying to fight us. Sevro has to choke out a Ceres boy who sits on a Red's chest, bludgeoning in his face with scarred fists. Two Grays are killed by Tactus when they try to fire on him. He dodges their scorchers and breaks their necks. A squad of seven Grays try to take me down. But my pulseShield protects me from their scorchers. Only if they concentrate fire and the shield overheats will I suffer. I dodge their fire and bring them down with my SlingBlade.

My army trickles in, slowly at first. But more are coming every four minutes. I'm nervous. It isn't fast enough. Jupiter could destroy us, as could Pluto and whoever else is left. My army is exultant because they have me; they think me immortal, unstoppable. Already they've heard that I killed Apollo. I hear nicknames rippling like currents through the army as we swarm through the gilded, vast halls. *Godslayer. Sunkiller,* they fancy me. But the Proctors hear these things too. The ones we've captured, even the ones a little bemused by the idea of students invading Olympus, now stare at me with pale faces. They realize they're part of the game they thought they escaped many years ago, and that there are no medBots directed toward Olympus. Funny thing, watching gods realize they've been mortal all along.

I send out dozens of scouts through the palace, telling them what I need. Already I can hear my plan being unwound in the halls beneath me. Jupiter, Pluto, Mercury, and Minerva remain. They are coming for me. Or am I coming for them? I do not know. I try to feel like the predator, but I cannot. My rage is calming. It is slowing and giving way to fear as the halls stretch on. They have Mustang; I remind myself of the smell of her hair. These are the Scarred who take bribes from the man who killed my wife. The blood pumps faster. My rage returns.

I meet Mercury in a hall. He is laughing hysterically and calling out bawdy drinking songs from the HC as he faces down a half dozen of my soldiers. He wears a bathrobe but is dancing like a maniac around the swordthrusts of three DeadHorses. I've not seen such grace beyond the mines. He moves as I mined. Fury balanced with physics. A kick, a crushing elbow, an application of force to dislocate kneecaps.

He slaps one of my soldiers in the face with his hand. Kicks another in the groin. And does a flip over one, grabs her hair when he is upside down, lands and slams her into the wall like a rag doll. Then he knees a boy in the face, cuts off a girl's thumb so she can't hold her sword, and tries backhanding me before dancing away. I'm faster than him, and stronger, despite his incredible gift with the razor; so as his hand goes at my face, I punch his forearm as hard as I can, cracking the bone. He yelps and tries to dance back, but I hold on to his hand and beat his arm with my fist till it breaks.

Then I let him spin away, wounded.

We're in a hall, my soldiers sprawled around him. I shout the rest back and heft my slingBlade. Mercury is a cherub of a man. Small, squat, with a face like a baby. His cheeks flush rosy. He's been drinking. His coiled golden hair droops over his eyes. He flips it back. I remember how he had wanted to pick me for his House but his Drafters had objected. Now he flourishes his razor like a poet with a quill, but his off hand is useless after I punched it.

"You're a wild one," he says through the pain.

"You should have picked me for your House."

"I told them not to push you. But did they listen? No no no no no. Silly Apollo. Pride can blind."

"So can swords."

"Through the eye?" Mercury looks at my armor. "Dead, then?" Someone shouts for me to kill him. "My, my. They are hungry. This duel may be fun."

I bow.

Mercury curtsies.

I like this Proctor. But I also don't want him to kill me with that razor.

So I sheathe my sword and shoot him in the chest with my pulseFist set to stun. Then we tie him up. He's still laughing. But farther down the hall behind him, I see Jupiter—a god of a man in full armor—storming forth with a crooked pulseShaft and a razor. Another armored Proctor is with him, Minerva, I think. We retreat. Still, they decimate my force. They come at us straight on in the long hall, knocking boys and girls down like boulders rolling through grain. We can't hurt them. My soldiers scamper back the way we came, back up the stairways, back to the higher levels, where we run over new packs of reinforcements. We scramble over each other, falling on the marble floor, running through golden suites to flee Jupiter and Minerva as they come up the stairs. Jupiter bellows laughter as our simple swords and spears ping off his armor.

Only my weapons can hurt him. They aren't enough. Jupiter's razor goes through my pulseShield and slips my recoilArmor on the thigh. I hiss with pain and shoot the pulseFist at him. His shield takes the pulse and holds, but barely. He flicks a razor at me like a whip. It grazes my eyelid, nearly taking my eye. Blood sheets from the small wound, and I roar in anger. I fly at him, past Minerva, breaking my pulseFist against his jaw. It ruins my weapon and my fist, but it dents his golden helmet and sends him reeling. I don't give him time to recover. I scream and hack in swirling arcs with my slingBlade even as I stab clumsily with my razor. It's a mad dance. I take him through the knee with the unfamiliar razor. He cuts open my thigh with his own. The armor closes around the wound, compressing it and administering painkillers.

We're at the end of a circular stairwell as I push him back. His long blade goes limp, then slithers around my leg like a lasso, about to constrict and slice my leg off at the hip. I push fast as I can into him. We go down the stairs. Then he rolls up and stands. I tackle him backward. Armor on armor.

We smash into a holoImmersion room. Sparks fly. I keep screaming and pushing so he cannot rip off my leg with the razor, still limp and looped around flesh and bone. He's backpedaling, off balance, when I take him through a window and we spill out into the open air. Neither of us have gravBoots, so we plummet a hundred feet into a snowbank on the mountain's side. We roll down the steep slope toward the one-mile drop, toward the flowing Argos.

I catch myself in the snow. I manage to stand. I can't see him. I think I hear his grunt in the distance. We're both muddled in the clouds. I crouch and listen, but my hearing still hasn't recovered from Apollo.

"You'll die for this, little boy," Jupiter says. It comes as if from underwater. Where is he? "Should have learned your place. Everything has an order. You're near the top. But you are not the top, little boy."

I say something pithy about merit not meaning much.

"You can't spend merit."

"So the Governor is paying you to do this?"

I hear a howl in the distance. My shadow.

"What do you think you're going to do, little boy? Going to kill all us Proctors? Going to make us let you win? It's not the way things work, little boy." Jupiter looks for me. "Soon the Governor's Crows will come in their ships, with their swords and guns. The real soldiers, little boy. The ones who have scars you can't dream of. The Obsidians led by Golden Legates and knights. You're just playing. But they'll think you've gone mad. And they will take you and hurt you and kill you."

"Not if I win before they get here." That is the key to everything. "There may be a delay on the holos before the Drafters see them, but how long a delay? Who is editing the gorydamn holos while you fight? We'll make sure the right message gets out."

I take my red sweatband off of my head and dab away the sweat on my face, then wrap it around my head once more.

Jupiter is silent.

"So the Drafters will see this conversation. They will see that the Governor is paying you to cheat. They will see that I am the first student to invade Olympus in history. And they will see me cut you down and take your armor and parade you naked through the snow, if you surrender. If not, I will throw your corpse from Olympus and piss golden showers down after you."

The clouds clear and Jupiter stands before me in the white. Red drips from his golden armor. He is tall, lean, violent. This place is his home. It is his playground. The children his playthings till they get their scars. He is like any other petty tyrant of history. A slave to his own whims. A master of nothing but selfishness. He is the Society—a monster dripping in decadence, yet seeing none of his own hypocrisy. He views all this wealth, all this power, as his right. He is deluded. They all are. But I cannot cut him down from the front. No, no matter how well I fight. He is too strong.

His razor hangs from his hand like a snake. With the press of a button it will go rigid, a meter in length. His armor shines. Morning breaks as we face one another. A smile splits his lips.

"You would have been something in my House. But you are a little stupid boy, angry and of House Mars. You cannot yet kill like I can, yet you challenge me. Pure rage. Pure stupidity."

"No. I can't challenge you." I toss my slingBlade down at his feet and throw my razor with it. I can barely use the razor anyway. "So I'll cheat." I nod. "Go ahead, Sevro."

The razor slithers up from the ground, stiffens, and goes through Jupiter's hamstrings as he wheels about. His slash goes two feet too high. He's used to fighting men. Invisible, Sevro wounds Jupiter's arms and takes the man's weapons. The recoilArmor flows into the wounds to stop their bleeding, but the tendons will need real work.

When Jupiter is silent, Sevro winks off Apollo's ghostCloak. We take Jupiter's weapons. His armor wouldn't have fit anyone except Pax. Poor Pax. He would have looked dashing in all this finery. We drag Jupiter back up the slope.

Inside, the tide of the battle has shifted. My scouts, it seems, have found what I told them to seek. Milia runs up to me, a content grin on her long face. Her voice, as ever, is a low drawl when she tells me the good news.

"We found their armory."

A host of Venus Housemembers, only just freed from slavery, thunders past. Their pulseFists and recoilArmor shimmer. Olympus is ours and Mustang has been found.

Now we have all the axes.

43

THE LAST TEST

I find her asleep in a suite beside Jupiter's own. Her golden hair is wild. Her cloak dirtier than my own. It hangs brown and gray, not white. She smells like smoke and hunger. She's destroyed the room, upturned a dish of food, buried her dagger into the door. The Brown and Pink servants are scared of her, and me. I watch them skitter away. My distant cousins. I see them move, alien things. Like ants. So void of emotion. I feel a pang. Perspective is a wicked creature. This is how Augustus saw Eo as he killed her. An ant. No. He called her a "Red bitch." She was like a dog in his eyes.

"The food was laced with something?" I ask one of the Pinks.

The beautiful boy murmurs something, looking at the ground.

"Speak like a man," I bark.

"*Sedatives, lord.*" He does not look at me. I don't blame him. I'm a Gold. A foot taller. Worlds stronger. And I look positively insane. How wicked he must think me. I tell him to go away. "Hide. My army does not always listen when I tell them not to toy with low-Colors."

The bed is grand. Sheets of silk. Mattress of feathers. Posts of ivory, ebony, and gold. Mustang sleeps on the floor in the corner. For so long we have had to hide where we sleep. It must have felt so wrong lying in perfect comfort, even with sedatives in her. She tried breaking the windows too. I'm glad she didn't. It's a far drop.

I sit beside her. The breath from her nose stirs a single coil of hair. How many times I've watched her sleep with a fever. How many times she's done the same. But there's no fever now. No cold. No pain in my stomach. Cassius's wound has healed. Winter is ended. Outside, I saw the first of the flowers blossoming. I picked one on the mountainside. It's in the hidden compartment of my cloak. I want to give it to Mustang. Want her to wake with the haemanthus by her lips. But when I take it out, a dagger slips into my heart. Worse than any metal blade. Eo. The pain will never go away. I don't know if it is supposed to. And I don't know if this guilt I feel is owed. I kiss the haemanthus and tuck it away. Not yet. Not yet.

I wake Mustang gently.

Her smile spreads before she even opens her eyes, as though she knows I am beside her. I say her name and brush the hair from her face. Her eyes flutter open. Golden flakes spiral there in the irises. So strange next to my callused, dirty fingers with their cracked nails. She nuzzles my hand and manages to sit up. A yawn. She looks around. I almost laugh as I see her digest what has happened.

"Well, I was going to tell you about a dream I had about dragons. They were purple and pretty and liked to sing songs." She flicks my armor with a finger. It rings. "Way to upstage me. Jerk. What happened?"

"I got mad."

She groans. "I've become the maiden in distress, haven't I? Slag! I hate those girls."

I tell her the news. The Jackal is split. His forces besiege Mars as he and Lilath hide in the deep mountains. We'll be able to find him easily.

"If you want, you can take our army and root the bastard out."

"Done," she smirks, and raises an eyebrow. "But can you trust me? Maybe I'll want to be big Primus of this weird army."

"I can trust you."

"How do you know?" she says again.

This is when I kiss her. I cannot give her the haemanthus. That is my heart, and it is of Mars—one of the only things born from the red soil. And it is still Eo's. But this girl, when they took her . . . I would have done anything to see her smirking again. Perhaps one day I'll have two hearts to give.

She tastes how she smells. Smoke and hunger. We do not pull apart. My fingers wend through her hair. Hers trace along my jaw, my neck, and scrape along the back of my scalp. There is a bed. There is time. And there's a hunger different from when I first kissed Eo. But I remember when the Gamma Helldiver, Dago, took a deep pull from his burner, turning it bright but dead in a few quick moments. He said, *This is you.*

I know I am impetuous. Rash. I process that. And I am full of many things—passion, regret, guilt, sorrow, longing, rage. At times they rule me, but not now. Not here. I wound up hanging on a scaffold because of my passion and sorrow. I ended up in the mud because of my guilt. I would have killed Augustus at first sight because of my rage. But now I am here. I know nothing of the Institute's history. But I know I have taken what no one else has taken. I took it with anger and cunning, with passion and rage. I won't take Mustang the same way. Love and war are two different battlefields.

So despite the hunger, I pull away from Mustang. Without a word, she knows my mind, and that's how I know it's in the right. She darts one more kiss into me. It lingers longer than it should, and then we stand together and leave. We hold hands till the door, then I turn to her.

"Fetch me the Jackal's standard, Mustang."

"Yes, Lord Reaper." She gives a mock bow and a little wink. Then she is gone.

The place is a madhouse of looting. In all the chaos, Sevro has found the holoTransmitter. It has our sensorial experiences stored in its hard drives and is queued to send them back to the Drafters wherever they may be. It is not a streaming feed, so the Drafters do not yet have today's events. There is a half-day delay. That is all it will take. I give Sevro instructions and have him get to work splicing out the story I want told. I would trust no one else.

I have Fitchner brought up from Castle Apollo's dungeons. He reclines in a chair in Olympus's dining hall. His face is purple from when I hit him. The floor is made of condensed air, so we are suspended above a mile vertical drop. His feet are on the table and his mouth twists into a smile.

"There's the manic boy," he calls, fingering his chin. "I knew I liked your odds."

I give him a greeting with my middle finger. "Liar."

He returns the finger. "Turd." He reaches for my hand. "Don't tell me you're still bitter about the poisoning, the sicknesses, the setup with Cassius, the bears in the woods, the shitty tech, the terrible weather, the assassination attempts, the spy."

"The spy?"

"Messing with you. Ha! Still a child. Speaking of which, where are your soldiers? Running around, eating themselves stupid, showering, sleeping, screwing, playing with the Pinks? This place is a honey trap, my boy. A honey trap that will make your army worthless."

"You're in a better mood."

"My son is safe," he says with a wink. "Now what are you up to?"

"I already sent Mustang to deal with the Jackal. And after this, I go to House Mars. Then it will all be over."

"Ooo. Except it won't be." Fitchner pops a familiar gumbubble and winces. I did a number on his jaw. It makes me laugh. I've felt like laughing since Sevro took down Jupiter. My leg throbs with pain from that blasted man. Even with the painkillers, I can hardly walk.

"No riddles. Why isn't it over?"

"Three things," Fitchner says. His hatchet face examines me for a moment. "You're a peculiar creature. You and the Jackal both. Everyone always wants to win. But you two stand apart, freaks. Golds won't die to win. We value our lives too much. You two don't. Where did it come from?"

I remind him he's my prisoner and he should answer my questions.

"Three things are not finished. Here's what's what. I'll tell you what they are if you answer my question: what drives you." He sighs. "The first thing, good man, is Cassius. He will simply *have* to duel you until one of you little sods keels over and dies."

I was afraid of that. I answer Fitchner's question.

I tell him the Jackal wanted to know the same thing. What drives me. The right-off answer is rage. From point to point, it is rage. If something happens, and if I was not anticipating it, I react like an animal—with violence. But the deepspine answer is love. Love drives me. So I must lie a bit to him.

"My mother had a dream that I could be greater than anyone in my family. Greater than the name Andromedus. The name of my father." Fake father. Fake family. Point still the same. "I am not a Bellona. Not an Augustus. Not an Octavia au Lune." I smile wickedly, something he can appreciate. "But I want to be able to stand above them and piss on all their gorydamn heads."

Fitchner likes that. He's always wanted the same, but he's found that without the pedigree, merit takes you only so far. That frustration is his condition.

"The second thing that is not finished is *this.*" Fitchner waves his hands about. I got the crust of this deal—he's making no revelations. I killed a Proctor. I have evidence that the ArchGovernor bribed others and threatened more so that his child could win. Nepotism. Manipulation of the sacred school. This is not idle news. It will shatter something. Perhaps even remove the ArchGovernor from office. Charges. Punishment? The Drafters will want blood. "And the ArchGovernor will want yours. This will embarrass him, and potentially make room for a Bellona ArchGovernor. Maybe Cassius's father."

Fitchner asks me why I trust the soldiers in my army who were slaves.

"They trust me because they've seen how they would have done in all this had I not come along. You think they want the Jackal as their master?"

"Good," Fitchner says. "You trust them all. Splendid, then there is no third complication. My mistake." I press him for what he means, so he sighs and relents. "Oh, only that you sent Mustang and half the army to deal with the Jackal."

"And?"

"It's really nothing. You trust her."

"No. Tell me. What do you mean?"

"Well, fine. If you must know, if there's simply no other way of going about it: she is the Jackal's twin sister."

Virginia au Augustus. Sister to the Jackal. Twin. An heir of the great family, the *gens Augusta*. The only daughter of ArchGovernor Nero au Augustus. The man who made all this happen. Kept cloistered and out of the public eye to ward off assassination attempts, just like her brother. That's why Cassius didn't know the daughter of his family's archrival. But when I sat with the Jackal, Mustang knew who he was. Her brother. Had she known before of the Jackal's identity? Nothing can explain her silence if she knew who he was and said nothing. Nothing except for family—which is a loyalty above friendship, above love, above a kiss in the corner of a room. I have sent half my army to the Jackal. I have given him recoilArmor, gravBoots, ghostCloaks, razors, pulseWeapons, enough tech for him to take Olympus. *Dammit.*

The Proctors all know. And when I pass them at a run, they are laughing. They laugh at my stupidity. The rage grows inside of me. I want to kill something. I marshal my forces. They are spread throughout the castle, eating its food, taking its pleasures. Fools. Fools. My best are where I need them. Sevro, left to his work. That is the most important thing. I order Tactus to hunt down the remnants of Venus and Mercury in the southern lowlands and enslave them, and I set Milia out to marshal the rest of my army with Nyla. I need to go to House Mars now. I cannot wait for my soldiers to assemble. I need fresh bodies, because when the Augustus twins come, they will have weapons and technology to match mine, and they may have more soldiers. The game has changed. I did not prepare for this. I feel a fool. How could I have kissed her? My heart is swallowed by darkness. What if I had given her the haemanthus? I tear it to ribbons as I jump from the edge of Mount Olympus in my gravBoots and let the petals fall.

I take only the Howlers with me, passing the petals as we soar down.

We wear gravBoots and armor and carry pulseFists and pulseBlades. The snow in the land of House Mars is gone. Muddy soil churned by the feet of invaders replaces it. The highlands are swaddled in mist. The smell is of earth and siege. Our towers, Phobos and Deimos, are rubble. The catapults gifted to the besiegers have done their work there. So too have they made progress on the walls of my old castle. The front façade is in ruin and strewn with arrows, broken pottery from pitch jars, swords, armor, and some students.

Nearly a hundred strong besiege Mars. Their camp is near the tree line, but an enclosing fence has been built around Mars Castle to prevent any sallies from the fortress. It has been a long winter for both sides, though I note the solar cooking pots, the portable heaters, the nutrition packets of the Jackal's besieging force—comprised of Jupiter, Apollo, and a quarter of House Pluto. Several crosses stand high at the bottom of the slope. They face the castle. On the crosses are three bodies. Crows tell me their state. The only sign of resistance I see from House Mars is our flag—the wolf of Mars, tattered and scorched. It hangs slack in the poor wind.

The Howlers and I come from the sky like golden gods. Our ragged cloaks flap behind us. But if the besiegers expected us to be Proctors bringing more gifts, they could not have been more mistaken. We land hard on the earth. The Howlers first, and I land at their head, and as I hit, the enemy scatter before me in utter terror.

Reaper has come home.

I let the Howlers make ruin of the enemies on our soil. This is as close as I've been to home, to Lykos, in months. I bend down and take a handful of House Mars soil as my men do my work around me. Mars. Home. I have flown a different banner, but I have missed my House. Enemies run to attack me. They see my blade, know who I am. I walk impervious. My pulseArmor is my shield. Sevro and the Howlers act as my sword.

I walk to the three crosses and peer up to see Antonia, Cassandra, and Vixus.

The betrayers. What did they do now?

Antonia is still alive, as is Vixus, barely. I have Thistle cut them down and take them back to Olympus for the medBots. They will have to live with the knowledge that they slit Lea's throat. I hope it hurts them. I stand for a moment at the bottom of the hill. I call up to tell them who I am. But they already know, because the flag of Mars comes down and in its place is raised a soiled bedsheet with a hastily drawn slingBlade arching across.

"The Reaper!" they cry, as I am their salvation. "Primus!"

The defenders are ragged, dirty, and thin. Some are so weak we have to carry them from the rubble of the castle. Those who can, come to salute me or tip their heads or kiss my cheeks. Those who cannot, touch my hand as I pass. There are broken legs and crushed arms. They will be mended. We ferry them back to Olympus. House Mars will not be useful in the coming battle, so I will use besiegers from Pluto, Jupiter, and Apollo. I have Clown and Pebble enslave them all with the standard of Mars. A thin boy I hardly recognize delivers it to me. But when he grabs me in a skeletal embrace, a hug so hard it hurts, I know who he is.

A silent sob echoes in my chest.

He is quiet as he hugs me. Then his body shudders like Pax's did as he met death. Except these shudders come from joy, not pain.

Roque lives.

"My brother," he sobs. "My brother."

"I thought you were dead," I tell him as I clutch his delicate frame. "Roque, I thought you were dead." I clasp him to me. His hair is so thin. I feel his bones through his clothing. He's like a wet rag around my armor.

"Brother," he says. "I knew you would come back. I knew it in my heart. This place was hollow without you." He grins at me with such pride. "How you now fill it."

The Primus of House Diana was right. House Mars is a wildfire. And it does starve. Roque has scars on his face. He shakes his head, and I know he has stories to tell—where he was, how he came back. But later. He limps away. Quinn, one-eared and tired, goes with him. She mouths a thank-you and puts her hand along the small of the thin poet's back in a manner that lets me know she's left Cassius.

"He told us you would return," she says. "Roque never lies."

Pollux is still humorous when I see him. His voice is gravel and he clasps my arm. Quinn and Roque kept the House together, he says. Cassius gave up a long while ago. He waits for me in the warroom.

"Don't kill him . . . please. It ate his mind up, man. Ate it all up what he did to you; we all found out. So just let him get some time away from this place, man. It does things to your head. Makes you forget we don't have a choice." Pollux kicks a piece of mud. "The bastards put me in with a little girl, you know."

"In the Passage?"

"Matched me with a little girl. I tried to kill her softly . . . but she wouldn't die." Pollux grunts something and claps me on the shoulder. He tries a sour chuckle. "We've got it raw, but at least we're not Reds, you register?"

Righto.

He leaves and I'm alone in my old castle. Titus died on the spot where I stand. I look at the keep. It's worse now than it was in his time. Everything is worse now, somehow.

Bloodyslag. Why did Mustang have to betray me? Everything is dark now that I know. A shadow cast over life. She could have told me so many times. But she never did. I know she wanted to speak with me when I was with the Jackal, but likely just to tell me something idle. Some tidbit. Or would she betray her blood for me? No. If she would have done that, then she would have told me before I gave her half my army. She took her standard too, and Ceres's. Why did she need so many except to make war with me? It feels like *she* killed Eo. It feels like she put the noose there and I jerked the feet. She is her father's daughter.

I feel that little snap go through my hands. I've betrayed Eo.

I spit on the stones. My mouth is dry. Haven't had anything to drink all morning. My head aches. Time to drop my balls, as Uncle Narol used to say. Time to see Cassius.

He sits with his ionBlade out on House Mars's table. He's in the seat I carved with my sigil. The old House flag lies across his knee. The Primus hand dangles around his neck. So much time has passed since he put that sword in my belly. The weapon looks silly now. A toy, a relic. I am so far past this room, past his blade, past his reach, yet his eyes stop my heart. The guilt is like black bile in my throat. Fills my chest and drains me.

"I'm sorry for Julian," I tell him.

His hair is golden curls but matted with grit and grease. Fleas make their home there. He is still beautiful, still more handsome than I ever will be. But I am the greater man. The spark in his eye has cooled. Time and space away from this place are what his soul needs. Months of siege. Months of anger and defeat. Months of loss and guilt have drained him of all that makes him Cassius. What a poor soul. I feel sorry for him. I almost laugh. After he put a sword in my belly, *I* pity *him*. He has never lost a battle. He alone of all the Primuses can say that. Yet he takes the badge and flips it to me.

"You've won. But was it worth it?" Cassius asks.

"Yes."

"No hesitation. . . ." He nods. "That's the difference between you and me."

He sets the standard and his sword down and walks close to me, so close I can smell the stink of his breath. I think he's going to hug me. I want to hug him, to apologize and beg for his forgiveness. Then he pulls open a scab on his knuckles, sucks the blood from it and spits in my face, startling me.

"This is a blood feud," he hisses in highLingo. "If ever again we meet, you are mine or I am yours. If ever again we draw breath in the same room, one breath shall cease. Hear me now, you wretched worm. We are devils to one another till one rots in hell."

It is a formal, cold declaration that requires one thing of me. I nod. And he leaves. I stand trembling for a moment after he's gone.

My heart thuds in my chest. So much pain. I had thought it would be over, but not all scars heal. Not all sins are forgiven.

I take the Mars flag and pin the Primus badge to myself. I watch the map on the wall. My slingBlade banner flutters over every castle there; my men secured the rest even as Tactus makes ready Olympus for Mustang's assault. Now those castles belong to me, not to the wolf of House Mars. My slingBlade looks like the *L* of Lambda. My clan. The place where my brother, my sister, my uncle, my mother, my friends, still toil. They feel a world apart, yet their symbol, a symbol of our rebellion—a working tool made into a weapon for war—flies over all the Houses of the Aureate except one. Pluto.

I leave the castle through the spire. I am a Red Helldiver of Lykos. I am Gold Primus of House Mars. And I am going to my last battle in this bloodydamn valley. After that the real war begins.

44

RISE

Tactus has assumed command in my absence. The man is a cruel beast, but he's my cruel beast. And with him at my side, my forces are fit for bloodshed. Our armor glistens. Three hundred strong. Ninety new slaves. They will not have a chance to earn their freedom. There were not enough gravBoots for all. Or enough armor. But everyone has something. The DeadHorses and the Howlers group together near the edge of Mount Olympus. They stare down, a thin arc of gold, at the ground a mile below. Our adversaries are in the mountains. When Mustang and the Jackal come from the snow peaks, they will be at a disadvantage. We have the highest ground. The rest of my force—Pax's former squad and Nyla's—guard the golden fortress and the Proctors. The slaves are there as well. I wish Pax were at my side. I always felt safer in his shadow.

I've sent Nyla and Milia and a dozen others in ghostCloaks to scout the mountains for the Jackal's movements. Who knows what intel Mustang has given her brother? He will know our weaknesses, our disposition, so I shift everything as much as possible. Whatever she knows will be useless. Alter the paradigm. I wonder if I could beat her as mercilessly as I beat Fitchner. The girl who hummed Eo's song? Never. I'm still Red at heart.

"Hate this gory part," Tactus sighs. He leans his wiry body past me to peer out over the edge of the floating mountain. "Waiting. Pfah. We need some optics."

"What?"

"Optics!" he says loudly.

My hearing goes in and out. Popped eardrums are nasty things.

He says something about Mustang and cutting her thumbs off for starters. I don't catch most of it. Probably don't want to; he's the sort to make braids of someone's entrails. "There!" Then we see a golden flier pierce a cloud. Three more follow. Nyla . . . Milia. Mustang . . . and something else.

"Hold!" I call to Sevro and his Howlers. They echo the command as Mustang approaches carrying something odd.

"Lo, Reaper," Mustang calls to me. I wait for her to land. Her boots bring her quickly to the ground.

"Lo, Mustang."

"So Milia says you figured it out." She looks around with a curious smile. "This must all be for me then?"

"Of course." I'm confused. "Thought there might be a scuffle between Augustus and Andromedus."

"No scuffle this time. I brought you a gift. May I present my brother, Adrius au Augustus, the Jackal of the Mountains, and his standard. And he's"—she looks at me with a hard smile as she realizes I thought she betrayed me—*"disarmed."*

She drops the Jackal, bound, gagged, and naked.

"Bugger my goryballs," Tactus hisses.

I have won.

Mustang stands beside me as the dropships come to Olympus. She's told me not to feel guilty about doubting her loyalty. She should have told me her family ties even though she doesn't claim the Jackal as her brother. Not in spirit. Her true brother, her older brother, was killed by one of Cassius's, a brute by the name of Karnus. Augustus and Bellona. The blood feud between the families runs deep, and I feel its riptide pulling at my legs.

Yet the question remains, is Mustang her father's daughter? Or is she the girl who hums Eo's song? I think I know the answer. She is what Golds can be, should be. Yet her father and brother are what Golds are. Eo never would have guessed it could be this complicated. There is goodness in Golds, because in many ways, they are the best humanity can offer. But they're also the worst. What does that do to her dream? Only time will tell.

My lieutenants flank me—Mustang, Nyla, Milia, Tactus, Sevro, even Roque and Quinn. We leave a space for Pax and Lea. My army flanks them. There is no need to embarrass the Pluto students. I want to. But I don't. They stand dispersed throughout my six units. We wait in a broad courtyard across from the landing pads. It is a spring day and so the snow melts fast.

Sevro is near me. In his eye, I see a subtle difference when he looks at me. The conversation we had when he finished editing the tapes was short and frightening. It echoes in my ears.

"The audio in the storm was scrambled," he said. "Couldn't make out the last words you said to Apollo. So I deleted them."

One of my last words was *bloodydamn*.

What does Sevro know? What does he think he knows? The fact that he deleted it means he thinks it is important enough to cover up.

ArchGovernor Augustus and Imperators Bellona and Adriatus and a host of other dignitaries to the sum of two hundred come from the shuttles, each with a cadre of attendants. The Director surveys us and laughs at the Proctors' condition. I have left them bound and gagged. There is no pity here. Any worry I had at punishment is swept away. Only Fitchner stands unbound. If there are any rewards given to the Proctors, he should reap them. They have seen the holoexperiences by now. Sevro made sure they were good. He knew well the story I wanted told. I made only a few adjustments.

Director Clintus is a small woman with a severe mountain peak of a face. She manages to crack a joke about this being the first time they have had the ceremony at so lofty a location. But she does think it will be the last. It is not the way the game is supposed to be played, yet it does speak to my creativity and cunning. She seems to like me very much and affectionately refers to me as "the Reaper." In fact, they all seem to like me very much. Though some, I can tell, are wary. Rulers tend to dislike those who break rules.

"The Drafters of all the Houses are clamoring to recruit you, my boy. You'll have a choice, though Mars has first offer. It will be up to you. So many choices for the Reaper!" Clintus titters.

Bellona and Augustus, blood enemies, both watch me as you would a snake. I killed one of their sons and embarrassed the other's. I do believe this may become awkward.

There is little ceremony. The attendants bustle about. This is but formality. The true ceremony will take place in Agea, where there will be a grand festival, a party to set fire to the heavens, and the holopresence of the Sovereign herself. Libations, dancers, racers, fire breathers, pleasure slaves, enhancers, spikedust, politicians, or so Mustang tells me. It seems strange to think others care about what happened to us here, strange to think that so many of the Golds are vapid creatures. They know nothing of what it is to earn the mark of a Peerless Scarred. To beat a boy to death in a cold room of stone. But they will celebrate us. For a moment, I forgot whom we were fighting for. I forgot this is a race that fights like hell to earn its frivolous things because it loves those things so much. I don't understand that drive. I understand the Institute. I understand war. But I don't understand what is coming in Agea, or what will come after that. Perhaps that's because I'm more like the Iron Golds. The best of the Peerless. Those like the Ancestors. Those who nuked a planet that rose against their rule. What a creature I've become.

When all is said and done, Director Clintus pins some badge on me. She winks and touches my shoulder. Then we disperse. Just like that. The game is through and we are told dropships are inbound for our departure to our own homes, where parents wait to give their approval or disown disappointing sons and daughters. Just like that. Until then, we mill about, feeling foolish in all our accumulated armor, all our weaponry that now means so little. I look at my slingBlade and wonder how useless it has just become. It's as though we're supposed to congratulate one another, cheer or something. But there is only silence. A hollow silence for victors and losers all.

I am empty.

What do I do now? There was always a fear, always a concern, always a reason to hoard weapons and food, always a quest or trial. Now, nothing. Just the wind sweeping in over our battlefield. An empty battlefield filled only with echoes of things lost and learned. Friends. Lessons. Soon it will be a memory. I feel like a lover has died. I yearn to cry. Feel hollow. Adrift. I look for Mustang. Will she still care for me? And then ArchGovernor Augustus suddenly takes me by the elbow and leads me away from the other stunned youth.

"I am a busy man, *Reaper,*" he says, mocking the word. "So I will be direct. You have created complications in my life."

His touch makes me want to scream. His thin mouth emotes nothing. His nose is straight. His eyes contemptuous and made from the embers of a dying sun. So peerless. Yet he is not beautiful. His is a face carved from granite. Deep cheeks. Manly, tough skin, not burnished like that of the fools on the HC or the Pixies who gallivant around the nightclubs. He reeks of power like Pinks reek of perfume. I want to make his face look like a broken puzzle.

"Yes," is all I say.

He does not smirk or smile. "My wife is a beggar. She pleaded with me to help her son win."

"Wait. He had help?" I ask.

His mouth slides into a soft smile. The sort reserved for simple amusements. "I'm assuming you are not sharing my involvement with others."

I want to break him. After all that has happened, he expects my cooperation, as though it is something due to him. As though it is his right that I help him. I unclench my fists. What would Dancer have me say?

"You're fine," I manage. "I can't help you on the domestic front, but I won't tell a soul that the Jackal had help from Daddy."

His chin rises. "Do not call him that name. The men of House Augustus are lions, not fleabitten carrion eaters."

"All the same, you should have put your money on Mustang," I say, intentionally not using her name.

"Don't tell me about my family, Darrow." He peers down his nose at me. "Now, the question is how much you want for your silence. I accept no gifts. Owe no man. So you will be taken care of on one condition."

"I stay away from your daughter?"

"No." He laughs sharply, surprising me. "The foolish families worry over blood. I care nothing for purity of family or ancestry. That is a vain thing. I care only for strength. What a man can do to other men, women. And that is something you have. Power. Strength." He leans closer, and in his pupils I see Eo dying. "I have enemies. They are strong. They are many."

"They are Bellona."

"And others. But yes, Imperator Tiberius au Bellona has more than fifty nieces and nephews. He has nine children. That Goliath, Karnus, the eldest. Cassius his favorite. His seed is strong. Mine is . . . less so. I had a son worth all of Tiberius's put together. But Karnus killed him," He's silent for a moment. "Now I have two nieces. A nephew. A son. A daughter. And that is it. So I collect apprentices.

"My condition is this. I will give you what you want for your silence. I will buy you Pinks, Obsidians, Grays, Greens. I will sponsor your application to the Academy, where you will learn to sail the ships that conquered the planets. I will provide you with funds and patronage requirements. I will introduce you to the Sovereign. I will do all these things for your silence if you become one of my lancers, an *aide-de-camp*, a member of my household."

He asks me to betray my name. To set aside my family for his. Mine is a false family, Andromedus, a family made for deception, yet some part of me aches.

I saw it coming. But I don't know what to say. "One of your son's soldiers might say something about your involvement, my lord."

He snorts. "I'm more concerned about your lieutenants."

I laugh. "Few of my army know the truth. And those that do will not say a word."

"So much trust."

"I am their ArchPrimus." I say it simply.

"Are you serious?" he asks in confusion as though I misunderstand something as basic as gravity. "Boy, allegiances crumble as soon as we board that shuttle. Some of your friends will be spirited away to the Moon Lords. Others will go to the Governors of the Gas Giants. Even a few to Luna. They will remember you as a legend of their youth, but that is it. And that legend will brook no loyalty. I've stood where you stand. I won my year, but loyalty isn't found in these halls. It is the way things are."

"It is the way things were," I say harshly, suprising him. But I believe what I say. "I am something different. I freed the enslaved and let the broken mend themselves. I gave them something you older generations can't understand."

He chuckles, irritating me. "That is the problem with youth, Darrow. You forget that every generation has thought the same."

"But for my generation it is true." No matter his confidence, I am right. He is wrong. I am the spark that will set the worlds afire. I am the hammer that cracks the chains.

"This school is not life," he recites to me. "It is not life. Here you are king. In life, there are no kings. There are many would-be-kings. But we Peerless lay them low. Many before you have won this game. And those many now excel beyond this school. So do not act as though when you graduate, you will be king, you will have loyal subjects—you will not. You will need me. You will need a foundation, a supporter to help you rise. There can be none better for you than I."

It's not my family I would betray, it is my people. The school was one thing, but to go beneath the dragon's wing . . . to let him hug me close, to sit in luxury while my own sweat and die and starve and burn . . . it's enough to rip my heart out.

Both his golden children watch us. So do Cassius and his father after they embrace one another. There are tears for Julian. I wish I were with my family instead of here. I wish I could feel Kieran's hand on my shoulder, feel Leanna's hand in mine as we watch Mother set dinner before us. That is a family. Love. These people are all about glory, victory, and family pride, yet they know nothing of love. Nothing of family. These are false families. They are just teams. Teams that play their games of pride. The ArchGovernor has not even said hello to his children. This vile man cares more to speak with me.

"Funny," I say.

"Funny?" he asks darkly.

I make something up. "Funny how a single word can change everything in your life."

"It is not funny at all. Steel is power. Money is power. But of all the things in all the worlds, words are power."

I look at him for a moment. Words are a weapon stronger than he knows. And songs are even greater. The words wake the mind. The melody wakes the heart. I come from a people of song and dance. I don't need him to tell me the power of words. But I smile nonetheless.

"What is your answer? Yes or no? I will not ask again."

I glance over at the dozens of Peerless Scarred who wait to have a word with me, no doubt to offer patronage or apprenticeships. Old Lorn au Arcos is there. I recognize him even without his Drafter's mask. The Rage Knight. The man who sent me my Pegasus and Dancer's ring. A man of perfect honor and leader of the third most powerful house on Mars. A man I could learn from.

"Will you rise with me?"

I look at the ArchGovernor's jugular. His heartbeat is strong. I imagine the Fading Dirge when Eo died. But when I hang him, he will not receive our song. His life will not echo. It will simply stop.

"I think, my lord, that it would present some interesting opportunities." I look up into his eyes, hoping he mistakes the fury there for excitement.

"You know the words?" he asks me.

I nod.

"Then you must say them. Here. Now. So all may witness that I have claimed the best of the school."

His pride reeks. I grit my teeth and convince myself this is the right path. With him, I will rise. I will attend the Academy. I will learn to lead fleets. I will win. I will sharpen myself into a sword. I will give my soul. I will dive to hell in hopes of one day rising to freedom. I will sacrifice. And I will grow my legend and spread it amongst the peoples of all the worlds until I am fit to lead the armies that will break the chains of bondage, because I am not simply an agent of the Sons of Ares. I am not simply a tactic or a device in Ares's schemes. I am the hope of my people. Of all people in bondage.

So I kneel before him, as is their way. And as is their way, he sets his hands upon my head. The words creep from my mouth and their echo is like broken glass into my ears.

"I will forsake my father. I will abandon my name. I will be your sword. Nero au Augustus, I will make my purpose your glory."

Those watching gasp at the sudden proclamation. Others curse at the impropriety, at the gall of Augustus. Does he have no sense of decency? My master kisses the top of my head and whispers their words and I do my best to cage the fury that has made me a thing sharper than Red. Harder than Gold.

"Darrow, Lancer of House Augustus. Rise, there are duties for you to fill. Rise, there are honors for you to take. Rise for glory, for power, for conquest and dominion over lesser men. Rise, my son. Rise."

ABOUT THE AUTHOR

PIERCE BROWN is the #1 *New York Times* bestselling author of *Red Rising, Golden Son, Morning Star, Iron Gold,* and *Dark Age.* His work has been published in thirty-three languages and in thirty-five territories. He lives in Los Angeles, where he is at work on his next novel.

piercebrownbooks.com
Twitter: @Pierce_Brown
Instagram.com/PierceBrownOfficial

To inquire about booking Pierce Brown for a speaking engagement, please contact the Penguin Random House Speakers Bureau at speakers@penguinrandomhouse.com.

ABOUT THE TYPE

This book was set in Sabon, a typeface designed by the well-known German typographer Jan Tschichold (1902–74). Sabon's design is based upon the original letter forms of Claude Garamond and was created specifically to be used for three sources: foundry type for hand composition, Linotype, and Monotype. Tschichold named his typeface for the famous Frankfurt typefounder Jacques Sabon, who died in 1580.